EVERYBODY'S OUT THERE

ROBERT M. MARCHESE

Black Rose Writing | Texas

ISBN: 978-1-68433-656-2
PUBLISHED BY BLACK ROSE WRITING
www.blackrosewriting.com

Printed in the United States of America
Suggested Retail Price (SRP) $20.95

Everybody's Out There is printed in Chaparral Pro

*As a planet-friendly publisher, Black Rose Writing does its best to eliminate unnecessary waste to reduce paper usage and energy costs, while never compromising the reading experience. As a result, the final word count vs. page count may not meet common expectations.

To Robbie and Riley, with endless love and loyalty.

EVERYBODY'S OUT THERE

CHAPTER 1

The worst place to be after a tragedy is confined to a car for fourteen hours. I'm convinced the body and brain need their space to roam, to breathe, to bleed. The road trip, however romanticized, is agony. Despair becomes trapped, turning wild and even dangerous. But when you're running away, you have no choice. So you wait it out, enduring the grueling drive from Illinois to Connecticut. There are the static radio stations you're unfamiliar with - a quarter of a Hendrix tune you used to know all the words to in college, half a Marvin Gaye song that reminds you of a girl from your past who had beautifully big lips, the barely audible melody of a Sinatra ballad that you know would make you ache with such longing if only the reception would clear up.

There are the other drivers with their dead-eyed glares and self-important hustle. There are the landscapes, dreary industrial slabs, boring suburban towns, lonesome rest stops and diners. But some lovely farms, too, with sprawling, graceful pastures that must've inspired countless strangers to contemplate some profound memory. And there are the bouts of imagination - the nonstop, riotous slideshows that always seem to illuminate the most unpleasant moments. Like the very recent ones between you and your ex-wife. It's imagination on such a drive that's the most brutal.

Only when I stop to grab a coffee or one of those shriveled, shrink-wrapped sandwiches, or to fill the tank, do I even realize that I've been thinking about Laura. Once I'm in the parking lot and I turn off the engine, and the buzz of the highway leaves my brain, do I begin to truly feel the loss. I stay with it for a few moments, convincing myself it's the mark of a dignified man to wade through the dense murk of heartache. Then I throw open the door to the Jeep and make as much noise as possible, creating a ridiculous diversion for myself. I'll sing or hum or rant. At a Mobile station in Sandusky, I yodeled, scaring a woman into walking point blank into a trashcan.

It's not just thoughts of Laura that consume me. It's also the idea of going back east after all these years - seeing the tiny town of Old Brookview; seeing the Old Man for the first time in almost four years; seeing the crazy goddamn kids he lives for and from whom he makes his modest fortune.

I had actually stopped calling Connecticut my home a few years ago. Laura told me I was being dramatic when I made the declaration. Illinois, I argued, was where I felt I belonged, where I felt I'd always been, and where I felt I'd always be. I secretly thought that cutting the cord between me and my past was giving her what she wanted. That she would see it as the mark of true contentment for my life with her. That she would find it romantic and sacrificial. *Dramatic* was the only word she used, and the matter was summarily dropped.

The Old Man and I barely kept in touch through the years. There was the occasional call on a holiday or birthday. And I was made aware of his stent only after his doctor badgered him into contacting me. On my end, I phoned when Laura and I got married. And when we bought into Grove Garden Estates. When we became pregnant, of course. As well as when we became *un*pregnant. One of my more urgent calls ended up being from an ashram outside of Aurora, when I revealed that I'd likely be heading back east once my affairs were in order.

As far as visits, there were few. Maybe two or three on my end. Not one on his. I lied about the wedding, telling him that Laura and I eloped. He told me this was a fine idea. Keep it simple, he said. I suspected he knew I was lying - that we did in fact have a traditional wedding with guests and a cake and all the frills and fanfare - but was looking for me to pardon him from having to act like we were close for even a day. To account for the lack of my family at the ceremony, I ended up telling Laura and her parents that Rollie had to recover from a spinal injury he sustained after falling off a ladder, something that had actually occurred when I was nine. On our honeymoon, which we took in Saint Croix, I told Laura it was for the best. She knew we weren't close, but nothing about how my father's wanderlust had actually deserted him long ago. I told her he hadn't traveled in over a decade. He was content to stay where he was, I said, doing what he did best, which was breathing life back into his collection of broken boys and girls. As far as what I was doing, he made it known that he felt it wasn't terribly important.

"So you're writing for a newspaper," he'd say. "Crossword puzzles and catastrophes."

The first Christmas after Laura and I were married, we surprised him by flying out east for a weekend. A few days before, I had received a small journalism award from the staff at the paper. Laura, wanting to brag about me, brought it up over a toast. Rollie hesitated for a bit, licked his lips, and clinked our glasses. Later, when we were alone, he told me he liked Laura. And then, as though he feared he needed something to weigh against his approval, he told me that if *I* wasn't writing my column, someone else would be.

"Isn't that the case with *any*one doing *any*thing?" I asked. "Doesn't the same apply to *you*?"

He looked at me like I had switched languages midway through what I had said.

"Of course not," he scoffed.

But I'm guilty as well. If he feels that what I'm doing is trivial, at least he's taking the time to consider it. I've been eight hundred miles away, writing my column for The Sun Times and submerging myself deeper into that parochial snobbery that disregards small town life; it's as though when I stepped from the shell of Old Brookview, its cracked remains split into a million fragments that blew away the moment I left. That's part of it. The other part is that I figured I knew where my father was at all times: He was in our hometown of *Old Brookview*, a sleepy, old-money town in southern Connecticut that on a map resembles a chipped diamond. And I knew what he was doing: He was overseeing the Hundred Acre School, or the *HAS* as it's called, cashing those enormous tuition checks, and lecturing a hundred or so adolescent basket cases from his wobbly podium he keeps at the head of the dining hall. Christ, I even knew what he was saying: *"What's the point of man's life? What sense can people make out of human existence? What's the purpose of human events? All important questions - but there're others you must first ask yourself: We'll discover those questions together, kids.*" It was commonplace for him to quote Kierkegaard or Descartes or Francis Bacon to a small sea of precocious, overly medicated lunatics.

So I suppose I felt that I had seen that show, knew the lines, the props, the stage direction, and didn't feel the need to see it again or even remember it any longer. I grew up among those lunatics. They tramped through my front yard on their way to class or mealtime. Or they huddled by the dense row of birch trees in my backyard to sneak a smoke before group therapy. There were only a hundred of them - "One student per acre; more than enough space to figure *some*thing out," as the Old Man put it - but they seemed everywhere. And in a sense, they were. I saw them not only on the campus, where my father and I lived - we had a tiny three bedroom Cape that crouched practically in the middle of five boys dormitories - but also in town at the Roarick Arts Cinema, Tiny's Drugstore, Cumberland Farms, Louden's Diner, and at Page Turners, the town's bookstore. To me, they were like pets I wasn't much interested in, knowing they were in the care of others who were. Not that I ever mistreated them. When I ate among them in the dining hall, which was often, I was courteous and mindful of my manners. They were responsible for serving the food and clearing the tables, so I'd say, "Just some pancakes and sausage, please," to the bipolar girl with the black eye shadow and permanent pout, or "Thank you very much," as I handed my cutlery over to the gangly misfit with the Army boots and freshly gauzed wrists.

They regarded my presence with unease. I was their opposite: a public school kid, who went just down the street, not even two miles away, to schools with courtyards and custodians and gleaming display cases holding pennant flags and trophies dating back to the 1940s. The Hundred Acre School, which is grades nine through twelve, is far too modest looking to be impressive. Classes are taught in one of two single-level schoolhouses. Essentially facsimiles of one another - the only difference is that one is fifteen years newer and was built to look identical to the other - they bookend the gymnasium. The older one has been named the Virginia House, after my late mother; the newer one is known as the Virginia II. Parked next to the Virginia II is a 1967 vintage, lime-green Winnebago the Old Man once drove around North America with my mother, courting her before they married. The vehicle no longer runs. Yet my father still washes it, refills its tires, and keeps its insurance active. It's all in the name of some tacit memorial to his late wife, who died of breast cancer when I was three.

When I grew up, my own peers thought nothing of wreaking havoc on the HAS kids. Often, their paths would cross downtown, which is a mile from the HAS campus. To their faces, they referred to the institution as "Straight-Jacket Central" or "Crazy-House High," and asked questions like, "Who's your mascot: *a Bipolar-Bear*?" In the presence of the HAS kids, they would feign epilepsy and disfigurement and mental conditions that always involved limps and lisps and drooling. They would call them "freaks," "misfits," and "weirdos."

Because the campus is on both sides of Wildwood Road, HAS students can be seen crossing at any time of day. Thus, these cruel gestures were often extended in drive-by fashion. It was not uncommon for students to be minding their own business, ready to cross the road, diligently checking for traffic, when out of nowhere came a bullet in the shape of a $30,000 Audi or Acura, which would spit out profane slogans at whiplash speed, followed by a glass bottle that would shatter at their feet. When I was nine or ten, I saw from my bedroom window a car fly by with shouting teenagers leaning from the windows, and, in its speeding wake, a HAS student fall over in the road after getting clubbed in the face with a raw, dead fish the size of a small pillow.

Despite any magnanimous attempts on behalf of the town of Old Brookview or the Hundred Acre School to occasionally integrate both groups of students in certain functions - fundraisers, assemblies - the results were often polarizing. I remember a guest speaker coming to town to talk about drugs and alcohol when I was a senior at Franklin Duval High School. He spoke in FDHS's gymnasium since it could accommodate its own students as well as the roughly hundred HAS kids, who were bused over. Minutes into the assembly, a brawl broke out between ten or more students, most of them girls. One of them, I remember, a HASER, as they call themselves, lost both of her front teeth. When I saw her in the dining hall the following day, I mentioned that I was sorry for the unfortunate melee. She studied me for a moment as she held her tray of food, wisps of steam rising from her soggy, Technicolor vegetables; then she opened her mouth and scowled at me, making sure to expose her hideous loss.

My teachers often assumed that because my father ran a therapeutic boarding school that I was somehow blessed with a remarkable talent for sympathy. That I must have possessed an insider's view of suffering. That I saw, firsthand, and on a daily basis, the intricacies involved in human dysfunction. "Grayson is lucky," Mrs. Boyle, my junior year English teacher, used to tell the class when someone consulted me as the mental health pundit while we studied *The Catcher in the Rye* or *One Flew Over the Cuckoo's Nest*. "He has privileged glimpses into what must be some intriguing stories, stories most of us will never know, but could most likely benefit from. Pathos is a rare mineral, children. Be envious." Then she'd look at me and tell me again how lucky I was.

Lucky was not something I considered myself. I always felt at the center of constant hysteria - highs and lows, and absurd, never-ending drama. I cared for none of it. None of it, after all, was *my* drama. It all belonged to a group of narcissistic strangers.

When I was a sophomore, I remember a peer asking me if I hated my father for making me grow up among crazy kids. "That must be some type of *abuse*," she said. "To live there with them. To expose you to that, *every*day. I can't even *imagine*." I don't recall my response. But if there *was* a benefit to it, I suppose it was the freedom it afforded me. When your parent is a firm believer in what he does, when he's utterly devoted, passionate to the end, and when the fragile neuroses of a hundred teens hangs in the balance, you can get away with murder. So as he dealt with unruly HASERS - kids who refused to go to class, take their meds, go to therapy, get out of bed, put down the razor blade - I was exploring pseudo-adult life. I never had a curfew; I socialized with too many college-aged kids. I scored a fake ID when I was seventeen and was initiated into the New Haven bar scene, which is barely half an hour from Old Brookview; I was able to succeed academically and socially without much parental guidance whatsoever.

Though Rollie never said as much to me, I must've looked pretty good when compared with the HASERS. I always imagined him, after a long, grueling day of suicide prevention and hackneyed pep talks, having an emotional outpouring with my mother's photograph, which he kept sufficiently dusted by his bedside: "We got pretty damn lucky with Gray," he might say. "Didn't we? Intelligent. Independent. Hard-working. He's got a good head on his shoulders, doesn't he, Virginia?" But I could only guess. He had busied himself raising other people's kids. As I discovered, depression wins out over two consecutive *Shoreline's Best Young Journalist* awards, and five-figure yearly tuition checks win out over just about anything.

The truth is this: The HAS kids needed my father more than I did. So I gave him up, lent him out, whatever you want to call it. But I did so with more than a bit of recalcitrance. I wore whatever antipathy I had for the arrangement like some hard-earned badge of courage. But I never spoke about it. Not once.

Going back now after years of being away does seem like the perfect irony. Anyone who knows me would agree to this. They would throw their head back and widen their eyes and say, "Really? You're going to work for Rollie at the *Hundred Acre School*? After all this time? Isn't that something?" They would wish me luck, walk away, and think, *poor fucker...he's hit rock bottom*. And though I know I could explore this irony, indulge its fresh fascination, I won't. I simply need to get away from Illinois and Laura and Grove Garden Estates. I need to put some distance between myself and the last year of my life. *Rock bottom*? Maybe. But the bottom seems appropriate for me right now. I wouldn't know what to do anywhere else.

There's not a doubt that the Old Man will be consumed with questions: "Have you spoken with Laura lately?" "Is she all right?" "How'd things leave off?" And then the nexus, the one that would come so close to breaking his silence: "Can't you two just try again to have more children?" He'll refrain from voicing any of these, though. He has discipline. I'll give him that. It's impressive. I suppose it's his business to know when to push, and how, and at what point, and when to simply back off and allow space. My defense will be simple: I'll look around the school and comment on what looks the same and what's changed. This will work. Rollie is famous for falling all over himself to point out even the slightest development in the Hundred Acre School, whether it's in the programming or the aesthetics. His pride in the place is remarkable, endearing even. Sometimes, though, it can be too much. I remember him telling me, and thinking he was justified, that he reproved a staff member for giving a tour to a prospective student and her family and forgetting to mention the new carpeting in two of the dormitories.

The truth is that it would be absurd to open up to my father about the Laura situation. Absurd for both of us. I have no practice in doing this, and now would be one hell of a time to start. I can barely sort it out for myself.

If it was just divorce, that would be one thing. Then I could at least fall back on common responses: "It just didn't work out." "We grew apart over the years." "It happens sometimes - people fall out of love." But it wasn't just divorce. And we didn't fall out of love or grow apart. And the Old Man knows as much. He knows enough to realize we were in love and that it was the real kind of love. The kind that lasts. The kind you can put in the fire and it will still come out smooth and shapely and unscathed. And he knows he'll never meet his unborn granddaughter, Emma Elizabeth. And though he thinks he does, he really doesn't know the reason for this, or much else for that matter.

So with my Jeep loaded with all I own, I head east on Interstate 80 into New Jersey. It's a few minutes past 1:00 a.m. and I've been traveling for over ten hours. The highway is dark and mostly deserted. I pass the occasional freighter and fellow traveler, but it's mostly just me. With the windows down, the cool June night air tumbles through the vehicle. The evening is moonless and the stars are sharp, fine points pinned to the sky in patterns and constellations I never tried to understand. The only station that comes in clearly plays jazz, which I never much cared for. Bursts of piano runs and bass lines and horn solos. No melody to speak of. Just a wild offering of freeform, spitfire noise. I need melody, a rhythm I can count on and comprehend and even predict after a while.

If I continue on to Connecticut, I'll arrive at the school at around 5:00 a.m. Rollie will be expecting me. I've gone over our reunion a thousand times in my head. He'll be cool yet inviting, all the while fighting the urge to show concern towards his poor, displaced son. I'll be taciturn and moody, pretending it's only due to the long drive behind me.

The decision to come back home was mine. It came to me in a spontaneous rush at the beginning of spring. It was as though the idea had sensed there were no others in my head, so it came tumbling along, with plenty of room to maneuver, and ended up in the form of a proposition to my father. Of course he was okay with it. He reacted with his typical nonchalance, as though it was a decision he felt quite sure I'd make one of these days. And now, as I close in on him, his school, my past life, I feel dread and joy and relief all at once. It's as though my insides are made up of a million tiny turnstiles, each with a memory attached. Laura. The Old Man. Emma Elizabeth. Grove Garden Estates. Laura's charming friend from Grove Garden Estates, Mr. Glenn Kilburn.

So I try focusing my attention on the phone call I had with the Old Man earlier this morning. I felt like I was underwater as we spoke, deluged by the notion that I would soon be returning to him. Gathering the last of my things - I had been staying at my friend Ben's house in Harwood Heights in a bonus room above his garage - I only half listened to my father's pleas to drive carefully and stop often. But I remember his tone, austere and inscrutable. It was as though he had sworn to himself that he was going to try the tough love approach and not give in to pity over my plight.

The Old Man. He must be glad I've decided to lick my wounds on his turf. Surprised, possibly, but mostly glad. So glad, in fact, that he's even created a temporary position at the school for me, one that doesn't involve my having to deal with any of his misanthropes. He's named the position Public Relations Director. We never got into what it involves, but he made it clear that I would not be working with any students.

"Don't worry," he said, when we spoke a few weeks earlier, "we'll stash you in an office as far away from the kids as possible. I'm even having a BEWARE OF MY SON: THE UNFRIENDLY BASTARD sign made for your door."

I told him to make all the jokes he wanted as long as he understood that the arrangement would only work, for however long it was destined to work, if I was granted this concession. As far as a timeline, I muttered something to him about staying on for just a few weeks, possibly until the end of the summer, or at least until I conceive some sort of game plan. I told him I was considering the west coast, that I met a friend of a colleague at a rooftop cocktail party in Chicago, who works for the San Francisco Chronicle. I said that they have a few openings and that the friend, Bob Nash, when he learned of my situation, offered me a job on the spot. The only true part of the story is that I *did* attend a rooftop cocktail party.

I'm not sure if I'm beaten with thoughts of everything, or if the jazz is putting me to sleep, but I start to feel the weight of exhaustion pulling at my eyes. Even the wind, which douses my face with switchblade speed, can't combat the fatigue. The last time I made this drive was about four years before Laura and I were engaged. That's close to ten years ago, and I knew as much about New Jersey's lodging situation as I know now. The thought of finding some depressing fleabag hovel is enough to make me decide to pull over and snooze for a bit in the Jeep. Rest stop or not. There's barely any traffic. I can pull off the interstate and tuck the vehicle snugly against the dark thicket of woods. I'll keep my hazards on while I sleep. After a few hours, I'll wake up, take a piss in the woods, psych myself up, and make it to the Hundred Acre School in time for breakfast.

So I pull off and find a clearing that's a safe distance from the breakdown lane. I kill the ignition and recline the seat as far as it will go with my things in the back. My body is tight with tension. My head feels warm and heavy. Like it's been playing host to some scalding hot thoughts that have finally burned out. Closing my eyes, I start to drift off. The steady click-clack of the hazards are soothing. After a moment, I hear a car approaching in the distance. It grows, sounding like a wave on the verge of crashing, and then it flies by. No other cars pass for a while.

It's quiet, a middle-of-nowhere quiet that tempts me with its forever quality. It's a quiet that tiptoes alongside those undreamt dreams that are still in the womb, waiting to be born into something worth remembering and talking about. My phone suddenly rings. It's the Old Man. He asks how my drive is going, mentioning that I'm probably in the Jersey area by now.

"Well done, sir," I said.

"Can you talk?"

"It's pitch black and I'm in New Jersey. There's nothing else to grab my attention at the moment."

"Good."

He sighs into the phone. Then he mumbles and starts to say something before stopping himself.

"What is it?"

"What part of Jersey are you in?"

"The part that probably inspired T.S. Eliot's masterpiece."

He laughs a little. I know he gets the reference. The Old Man and I have next to nothing in common, but he's no dummy.

"I wanted to talk to you about something," he said.

"Okay."

"I wanted to tell you this morning on the phone."

"All right."

"Things have been busy here. It's been a pretty busy couple of days."

"Okay."

"More so than usual, I mean."

"So you've had to actually *earn* those enormous tuition checks?"

"Something's happened, Gray."

"Okay."

His tone is neutral. It has a hushed quality that perfectly suits the desolation of the dark interstate. I adjust my seat to its upright position.

"I wanted to tell you before you got here. I wanted to tell you this morning—"

He cuts himself off. Then he heaves another sigh into the phone.

"There was an accident."

"What do you mean *an accident*? Are you all right?"

"A girl was killed," he said.

"Jesus."

"Murdered actually."

"Murdered?"

"Hard to believe, isn't it? In this town of all places."

"So maybe *accident* isn't exactly the word you're going for."

He sighs again. I apologize for the mockery. He says she was not one of his students. Then he tells me the story of a recently missing local girl, a teenager, Nicole D'Ambrosio, and the massive search parties that began last Sunday when she disappeared. He tells me about how it made the local papers right away, and how the girl's folks are bigwigs in town: Her mother is some local artist and her father an attorney. He tells me about the colorful and professional looking HAVE YOU SEEN OUR DAUGHTER? posters downtown in every storefront window, on every telephone pole and windshield, and even on every cart at Stop & Shop. He tells me the girl was a typical Old Brookview girl, blonde and blue-eyed, and how she was co-captain of her high school soccer team, played the clarinet, and was one of the newest members of the National Honor Society.

Then he tells me about a student named Dan Hart, who the other HASERS call Dan Juan. The Old Man puts it bluntly: The kid likes pussy, he says, no two ways about it. He rattles off Dan's stats: been a student for a year; mostly a good kid; bright; funny; lazy; has ADD and bipolar disorder; parents still married; older sister killed herself three years ago. And this Dan Hart - or *Dan Juan* - is known for extended disappearing acts, Rollie tells me; he often takes long strolls on the hundred acre campus, always with a curious and willing female in tow. And it was on such an excursion, just three days after Nicole's disappearance, at 11:15 p.m., that he and his latest conquest, a fifteen-year-old girl named Jessica, discovered Nicole D'Ambrosio's body on a remote part of campus adjacent to the interstate. Curled into a near fetal position by a line of pine trees, the body was covered with branches and dead leaves. She was murdered, he tells me. Strangled.

"So when do you think you'll be here?"

"Jesus Christ."

"When?"

"Soon. Okay? I'll be there soon."

"Because things are a little out of hand here as you can imagine. I've got a hundred kids who are petrified; they're either playing Sherlock Holmes to prove their innocence, or they're telling every authority figure who gets within ten feet of this place to go fuck themselves. I have a faculty who's on edge, to say the least, a police department who's breaking my balls, and an entire town who's turned on me."

When he's done, there's a pause. It's not a long pause, but it's long enough for me to consider how I'll respond. So, without censor, I say the thing that seems to punctuate the gulf that's existed between me and my father for as long as I can remember:

"What do you expect *me* to do about any of this?"

Another pause.

"Will you just get here, please?"

When we hang up, I'm confronted with the thought that he must've waited to tell me this. Waited for me to be on the road, well on my way, most of the drive done with, and now forced with the obvious decision to either turn around or continue on to the Hundred Acre School. I picture him mapping out my route and travel schedule, all the while the phone by his side, waiting for that moment to make the call.

I *could* turn around. I could find a gas station and fill up on coffee and then head west. I could find a cheap motel where I could stay the night. Then I could call the Old Man in the morning and explain. There's already too much disorder in my own life, I would say. I appreciate your situation, I would tell him, but I don't feel like it's in my best interest to be part of such a controversy. Good luck and let me know how it all turns out.

For the next ten minutes I sit in the Jeep, trying to arrive at a decision. When it's evident that nothing will help me decide, no sign or sudden flash of inspiration, I start the car and pull onto the deserted interstate. The pavement, stretched out before me, looks ominous, like some blackened tongue ready to lap me up and spew me into the middle of a whole new chaos. I realize I'm now fully awake. As I accelerate, putting the darkness and the distance behind me, I find myself wanting to feel for this poor local girl and her family, and even for Rollie, who must be enduring a hellish ordeal with his fiercely unstable misfits, but almost immediately thinking again of my ex-wife and our own recent tragedy.

CHAPTER 2

When Laura and I decided to build a house and have children, I remember being thankful that my own family was too far away to ever share in our domesticity. Besides Rollie, I have three cousins, Meg, Walter Jr., and Sonny, as well as an aunt and uncle, Jeanne and Walter. They all live in or around some remote hick town in New Hampshire, and I wouldn't recognize any of them today if they were to fall from the sky and land on me. Jeanne is my mother's older sister, and the Old Man and I lost touch with her family a few years after my mother passed. I'm sure this happened once it became apparent that grief was all we shared. How often can you memorialize someone during small talk over the phone, or reminisce about their good nature and intellect during the occasional Thanksgiving dinner? I was around seven or eight the last time we all got together. The few memories I have of my New Hampshire family are slight and mostly faded. My cousin Sonny's obsession with ninjas. His sister, Meg, shocking her parents by shaving her head. And my Uncle Walter's presence was never without the stubby end of a cigar sticking out the side of his mouth.

As for the life Laura and I led, I wanted it all for myself. Which is to say I was okay sharing it with friends; friends, at our age, are noncommittal. They're only interested in a dinner party here and there, or a celebratory shindig to raise your glasses to that new well-deserved promotion, or a New Year's bash, where you say the hell with it and break out the good china.

Laura is a different story. Her family all live in the city. Her parents, Luke and Abby, are Chicago born and bred. And she has two brothers, Rick and Lyle, and a sister, Stevie, all of whom live minutes apart. The affection they have for one another used to make me blush. But its foreignness eventually caused me to develop the type of cynicism that is so private and repressed that you sometimes question its existence. I never shared this with Laura. She always thought whatever reticence I expressed was based on a lack of familiarity over a family who has regular Sunday dinners and vacations together and pulls the kind of pranks you only pull when you're willing to put in quality time and even spend a few bucks. Of course I was unfamiliar with all of this. But it went beyond that. The roots that bore these relationships were watered with something I could hardly fathom.

We were living in a townhouse on Southport, which is in Wrigleyville. It's a sought-after area, being that it's walking distance to just about everything: markets, book stores, bars, two great Thai places, and, most notably, home of the city's beloved Cubs. And though Laura never shared my enthusiasm for the sport, she placated me by attending a dozen or more games each season. This became a ritual, and I think over time she developed an interest in the game, appreciating, if nothing else, its storied traditions.

We were renting the townhouse from Dana Knowles, one of Laura's roommates from Columbia. This was as fine an arrangement as we could've asked for. Dana's parents, in an effort to teach their daughter to be fiscally savvy, gave her various properties in and around the city, instructing her on the art of landlording. Luckily for us, Dana's interests were steeped more in being a socialite than a businesswoman. So she rented us the airy and spacious townhouse for a pittance. Her folks, I imagine, had amassed such a portfolio that they wouldn't have noticed if their Southport place burned to the ground.

And though we were happy in our rental, I began house hunting almost as soon as we had unpacked our last box. We knew we weren't interested in raising children in the city. Born just a few blocks north of the Knowles' condo, Laura got her fill of Chicago's hustle by the time we were married. As for me, I simply wanted to get away from her family. Besides, though I had fled from an east coast suburb years earlier, I knew the value of having a yard and a lawn and a broad sweeping view of the sky and stars. The way I saw it was that I would be given the opportunity to do it the way I thought it ought to be done: without bipolar nutcases running across your lawn at midnight, plotting illicit rendezvous that would make most people blanch. When I told this to Laura, she smiled and shook her head. Then she told me that I hadn't even come close to escaping the madness; the city, she said, had more nutcases than my father's Hundred Acre School.

During the weekends, we'd drive through neighborhoods in the more desirable outskirts - Wheaton, Glen Ellyn, Naperville, Lisle, Elmhurst. Nothing much appealed to us. Wheaton was too far. Naperville was too expensive. Elmhurst was too blah. And the others seemed to have too few suitable properties for sale. So we held off. The upside was that having such a meager monthly rent allowed us to save for a future down payment.

Then two things happened inside of a week that would inspire what Laura and I came to call our newborn plan. The first one was that we became fed up after looking at what turned out to be our last in a series of marginal homes; it was an overpriced Dutch Colonial with a cracked foundation and a master-bath bidet as its only amenity. The second was we had attended a dinner party in Highland Park, a gorgeous suburb twenty-five miles north of the city. Ed and Jan Singer, friends of friends, and the hosts of the party, were famous for their potent homemade libations, which consisted of strawberry wine for the women and a stout that was darker than burnt molasses for the men. Needless to say, Laura and I were buzzed on our way back into the city. And after a series of wrong turns, we found ourselves face-to-face with a half-dozen bulldozers and backhoes parked peacefully near a hastily planted sign that read, GROVE GARDEN ESTATES – LET US BUILD YOUR DREAM HOME. When I flipped on the high beams, there was the name of the development company, Cadman Builders, and a phone number, both at the bottom of the sign. Laura and I didn't say a word; she just reached into her purse, fished around for her phone, and snapped a photo of the sign.

We found out that the property - over a dozen prime acres of level farmland - was owned and in the process of being developed by two brothers from Pennsylvania. The brothers, Abe and Caleb Cadman, probably in their early forties, had inherited the land from their grandfather years earlier; they had resisted selling for sentimental reasons, and resisted building for logistical ones - the main one being, simply, they lived in Pennsylvania. They owned a construction company out of Harrisburg, PA, and specialized in middle-of-the-road single family homes. After finishing some projects on the east coast, they decided it was doable to go west for a while and make something of their farmland.

They both flirted with Laura when we all met in their trailer, which was situated on the periphery of the building site. It was cramped and humid with beach chairs and a broken AC unit. The brothers called her *Princess* and told her they'd love to build her the palace they knew she deserved. They stared at her chest and complimented her smile; one of the brothers stroked her wrist when he handed her a pen to sign the contracts.

I didn't mind any of this as much as I did their heavy musk-scented cologne, which was stifling in such an enclosed space. They were characters, though, ready to pounce on one another for interrupting or quoting an erroneous price for an extra window in the living room or granite countertops in the guest bath. One of them - I think it was Abe - even smacked the other in the back of the head with a binder filled with carpet swatches after he inadvertently revealed how much they stood to profit from the entire development.

It's true that they were hardly the professionals we envisioned working with, but they laid out an attractive offer and set an affordable price for a hell of a lot of house. So we were stuck with them for one year. That's how long they said they'd need to build our home. One year. This seemed reasonable.

I'm not sure what couples do in mental preparation for starting a family. They may have discussions about value systems and finances and whether it'll be a Lucy or a Logan and who each might look like and act like and would do to Mommy's and Daddy's social life and sleep habits. Or they could read manuals and articles and books on childbirth and potty training. They might babysit for friends to ensure their decision is steeped in true, wise hearts. Hell, they may even consult their priest or therapist for advice - as though anybody, even the most sound-minded, can say for sure what lies ahead. Laura and I did none of this. We knew from the beginning that we wanted a family. Being that I was an only child, I was intent on having several children. Up to three or four. Laura wanted the same. We avoided seeking advice or reading books or even discussing it much with one another. Maybe that sounds haphazard. Maybe we sound like we were daunted by adult matters, so we evaded them completely. But it never felt that way. The whole thing had a spontaneity to it; in a way it seemed even holy.

When I was a teenager, I slept in an abandoned church a few towns north of Old Brookview. It was to be torn down that summer, so a few of us grabbed some candles and cheap beer and found a way in near the rear entrance and stayed overnight. And though I wasn't the least bit pious, I recall waking up in the night, silently staring at the cavernous church ceiling, and feeling, probably for the first time in my young life, the true spirit of something sacred beaming down from those splintered rafters. Not necessarily religious, but spiritual. And that's how it felt with Laura. Like there was the presence of something beautiful and watchful, something that required no belabored introspection. It was just there, and it seemed all around us.

"I'm not going to renew my birth control," Laura said to me during one of our Sunday morning walks. "Okay?"

We were married for just two years before any earnest attempts at having a child. We gladly christened every square foot of the Knowles' townhouse, proclaiming that each effort would be the one we'd frame in our minds as the moment of conception. But it wasn't that easy. It simply wasn't happening. Yet we avoided discussions and subtle accusations; we also stayed away from fertility pundits. This suited me just fine. I can't imagine anything more debasing than being asked to ejaculate into a vial so your semen can be scrutinized by experts whose job becomes making you feel like you're not failing your wife.

We tried to conceive right through the construction of the Grove Garden house, which ended up taking nearly two years. There was a glitch in the Cadman's original plan, which was to build half a dozen homes, some spec houses and some custom. After the first month, when the clearing of the lots had wrapped, the brothers were given an ultimatum by their crew: more money or else they'd strike. The brothers, one could immediately tell, would sooner cease with their licentious behavior than acquiesce to any type of threats, especially ones involving their business, in which they did seem to take pride. Abe and Caleb held their ground, losing their workers in the process. Rather than hire a new crew, the brothers opted to do the work themselves. All of it. There was no doubt that they were quite capable - so they assured us - but the simple fact remained: six houses of considerable size and detail, two men, a promise of one year. It was ridiculous.

"This way, we can personally oversee every detail of the Princess's castle," they told us.

We had nothing to lose. We weren't in a hurry to move, so we agreed to the arrangement. The truth is that we were more intent on starting a family than picking out flooring and fixtures. Besides, we thought it would be entertaining to see how the matter played out: six houses, two men, one year. What could possibly go wrong?

CHAPTER 3

The mission statement for the Hundred Acre School reads as follows: *The intent of the Hundred Acre School is to foster positive, constructive, and healthy development in its students. Our focus is on the student and his or her social and emotional growth and well-being. We are committed to the task of helping each student reach their potential, thus becoming an independent, self-motivated, responsible, and healthy individual. We encourage all students to build lasting, productive relationships with faculty, family, friends, and peers. We also encourage all students to self-assess behaviors, seek help when necessary, help others when appropriate, and respect the educational and therapeutic process. Our aim is steeped in creating a least restrictive environment for students to feel safe, uninhibited, and able to express themselves freely and without limitation.*

I authored this sanctimonious bullshit when I was a sophomore in high school. The Old Man was going through a rigorous state accreditation process at the time, and part of this process involved updating the curriculum, extending the school day, hiring only certified staff, and creating a mission statement.

"You're the wordsmith, Gray," he said. "This kind of stuff should be second nature for you."

Then he told me the ground it needed to cover and gave me free rein. Besides an overuse of the word "student(s)," I was happy with how it turned out; not bad for a fifteen-year-old. Still, who could resist the quiet hilarity of the notion that I, Grayson Loveland, known for his apathy towards the HAS, created such a sensitive manifesto?

The words are embossed in yellow letters on a large tapestry hanging over the piano in the dining hall. If Rollie looks up at any point during his meal, he will behold my prose. As will most anyone whose back is not turned towards it. I can recall eating among the students and watching sets of aimless eyes staring dumbly at the banner as though considering the veracity of its words. And not that I ever would've asked, but I did wonder what they thought of them. Moreover, I wondered how they'd have felt if they knew I had written them.

But now the words are everywhere. They're on sheets of laminated cardstock, which are pinned to bulletin boards in each of the classrooms and offices. They're scrawled on the back of t-shirts for sale and on display at the Staff on Duty (SOD) office, a tiny, one windowed room adjacent to the infirmary and dining hall. And they adorn large, see-through stickers, which are stuck to everything from windows to the backboards of the basketball hoops. Clearly, the Old Man has toyed with the notion of building morale by smearing this jargon everywhere but across the skyline.

I arrive at the school at a little after 5:00 a.m. After parking in the visitor lot - the Old Man finally had it paved - I roam the campus, which is quietly humming beneath sharp bolts of the early June twilight that stab through the treetops and into the dew covered ground. Breakfast isn't until 7:00, so the students are still clawing at the precarious rubber walls of their strange dreams. What do these kids dream about, anyway? More meds? More freedom? More cigarettes? More something, no doubt. Or maybe less. How the hell should I know? What I do know is they crave sleep like most of us crave oxygen. Rollie used to get calls in the morning from the dorm staff - he probably still does - explaining how so and so refuses to wake up and come to breakfast. Did you try this? Did you try that? Did you use finesse? Humor? Tact? Leverage? The Old Man would go through a litany of questions before paying a housecall to the stubborn sleeper. Then, nearly minutes before breakfast was over, he'd enter the dining hall, that look of triumph curling his lips into some puckered punctuation mark, and in tow would be a bummed out, somewhat disheveled teenager, who'd skulk over to the food line and extend their empty plate like they were the victim of some petty prank.

Before noon, this place will be a hotbed for every imaginable teenage catastrophe: breakdowns from those who hate it here; those who say they don't belong here; those who won't take their meds; those who tried to trade their meds; those who can't get along with their classmates or their dorm mates or their therapists or their teachers or their faculty advisors; those who are haunted by severe bouts of depression, anxiety, fear, obstinacy, paranoia, and any conceivable malady in between. So the peacefulness here, at this hour, is something to relish.

In high school, on the weekends, I used to bring my girlfriend, Erin, to campus. We'd go to a movie or a party and I'd drop her back at her house at exactly 11:00 p.m. Her father was a state cop and strict as hell about her curfew. This didn't stop us, though, from having a regular after-hours party. We'd wait until around 1:00 a.m. when she'd sneak out of her first floor bedroom window and meet me at the end of her driveway. We'd then make our way to the HAS, where we'd roam the campus, sometimes for hours, bringing some alcoholic concoction and a blanket, which we'd spread out under the stars, either by the baseball diamond or near the maintenance shed. And as we lay there, naked, half drunk, and woozy in our teenage ebullience, we'd surmise the calamities that would befall the school by daybreak. Erin, who had an astute handle on the place - she listened to my tirades on a regular basis - likened such tranquility to the dusky early morning hush that must've pervaded Omaha Beach on that fateful June day back in 1944. And though the comparison soon became hackneyed, it nevertheless made us laugh every time.

It's been four years since I've seen the Hundred Acre School. The Old Man has obviously done some work in that time. The shrubs that lined the face of the dining hall have been torn out and replaced with a rose garden and a couple of wooden benches. Fresh new white siding has been put on two of the girls dorms: the Joni House and the Helen House. Each of the buildings is named after an influential figure in Rollie's life. There's the Joni House, named after Joni Mitchell, whom he adores and actually met twice at her art shows in NYC; two of her paintings are hanging behind a plexiglass case in the dorm's common room. The Old Man named the Helen House after his mother, my grandmother, whom I never met; she died when my father was an undergrad. The largest dorm on campus, the Priscilla House, is named after a now deceased Old Brookview resident, Priscilla Danford, a wealthy widow who donated generous sums of money to the HAS in the 1980s. The Minnie House is named after Rollie's beloved college professor, Filomena Perucio, a preeminent figure in the annals of Cornell's faculty, and the woman who inspired him to change his major from philosophy to education. And the Missouri House is named after a quirky, half-mad literary character from *Other Voices, Other Rooms*, a Truman Capote novel the Old Man rereads every couple of years, claiming its gothic enigmas, forlorn atmosphere, and offbeat characters somehow remind him of the Hundred Acre School.

The boys dorms, like the girls, were all named in the early 1990s, twenty years after the school was established, and bear their titles after those who, as Rollie puts it, "contributed to the betterment of the HAS in some extraordinary way." There's the Miles House, named after the first teacher the Old Man hired when he opened the place in the early 1970s. Miles Katz stayed on, teaching history and coaching girls softball for a decade, establishing a rare precedent; most teachers regard the place as a stepping stone and stay on for no more than a couple of years. There's the Alan House, named after a local musician, Alan Browne, who volunteered his time several days a week to teaching the kids how to play whatever instrument they owned, or how to set the sophomoric prose of their suicide letter to lovely guitar accompaniment. There's the Homer House, named after Dr. Homer Wald, a therapist whose charm, wit, and avuncular demeanor ingratiated him to anyone graced by his presence. His death, brought about by an unexpected aneurism - I was a senior in high school at the time of his passing - caused the Old Man to lower the school's flag to half mast and cancel classes for the rest of that day. There's the Charles House, named after Charles Burr, HAS's bellicose principal from 1983-2000. He and Rollie were constantly at odds over this or that, but Burr's tough-love approach with the students, his unyielding candor with his staff, and his effectiveness as an all around leader, won out and endured the better part of two decades. There's the Mickey House, named after Mickey Kinnon, HAS's crotchety, pot-bellied cook, who I know is still banging around his pots and pans, hollering at those who neglect to prep his grill with non-stick spray, and blasting anyone out of his kitchen who attempts to tell him their omelet is runny or their London Broil chewy. Mickey, a war vet who lost three fingers on his left hand, has always had the ability to crack up the Old Man with his colorful stories.

Other improvements Rollie has made are the new windows in the therapy lounge and main office, both small, aluminum-sided buildings that are adjacent to one another. He's had the exterior of the gymnasium painted a fresh cream color. A small addition has been added to the maintenance shed. The basketball court has been re-tarred. The Virginia House has been re-roofed. The Old Man has completely refurbished the pavilion, which is HAS's rec room; it's replete not only with an enormous flat-screen TV and surround sound, but with a ping-pong, foosball, and pool table.

Smiling to myself, I recognize the time and money he's put into the place. He's on a mission to update and upsize and get more upscale, probably an attempt to justify charging students nearly $100,000 a year. They come from all over, too - not just from the east coast. The Old Man has had kids from Texas and Canada and Florida and North Dakota. One year, he even had a European student all the way from Belgium.

I poke around a bit, peering in windows, pulling on the occasional door, which I know will be locked. The Old Man keeps a stranglehold on security. He has ever since an incident that befell the Homer House back in the 1990s. It was a morning like any other at the HAS - refusals to get out of bed; petulant fits and freakouts; steadfast commitments to being deep and dolorous, all of which are so routine that you could set your watch to them. The Homer House boys, upon waking, noticed that the windows to their common room were obscured by some dark, smeary blur from top to bottom. It must've looked like the end of the world - or like an eclipse had occurred and the sky exploded, its gelatinous shrapnel sticking all over an unsuspecting earth. They informed Reg, their dorm staff, who was no doubt burdened by his efforts to rouse ten or so adolescents into facing the new day. Reg thus ventured outside to discover the source of confusion. It was shit. And it was no mere fling and flee job, either; it was laboriously coated with deft precision.

During the week, before school each morning, I'd eat breakfast with my father and the students in the dining hall. The Old Man wanted it this way. My presence, he told me, would be good for the students; they'd be inspired by how together I was. He added that I would somehow become enlightened by sharing in their world, possibly earning some humility along the way. His final reason - and this one I suspected on my own - was so he and I could bond before he embarked on a typical fifteen-hour work day. Of course, none of this ever happened. I ate quickly, usually at Rollie's table, which he shares with administrators and therapists, mostly with my nose in a book, looking up on occasion, giving terse answers to anyone who tried to engage me in conversation. Meanwhile, the Old Man would circle the dining hall for most of the meal, clutching a bagel and coffee, asking students about the night before or the day ahead.

On the morning of the incident, I remember hearing the buzz of the kids' conversations about the foul prank. They didn't appear to be offended or humiliated; rather, they seemed impressed and bewildered over the amount of effort and excrement used in such a scheme. I recall going to school that day and regarding each one of my peers as a possible suspect.

Later that night, the Old Man told me another sick discovery had been made; thankfully, he said, this one was not revealed to the students. That same morning, when the therapy lounge was opened by one of the psychiatrists, the words CRAZY COCKSUCKERS were scrawled in red spray paint across the wall in enormous letters. It was soon discovered that a back window had been easily removed to gain entrance. The Old Man never called the cops. He called his maintenance crew instead, had a meeting with his faculty, and decided to hire night staff, which he did, that week. They were - and probably still are - a motley cadre of men and women. He hires those who aren't afraid to wield a club or shine a light in some punk's face while telling him he's trespassing and about to get his goddamn head split open. Two of them work at a time, from 11:00 p.m. to daybreak, patrolling the campus, setting up shop in the SOD office, where they drink coffee, read the tabloids, and pretend to be omnipotent overseers of some slumbering kingdom.

I couldn't help but immediately loathe their presence, as their being hired put an abrupt end to my late night rendezvousing with Erin. On a positive note, I suppose, since the Old Man brought in his geriatric mob squad, there have been - as far as I know - only a few minor incidents since the shit and CRAZY COCKSUCKERS stunts. Except, of course, one dead Old Brookview girl found in the woods on a remote part of campus.

The school lines both sides of Wildwood Road for about a quarter mile. The five boys dormitories, as well as my father's house, reside on the north side. This is a modest Cape with yellowish clapboard siding, burgundy shutters, and a front porch that was built one summer by the Old Man. This is the home in which I grew up, and now looks like something that came crashing out of my memory, landing miraculously upright and intact. It's true I came of age in this house. I drank my first alcohol in its basement; smoked my first joint in its upstairs bathroom; stashed my fair share of contraband in my bedroom crawl space; but what I remember best is the sensation of being utterly surrounded at all hours by hordes of troubled teenagers.

The rest of the campus resides on the south side. This includes the five girls dorms, the dining hall and its attachment - which is the SOD office - the maintenance shed, the gymnasium, the pavilion, the main office and therapy lounge, the nurse's office, schoolhouses, the Winnebago, and a baseball diamond, which sits on the southernmost tip of the campus proper, its backstop essentially a hundred or so feet behind the Pricilla House. At the moment, yellow police tape snakes around the backstop, dragging and twisting its way to some oaks on both sides, cordoning off the field as well as the seventy or so acres beyond.

The Hundred Acre School was a Christian summer camp from 1951 to 1963. After some highly publicized financial debacle, it closed, much to the delight of the mostly secular locals of Old Brookview. Almost immediately following the closing, a man named William Hannah purchased the land and planned on using it to simulate hunting excursions after stocking it with wildlife he said he knew how to procure. The town might've been intrigued by this, but they petitioned against Hannah and his inane money-making ploy. The land was then sold to the town and was all but abandoned for over eight years. Offers were made and propositions entertained. An entrepreneur from New York wanted to scoop up the property for a sportsplex, a dozen or so baseball and football fields for recreational league play. A shooting range was proposed by a local chapter of the NRA. A deal for a Herb's Par Three, a small east coast chain of golf courses, nearly went through. The last venture to be turned down was concocted by Al Moakley, a local resident who expressed interest in buying the property with the intention of leveling the buildings to plant an enormous corn maze to which locals and outsiders alike would naturally flock in order to get lost for $15 a head. The fate of the property seemed elsewhere.

In the late summer of 1972, a young man and his pretty girlfriend, fresh out of Cornell's grad school, pulled their Winnebago into Old Brookview when its transmission hacked its final breath along the interstate. With swells of that early 1970's wanderlust in their system, the couple had been traveling through North America for a few months, crossing its highways and backroads, turning heads in small town diners in Kansas, making friends with their northern brethren in Saskatchewan, getting homesick in Detroit. That they ended up in Connecticut was fortuitous. It simply happened to be where their 1967 Winnebago, only five years old at the time - but sporting a mostly rebuilt engine - sputtered out and slowly died. It happened on I-95, about a quarter of a mile before the Old Brookview exit.

The couple pushed their smoking vehicle in the searing early morning sun, arriving safely at Shaded Corners Professional Complex, which was, and still is, a community of local small town businesses - doctor's offices, attorneys, accountants, massage therapists, and at one point, a Native spiritual healer, Wandering Wolf, who later scandalized the town when it was discovered he had impregnated two teenage girls inside of a few weeks. Rumor has it he was run out of town after being threatened at knifepoint by the father of one of the teens.

The sign at the end of the off ramp to Old Brookview says *Welcome to Old Brookview, Connecticut's Best Kept Secret*. The couple, not particularly intent on cutting their journey short due to a bum engine, which included the transmission, starter, and fuel line, found, after hitching a ride into town and poking around a bit, that they immediately agreed with this sentiment. So they decided to stay for a while in the small shoreline town. The girl, Virginia Gardner, was, by all accounts and photos, a slim, freckled blonde with bright eyes and a blinding smile. She came from the tiny town of Lincoln, New Hampshire, so she was happy to be back in New England, only a few hours away from her parents and older sister. She was twenty-eight around this time.

The man, Rollie Loveland, was scholarly looking and serious, even back then. With his long mane of hair and his wild, untamed beard, the Old Man resembled a sort of roguish intellectual with abstruse theories he hadn't the patience to ever explain to anyone. His hair has since thinned into smooth wisps of graying silk, and he's kept the beard all these years, which he calls the one relic of his halcyon days. He comes from East Hanover, New Jersey, so for him, too, their east coast drifting was a welcomed homecoming. At just twenty-four, he was several years younger than my mother.

The *Tit for Tat Diner*, apparently called *Tits* by most residents, was looking for a waitress and dishwasher. So my parents, just barely a year away from being married, took the jobs and lived out of their Winnebago, which they had towed to the back of the restaurant by the owner, who took an instant shine to the couple - especially my mother.

James Roarick III was, and still is, the wealthiest man in Old Brookview. His name alone connotes almost legendary shrewdness. Roarick's story is well known around town. An irascible yet charismatic man with large appetites, he most likely created his own mythology over a strategic series of deliberate catharses to just the right person at just the right time. Like his father before him, who suffered a fatal heart attack while on a business venture in the Netherlands, Roarick has a talent for making a buck, particularly in real estate. He and his younger brother inherited a small fortune by J.R. Jr., whose own wealth and professional savvy garnered him a modest portfolio - *modest* only when compared to what his oldest son would achieve.

James' brother, rumored to never have had the stomach for canny business dealings, took his share of the inheritance and headed out west to a Montana cattle ranch. The boys' mother had run off when they were babies, so J.R. III - which he began calling himself after his father's death - a recent Air Force graduate and still in his early twenties when officially parentless, was left to his own devices.

Roarick's personal life was always a source of local intrigue. A deeply private man, he would become known as much for the cryptic ways in which he spoke of his wife and only child, Austin, as he would his business ventures. Gretchen Roarick, according to those who knew her, spent more than half the year in Nassau, where the family owned a home. When she *was* in Old Brookview, flitting about in her convertible or chauffeured sedan, marching down Main Street with her pearls swinging to the rhythm of her shopping bags, she was as easily spotted as any idiosyncratic snob might be who lives among mostly grounded people. Considerably younger than J.R. III, Mrs. Roarick had little interest in standing by her husband's side as he amassed his fortune. Nor did she wish to devote herself to philanthropy or motherhood.

Austin was only a couple of years older than me. My memories of him are limited. He always seemed to be starting and stopping school at odd times, in the throes of a long New England winter, or days after our annual benchmark tests, which were always in the first week of April. One day, he would be skulking through the halls of Old Brookview Middle School or Franklin Duval High School, sneering, mumbling to himself, aloof from his peers, and always absurdly dressed in a sport jacket and pleated pants, and then he'd be gone the next, plucked out of not only the school, but the town, and sent to some elite and expensive prep school in Pennsylvania or upstate New York. Rumors would always accompany these sudden acts of disappearing and reappearing. Trouble with the law. Drugs. Vandalism. But no one ever seemed to know for sure. As far as we were concerned, Austin, like his mother, was something of a gray ghost in Old Brookview. Transient. Elusive. Always a source of interest to locals.

Though an air of mystery surrounded Austin, he did manage to become known by his peers for a bizarre yet somewhat impressive feat. He'd obsess over a particular classmate for one reason or another - maybe their appearance, their mannerisms, their reputation - and commemorate them by authoring a singular alliterative phrase of graphic prose that would fill pages upon pages of his notebook that he'd show off like it was some miraculous artistic effort. It was a strange exercise, revealing an eerie discipline that most adolescents, ill-equipped to articulate such strangeness, would simply shrug over, albeit a bit wide-eyed and suspicious.

Edie Carlson, a frumpy, lonely girl rumored to have had sex with her first cousin, was possibly one of Austin's most conspicuous targets; thus, "Cousin-humping Carlson bore an inbred baby," consuming a novella's worth of pages, nearly became a mantra one year until it was shut down by the administration. What ended up being as memorable as Austin's writings was the nickname this odd literary tic bestowed upon him. Repeat Offender. Given his predilection for repetition, not to mention his constant treks to the principal's office, Repeat Offender seemed befitting.

James Roarick III's professional exploits had become legendary by the time he was just shy of his twenty-fourth birthday. With the help of a team of attorneys, he supposedly strong-armed the owner of the local movie theatre out of business before scooping up the gorgeous Mock Tudor style building on the front street. He did some light renovations, renamed the place Roarick Art Cinemas, and opened its doors a few weeks later. This became standard for J.R III. He was a hustler, never beneath threatening anyone in his way. By the time he was in his early thirties, he owned most of Old Brookview's businesses: Page Turners, the town's bookstore, Tits, which became Louden's Diner, renamed after his black lab, the professional building, the movie theatre, four gas stations, several apartments and houses in and around town, and Tiny's Drugstore, given its name after his own ironic military moniker; J.R. III, at well over six feet tall with a broad, barrel chest and powerful limbs, is a hulking figure who can palm the average man's head while towering over him.

Most importantly - especially for my father and his soon-to-be bride - J.R. III owned a hundred acres off of Wildwood Road, a rustic area that runs along the interstate, and yet is remote from the rest of the town. Roarick is rumored to have acquired the property in one of his infamous cutthroat deals, which supposedly involved him dangling a man from his boat when they went yachting to discuss the abandoned land.

Roarick sat on the property for nearly three years, no doubt contemplating his options. The obvious must've occurred to him: level it, including every outbuilding, and install a few housing developments, boasting high-end homes with three car garages, cathedral ceilings, and master suites. This would've been a lucrative venture. And J.R. III could've gotten around the permits he would need to pull, as well as the obscene amount of capital he'd have to come up with to get the project off the ground. Instead, he became inspired by two bright-eyed Cornell grads who were squandering their talents by slinging home fries and scrubbing pots and pans in his diner.

My parents were not too proud to work manual labor jobs, even with the ink barely dry on their graduate degrees. Years later, Rollie told me that working at the diner was one of the happiest times of his life. This was the early 1970s when it was easier to be a nomad. It was pre-internet and pre-cell phone. The romance of America might've been blunted by recent political assassinations and the looming catastrophe of Vietnam, but not snuffed out completely. My parents deliberately gave themselves the time to read and think and grow not only their ideals, but the love they shared with one another.

Roarick, who owned the diner, could be found there daily. The place functioned as his ersatz office. His business meetings were held at a reserved table by a window, away from other patrons. They were public displays of clandestine affairs. It became typical for Old Brookview residents to witness J.R. III storm out of the diner in a huff of impatience after gathering his briefcase and throwing a handful of bills on the table. When he wasn't meeting with attorneys or investors, he was often seen at his spot, poring over a scattered mess of paperwork while nursing a cup of coffee into which he'd occasionally drop a bit of brandy.

Roarick, nearly a decade older than my mother, called her Ginny, which, according to my father, no one had ever called her before. Roarick also told her she reminded him of Mia Farrow, only a prettier version. And he left her twenty dollar tips for refilling his coffee or fetching him a corn muffin. The Old Man was never put off by any of this; J.R. III knew Ginny was spoken for, and his advances were therefore nothing more than playful gestures.

"He was interested in us equally," my father has told me. "He was curious about our studies and our travels and our domicile on wheels. He jokingly referred to it as our green monstrosity."

It was this very monstrosity, this 1967 lime-green Winnebago, that was the catalyst in establishing what would prove to be an alliance for all parties. Roarick would tease my mother about the place she called home. How did she live in such tight quarters with Rollie? Sleeping, eating, bathing. Not to mention the wormy-looking heap didn't even run, so how did she and the Old Man get around? Errands, shopping, outings. He was genuinely intrigued, he told her. So one morning, after humoring another series of comments and inquiries over the vehicle, my parents invited Roarick for a personal tour of their humble abode.

J.R. III was polite as they pointed out where they ate, slept, read, played cards, used the bathroom. Ducking and sliding his large frame at every tight space, Roarick took the short tour with gasps of awed wonderment at their ability to live so free and Spartan-like. Noticing an impressive collection of books on some shelves above the tiny dinette, Roarick, himself a voracious reader, inspected the types of literary fodder his employees took to. He was taken with the results, which were mostly ponderous textbooks on philosophy, education, and psychology. Between my parents, they had a veritable library crammed into the vehicle. There were texts on Plato and John Locke and Descartes and moral philosophy and critical thinking; there were those on behavior and classroom management; child and adolescent psychology; assessment; curriculum; human exceptionalities; and children with mild to severe disabilities.

Roarick must have sensed his employees were bookish, but he knew little else about them - their background, their pursuits, and their design for their futures. Roarick asked them about their studies at Cornell. He asked about their internships and their aspirations. They told him where and how they had met, which was at a Don McLean concert at the university. This was during their first year at Cornell, and, as my father tells the story, which he has on numerous occasions, McLean, supposedly, performed his famed paean "American Pie" for the first time that evening, nearly one year before it would be released to the public.

"So," Roarick must've said, taking in the couple's history as well as obvious expertise, "what's it all mean? What are you going to do with it?"

The truth was, according to the Old Man, he and my mother had talked only a few times about opening their own school. Mostly, though, it was a pipedream, steeped in the earnest if somewhat idealistic notion that they could pool their passion and knowledge and change a small corner of the world. My father figured he'd teach - probably high school, and definitely to a special ed. population - while my mother seemed interested in being a child psychologist.

Sensing who they were talking to, a powerful man with money and connections, they took on the roles of two visionaries. According to Rollie, it was my mother who steered the conversation, presenting to Roarick copious ideas about a very unique type of boarding school. One that would be a therapeutic as well as educational milieu. One that would serve adolescents who were less than successful in a mainstream school setting. It would employ a full staff of licensed psychiatrists, teachers - who would also be dorm staff - and administrators, who would be general overseers and case managers. And it would capitalize on and combine the talents and expertise of two Cornell grads, who had earned respective degrees in psychology and education.

Much of this, according to Rollie, was extemporized. The heart of the idea *was* genuine, but most of the specifics were born at that moment. My mother's muse was nothing more than possibility. She recognized Roarick as a man who could make things happen. According to my father, she was anything but a sycophant. "She simply played the situation beautifully," he's bragged to me through the years. Though she couldn't have known that at the time. Most likely, she expected nothing from this man, who probably negotiated multimillion-dollar deals over breakfast; it was too fantastical to concede that he would ever get involved with two ivy-league drifters who worked in his diner for minimum wage. My father tells me his role was to go along with everything my mother said, agreeing with this or that, backing her up, adding in a detail or two. Roarick, listening, simply nodded his head in approval over the couple's lofty design, complimented them on their Winnebago, and saw himself out.

Nearly a full month passed before J.R. III invited my parents to dinner at his home in town. He told them the affair would be business mixed with pleasure. They accepted and were picked up by a chauffeur and driven to their host's waterfront property, a now legendary landmark in town, and where he still resides today. There, over drinks and hors d'oeuvres, Roarick got down to it, submitting his proposal. He had one-hundred prime acres in town; it was good land with great possibility, he told them. It needed some upkeep - a little mowing, planting, painting, rebuilding - but it was nothing a few dollars couldn't take care of.

"I see *your* school on *my* property," Roarick told them. "Think of it as your own playground. Do what you know how to do, however you want to do it, with no interference from me."

This was a real offer. A once-in-a-lifetime offer. They knew Roarick could make it happen - a few phone calls, probably; maybe a meeting with his accountant over coffee and brandy. They knew, running on romantic grandeur and the fumes of flower power, that they could bring their tenuous vision to light, that they could play the parts of academic and therapeutic luminaries until they paid their dues for real and could legitimize their positions as overseers of their own school. For now, though, they thought, *hell yes*. Toasts were made that evening. Hands were shaken. A deal was sealed.

Either Rollie had the pool table inside the pavilion re-felted, or else he bought a new one. Cupping my hands against the window and peering into the rec room, I can't tell. But the felt used to be green and now it's a deep, flashy red. Who knows if they do this anymore, but when I was a kid, the HAS would have an annual pool tournament in the spring. Faculty versus students. And every year the Old Man would drag me to the event as though it was a red-carpet gala. During the walk over from our house, he'd talk about the student players like they were first-round draft picks from some elite billiard squad. The entire affair bored me to tears. I'd always end up slumping in one of the sofas and removing a paperback from my back pocket. Then I'd quietly read next to some melancholy kid who'd stare off into the void with an agonized expression on his face. The loud crack of the pool balls would occasionally jar me. So I'd look over at the Old Man, who was often eliminated after the first round, but still liked to rally around the action that would dominate the room. He never seemed to notice, or mind, that I wasn't part of it. On our walk home, he'd talk about the student who won - he always saw to it that the stubby little gold trophy went to a HASER - as well as all of the close shots and lucky breaks. Never, though, did he comment on my apathy.

It was only until I was older that I was able to fully appreciate the pavilion. When the school shuts down for vacation - two weeks around Christmas, two in March, June, and August - the student body goes home. Rollie encourages the kids to use this time to employ whatever coping strategies they've learned in therapy. Who knows the ratio of success stories to catastrophes during these reprieves, but I do recall my father getting frantic phone calls from parents, pleading with him to allow their child to return early. The Old Man, firm in his conviction that families need to weather the acrimony until the break is over, never relented. This, for me, was a God-send. It meant the campus would be deserted. I took full advantage of this. The pavilion, as far as I could see, was the only real perk the school could offer me. Rollie would thus give me my own key, allowing me access whenever I felt the desire to shoot pool or play some foosball with friends. We'd throw back some shitty second-rate beer while reveling in having the place to ourselves. Though my disgust for the HAS was known among my peers, I was nevertheless conflicted when one of them, Pete Slattery, spat a wad of phlegm on the pavilion's floor one evening.

A far more memorable time was when I brought along Tiffany Luster, a doe-eyed, busty brunette with a killer smile and a penchant for fellatio. Hardly a neophyte - even at just seventeen - she was rumored to be something of a teenage prodigy in this realm. And though Erin, my first, was my only other means of comparison - she had broken up with me our senior year to date a University of Connecticut soccer star - I felt I had no right to challenge such an accolade.

Suddenly, in the midst of my pornographic musing, I'm tapped hard on the shoulder. Turning around, I'm face-to-face with a short, pudgy woman with shoulder-length hair and a red bandana wrapped around her forehead. She wields one of those long police flashlights, and even though daylight has fully emerged in a quiet, catlike furtiveness, she clicks its black button on and off, shining a sharp sword of light off to her side and into the overhanging branches. A walkie-talkie dangles from her side, pulling at her too-tight jean shorts, which are bursting with pale, pasty flesh. This, clearly, is the Old Man's top-notch security.

She stares me down, pressing me with a wiry, loathsome look. I catch a glance at her shadow, a bulbous tar spill that grows out from behind her, making a mess of the cement walkway.

"And your business here is what exactly?" she asks. "In other words, can I help you with something?"

"I was just looking around," I tell her, smirking over her truculence. "Reminiscing, really."

"This campus is private property," she tells me, holstering her flashlight. "In other words, you can't be here."

I tell her she's doing a hell of a job in keeping the place safe from crazy people. Then I add that they could hurt the other crazy people. She finds none of this amusing, so I relent and tell her I'm Rollie's son from Chicago.

"We'll see about that," she said, lifting the walkie-talkie from her side. "In other words, stay put."

She calls what she refers to as home base, asking that they contact the boss to see if he's expecting his son. When she's done with the call, she continues to stare at me. This time more pensively, like she's trying to place whether she's seen me before. Gone is the hard, distrustful look. Clearly she believes me. But she has to follow procedure, I'm sure. After a few moments, a man's voice comes back to her, saying it's okay, adding that Rollie is at home and has been waiting for me; he wants me to walk over, the voice tells her. She clips the walkie-talkie to her side and continues to turn the flashlight on and off.

"I didn't know Rollie even had a son."

I nod and walk past her, apologizing for any trouble I might've caused. When I'm barely a few feet away, she calls out to me:

"Chicago, huh? I've never been before. I hear it's a fun city."

I stop walking and wheel around to face her.

"It's not," I tell her, shaking my head. "In other words, it sucks."

The Old Man is standing on his front porch, drinking from a bright, yellow mug, staring out at the road, which runs parallel a couple hundred feet away. He's dressed for the day, wearing a pressed black short-sleeved shirt, khaki pants, and a black tie, which has dripping silver beads of water as its pattern.

"What the hell's the matter with you?" he asks, setting the mug on the railing. "Snooping around like a goddamn cat burglar after what this place is going through. Do I need to tell you how on edge my staff are? And the kids? You know better than to sneak around like that. Louise was gonna call the cops, you know. I should've had her shoot you."

The Old Man looks good. Tired, maybe. And certainly worried. But fit and healthy. His skin has already turned to that pie crust brown it turns every summer, even after only a few days of digging around in his gardens. It looks like he's dropped a few pounds since I last saw him four years ago. I wonder if he thinks it's a shame that it's been so long. I wonder if I do, too.

"You look good," I tell him, my voice laden with surprise.

I begin to think about my own appearance and what's changed in the last few years. I now wear glasses, which I tried to avoid for some time, and I wear my hair a little shorter than I might've when Rollie last saw me, convinced this will make imminent graying less apparent.

He offers me some green tea, which I refuse, so he takes me on a tour of the campus. I have neither the heart nor the energy to tell him I'd just completed my own private one when Louise, in all her chubby glory, came upon me at the pavilion.

As we start walking around the place, things begin to emerge from their dusky a.m. withering and come to life. There's a maintenance man pitching a freshly painted sign in front of the Minnie House, which bears the dormitory's name in straight, neat, yellow letters. His name is Diego and the Old Man introduces me, calling me his long lost son from Chicago. Diego, smiling - I can tell his English is shaky at best - offers his hand, which I accept before we move on.

"We've had the inside of every dorm updated. New bathroom fixtures; new carpets; mostly new furniture, too."

A young woman, probably in her early twenties, wearing tight black shorts and a long-sleeved shirt, is race-walking on the narrow road that cuts through the heart of the campus. She's wearing earbuds, and I can hear the bass and drums of her music as she flashes a smile at us and moves briskly past. The Old Man tells me her name is Carrie; she teaches math and resides at the Helen House.

Each dormitory has two staffers, both of whom are also teachers. They work in the dorm on a rotating schedule; the first will be on duty one night, fielding complaints, breaking up fights, pleading with wired, rambunctious insurgents to close their eyes and go to bed - as well as work the following morning, having similar responsibilities - before switching with their counterpart. Weekends, where the staff clocks in dozens of weary hours, function the same way: one weekend on, one weekend off. It seems like a grueling schedule, which is probably why the turnover rate is so high. Teachers stick around, on average, two to three years. Any more than that and there will be a need to start usurping the kids' meds: *one for you, two for me*...

The Old Man continues to point out improvements and additions. The gym floor was stripped and refinished. A small plot was cleared behind the Helen and Minnie Houses, where a Gazebo has been installed. A new garden of impatiens here. A new walkway there.

"We've even got t-shirts now. And take a guess what it says on them?"

"School's mission statement."

"You're a goddamn clairvoyant."

"Seems like you're spending a lot of dough on the place. Too much, maybe."

Since he doesn't own the school, every improvement made, every nickel spent, every headache and backache endured, is strictly in the name of J.R. III.

"It's money well spent."

What a saint he is. Just like some superhero or fairy-tale character. Do for others no matter the cost. Be selfless. Be righteous. Be magnanimous. What lessons. What inspirations. We're not living in one another's worlds. We never have, either.

Money is something we don't often talk about. And though I know he's not hurting, and never has, I couldn't say what he's worth. He lives simply. The car he drives and the clothes he wears are modest. He doesn't travel or gamble or make unwise investments. He could easily splurge and buy a villa in St. Thomas, or maybe that '59 Thunderbird he's fantasized about over the years. None of this appeals to him. Decadence. Self-reward. These do not register with the man.

"Well, I suppose when you're collecting $100,000 per student, you can afford to buy a few new windows or desks or gallons of paint. Right?"

Ignoring my comment, he puts his hand on my back - the first physical contact we've made since seeing one another - and eases me into resuming our tour. We walk behind the Joni House, where two female students are crouched by the bulkhead door, smoking cigarettes and talking in low whispers. Rollie steers me in their direction. They don't extinguish their smokes when we approach them. One of the girls is pretty with straight, shoulder-length hair and high cheekbones that look to be chiseled from white slate. She clutches a pack of Marlboros and a chrome lighter. The other girl is a behemoth with a long face and dark, brooding eyes.

"I see Alyssa here is a fine influence on you, Desi," the Old Man says.

The girl I imagine to be Alyssa - the attractive one - rolls her eyes and exhales a steady stream of smoke. The large girl, Desi, at least makes an effort to show her shame by hiding the lit cigarette behind her back.

"Does Tennille know where you girls are?" Rollie asks.

"She thinks we're taking out the trash," says the pretty girl, still smoking. "She's clueless."

Rollie puts his hand out and asks for their cigarettes. They both stand up. Alyssa takes a final drag before dropping the butt and handing over the pack and the lighter. Desi extinguishes hers into the ground before flicking it behind her.

"A real nasty habit," says the Old Man, crushing the pack in his hand. "And something I think we've spoken about one too many times. I think we need to look into that nicotine gum. It worked for your pal Sloane."

Alyssa, I realize, is staring at me. She asks my father who I am. He again introduces me as his long lost son from Chicago. He tells her that I'll be working at the Hundred Acre School for the time being. She stares another moment and then tells me I should go back to Chicago.

"Haven't you heard there's a killer on the loose?" she asks. "And it could even be a HAS student. Who the fuck knows, it could even be me. Or Desi."

Desi's mouth turns into a fleshy, oblong hole as she shoots her friend an incredulous stare.

"Smoking *and* swearing," says the Old Man, his voice filled with stern affection. "Going for Miss Congeniality again this year, Alyssa?"

The girl rolls her eyes and tells him she'd rather go blind and insane. The Old Man wishes the girls a pleasant morning and says he'll see them at breakfast. As we turn away, Alyssa calls out to me, addressing me as Rollie's long lost son from Chicago:

"I was serious about what I told you before. You should go back to Chicago. *I* would."

The girls turn away and walk around the house and out of sight. My father and I continue our walk. He tells me about both students. Desi, the heavy one, suffers from severe depression and has struggled with a school phobia her entire life. When she was in eighth-grade, she tried to stab one of her teachers with a broken test tube; that was two years ago.

"She's made a lot of progress."

As for Alyssa, she has a clinical diagnosis of borderline personality disorder.

"It means she's impulsive as hell. And she struggles with interpersonal relationships. Rapid mood changes - you name it."

The Old Man adds that she's attempted suicide a handful of times. On the upside, he tells me proudly, she has yet to make any attempts while a student at the HAS, which has been for just over eight months.

"You can imagine how our recent tragedy is affecting these kids," he says. "They're kids who need stability and safety. This has really fucked with them. We're naturally concerned that some of our good work might be undone. And we're going to do whatever it takes to see that that doesn't happen."

As we approach the Winnebago, Rollie asks if I notice anything different about it. I study it for a moment before shaking my head. The tires, he tells me. They're new. He laughs at himself for the purchase, but adds that he no longer has to refill the air every few weeks.

"Looks pretty good," he said. "Doesn't it?"

Carefully running his hand along its side, he mentions that he has it washed every week or so by Adam and Matt, two handy students who regularly try to coax him into letting them get under the vehicle's hood. Scoffing, he tells me how the boys swear they can restore it to running condition. My stomach suddenly grumbles, which reminds me I haven't eaten anything since a granola bar a few hours earlier.

"When's breakfast?" I ask, looking at my watch.

Tolerating Rollie's passions - his students as well as nostalgia over my mother - will be sufferable only with a plate of food in front of me. He scrapes something off the Winnebago with his fingernail before we move along towards the baseball field, where we stop in front of the yellow police tape. My father puts out his hand as if to say *here you have it*.

"The coroner's report isn't in yet," he tells me. "So nothing's official. But I have a friend downtown and he's hinting at a strangulation. We'll see."

He curses a bit and says a prayer for the dead girl, Nicole D'Ambrosio.

"One hell of a way to begin the summer, don't you think?" he says.

"I don't even know what to say."

"Listen," he says, putting his hand on my back, "what's that thing about bad luck coming in threes? Because we had something happen here a few weeks ago with one of our dorm staff, a guy named Dimitri."

We continue our walk as he launches into the story of his former employee, Homer House dorm staff and English teacher, Dimitri Ames, a young man he hired five months earlier, right after the new-year. He was just out of college, the Old Man tells me, and a talented kid: He's a skilled martial artist; plays the piano; lacrosse; and is an expert sailor and fisherman.

Whenever he interviews for positions, Rollie scours resumes in search of skills that might benefit as many of his kids as possible. He likes to hire staff who can play instruments and sports. He likes to hire those who appreciate and partake in the arts: dancing, painting, acting, sculpting, playing the goddamn oboe. This all apparently comes in handy when you're trying to fill the hours with a bunch of kids who either want to sleep their lives away or swallow a box of poison to end them.

"He seemed well-liked," he says, leading me past the gymnasium. "Good teacher, good dorm staff. Got solid evaluations."

As he talks about this Dimitri character, I take notice of the gym, which is where I'll be staying. The building has a small second floor apartment with a kitchenette and pull-out sofa. It was once used as a storage space, but the Old Man had it converted so he could occasionally offer parents a place to spend the night. It has its own entrance in the way of a long, narrow staircase in the rear.

Rollie sent me a text a couple of weeks ago that read, "We've avoided talking about the living arrangement. You're welcome to stay with me, but I'll understand if you need your own space." My response was as tactful as I could manage: "I don't want to put you out. The gym apt. will work fine." This arrangement might be the lesser of two evils, but I'm uncertain. I'm not thrilled about being so close in proximity to the students, as the gymnasium is in plain view of every girls dormitory, but living under the same roof as my father is the brashest acknowledgement of my failures that I can imagine.

We continue our walk, crossing Wildwood Road, which is lifeless at the moment, and make our way along the north side of campus. We pass Rollie's place, which he points to, mentioning how he had the basement finished into living space. Admitting its absurdity - after all, he has the entire three bedroom house to himself - he laughs and tells me he's created a haven for those looking for a little grown-up reprieve. Replete with a card table, jukebox, and mini-bar, the Old Man says many good times have already been had there. His staff, he tells me, work hard and deserve a good time without always having to leave campus.

"Don't think I fool myself into believing that my little card games are the *only* adult fun being had on this campus. I know what else is going on, and they're entitled to it all with the way they work."

He stops to pick up a soda can from off the ground.

"I pride myself on my ability to judge character," he tells me. "And you sure as hell need to know how to do that when you're running a business. I'd say my track record speaks for itself. But this time I was duped."

"We're talking about this Dimitri guy?"

He doesn't answer. Crinkling his forehead, he turns to me. Looking at my watch again, I ask about breakfast.

"We're fine. It starts at 7:00."

I follow his lead to the staff entrance of the Homer House. A converted Cape that has been eviscerated and made to accommodate up to ten students, it's one of the school's larger dormitories. Each dorm has two or three bedrooms, a common room, a large bathroom, and two small, fully equipped staff apartments.

The Old Man pulls a key from his pocket and unlocks the door before ushering me into the faculty apartment. It's barely five-hundred square feet. The kitchen, just off the entrance, has dated yellow appliances and white countertops with an outbreak of some gold speckled pattern that resembles measles. The cabinets are stained a dark chocolate finish, and the linoleum floor, though sparkling in its yellow and green octagonal patterns, could be some giant 1970's board game.

"What are we doing here?" I ask, trying to recall my memory of this place from when I saw it as a kid.

Rollie leads me through the apartment. Aside from the kitchen, there's a tiny bedroom with a futon and nightstand, an office or living room with a teal loveseat and an old TV atop a cheap, black wooden stand, and a bathroom, which is top to bottom in an off-white subway tile. The place will never win any awards, but it's clean and well-kept. It's also empty. Besides the furniture, there are no personal effects. Nothing hangs on the walls except a blank bulletin board above a small writing desk.

"Do you have any idea how long I deliberate over the hiring of my staff?"

"I do not."

"Sometimes it takes me a few weeks just to respond to a resume. I know the world moves quicker than this, and I know I run the risk of losing some good people with my pussyfooting around."

"I suppose you would."

"And I'm a man who trusts his instincts."

"I know you are."

"But sometimes they go to sleep on you."

"I know they do."

He turns and walks into the kitchen where he sets the soda can he's been holding on the countertop. I watch him from the living room. He strokes his beard and lifts his glasses from his nose to check the lenses. Then he launches into something. *Ethics and ethical theories. Hedonism. Plato and absolutism. Evil.* And finally, *the good*, which, he mentions, is Plato's wording. And it's on this he focuses.

"How simple is *that*?" he asks, spinning the can around on the counter. "*The good*. Just the name alone: the good. Nothing too lofty. If people can discover what's good, and this is according to Plato, then they will never act wickedly. The question then becomes how do we define *good*? A lot of us assume that the world has long ago decided on a definition, right?"

My stomach grumbles.

"Right?" he asks again.

He picks the can off the counter and turns it over in his hand.

"I'm not sure what you're getting at. In fact, I think you lost me back at the Winnebago."

"He was fucking around with her. A student. An eighteen-year-old student. In here, for Christ's sake. He was fucking around with her, probably in these rooms."

"We're back on Dimitri, right?"

My father tells me the story. The student's name is Lindsay Lowe. Depression. Anxiety. Some oppositional behaviors. Bright girl, though. Affluent family. Dysfunctional, yet affluent. Brother seems to have his shit together. He goes to Yale and visits her on occasion. Lindsay was a member of the school's ill-fated and short-lived lacrosse club, where it was discovered - after a series of interviews with the other students on the team - that coach and athlete would engage in steady one-on-one dialogues, heavy with innuendo and suggestive glances. None of it ever had anything to do with lacrosse. The girl, who Rollie describes as pretty and vulnerable, was the perfect target.

"They all are," he adds. "They're all looking for the same thing. And they'll search high and low for anyone who'll offer it to them. Well, this fucking guy was offering."

The sound of voices beyond Dimitri Ames' apartment seems to rise out of nowhere. I hear a voice of authority mention something about vacuuming the carpets before breakfast. It's the HASERS, who are just beyond these walls, probably trying to fleece their way out of morning chores.

"They would come in here during his prep period - most mornings at about 10:00. He'd be in here, and she'd skip her calculus class and pay him a visit. The rest of the dorm was empty, so they had the place to themselves.

When she was confronted about all the cuts, she said she was roaming the campus, thinking, smoking, crying. This went on for almost two months. *Two months.*"

I can remember through the years the Old Man dealing with a few flirty staffers - mostly males - who either made a remark, an advance, whatever. It wasn't the norm, but it did happen from time to time. The energy that pervades the Hundred Acre School stems from its commune-like vibe, everyone living and eating together; this hardly negates the underbelly of the place, which are the secrets, fears, and failures lurking in so many shadows and belonging to adults and children alike. From my vantage point, trust and loyalty among staff and students always seem to be on trial. And more often than not, the outcome is that of a hung jury. Those who work at the HAS do their best to sell themselves, to convince everyone of their pure and altruistic heart. And in a medicated blur, the students won't think twice about shucking away their old life for a newer one in the arms of whoever can make them feel the steps of some endless, euphoric dance.

"She told us *every*thing. She cooperated. But he was another story. Would you believe he threatened me? That little pissant."

And though Ames couldn't be brought up on formal legal charges - the girl's not a minor, the Old Man points out - a lawsuit is certainly possible. The parents could sue the school, he says in almost a whisper. He adds that the likelihood of that is slim - the girl's parents are going through an epic divorce and are caught up with that at the moment.

"I had to move a few things around to get his classes covered these past couple of weeks. And Ryan, the other dorm staff - that's him you just heard out there - well, he's been working to the bone, nonstop really. But it's time to find a replacement. Which hasn't been easy, by the way. I can't bring myself to take much of a risk right now in hiring just anyone. There's too much at stake. Too much going on. Too much fucking chaos. These kids are just looking for any excuse to burn and loot. I've got the police up my ass - the whole town really. That D'Ambrosio girl was a local princess and they need a scapegoat. Do you see what I'm saying, Grayson? I do for you and you do for me. Hell, it's English, for Christ's sake. You were a fucking journalism major. It's nearly perfect."

The vacuum starts in the other room. My father is looking at me, waiting for a response. Producing one should be as easy as telling an obnoxious salesman you're uninterested in their pitch. Or telling some nameless, faceless voice over the phone you're not only tapped out, but you gave at work, so thanks but no thanks and good luck. But for some reason, the words aren't that forthcoming.

"C'mon," I said, which is the only thing that comes to mind.

"Free rent, free food, free utilities. *You* know how this works as well as anyone. Plus a nice little salary. Not bad."

He goes on to tell me about the kids in the Homer House. There are nine boys; the youngest is sixteen and the oldest is eighteen. They have a broad spectrum of diagnoses, ranging from OCD and bipolar disorder to mild autism and severe ADD. He says that they're a wild bunch, but they've been tamed pretty well by Ryan. Except for Nick Russo, he adds; he's the eighteen-year-old.

"He's got some anger issues we're working on. Must've broken half a dozen windows around campus over the last few months. But he's an interesting kid."

"This is your sales pitch? Autism? Bipolar? Broken windows?"

From the other room, the vacuum emits that shredding sound it makes when it sucks up shards of debris. Rollie tells me he can finagle what's called a Durational Shortage Permit through the state of Connecticut. This will allow him to hire an uncertified teacher due to either extreme circumstances or lack of desirable candidates.

"I've done it before," he tells me.

I shake my head at him.

"You know what Spinoza's contention was?"

"Unfuckingbelievable. You're going to wield your philosophical drivel until I'm overcome with mental fatigue and become a relenting slob? Give me a break with that stuff."

"That all actions are determined by past experiences, by physical and mental constitution, and by the state of nature's laws at *that* moment."

I'm still shaking my head at him. The vacuum continues to bellow a steady drone in the other room.

"I don't know exactly what it was, Gray, but something led you back to this place. Something did."

"A divorce did. It was a divorce. There's no philosophy in that."

He tells me he believes it goes deeper than that. Then he tells me he spoke with two parents earlier in the day who are considering withdrawing their children from the school. It always surprises me when I hear about students' parents. It rarely occurs to me that these kids even have parents. They're trapped in my brain as wayward misfits, castaways, abandoned on the Old Man's doorstep. I have trouble envisioning them sitting Indian style beside a Christmas tree with shreds of paper strewn about; or seated at the dinner table, eating and talking with levity; or just saying goodnight to one another and meaning it. It truly strikes me that they have parents. Parents who love and worry and doubt and remember.

"And I'm not sure I can blame them," he adds.

A posting was put on the school's website. A letter was sent home. And calls were made, all explaining what had happened with the D'Ambrosio girl.

"We're going to lose a few students. It's inevitable."

"You might have to moonlight," I tell him. "Find a way to recoup that lost revenue."

Ignoring my sarcasm, he checks his phone before telling me he's heading over to the dining hall. He encourages me to look over my new place before joining him.

"I'll introduce you to the staff throughout the day. And I'll show you your classroom after breakfast."

He swipes the soda can off the counter, gives me a nod, and leaves me alone in Dimitri Ames' old staff apartment. The moment he shuts the door, the vacuum cleaner ceases its hacking cough. And I'm left hearing a lone voice, mumbled at first, then more audible. It builds into a hostile whine, careening through the air in prepubescent squawks and expletives. Then another harmonizes with it, creating a caustic, discordant tangle. Then another. Then another.

Sitting on the teal loveseat, I can't help but think what Dimitri Ames probably did on it some mornings with a willing eighteen-year-old student over a two month stretch. And though I haven't eaten anything substantial in hours, my appetite is suddenly gone.

CHAPTER 4

It was a few days before spring when Laura and I met with the Cadman brothers to plan our kitchen. There were decisions to be made. Island or breakfast bar? Granite or marble countertops? Appliances. Cabinets. Lighting. Flooring. We sat in their dingy trailer, across from the brothers, and perused stacks of three-ring binders. Both men, chewing on sunflower seeds and spitting the shells into their palms, would either nod and mumble in agreement over our taste, or else scoff, confiding in us in a sort of menacing whisper, that the particular distributor we were considering made a sub-par product.

"I can't imagine the missus here would settle for *subpar*," one of the brothers said, a speck of shell in the corner of his mouth. "She deserves topnotch. Doesn't she?"

Laura was always polite about the flattery. Even though she knew it was overflowing with sleazy intent. But she would smile and be agreeable, never letting them dissuade her from her choices. We were first-time buyers, but savvy enough to understand that the Cadmans were working tactfully to not only flirt with my wife, but to encourage us to exceed our allowances. They mostly ignored me, focusing instead on the *princess*, as they continued to call her.

In the beginning, we met with them an average of a few times a month. Each meeting revealed some newly bizarre behavior. Like one of them repeatedly discussing his ex-wife, even referring to her on one occasion as a "dishrag slut." Or they would curse at one another over pricing or timeline quotes. One afternoon, while we were meeting with one of the brothers to pick out lighting fixtures, he reached into a small duffel bag on his desk and produced some rolling papers and a mason jar full of pot. Then he rolled the world's fattest joint and proceeded to smoke it in front of us, explaining that it was medicinal.

There was a lot to laugh at during this time. And our laughter was that rare type that had within it subtle traces of delirium that might've been masquerading behind a wayward kind of hopefulness. Just like building a new home, though, conceiving a child didn't turn out the way we thought it would. Conception proved more complicated than we had imagined. But we enjoyed the process; our physical relationship had always been healthy, and though its purpose did somewhat change, we maintained a steadfast attraction to one another.

Laura. Graceful Laura. Her sweet, brown cookie-dough eyes; her perfect breasts and body; her heavy, ruler-straight hair that falls around her heart-shaped face in exotic, wavelike motion whenever she moves or mindlessly throws it from side to side. I loved to look at her from across a room when she was reading or sleeping or on the computer. She was able to be still and silent and yet somehow inspire in me an almost manic burst of worry and elation over what the future might hold for us. There was a magic to Laura, a reservoir of grace and goodwill that made me feel like I deserved her, which I probably didn't.

It was during one of our early meetings with the brothers when we discovered we were the first to buy into Grove Garden Estates. Covering one of the trailer's walls was a map of the development, each of the six properties delineated in thick, red marker. Our lot, number three, had a black asterisk next to it, which meant it was under contract. Like the others, it was level, wooded in the rear, and had two full acres. We chose it simply because the road in front of it, once paved, would resemble a sort of cul-de-sac. This, we imagined, would someday be ideal for tricycles and hopscotch and mosaics sketched out in sidewalk chalk. Laura's parents approved of our plan.

"That's the way to do it," Laura's father, Luke, told me one evening when we had them over for dinner. "You get yourself in the door, get settled, and watch the price of the rest of those homes get jacked up, thirty, forty grand. Meanwhile, you've got the most equity."

I nodded as if I had planned it this way. What the hell did I know about what we were doing? In my mind, we just seemed to be on the verge of learning how to behave like adults.

Laura's parents always let me think I was somehow gifted in the art of caring for their daughter. Like I had lived up to the solemn vows I had pledged in front of God and Grandma and Cousin Lou. They never hesitated to celebrate our good fortune or Laura's contentment, which she would display to her entire family. So I'd receive a clap on the back from Luke, or a warm, inviting smile from Abby, her mother. These gestures were alien enough to me that they would almost always make me blush or secretly recoil.

The Cadman brothers must've felt a sense of relief when we were their only buyers. They were, after all, doing every bit of the work themselves. Laura and I would drive out to the development to check on the progress and behold the sight of two average sized men digging the foundation, laying the concrete, framing the house. And it would be them, they told us, who would be doing the electrical, plumbing, drywall, roofing, flooring. They'd put in twelve and fifteen hour days, so by the time we got to them, they'd be spent, head to toe in sawdust and sweat, and ready to pounce on a couple of six-packs.

We had mixed feelings about this arrangement; on the one hand, we were glad for the individual attention. Working on a single home allowed the brothers to focus their energies on the slightest of details. They could afford to be fastidious. Yet we were eager to be part of a community and begin meeting our future neighbors. Laura and I looked forward to the days of barbeques and block parties; to friendly waves during evening walks or quick trips to the grocery store; to tying a balloon to our mailbox after the birth of our children and receiving congratulations and offers of gently worn hand-me-downs. And we were looking forward to seeing who these people would be.

It became comical to enter Grove Garden Estates and behold the half dozen cleared lots with only one house under construction. When we asked the brothers about the lack of interest, they blamed a slow market, but they were optimistic they'd sell more lots by spring. You didn't have to be in real estate to have faith in this assumption. Grove Garden Estates was a beautiful subdivision, offering well-priced homes in a wonderful town. As for the brothers, they might've been eccentrics, but they clearly knew their craft.

Late one afternoon, with the framing scheduled the following day, Laura and I went to the trailer to sign some papers and cut the brothers a new check for a few grand. Abe and Caleb, standing side by side, each covered in sweat, hovered over us as we read through the fine print. Through the stiff aroma of sun-baked fatigue and beer breath, we could smell their musky cologne. When one of them snatched the check from my hand, we said our goodnights and stood to leave. It was then that Laura noticed the map of the development. Another lot had a black asterisk next to it. Lot number four.

"We've got neighbors!" she proclaimed, walking past the Cadmans and over to the map. "Hallelujah! When did this happen?"

They told us all they knew about our future neighbors, Glenn and Linda Kilburn. They'd moved out from Maryland and were renting a place in the city for the time being. He was a doctor. An oncologist. As for the wife, they weren't sure about her. No kids, though. But a nice couple. Laura, as though she was just promised a reunion with dear old friends, was beaming.

"Neighbors!" she said. "Gray, we've got neighbors!"

. . .

We met the Kilburns a few weeks later when we pulled up to our lot one early evening to check on the progress. The framing was underway, but had stalled since the brothers commenced on lot number four. The Cadmans were leading Mr. and Mrs. Kilburn around their property - at this point, only the foundation had been dug - pointing to spaces off in the distance and spitting sunflower shells onto the ground.

"Speak of the devils," one of the brothers said as we got out of our car and approached them. "We were just talking about you folks."

I introduced myself first, putting my hand out to Glenn, who took his glove off and gave me a firm grip and an easy grin. He was tall and lean with a smooth face and large, bright eyes that looked like a swirling blue concoction of kindness and mischief. Laura shook his hand as well before he introduced us to his wife, Linda. Hugging herself against the chill of the air, she was bundled in a heavy, black cashmere coat and matching gloves and hat. Forcing a smile at us, she mentioned how she was cold. A pretty woman,

Mrs. Kilburn had colorless eyes and the kind of fair skin that made me guess she was the type to arm herself with silk scarves and expensive creams against the sunlight. She looked older than her husband. She looked like a doctor's wife.

Laura asked Mrs. Kilburn which model home they had chosen. The Cadmans offered five different models, all variations of a Colonial. There was the Sheraton, the Marriott, the Radisson, the Windsor, and the Hilton.

"The Radisson," she said flatly, her voice like a bored hypnotist's.

This was the most expensive of the models. Boasting nearly six-thousand square feet, some of its extras included a plush master suite with a propane fireplace, a large bonus-room above the garage, a first floor office, a sun-porch, and a private bathroom for each of the additional four bedrooms. The Marriott, our choice, was the most modest.

"Congratulations," Laura said. "You must be excited."

"Anything will be better than Port Deposit," the woman said. "If you're at all interested in a town whose claim to fame is that it has no claim to fame, then that's your spot."

Glenn nodded his head and assured us they were happy about the move. Then he said he had a fine idea: He said their business with the Cadman brothers was just about over, and when it was - as well as ours - he and Linda would love to meet us for dinner at a quaint spot they had discovered in town. Mrs. Kilburn looked a little surprised over her husband's conviviality, but commented again on the cold and said she was eager to be indoors. She began walking towards their sporty silver coupe, which was parked alongside the trailer. She called over her shoulder to her husband, telling him he could finish up with the brothers and that she'd be in the car.

We spent a couple of hours with the Kilburns at the restaurant, a little place on the front street called the Blue Rose Café. We chatted and ate and Glenn and I had a few beers apiece while the women drank red wine. We joked about the Cadman brothers, laughing over their machismo. Glenn even did a spot-on impersonation of the two of them arguing with one another.

In between sips of his beer, Glenn told us about the position he had accepted at Northwestern Memorial. As he spoke about his schooling and recent transfer, he served up his words like they were fine, crystal wares for me and Laura to marvel over. Clearly, he enjoyed being the young, handsome, sought-after physician, who had just moved to the Windy City while awaiting his expensive suburban home to be built. Mrs. Kilburn, meanwhile, seemed to grow bored with her husband's hubris; she would either interrupt him with non sequiturs or gesture to the waiter, indifferent over the malaise she was clearly exuding.

We talked about filling those additional bedrooms in our eventual homes. Laura told Mrs. Kilburn we were trying to start a family. Glenn raised his glass and made a toast to this. But never did he, nor his wife, mention their own plans to do the same.

The Kilburns weren't our type of people. They golfed and wore expensive jewelry and perplexed common run-of-the-mill snobs like me and Laura, whose snobbery was private and necessary as a means of propriety.

I remember that afternoon vividly. I remember Laura kicking me under the table whenever Glenn's talk about his golf game or collection of vintage beer steins became boastful. I remember Mrs. Kilburn barely smiling and never actually touching anyone's glass when her husband made a toast to new neighbors. I remember my chicken was overpriced and undercooked. But what stands out most clearly was what Laura said to me in the car as we were driving back to the city.

Leaning against the headrest, she laughed to herself and said, "Well, there's still hope for lots one, two, five, and six. Isn't there?"

My thoughts exactly. The truth is that her comment would prove ironic for more than one miserable reason. As we waited for our Marriott model to be built, we continued to work on starting a family. Both of these feats proved to take longer than we had imagined. The Cadman brothers were working on lots three and four. One week would be devoted to each house at a time, while the other, during that period, saw no progress. The brothers, true to their word that they would oversee every detail, did just that. Two men constructing two homes with no outside help. This arrangement caused tensions among Abe and Caleb to soar. Each time Laura and I visited the property, the brothers would be at odds, debating costs, calculations, and methods of construction.

One evening we found the Cadmans walking towards the trailer, one brother several yards behind the other. They each stormed past us without a word, and we saw that they were both disheveled beyond normal and had split lips and bloody fists and faces.

When fourteen months had passed, there was still much work to be done. The brothers promised we'd be closing on the house after one year, which meant around Christmas. Clearly, this would not be happening. As for the Kilburn's home, it was just behind being neck-and-neck with ours. We surmised that Glenn, in some suave display of smiting the bourgeois, handed over an envelope stuffed with cash as an incentive for the brothers to remember that money talks.

Meanwhile, baby-making wasn't any easier. We were tenacious about it, yet our futile efforts were beginning to wear us down. Still refusing to call in specialists, we opted for an existentialist approach. So without ever saying it, we resigned to the belief that perhaps we weren't meant to be parents. It was through sober glances at one another after yet another negative pregnancy test. Or even how during our repeated love-making we'd sneak looks at one another that revealed worry and sorrow. Even the Old Man got in on the disappointment.

"How about a grandkid, Gray?" he said one evening over the phone. "For Christ's sake, the two of you are building that big house with all those rooms. What's the point?"

Laura and I, pragmatists to a degree, had of course considered this. Then, in the middle of May, the Cadman brothers, with a great deal of work to be done on both homes, ceased all activity and flew back to Pennsylvania. They explained to us in a rambling text that their father, Abe Sr., had suffered a stroke and that they needed to be with him at once. They would seal up the properties and be in touch with us as well as the Kilburns.

Progress ended up being delayed for months. For the first few weeks, we heard nothing from them. Then after a month we received a phone call from a woman back in Harrisburg, PA, who said her name was Janice and she was the Cadman's secretary. Abe Sr. had suffered a hemorrhagic stroke, she told me. He eventually developed pneumonia and died. The family, she said, practically whispering into the phone, was devastated. I offered my condolences. Janice asked if I wanted the address to the funeral home in case I wished to send flowers. I told her I did and then pretended to look for a pen and paper.

The brothers, she told me, would be tied up for another week, but would be fulfilling their obligations after that. They ended up returning a little over a month later. Abe called us in the middle of the night to report that construction would be delayed further. In a slow, gravelly voice, which sounded nothing like I remembered, he explained that there had been quite a bit of vandalism to both houses. Windows had been smashed throughout each, and the kitchen cabinets and bathroom fixtures, which had been delivered, stored, and locked in the garages of the homes, had been spray painted. Equipment, too, he said, had gone missing. Hand tools and electric saws and boxes of nails and even bags of lawn seed and mulch. I told him Laura and I visited the house just a few days before and everything was exactly as they had left it. I thought I heard him crying on the other end of the line. But he didn't say anything for a long while. Finally, he told me he or his brother would be in touch before he hung up.

Nearly two weeks went by and we heard nothing from the Cadmans. Our texts and calls went unanswered. One night, an hour into a dinner party we were hosting, one of the brothers showed up at our place. It was Laura's mother, Abby, who answered the door to a weary and frayed looking man. Clearly drunk, he sidestepped Abby and entered the condo, asking no one in particular if the princess wanted him to enlarge the size of her walk-in closet. He could do this, he said. And it would be no trouble or additional cost. He said he knew princesses liked walk-in closets and his brother didn't need to know about it. She deserved an extra large walk-in closet, he announced. He kneaded his eye sockets with his fists and swayed back and forth as he spoke with slurred speech. We ended up filling him full of coffee and calling him an Uber. Laura's father, Luke, suggested we hire an attorney.

It became typical for the brothers to schedule appointments with us at the lot and then fail to show up. If they did make an appearance - usually buzzed and reeking of hard liquor and pot - they'd scowl at us as though we were putting them out with the questions or concerns we had. During one such meeting, one of the brothers, as they rushed us hastily through our house, projectile vomited on the plywood flooring in the dining room. Matters escalated when it came to monetary issues. They would demand payment for work that hadn't yet been done, or for work they'd already been paid for weeks earlier.

One August evening, Laura and I visited the trailer to discuss landscaping. This seemed inane to us, considering the skeletal state of the house's interior. But it was an appointment to discuss *progress*, a principle that had eluded the brothers. So we kept the meeting and even showed up ten minutes early. After our repeated banging on the trailer door, we were met by a feisty, half-naked brunette with the stub of a lit cigarette squished between rust-colored lips that looked like bear traps. The smoke filled her eyes, causing her to squint through it as she asked us who we were and what we wanted. We told her we had an appointment and that our house was being built by the Cadmans. She scratched her exposed stomach, which was trim and tanned, and looked past us towards our lot. I decided she probably had a few ex-husbands, several tattoos, and a custody battle she secretly didn't give a shit about.

Studying Laura as though she could be unwanted womanly competition, she yelled for Caleb. When he didn't answer, she said he was unavailable, that it had been one hell of a night and he was sleeping it off. She told us he had officially moved into the trailer, so we shouldn't have difficulty tracking him down. Flicking her cigarette over Laura's head, she sniffed hard, scrunching her face like some wrinkled rodent, and slammed the door in our faces.

By the time summer had ended, we contacted David Bell, an attorney and old college friend of Laura's. We weighed our options, which we soon learned were slim. The wording in our contract precluded us from recouping any capital we put down after the initial stages of construction, which, according to the fine print, was the clearing of the lot, the pouring of the foundation, and the basic framing of the house. Moreover, the parameters on the closing date were left wide open. If the Cadmans were so inclined, they could've opted to drive a single nail every other day for the next ten years without breaching a word of what we now regarded as an absurd contract.

We were left with two choices: We could walk away, losing a great sum of money, or we could hold out, pray for enough emotional rehabilitation for the brothers to finish building, and hope to have a housewarming party prior to dementia setting in. Before we could decide, something unexpected occurred. The Cadmans began working again. They put in a flurry of twelve-hour days. In one week alone, they finished the lighting, plumbing, and flooring in both houses. Their pace was astounding, their focus remarkable, their craftsmanship flawless. Conscious to not disrupt the mad geniuses, we tiptoed around this newfound luck in hushed hopes that it would continue. Upon receiving a second call from Janice, the brothers' secretary, we were to soon learn it would not. She was crying on the other line. The Cadman family was devastated, she told me. Another tragedy. After an all-night bender, Abe, in a blinding fit of rage, torched the trailer in which his younger brother slept. I was speechless. It happened the previous night, she added. Upon daybreak, Abe, contrite and forlorn, had turned himself in to authorities. Janice cried in soft static bursts like some forsaken lover trying to salvage her dignity. Because I didn't know what else to say, I asked if Caleb was all right. There was a momentary pause.

"He's in critical condition," she said.

As I sat there, listening to this faceless woman reveal to me the dysfunction of the Cadman family, all I could think of was how I was going to break it to Laura that our house would be delayed even further. Shameful and insensitive, but these were my thoughts nonetheless. Janice, probably sensing my apprehension, pulled herself together long enough to tell me that despite this misfortune, Cadman Builders intended to honor their commitment to us.

"That's a guarantee, Mr. Loveland. An absolute guarantee."

This promise was spoken with such maudlin pride that it embarrassed me to even respond.

"Fine," was all I could muster.

"We'll be in touch and get you squared away."

Before we hung up the phone, she asked if I wanted the necessary info to send my condolences to the Cadman family. I told her no, I did not.

A week and a half later, we received a call from a man named Joel Sandburg, who claimed he was the Cadman's right hand man for their Harrisburg operations. He was calling from the site of the new trailer, placed just fifty feet from the old one, which, at that point, was a charred mound of ash and twisted metal. With him, he mentioned, was a crew of four more men, all ready to go to work.

The crew commenced on Halloween day. They promised a closing date for us on or before January 10th. With work ethics that more than made up for their errant bosses, the new crew proved efficient. The house was finished two days before Christmas and we moved in on January 2nd, a full year later than had been anticipated.

The move was bittersweet. There were all the delays. There were the bizarre antics of the brothers we endured for far too long. And, most upsetting to me and Laura, there was to be no neighborhood after all. Two houses. That would be it. There would be no couples walking after supper; no children playing home run derby; no solidarity or security that inspires such suburban moves in the first place. These notions had exploded into wild plumes of smoke the night Abe Cadman went off the deep end. And there would be, for some time, a reminder of this on the ground where the trailer once sat; it was now blackened, and poorly concealed with a lopsided floating garden.

The Kilburn's house was finished just days after our own. They ended up moving in two weeks later, the day after a record-breaking snow storm. Laura brought over homemade cookies and hot chocolate. She suggested we have dinner soon. We didn't see the Kilburns for weeks after that. Holed up in our own homes, we let the cold swells of winter keep us divided until the weather warmed and the ground thawed.

So on a mid-April morning, I saw Glenn in his newly paved driveway, washing a vintage black Corvette. Whistling some tune, he watched me approach him from across our thawed lawns. It's true that we were not destined to be close friends - this was evident upon our first meeting when I learned that he golfed and was an antique enthusiast - yet I had every intention of being neighborly. We shook hands and greeted one another, joking about the end of our hibernations. Dropping the chambray into a blue bucket, Glenn stretched his arms, circling them in the direction of the newly polished Corvette. He then took a deep sigh and surveyed his work.

"Nice looking car."

"I appreciate that. It's a '66."

"Your seasonal car, I assume?"

"You assume correctly."

"Very nice."

"How about a drive once the weather gets a little warmer?"

Fighting against the moment that had turned me into some awestruck little boy, I nodded before waiting for the talk to turn adultlike. Glenn kicked it off by telling me about the landscaping company he planned on using. We talked about our wives and the local grocer and the amenities of our new town, including the used book store and the retro burger joint with the Elvis motif. Glenn mentioned taxes, saying how he figured ours might increase. He said the town would most likely take it out on us that there would be no additional homes built on our street. That Abe Cadman's wanton act of violence had in fact cost us dollars. The thought of having one and only one neighbor made me uneasy, especially neighbors like the Kilburns. I blurted out that they would most likely build on the vacant lots already primed for construction. They wouldn't let perfectly good land waste away, I said. Glenn smiled and shook his head.

"No way," he said, "at least not for a few years. The Cadmans are done for. Finished."

I suggested that the brothers would sell the remaining land to new developers.

"Eventually," Glenn said. "But that'll take time. Trust me. There's going to be new permits and logistics and a shit load of red tape involved. I'm afraid it's just the four of us - for now, anyway."

I would remember this final declaration many times, recalling the way he said it, which seemed almost sinister. Like he was privy to my disappointment and was glad for it. Like me, he must've known we were vastly different from one another. So there was likely a shared feeling that the other man must somehow be flawed.

Glenn's math would prove to be just slightly off. I didn't know it the moment I was talking to him - I would find out a few days later when Laura nearly fainted at work and went to the doctor - but there would be one additional member to the Grove Garden community. It suddenly felt as though a new language had developed between me and Laura. When I think back on that time now, I recall a lot of silences that would give way to joyous bursts of talking. Ideas on parenting styles and baby names were presented with little forethought and then abandoned the second a better one surfaced. In my prideful haste, I even bought balloons - blue and pink ones - and tied them to our mailbox. Laura laughed at this and informed me that such a tradition was for *after* the child was born.

We joked that the pregnancy must've been fate's intervention. After all, we endured so many fruitless attempts at conceiving. We endured the Cadman brothers and the delay in building our new home. We endured having Glenn and Linda Kilburn as our only neighbors. So I suppose we felt as though we deserved this child and this feeling that our world had just been born out of some cosmically divine womb, and all its greatness and justice and cheer was for us and us alone.

But before the year's end, Laura and I would be tested like never before; the hourglass had been tipped, and all the optimism and renewal that had rushed at us with a boundless overflowing had suddenly been dammed at the very moment we decided to count our blessings.

CHAPTER 5

Those who work at the Hundred Acre School inhabit a world that is rarely understood by outsiders. It's a world you cannot prepare for with classes or mentors or manuals. It's a world that has indefinable questions and answers. After barely two weeks at the HAS, I've encountered the cast of a reality show I would never opt to watch on my volition. There Cliff, a chronic masturbator who favors his dorm-mates' clothing as a receptacle. Albert is a pimply-faced wizkid who puked yellow bile at my doorstep not once, not twice, but three times since my tenure began. Vicki is a chain smoking goth-queen who loiters by the Homer House, casually describing to its residents the size and smell of her genitalia. Andrew is a dazed sleep junkie who not only refuses to rise with his peers, but who pretends to be deaf, dumb, and blind with the skill and ease of some masterful thespian.

I imagine my father watching my every move, my every interaction with his students - how I look at them and teach them and talk to them, asking them to please pick up their dirty socks or to extinguish their cigarettes or take their hands off of one another or get to class or get to sleep or get out of bed or to not let me catch them swapping their Adderall for another's Ritalin. Yet the truth is I haven't seen much of Rollie during my first two weeks. I imagine he's got a system worked out. He's close with these kids. And his staff, too. He's probably snatching them away, one by one, and asking what they've heard about the new guy. He'll tell them to forget the fact that he's the son of the school's overseer. Be candid, he'll tell them.

What could they possibly say? The truth is I've been nothing but cordial. To the kids and staff alike. Which is to say I'm so out of my element - and in a state of bewilderment over being here - that I'm too sulky to be standoffish. Everyone must sense it. It's already been pointed out several times that I must be in my thirties, more than a few years older than the average Hundred Acre School teacher.

The way solitary men drive eighteen wheelers, or the way extroverts sell themselves along with some pitiful product to the public: This is the way the Old Man's faculty ease towards a job where in a single day they can be told to fuck themselves, witness a rancid sexual swap of some fellatio for a Marlboro, and partake in a therapeutic breakthrough. I know these people. Growing up among them, I was their boss's son; my role was limited to being seen here and there on occasion, being told what a great father I had, and being asked if I planned on following in his footsteps.

I've often wondered where Rollie finds these people. Or rather, how do *they* find him? The truth is that most of them are not from the area. A lot of them are recent college grads who share stories of backpacking excursions in Costa Rica or kayaking exploits in Dubrovnik or making and selling jewelry in remote parts of Alaska. For them, Old Brookview is a stopover, an emotional filling station for the searcher, the drifter, the idealist, who thrives on saving its needy, broken-down adolescents. These people become a collection of selfless do-gooders, a batch of close-knit fraternities and sororities working roughly eighty hours a week, hellbent on imparting their freewheeling notions about travel and liberty and destiny and healing as though on missionary work. It's not a place for narcissists or prudes. For that matter, I can't imagine the weak-willed fitting in, either. I believe the more eccentric and even slightly damaged individual finds they are somewhat at home within HAS's sprawling chaos. It's for the type who, if asked their life philosophy, would respond with an immediate, relieved passion, a studied, almost mechanical stoicism, as though they've been waiting patiently to share their dissertation with just one more person.

My presence here mocks all of this. Not that anyone besides Rollie is privy to that notion. For now, I'm sure I'm regarded simply as the outsider who's biding his time. The word *nepotism* is sure to have come up in at least a few conversations about the new guy. But I know I'm flattering myself to think that anyone is paying more than a little attention to my presence. Under normal circumstances it would've been the subject of great conflict and brazen juvenile stare-downs; these kids hate deviations to their routines. The truth is that they hate their routines, period. But they hate it when at the very least they cannot count on that which they hate. Yes, I'm the new guy who's replaced Dimiti Ames. And yes, it's well known that he was fucking around with Lindsay Lowe, a mature and attractive student. It's a scandal for sure. Not to mention currency for committing deeds of egregious misbehavior. But their minds, naturally, are on the murder of Nicole D'Ambrosio. And how their little asylum has become the subject of great fear and suspicion - even more so than usual. The girl was not one of their own. In age, yes. But she was a public school princess with an impeccable reputation and a nuclear family and a promising future. Sympathy, I have to imagine, might not be their first reaction. Probably it's more dread over being suspected of the crime.

One of my classes - American Literature for juniors - nearly erupted over the matter just the other day. Vanessa, a tall, petulant girl with soft brown eyes who always wears her pajamas to class, led the discussion.

"I'm not saying that one of us *didn't* do it. That's not the point. And I'm willing to bet that one of us *did* do it. But we were fucking branded before they found that girl. And we're fucking branded after. And you know what the brands say?"

"Yeah, they say *eat my dick,*" said Josh, a broad shouldered, rambunctious spaz with an angel's face and a trucker's mouth.

This kid is a student of sardonic comedians: Carlin, Pryor, Bruce. He quotes their material often and with his own affectations, much to the approval of his peers, who know the jokes are lifted, but give him points for memorization, delivery, and timing.

"That's *fucked up* that you're so quick to accuse one of us, Vanessa," said Bridget, a blonde hippie chick whose dreadlocks are in their early stages. "Do you think that makes you a realist? Because it doesn't. It makes you a bitch."

The nine boys in my dorm are far less polemical. Aged sixteen to eighteen, the Homer House boys are regarded as HAS's macho veterans; they strut, swear, and start fights with younger, less cocky kids. I've overheard a few conversations during lunch or morning cleanup where they've surmised over the murdered girl's anatomy. The boys, as well as the entire town of Old Brookview, have had plenty of chances to commit Nicole D'Ambrosio's appearance to memory; her parents deluged the town with professionally made posters with their daughter's beatific face staring out into streets she will never walk again.

"I bet her tits were like scoops of heaven," I overheard Noah say one morning as he mopped the bathroom floor. "What a waste."

A short, brash, arrogant kid with big white teeth and a raspy smoker's voice, Noah Calash hails all the way from Oahu, but has recently moved to upstate New York with his mother. The kids call him Hawaiian Punch, or sometimes just Punch.

"Forget her tits," Cal said. "Who needs tits? *I've* got tits. The real waste is between her legs. You know these rich chicks wax and sculpt down there like it's up for consideration in the pussy museum."

Cal Henry: a chubby rich kid with a penchant for smut - I discovered a stash of dirty magazines in the soundhole of a beat-up acoustic guitar in his closet - and a gift for offending the opposite sex with his misogynistic quips.

The oldest of the bunch, Nick Russo, a quiet brooder with a reputation as a daredevil - in his old life, he supposedly jumped a motorcycle from the rooftop of a friend's house - appears especially pensive. He contemplates saying something; his focus suggests that he thinks his words will be permanently etched somewhere for all to see, and he will be forever known by these words alone. He ends up walking away from the conversation altogether.

My reaction to all of this is the same. I ignore it. I either feign distractedness and walk away like Nick, or I yawn and rub my eyes, showing boredom over their banal pleasure. Why would I discipline them? *How* would I discipline them? The truth is that I can't even fathom the notion of delivering some absurd pep talk about scruples and then having to deliver it with a straight face.

Conversations with my students are limited to literature. We'll read a few pages of Kerouac or Thoreau, watch a few online clips, and I'll sit back and listen to them duke it out over what means what. Once this grows wearisome, they'll work on the questions Dimitri Ames left in yellow folders in his classroom.

The boys in the Homer House are inquisitive in a self-serving way. They ask for extra dorm snacks or if they can sleep for fifteen more minutes or if they can finish a movie even though it ends at 11:30, a full hour past curfew. My response is always to let them have their way. Why wouldn't I? Being agreeable makes for shorter interactions. It's win win.

I feel like an off-duty cop at an after-hours party where someone breaks out a little cocaine; sure, I have some power, but everybody knows it's in check and that I won't be using it. I imagine the Old Man a day or two before my arrival. I imagine him gathering the students and staff and telling them to not mind me, that I'm a curmudgeon and to make my life as hassle-free as possible. This place is simply a layover for me, he'd tell them, and I'll be gone soon enough and everyone can forget about the brief, harmless, and strange appearance of the overseer's son.

My father did introduce me to the school. It was my second full day when he dragged me up to the podium after breakfast:

"I'd like to introduce you to Grayson. He'll be with us for a bit in the Homer House - as well as teaching English in the Virginia House. Welcome, Gray."

There are no formal salutations at the HAS. It's all first name basis. Part of Rollie's grand design to create unity through familial vibes. There was silence after the introduction. No polite applause. No *Hello, Grayson* in awkward, half-assed unison. And then he said, "That's it," and the students were dismissed. The Old Man then walked past me, sat down, and went to work on finishing his pancakes. He never made mention that I happened to be his son.

The routines I've fallen into have already been created for me. They've always existed. Morning: gently rouse kids to wake, bathe, dress, do chores, take meds, and be on time for breakfast. Teaching: attempt to convince my classes that theme and symbolism are as interesting as their own lives. Afternoon: lunch, group therapy, meds, embark on activity - some on campus: billiards, basketball; some off campus: beach, movie - and sell the idea that the distraction will bring them something everlasting. Evening: dinner, second activity, help with homework, meds, showing enough leniency towards study time, curfew, and allotted phone calls to ensure there won't be an insurrection so I can close my door sometime before midnight.

Then comes the dorm report. This involves writing a narrative about each boy's night. The purpose of the report is to discuss behavior; the Old Man asks his staff to remember the acronym C.O.P.

"It all comes out at night - every type of behavior. There's a subconscious anxiety about waking up the next day to do it all over again," he says. "The classes, the therapy, the routines. So any *concerns*, *observations*, and even *praise*, are essential to these reports. C.O.P."

It's not likely that the night will go smoothly, especially in the Homer House. Nine emotionally unstable boys. Two or three per room. Nightmares, pranks, midnight scuffles. During my on-duty nights - I alternate with Ryan, the other dorm staff, a twenty-something optimist with a peach-fuzz goatee and watery, sympathetic eyes - it's common for me to be woken up at 2:00 a.m. with a furious pounding at my door. So I drag myself out of bed, stumble through the dark, and find a few of them in the hallway - one of them always has their hands flailing about, their bare chest heaving with anger.

Two nights ago is as good an example as any:

"Gray, Noah keeps farting and using his fan to blow it in my face," said J.J., a miserable redhead with sharp, bony fingers he likes to stick in your direction to make his points.

Noah, smiling, denied the charge and told me that J.J. takes it up the ass. I rubbed my eyes and swayed to the dull hum of the light burning above me. After coaxing them back to bed, I returned to the dorm report. Seated at my desk, my mouth dry and my head empty, I made an addendum for the farting.

• • •

I recall J.R. III's occasional appearances at the school as something of an event. Always unannounced, always alone, Roarick would show up, usually during mealtimes or some schoolwide function, slowly stroll through a sea of questioning faces, barely speak to anyone, and survey his surroundings as though trying to commit them to memory. When he seemed satisfied, he'd huddle with the Old Man for a moment, take one last look around, and head to his vehicle, always appearing content that he inspired confusion. The kids knew who he was. And though he may have owned most of Old Brookview, including the very campus on which they resided, he must've been another mysterious figure to them, one who lived in the real world and had something they couldn't relate to in any way whatsoever: power.

All these years later, all that's changed about Roarick's visits is that he now brings his son, Austin. They stop by one evening during dinner. Ryan mentions that he's heard Roarick is uneasy about the murder on his property, and it's this that has prompted his presence. The boys in the Homer House, as well as many of the other students, study the two men as they approach Rollie, who sits at his table with admins and therapists.

Roarick appears larger than I remember him. Meticulously dressed in a maroon short-sleeved polo shirt tucked into pressed khaki pants, his body appears fit, proportioned, and powerful. His hair, obviously dyed black, is neatly parted along one side, and he has a clean shaven face that is reddened at his cheekbones. His son, dutifully at his side, wheels his head around as he scans the dining hall like some nervous bird; he has the appearance of a younger brother rather than a child. Probably thirty pounds overweight, Austin, who is several inches shorter than his father, is already mostly gray. His face, unlike that of J.R. III, who could be described as handsome, is squarish without looking the least bit chiseled. And though his style is similar to his father's - black polo shirt tucked into brown pants - he doesn't pull off the wealthy weekend golfer look he's clearly going for. He's clumsy, weathered, and seems to be stained with a look of omnipresent fatigue. My own memory of him is so slight that seeing him now barely registers.

His name, though, has come up a few times over the years. Rollie, usually in a sardonic tone, would talk about him like he was little more than a nuisance.

"You remember him, don't you?" my father would ask. "You two went to school together for a bit. He was a fucking weirdo even then, from what I recall."

Austin, according to the Old Man, had been trying to extricate himself for years from his father's business affairs - though he was hardly an integral part to begin with. He had tried his hand, and failed, at a host of his own ventures. An online jewelry exchange. Firecrackers at wholesale prices. Refurbished patio furniture. Pool supply delivery. Each enterprise put him further in debt - for which J.R. III openly refused to pay - and thus helped cement his position as nothing more than overseer of his father's many accomplishments.

Among the students, Austin is known simply as a cheapskate. He will hire out kids to do odd jobs and pay them insultingly low wages. Given the difficulty in earning an honest buck, they always accept the work. Fifty dollars for spending countless hours creating a website. Twenty dollars for designing business logos. Five or ten dollars for lugging this or that or washing his car or even deejaying a private party for a few hours.

Noah, sitting next to me, and focused on Austin, gives an apt description:

"He looks like a cartoon criminal."

The other boys agree. They then try to top it with further comparisons. Most are crude. I notice that Nick is the only one who doesn't participate. Staring at his half-eaten cheeseburger in front of him, he wears a fixed look in his eyes, like he expects to soon be on the threshold of some fantastic discovery. I also take notice of my father, who's looking in my direction and pointing. Austin nods before walking towards me, a dangerous looking, off-centered smile transforming him into some petty outlaw. I watch him approach. He extends his hand and introduces himself as J.R. III's son. The hand, curled downward into a slight claw, all open fingers, hangs there in front of poor Albert's face, suspended and aimless. It takes me a moment to register that he's looking at and speaking to me. I pardon myself and finally shake his hand.

"We went to school together," he said, a trace of pride in his ability to speak the truth. "Like a hundred years ago. You're Gray."

I tell him I remember him well. Probably flattered by the lie, he begins to ramble at breakneck speed. He reminisces about people from the past - I am familiar with only one girl's name he mentions - parties he could recall, and popular gathering spots back then.

"That was a hundred years ago, wasn't it?" he said.

"Feels like it."

"And look at us now, Gray. Both working in the family business. Working for the greater good. For nuestros padres."

This Spanish affectation clearly pleases him; he takes a step back with what seems like a transitory and minute burst of inspiration, rights himself a little, and steps forward again. I'm too embarrassed to do anything but offer a convivial gesture. So I introduce him to Ryan. As they shake hands, I quickly realize the distraction will be too short, so I introduce him to all the boys in the Homer House.

Austin's face changes as he stares down at the boys. As does his tone. They both seem to now bear a different type of confidence than what he's exuded with me. It's looser and bolder. His eyes, as he scans the table, offer a distrustful look that shows not even a pretense of what should be tacit sensitivity towards young people who are clearly troubled. And his voice, which suddenly becomes hollow and quietly fierce, condescends as it says, "Evening, boys." He seems to forget that this greeting is being supervised by me and Ryan.

"Not too hungry?" he said, focusing on Nick, who's playing with his food.

Nick, avoiding any eye contact with Austin, forces a grin.

"I don't blame you," Austin said, lowering his voice and leaning in towards the table. "Who knows what goes on back there in that kitchen? When I was a kid, I used to hear crazy stories about this place. I'm sure Gray here can vouch for that."

He looks back and forth between me and Nick.

"I remember hearing about the critters they used to find. Big old bastards, too. Old Rollie wasn't too into maintaining shit back then, huh?"

Both lies are so absurd that I find myself waiting for a punchline that never comes. I don't know which one to respond to first - the critters or my father's negligence - or even *how* to respond. So I play it safe:

"Well, like you said, that was a hundred years ago."

"How do you like working for your old man?" he asks.

"It's okay."

"Just okay?"

"It's fine."

"I'll be honest with you," he said, lowering his voice again, but not enough to be discreet, "I'm surprised as hell to find you here. I remember talking to you - hell, we must've been sixteen - and you told me your thoughts on this place. Let's just say your description stuck with me all these years. Probably because I felt the same way."

The boys are looking at me, waiting for me to respond. It occurs to me to remind him of his days as the Repeat Offender, the misfit outcast who brazenly shared notebooks full of his perverse poetry. There's a good chance this wouldn't even humiliate him; hell, it might inspire him to pull up a chair and spout out more nonsense. So I settle on a compliment:

"Your memory is impressive."

"What can I say?"

Straightening his posture, he takes a step backwards and runs his hands along his protruding stomach. Attempting levity, he mentions how he's sort of like my boss because of who he is and who I am and our respective positions. I'm only half listening since I'm focused on Nick, who looks dazed and spent, like he's just been interrogated by some autocrat.

"Take care, boys," Austin says, "Gray. Nick."

With this, he turns around and rejoins his father and the Old Man, who are standing by the rear exit. Ignored, he lingers on the periphery of their meeting for a few moments before heading out the door and into the cool, orange evening. Again, Noah creatively articulates the essence of this man:

"He sucks."

No one disagrees.

• • •

I run into Dr. Nussbaum in the dining hall during lunch one afternoon. I barely recognize him. He appears to have lost forty or fifty pounds since I'd last seen him, which is probably shortly after I graduated from college. He's grown a thick beard, which is graying, and he wears dark framed glasses. He looks the part of a psychiatrist - erudite yet compassionate.

Nuss has been a therapist at the Hundred Acre School since I was a kid. It's common for HAS therapists to come and go; most of them have their own private practice in addition to working for Rollie. Nuss never went that route. He devoted himself to the Hundred Acre School. He's as regular a fixture on the place as the Old Man himself. I can recall my father racking his brain in an effort to memorialize the revered doctor. He was hellbent on naming a part of the campus after him, but as no parts were without a name, he settled on a plaque and honorary dinner.

As a kid growing up in this environment, my responsibility was to be respectful to those who worked for its cause. As I matured, this became a more labored effort. But for some reason, I always liked Nuss. Rollie would have him over the house for supper on occasion. Maybe he felt bad about

Nuss's wife leaving him. For this reason, I imagine, they were kindred spirits; both were womanless, and bewildered that men like them, bright and ambitious, could be alone. I recall a lot of wine and humor at these dinners; not to mention being badgered with advice by the two - girls, college, my future. And when the Old Man would hint about my taking over the HAS - a prospect we both knew was laughable - Nuss would sober up, right his posture, and speak in an earnest, lucid voice:

"All you need to do, Gray," he'd say, affecting a slight pause, "is walk. That's it. Just walk and you'll be fine."

To this, my father would roll his eyes and tell Nussbaum he was cut off from the wine. This would force the doctor to explain himself:

"I mean it. If you keep walking, you're bound to walk into *something*. Look at Rollie here. You know how he came into this place? I think he *literally* walked into it. Trust me, Gray."

He was certainly succinct. This was a nice contrast to my father's garrulousness. I respected Nuss. This was forever cemented during one of these dinners when the topic of my upcoming senior prom was brought up. I mentioned how my date would be driving us in her green Ford Taurus, which would not make much of an impression. Thinking about this for a moment, Nuss looked at my father and asked if he could lend me his car, a fully restored, sky blue, 1970 Mercedes convertible. I had seen it a few times at the school, gleaming with pristine antiquity in its *Reserved for Therapists Only* parking spot. The Old Man told Nuss and I to work it out between the two of us; smiling, he said he wanted no part of it. What we worked out was that I would return the car without so much as a scratch on it and with a full tank of gas.

With a plate in one hand and a glass in the other, he walks towards me from the serving line. A girl with bleached blonde hair and a pierced lip says hello to him as he passes her. He stops for a moment to tell her something. She smiles at whatever it is and walks past.

"In the flesh," he says as he approaches me. "Mr. Grayson Loveland."

"I barely recognized you."

He nods and tells me he's discovered exercise.

"And these crazy things called vegetables," he adds, holding up his plate, which is made up of a garden salad with a wedge of bread pushed into one corner.

And, he mentions, he quit smoking.

"They say the cigarettes keep you trim, but not when you use them as chasers for cheesecake."

He takes a sip of his drink, which looks like fruit punch, and nods at me a few times. Neither of us says anything for a moment. A pudgy and pimply kid from the Miles House begins shouting obscenities at his dorm staff. The other boys at his table are laughing, which further inspires the boy's outburst. Only a few other students in the dining hall bother to take notice of the one-man show. Most go about their business of socializing, eating, or slumping in their seats. Victor, one of the administrators, a tall, handsome man with a neat blonde goatee and a trim build, rushes over to the table. He and one of the boy's dorm staff escort the kid out of the building. His entourage boos and hisses.

"Never a dull moment," Nuss says, raising his eyebrows.

"I can see that."

Sipping his drink again, Nuss looks me over. After a moment, he tells me to make certain I try to work some sleep into my schedule whenever possible.

"As often as you can, is all I mean. You know as good as anyone how this place can take its toll."

"I do."

Taking in a deep breath, I tell Nuss it's been good seeing him and to have a nice afternoon.

"I'm always around. So track me down if you need something - while you're living and teaching here, I mean. Okay?"

A kind offer, yes, but to hear someone tell me I'm *teaching and living at the HAS* sounds strange; it actually comes off as glib misinformation.

"Advice on dealing with the kids - tips, suggestions, whatever. Let me know. That's why Rollie keeps me around, you know. Because I put his new staff at ease."

"Understood."

"My offer is not out of deference to Rollie. Or because I'm a friend of the family."

The phrase *friend of the family* sounds funny to me. What family? It's me and the Old Man.

"I know."

"I've known you since you were a boy, Gray. But that's got nothing to do with it."

"Nothing to do with what?"

"Talking."

"Talking about what, exactly?"

"About whatever you feel the need to talk about - whether it has to do with this place or with anything else that might be on your mind."

"Do I look like I have something on my mind?"

"Yes. You actually do."

"Okay."

"I guess what I'm saying," he says, "is to take advantage of having so many therapists around."

The Old Man comes to mind as I head to my dorm after lunch. He must've confided in the good doctor that his son has endured the hardship of a recent divorce and has crawled back to the east coast, exhausted and heartbroken. But there's something more he probably would've told Nussbaum. Something besides the divorce. The Old Man has a strong sense for any type of suffering. He knows. He knows there's more to my story. And now Dr. Nussbaum knows.

The thundering roar of an engine suddenly sounds in the distance. It grows louder while a handful of students gather along the edge of the street as though they're spectators at a road race. I take a few steps towards them as the vehicle approaches. Its tires screech against the hot pavement as it rounds a corner by the main office. I take a few more steps to get a closer glimpse of the scene. The car, which is a metallic blue SUV, flies by the kids at probably quadruple the 15 mph speed limit, causing them to lurch back a few paces. Several bodies are hanging out of the windows, shouting expletives at the onlookers. The license plate is covered with what looks like a brown paper bag. The words FUCK YOU are written in thick black marker.

An explosion sounds a moment after the vehicle flies past the crowd. The SLOW SCHOOL ZONE sign suddenly becomes engulfed in flames. Shattered glass sprays around it and falls to the pavement. The passenger in the front has thrown a Molotov cocktail with deft accuracy. The students watch the vehicle speed away. They don't shout or give chase or search the area for good throwing rocks. One boy walks towards the flaming sign and stares up at it as though the sun itself has fallen from the sky and landed essentially in his backyard. The fire, which looks nearly translucent in the daylight, does an ominous belly dance.

A young teacher named Angela is running towards those who've witnessed the incident. The dining hall door flings open. It's the Old Man and a few others behind him. They arrive on the scene in a matter of seconds. But because I know the matter is being handled - plus, the fire is in no danger of spreading, and no one is hurt - I turn from the crowd and make my way towards the Homer House.

CHAPTER 6

I imagine that only some women are good at being pregnant. Their grace can turn the heads of strangers; their loveliness can inspire private moments of optimism in even the most downhearted. The light they are lucky enough to generate flows freely as they walk and talk and eat and work.

Laura was one of these women. There was an ease in her movements; a pride in the way she touched things around her; an effortless magnitude she claimed without being the slightest bit aware. If she innately possessed both an inner and outer glow by being pregnant, she also seemed to have a ravenous desire to get the full experience out of carrying our child. And I don't mean with pregnancy massages or binge eating or frequent demands for the red carpet treatment.

Laura, always a woman in tune with her sexuality as well as her body, derived an entirely new sensation from herself. Pleased with how she looked, she hired a photographer to capture her blissful state once she began showing. This was in the early stages of her second trimester. The pictures, done in sharp black and white, were tasteful and expressive shots - mostly they were of her holding her bare stomach with a slight and pensive smile. She meant to chronicle the phases of her pregnancy with a few photos every month or so. Her intention, she told me, was to create a pre-pregnancy scrapbook. It was to include not only photos, but her personal thoughts as well. So she bought a bounded, charcoal colored journal in which to write.

And she could be found at the roll top desk in the living room, or with a cup of tea at the kitchen table, or lying in our bed with the lamplight dousing the freshly inked pages that were filled with her private motherly musings.

Laura, I quickly discovered, was in the habit of using the "us" and "we" pronouns whenever discussing baby matters. The way she put it - to family, friends, or physicians - was *we* were pregnant; *we* were ecstatic; *we* had a question.

"We're having a baby shower," she told me one afternoon. "My mother and Stevie's idea. They're planning the whole thing for us."

Her mother and sister cut no corners with the shower. They rented out the private dining room in Les Nomades, a swanky French restaurant in the city. They made favors, baked a cake, and organized games. And though the gathering wasn't a surprise, they placed me in charge of compiling the guest list of friends and co-workers. Laura's sister Stevie reminded me that after this charge was fulfilled, my service, as well as presence, was no longer required.

"Just disappear from noon till around three," she reminded me. "And be sure to pick up your wife in that Jeep of yours. You'll need it."

That Jeep of mine was able to hold about half of the gifts we received. Though some deviated from our tastes and needs - three of Laura's co-workers chipped in on a menagerie of snowbabies - most were practical and tasteful.

Laura saw to involve me in the registry as well. Clothes; bedding; a highchair; a stroller; a carseat: My involvement was to accompany her to stores and provide reassurance that she was making the right choices. She had carte blanche. She could've told me we needed a laptop for the newborn and I would've driven her to the nearest retail store and watched her select one without question. The truth is that Laura did all the research on what we needed. So aside from allowing her to appease me with my role, I took delight in watching her register. She maneuvered around the merchandise with ease, like she stocked the shelves and racks herself and knew the arrangement most suitable for making women like her blush with elation. She would examine a bassinet or peel some pajamas from a hanger and then look at me for my reaction.

After the shower, the next task was the baby's room. We decided to use the small bedroom closest to our own. Laura hired a coworker's son to paint the walls a neutral greenish color called Creeping Willow. Then she learned how to stencil and in a single afternoon accented the room with clouds and stars and the Man in the Moon. My father told me over the phone that he wanted to buy us a crib for his first grandchild.

"Christ!" he cried over the phone, "I haven't even been out to see your new place."

"It's definitely been a while."

"Don't sound so heartbroken."

I was fine with our arrangement. We both were. He tended to the needs and lives of strangers' kids while occasionally expressing contrition about missing out on mine. And I helped flesh out his excuses so he wouldn't have to embarrass himself with half-assed apologies. He ended up sending me a check with an accompanying note that told me to read Consumer Reports for safety tips. Laura's parents, not to be outdone by Rollie, furnished the rest of the nursery.

The room, with its "Twinkle, Twinkle, Little Star" theme, was completed three months before our due date. There were times when I'd find Laura in the room by herself, quietly rocking in the chair her father had rescued from their basement and refinished himself, or examining the board books we bought, or reorganizing the closet, which was well stocked with outfits for all seasons and stages, boxes of wipes and diapers, and more bedware and blankets than we knew what to do with.

Then there were the classes and groups we joined. Through our hospital, we obtained a catalogue of the many offerings. Laura was advised by her sister-in-law on which classes were useful. We avoided the *Moms and Emotions* class, which, according to the description, stated that "14% of pregnant and postpartum women become clinically depressed." It commented on new mothers as well, citing that a similar percentage develop serious anxiety disorders. Laura, admitting naiveté, blasted these statistics.

"*Depression* and *anxiety*? This is the happiest I've ever been. It's only going to get better from here."

We opted for *Prepared Childbirth* and *Newborn Care*. Each class, which met one night a week at our hospital, was taught by Elaine, a middle-aged hippie stick-figure. Everything, according to Elaine, was "far out" or "out of sight." The courses, attended by other young couples expecting their first, should've been called *Tips Only Shell Shocked Imbeciles May Not Know*.

Massages, easy breathing, pleasant thoughts, relaxing music: This was the substance of the first course. The other one - slightly more useful - involved little more than learning how to diaper and hold a newborn.

My baby experience was limited to giving up my seat on the 'L' train for a mother holding her sleeping infant or toddler to her breast. Laura's was a bit more extensive. Her brother Rick and his wife Juliet have a small daughter, Ashley. And her other brother, Lyle, and his wife Pam, have a daughter, Morgan. Not to mention, she reminded me, babysitting all through high school and even some in college was how she earned enough money to buy her first car.

I was content to follow my wife's lead with all baby matters. *Her* instincts. *Her* knowledge. The only expectation for me was that I'd listen. Despite my novice status, I found myself filled with confidence and even a strange nostalgia for my own childhood. I secretly wished we were having a boy, so I could buy him Matchbox cars and sports cards and throw a baseball around with him in our backyard. Then I would secretly wish it was a girl, who would look and act just like her mother and love her daddy with an undying forever kind of love and stare at me with big blue eyes as though I was her one and only.

I had heard about men who feel suffocated by impending doom when they're about to embark on fatherhood. They feel fear and uncertainty. They long for their single life. They look at their wife with secret disdain - as though her eventual machination to sabotage their freedom has nearly come to fruition - and they become aloof and sometimes lustful of other women. This was not me. I knew what kind of father I was going to be. I knew what kind of family we were going to be. So I ignored the cynicism of some of my male coworkers - tired, jaded slobs with energy only for scare tactics veiled in banal jocularity - who would harass me about changing shitty diapers, being awoken at all hours of the night, and barely finding the time or stamina to resume any kind of sex life. I humored them. Widening my eyes as if to exude shock or incredulity, I'd listen and smile and then change the subject. How could I tell them I was so taken with the experience? Which I was. I loved looking at my wife more than ever; she was sexier and more magnetic than I could remember. We were closer now than ever before. I loved hearing her tell me in our second month that our baby had a heartbeat; that in our third, our baby's bones were ossifying and ears had formed; that in our fourth, our baby made its own insulin and was urinating in the amniotic sac.

I became accustomed to riding this high, to having my senses sharper than ever, to plotting my family, that it was startling when it was all challenged. It began during Laura's second trimester with a routine checkup with our OB/GYN, Dr. Rose, who, upon our first visit, told us to call her Hilary. Hilary, a subdued woman with short graying hair and a voice like a barely audible woodwind instrument, told us things were looking fine. The ultrasound, she said, was showing all the appropriate developments. As she consulted her chart, she asked if the nurse had gone over the upcoming test that was available. Laura shook her head, but said she had read about it in one of her pregnancy books. She knew it was referred to as a maternal serum.

"That's right," said Hilary, "maternal-serum-alpha-fetoprotein test, or MSAFP."

Hilary explained the test to us:

"The MSAFP is a routine blood test that screens for certain fetal disorders. It's generally offered to women between the fifteenth and twentieth week of pregnancy. It's most accurate when performed between fifteen and eighteen weeks gestation. Which is right around where you are. Abnormal MSAFP levels are associated with genetic conditions, birth defects, retardation, and late-pregnancy complications. Because seventy to eighty percent of all trisomies - a type of inherited genetic defects - occur in women under the age of thirty-five, MSAFP is typically offered to pregnant women of all ages. Which is to say that the test is optional."

Laura spoke up almost immediately:

"I think we'll pass."

I looked at her. She was wiping the ultrasound lubricant from her belly. I asked Hilary if most couples opted for the test. She told me some did and some did not.

"But it couldn't hurt," I said. "Right?"

"Some people like to exercise their right to gather as much information as possible about their unborn child. And others—"

"And others don't," I said.

"Right."

"What would *you* do?" I asked.

Laura slid off the examination table and began to dress. She was looking at me. Dr. Rose smiled a polite smile, the fragile, weightless kind you extend when you're in a hurry or when you've decided not to waste many words.

"I'd talk to my spouse about it," she said.

Then she wheeled around and drew the curtain, separating herself from me and Laura. Opening the door to the examination room, she told us to let her know our decision, that she would schedule the appointment for us should we choose to go that route.

"It's a routine blood test," I said quietly to Laura.

"An *optional* routine blood test," she said.

"I think we should do it."

"You mean you think *I* should do it."

I watched her slide her shirt over her head and pull her hair out from its back. She was looking down towards her belly.

"Yes, I think *you* should do it."

"I honestly don't see a point," she said, picking up her purse from the floor.

"The point is that I'm one of those people who likes to gather as much information as possible about his unborn child."

"Would the results change anything?"

Laura looked beautiful standing there in that office. Like the life inside her had at that moment produced a magical energy that surrounded her and multiplied and couldn't be tampered with or turned off.

"Of course not."

She studied my face for a moment. I wasn't sure how I looked. Yet I'm positive I did my best to give off an air of insouciance.

"A routine blood test," Laura said, sighing.

She moved past me towards the curtain. Following her, I offered to take her to our favorite restaurant, Great Caesar's, a quaint and charming tavern we recently discovered in the center of town.

"A bribe?"

"Absolutely."

"Shameless."

"Absolutely."

Laura turned to face me as she opened the door, declaring that I would have to sweeten the deal further. She was smiling.

Laura took the test two days after our visit with Hilary. The results would take up to seventy-two hours. We waited. Life went on. Distractions arose. I came home early one evening to find Glenn Kilburn sitting in my family room, hunched forward, a drink dangling from one hand, talking to Laura. He stayed seated when I entered the room.

"There he is," he said, swigging from his glass. "I was just telling Laura here that your place is looking good. Classy. Sharp. Good taste."

He looked around and pointed out what he liked: the matching jelly cabinets, the medallion Oriental rug, the green paint, which he knew, thanks to Laura, was called Mountain Botanical.

"Classy," he said again, nodding his head this time. "You should see what we've got going on over there at the Kilburn residence. Antiques, antiques, and more antiques. I should call it a museum and charge admission."

Laura stood and walked over to me. She explained that Glenn stopped over not too long before. So she offered him a few drinks and they got to talking.

"Just wanted to plead with you folks not to call the authorities on me if you see it getting too wild over there," he said. "A frat party or two might be in my immediate future."

It was difficult to tell if he was drunk or not. Laura turned to him and then back at me. Then she told me in a sobering tone that Glenn and his wife had split up.

"She went back to Maryland," Glenn said, raising his glass. "Moved in with her parents."

"It happened this past weekend," Laura said.

Finishing his drink, Glenn began to suck on the ice. Laura walked to the liquor cabinet and removed a bottle of Irish whiskey I received as a secret Santa gift from a coworker. Then she filled Glenn's glass and set the bottle on the coffee table. He thanked her and told me I was lucky to have a wife who didn't love antiques. Leaning back on the sofa, Glenn sipped his drink and sighed to himself. Laura announced she had an idea: Glenn should stay for supper. She told him we were having lasagna.

"It's become my latest craving," she said, rubbing her stomach.

"I appreciate the offer," Glenn said, "but how about a rain check?"

He was looking at me when he said this. I turned to Laura. She insisted again that Glenn join us.

"Maybe another time. But this was just what I needed, and I'm grateful."

I wasn't sure if he meant the alcohol or the company of a woman. He stood up as he drank his whiskey. Laura told him to call on us if he needed anything. Then she looked at me and smiled as she ran a hand through her hair. Glenn moved past me and I could smell the booze on his breath. He suddenly turned around and put his hand on my shoulder.

"You're a lucky man," he said, slurring a bit over his words. "Laura here has good taste. You ought to see my place."

Then he leaned in towards me and softly cursed his wife, telling me the interior of their house was painted in the most antiseptic, lifeless color called Cool Gray. He looked around the room again as he finished his drink. Then he turned back to me and extended his hand, mentioning that he forgot to congratulate me. He asked if we had names picked out. We told him we had a few. He nodded and said goodnight. As he walked out the door, he still held onto the empty glass.

Laura said two things that night that bothered me. The first was that she was beginning to find Glenn Kilburn charming. It was his wife, she said, who must've been the supercilious one. The second was that Glenn agreed with her about maternal-serums. They both felt strongly that they were unnatural. And after all, she mentioned, he's a doctor.

. . .

A nurse named Jody called us with the test results. It was early on a Tuesday evening. She spoke with Laura while I sidled up next to her so I could hear their conversation. The results were positive, she said.

"Which only means that the risk factor for Down Syndrome has increased," she explained. "It does not necessarily mean your child will *have* Down Syndrome."

Jody explained that the initial risk factor for serious birth defects is about 1/700. After Laura's test results, the risk factor was now 1/71.

"Understand, though," she said in a reassuring voice, "I see more false-positives than anything else."

Jody explained our options. The next logical step, she said, was a fetal ultrasound. This would look for abnormalities like the lack of a nasal bone, overly thick neck skin, webbed feet, and so on. Without thinking, I blurted out that we wanted the next available appointment. Laura pulled the phone from her ear and threw her forefinger up in front of my face.

"Make the next available appointment!" I shouted.

Laura apologized to the nurse while shooting me a deadly look. I hurried upstairs to my laptop and went online to find any information I could about these prenatal tests and birth defects and percentages of this and that. I was deluged with information. After a few moments, I gave that up. I sat on the edge of our bed, listening. Laura was off the phone and I could hear her quietly below me on the first floor. I heard the refrigerator door open and a chair being pushed in and a dish being set in the sink.

I wondered what she had told the nurse. Or if her attitude had changed - if she was now grateful for the maternal-serum. Or if she would oppose me when I demanded that we move forward with the next test. Laura and I didn't see one another for the rest of that evening. She slipped into some quiet activity downstairs while I fell asleep earlier than I had in years.

CHAPTER 7

Dan Hart is a campus celebrity. First there's his promiscuity, which is well known - and even well documented. He's rumored to have seduced handfuls of female students, both younger and older, and has been seduced himself by many more. At only sixteen, it appears he's well on his way to penicillin and paternity tests. A nice looking boy, Dan stands nearly six feet tall, has shaggy blonde hair, a slight build, and deep green eyes. His smile, which he wears on most occasions, looks like a magnet he's crookedly fixed to his face and forgotten to remove. Some of his peers call him Dan Juan.

Another reason for this fame is that he is the one to have discovered the dead body of the local girl. Never a suspect himself, Dan cooperated with the police and with Rollie. He and his female companion, a sophomore named Jessica Levesque, answered the questions put to them before they slipped back into campus life.

But this doesn't stop Dan's classmates from asking him about his disturbing discovery. "Were you freaked out?" "What did she look like?" "Did you know she was dead?" "Are you having nightmares?" These are some of the questions I overheard as I attempted to engage a group of students - two boys and two girls - in a discussion on a Flannery O'Connor story I assigned. It took a week for me to learn that the Dan Hart I had heard so much about was actually my student. With the boys in the Homer House, it was different; I *had* to learn their names for the dorm reports. Not to mention I heard them constantly in and around the dorm and during mealtimes. Noah would ask

Dustin how long he's liked banging little boys. Alex would tell Cal he found Cliff's tampon floating in the toilet. Cliff would berate Andrew for being what he called "a little bitch on training wheels."

But the students I teach are another story. We might be holed up together, sweating miserably inside a tiny classroom on Monday through Friday, but I put little effort into learning their names. It's true that I began grading their work and even passing it back to them, but I do so after leaving it in a pile on my desk and asking them to retrieve it themselves. Yet my three classes know *my* name, which, for some reason, they say in its entirety: "Grayson Loveland, do you miss Chicago?" "Grayson Loveland, do you mind working for your daddy?" "Grayson Loveland, did you mind growing up on the HAS campus?" My answers are terse at best.

One afternoon, Rollie held a staff meeting after lunch - something he began doing often ever since the D'Ambrosio girl's body was discovered - and enforced accountability for all students at all times.

"We need to know where our children are," he said, "at all times. I want constant head counts during meals and constant attendance during classes and activities. And I want immediate action taken if anyone's missing. Call the SOD office. Contact an administrator. Hell, call me. We need to know where our children are."

Roger, a math teacher and dorm staff in the Miles House, leaned towards a pretty, young Asian teacher named Sandra and whispered something. Smiling, she nodded. The Old Man told us that he'd recently spoken with parents who feared for the safety of their child. Two students, he added, have officially withdrawn from the school. Roger, the math teacher, again leaned towards Sandra. This time I heard what he said:

"What about *our* safety?"

The Old Man heard him.

"I'm glad you mentioned that," he said, looking at Roger. "Because we're in the process of hiring additional night staff. Louise and I will be interviewing this week, in fact. We're all uneasy about this thing. But in the meantime, please be on top of your attendance."

On the way out of the dining hall, I was on the heels of Roger and Sandra, who continued with their conversation. Sandra, with flawless sarcasm, said something that made me laugh out loud:

"Have a good class. And try not to let a little thing like having a murderer on the loose distract you from your lesson."

• • •

Dan Hart, whose name heads the roster for my afternoon class, is missing today.

"Anyone know the whereabouts of Mr. Hart?"

The three other students offer sheepish grins before one of them, a short, dark-haired diva with a lip ring, speaks up:

"He's not here."

"I see that. Does anyone know where he is?"

They eye one another as though the secret they share has the power to bring a man to his knees.

"Yes," the girl says.

I look at her, waiting for a response. She stares back at me, any trace of a smile now gone. It's replaced with contempt. Contempt for a stranger who stands before her, weakly asserting whatever vague power he may have, and daring to ask her about Dan Hart, her peer or boyfriend or whatever. Still no answer. I try to recall the handsome, wiry boy who did attend my class a few times - always late, always without an excuse, and always to the resounding cheer of the other students. *Dan Juan*! they would chant when the classroom door swung open and he'd enter, his eyes mostly hidden under unruly tufts of hair.

"What's your name?" I ask, examining my roster. "Are you Meredith or Molly?"

"Meredith."

"*I'm* Molly," the other girl says, raising her arm at half mast. "And Dan's likely busy."

"Your elusiveness just misses the mark of being charming," I tell her.

"Well *fuck me*," says Molly, "because charming is all I've ever wanted to be. Truly."

The other student in the class, a broad-shouldered sourpuss with long sideburns and black framed glasses, laughs to himself. Their loyalty is fascinating. They behave as though Dan is some terribly misunderstood figurehead rather than a troubled teen who likes to ditch class so he can get laid. It's as though their peer's sexual plights have vicariously become their own. I wonder if these kids have grown so unaccustomed to victory that they've decided to redefine what it means. Maybe it now means that if one of their own is lucky enough to feel good - even if just for a moment - then they have to do whatever is necessary to allow that to happen. Maybe this gives them hope that their turn to feel good is just around the corner.

As I pick up the phone to call the SOD office, in walks Dan Hart; he's licking his lips, which are twisted into a cocky, impish grin.

"Dan Juan!" the others call out.

Hanging up the phone, I turn to the boy, who has snuck by me and taken a seat in between the two girls.

"Mr. Hart."

He looks up at me, smiling and massaging the hairs on his chin with his thumb and forefinger.

"They're getting strict with attendance. They want you guys in class on time."

"I can't give you any guarantees. Lateness is part of my charm."

"We were just discussing charm," Molly points out.

"I just told you, they're getting stricter about it."

Meredith asks why I'm using the pronoun "they" when talking about the Hundred Acre School. She says she finds this interesting.

"Shouldn't you be using *we*?"

I tell her I don't know and that it's not important at the moment. Looking back towards Dan, I once again explain the school's position on attendance.

"There'll be consequences in the future."

He looks at me for a moment, his smile sliding around his face as though it's chasing the right words he wants to use. The other kids watch him, knowing they're about to be entertained. When it seems like he's without a comeback, I look down and pretend to organize the papers on my desk.

"Would you encourage me if you discovered I was an outstanding student?"

"Excuse me?"

"If you found out I was some fucking wunderkind - if I was all over this academic stuff?"

"Would I encourage you?"

"If I excelled in class," he said, respectfully losing his patience with me. "Or in *any* area, really - literature or basketball or cooking? The question is this: Would you help me realize my potential by creating situations where I could do so?"

He threw me off guard. *Wunderkind*? *Realize my potential*? What could I say? Bullshit aside, I *was* the boy's teacher.

"Sure."

"Then forget this attendance nonsense," he said, "with *me* anyway."

"And why should I do that?"

"Because it's your job to encourage us. Even if it's a fucking job you don't want; it's still your job. And you need to respect that, and help me realize my potential."

The others lean into our conversation. I'm struck by their restraint.

"Are you kidding me?"

"Don't you see? I'm trying to help *you* help *me*."

"I don't even know what you're talking about."

This, of course, is a lie. I know what he wants. His exploits are well known, even to someone who's been at the school for only a short time. Not to mention I recall what Rollie told me about him.

It occurs to me that I'm toying with Dan for a couple of reasons. One is that I'm floored that such a young kid can articulate his case the way he does - or, at the very least, believe wholeheartedly that he's making a valid proposition. Another is I'm intrigued over the loyalty his peers have towards him. I'm curious to learn how well they'll work in concert in trying to conceal his licentious intent.

He says all I have to do is not hassle him or report him for being late. And this, he tells me, will help him *realize his potential*.

"For what?" I ask, daring him to tell me.

Dan looks at his peers. Meredith and Molly are shaking their heads, their gazes wide-eyed and fixed on Dan, waiting to see how far he might go. Dan sighs. For the remaining minutes of class, the four of them sit at their desks and work mostly in silence, the weight of my still unanswered question hanging like some tinny echo. On occasion, there's a whisper or snicker. When the passing bell sounds, they slam their anthologies shut, gather their belongings, and slide past me to the exit. Dan is the last in the procession, and he stops in front of me after the others have gone. With that grin that has probably gotten him laid dozens of times, he smooths his hair and shifts his book bag to his opposite shoulder. He's making perfect eye contact with me. Then, as though it's fallen to the floor, it quickly vanishes, and I'm looking at a young boy who wants more than anything to appear as a man. His disabilities suddenly come to mind: ADD, bipolar.

"It's not like I can do it at the talent show this weekend," he says. "And it'll never get me any awards, but it *is* my thing. And I'm good at it, so why bust my balls? Respect it. Besides, I *know* all this literature shit from my other school. So what's the problem?"

Interesting scenario: specious plea from a horny, depressed adolescent, advocating for his right to cut class and have sex in the woods. He's serious, too. And has been the entire time. This is evident in the way his voice trembles a little. And his eyes, which moments earlier, with his modest entourage present, were lit with confidence and intellect, now resemble two tiny bowls of crushed glass.

I stare at him and furrow my brow. He's a handsome boy. I'll give him that. And he presents a compelling, if not inane, argument. After a moment, he smiles once again and begins to move past me. But because I can't leave things alone, unresolved, with Dan having the upper hand, I decide to ask him a question of my own:

"Why do you think this is a job I don't want?"

Turning around to face me, he hoists up the other shoulder strap to his book bag and tucks his thumb underneath. He tells me he'll make me a deal if I want. And before I can even question his audacity, he comes out with it:

"You use discretion with my shit," he said, dropping his hands to his side, "and I'll use discretion with yours."

. . .

Old Brookview hasn't been my home for more than fifteen years. And in that time, I've felt victorious for having left. Like my liberty was hard-earned and well deserved. The truth is I was just another suburban brat with a callow worldview and a sense of entitlement. Which is not to say that I don't cringe at the thought of being back here now after so long, but I'd like to think that my perspective is more sophisticated. Old Brookview is, after all, a well-regarded town. *Connecticut* magazine keeps it on their "Top Ten Places to

Live" list year after year; or so my father tells me. The public schools often garner enough accolades over academics and athletics to entice local businesses and philanthropists to make generous donations.

The town has a practical purpose for me now. Its fine green lawns, scrubbed white fences, and lovingly-cared-for homes are monuments of domestic privilege. At one time, they represented what I took to be a vain contrast to whatever my generation's cause became. And though I never took the time to find out what it was, I did see life in suburbia as a sort of dreadful complacency. But like I said, I was callow and entitled.

Driving around now on my weekend off is not the nostalgia trip one might hope for. My memories are not adrift on its streets or in its hangouts. They are not lazing on its beaches or within the homes probably occupied now by strangers. The truth is that this town has always had one meaning for me. The Hundred Acre School. It's the heart, blood, and bone for me. That's not at all by choice.

Main Street in Old Brookview is postcard perfect. There's Sali's Pizza Joint, which is currently under renovation. There's Page Turners and Roarick Art Cinema and Tiny's Drugstore. These are places very much intact from my youth. But I feel anything but a rush of romanticism at their sight now. It's true I ate my share of calzones and other junk food at Sali's, and loitered in Tiny's, buying candy and condoms, and sat through more than enough mediocre films we settled on when free tickets were given to us by friends who worked at the door. I did all of this the way adolescents should - with girls and guys, after school or late at night, and with impatient sneers from adults when we were too loud or too indulgent with our agendas of sex and freedom.

It was all fine. But it was never more than that for me. I always knew I didn't want to stay - or even return. Still, though, I wonder about those I drank with and slept with and saw in the nude and swam with in the ocean under perfect summer starlight.

There was Nadine and Val Candee, identical twins who left school for two months to accompany their father, a university professor, around the United States during a book tour. Always the ones to buy or supply the booze, they were two years ahead of me and called me "Little Brother."

There was Anita Gregory, a chic Amazonian with a wicked sense of humor and precocious sexual mores. She and I managed a nice reciprocal arrangement when we were both bored and single. I always imagined her destined for a rude awakening once her looks ran their course.

There was Justin Mann, one of my closest friends, even into college, which is where we eventually lost touch. It was with Justin that I was able to unburden myself and lose any inhibitions that are part and parcel of adolescence. Any sophomoric musing or surly teenage diatribe was safe in the company of Justin. He would gladly agree, making a toast to your sentiment, and throw back a shot or two of whatever he stole from his mother's liquor cabinet.

And there was Erin Stevens, my high school sweetheart. Together we made a fine, proud couple. We figured we were in love, so we did what any teenagers do who find themselves considering the rest of their lives: We intensified our commitment until it turned disastrous. With her, though, I shared my contempt over the HAS, my sorrow over my mother, and my indifference towards the Old Man. To this day, she remains the only girl - besides Laura, naturally - who I ever introduced to my father.

If I think of those times now, which I do less and less these days, it's not because they weren't filled with the sweet spirit of recklessness. They were. It's because my past is so transfixed with the Old Man's Hundred Acre School. The way the place would sound like a frenzied dress rehearsal for some absurd soap opera. Or the way it looked during the fall when the yellow sugar maples would bloom with their fiery leaves. And the way Mickey's cooking would seem to stick to your guts for days.

I never appreciated being unique in the ways in which I was: having nearly one hundred siblings, as the Old Man used to put it, and sharing my home and my father with each of them. To some, this might build character or foster acceptance. To me, it meant I had no control over my home life. When I think about that home life these days, all I have are recollections of strangers in a strange place. What confounds me is that my memory has actually allowed the HAS to bulldoze what were some good times with some good people. It's cleared some vast spaces and planted itself there, firmly, proudly, and without explanation, as though it's conspiring to teach me a lesson about what's somehow really responsible for shaping my virtues and giving me this life.

Parking in front of the movie theatre, I explore the downtown. An older woman with a pie face and large-framed glasses smokes a cigarette outside the small art gallery. She smiles as I walk past. A young couple pulls their toddler in a wooden wagon. A man brushes past me, towards the post office, with a box of envelopes tucked under his arm.

I stop in front of Louden's, where a college-age kid is washing the large plate glass window with a squeegee. Peering inside, I can see the same old faded green sign above the register - it's been there as long as I've known the place - that bears the diner's former name: *Tit for Tat Diner*. So much better than *Louden's*, I think. Watching a waitress dole out plates of food to a corner booth, I'm reminded of my mother. The Old Man always made a point of telling me - if we ever ate here or even just walked past - that "Virginia was one fine waitress, a real pro; they all loved her to pieces." He said this every chance he got, even getting specific with endearing stories about her fancy coffee pouring technique, or how pretty she looked in her skirt and apron, or how after hours she'd dance from one end of the place to the other to the sounds of Otis Redding or Sam Cooke, two of her favorites. I never took the bait. I knew full well he was trying to flesh out my mind's image of her. And it worked. Thankfully. At the time, though, I wanted him to think that such recollections were prosaic. My mother, *the waitress*? This was beneath her. She was a woman of depth and grace. I would simply remind him that she was a Cornell grad and worked at the diner for only a short time.

"I know," he'd say. "I was there. Remember?"

He *was* there. And I was not, having nearly no memories of her at all.

A couple of high school kids appear on skateboards. They kick their boards into the air with a frenzied deftness that somehow just misses being poetic. After loitering by the diner for a few moments, perfecting their routine, they move on down the sidewalk. I head the opposite way, towards the fire station. As I walk past Isla's, a ladies boutique, I hear my name being called. The voice, a male's, says my last name, too. I turn around to face a husky young man with a military crew cut and sunglasses atop his blocky head; he's walking towards me. Though he looks familiar, I can't place him.

"Thought that was you," he said, stopping a few feet in front of me.

He's chewing on the last piece of a bagel and panting at the same time. Smiling, he brushes some crumbs off his shirt. Probably in his early to mid-twenties, he looks like a powerhouse. Like he may have boxed or played rugby in college. He tells me about a wonderful coffee and bagel shop just around the corner. Reasonably priced, he says. For Old Brookview, he adds.

Then he cringes a little and says how he momentarily forgot I probably know the town better than he does. It's clear from the way he's talking, and how he's settled into the conversation, that he will not introduce himself. The face, more than the voice or mannerisms, is what I seem to remember.

"I haven't lived here in a long time," I tell him.

He nods. After a few moments, he pulls his sunglasses from his head and slides them over his eyes. A mother and her teenage daughter pass us, each of them swinging a bundle of shopping bags.

"What a shame about that poor girl they found, huh?" he said, lifting the sunglasses back to the top of his head. "Unbelievable. I have a sister a year older than she was."

I agree that it's a shame. He tells me the boys in the Alan House have all been sleeping with their lights on ever since the murder was discovered. He snickers a little, mentioning how the Alan House boys aren't the bravest to begin with. So he works for the Old Man. One of my colleagues, too, I suppose.

"It's a hell of a thing, you helping Rollie out the way you are. I know it means a lot to him."

Taking a step towards me, he lowers his voice and says how he never fully trusted Dimitri Ames. That he sensed something was wrong with him and that he never really fit in at the HAS.

"Clearly the guy has some problems."

"Anyway, it's good to have you as his replacement."

"It's only temporary."

Pausing for a bit, he nods.

"I've been working for your father for just over two years."

"I'm sure he appreciates your loyalty."

"It's been a godsend."

"Yeah?"

He doesn't offer anything further. Slapping his belly with both hands and exhaling, the young man, my fellow colleague, must sense that I'm ready for our conversation to end. Taking a step backwards, he says how it was good talking to me. He adds that it's nice to know we both have the same weekends off and if I ever want to have a beer or shoot pool, to let him know.

"Actually," he adds, "I'm not sure what your plans are later, but we're all getting together at around 10:00 tonight."

Pretending to think about it for a bit, I tell him that tonight might not work. He says it's no problem and that he understands. He adds that the poker games are a weekly event and that I can always come during my next weekend off.

"Poker?"

"Rollie's got a regular Robstown in his basement."

When I don't respond, he says that Robstown is a small Texas town that claims to be the birthplace of Texas Hold'em.

"Some of us are a bit fanatical," he tells me, laughing. "Scotty - I don't know if you know Scotty; he lives in the Miles House - he bought a book on strategies, for Christ's sake."

It's remarkable to think how I've just been extended a last minute proposal to socialize in my childhood home where my own father still lives. I paw in silence at my scratchy, unshaven face. The young man begins telling me a story about one of the last games where Scotty won nine hands in a row. Interrupting him, I tell him I can shift some things around in my schedule and that I'll see him later tonight. Then I walk past him and make my way to Page Turners. Nevermind a book on strategies: I need to see if they carry one for novices.

• • •

My father doesn't embarrass himself by exploiting the role of host to his staff, all of whom must be only a few years out of college. For this, I'm thankful. A few absurd scenarios did cross my mind, one of which being the Old Man in a half-buttoned silk shirt, sitting at the head of the card table, chomping on a cigar and holding court with his philosophical rants and fancy shuffling technique. Not that he's known for imposing himself socially on people. There just seems to be a type of guru-esque persona bestowed by his loyal staff. I've seen it in the dining hall in the way they listen to his morning monologues. Or during meetings when he makes some intentional Freudian slip at the expense of one of the students. They eat it up. All of it.

Instead, he unfolds the card table, fires up the jukebox, and fills a cooler with ice cubes and bottles of assorted beer. Then he disappears upstairs, leaving his seven employees to their evening. Before he goes, he offers some words of wisdom, said in a half-smirk, as though self-conscious of his pedantry:

"Make certain that money is all that gets lost here tonight," he says. "Everything else is indispensable."

Enticements are made to keep Rollie in the basement to play a few hands. They sound like well-rehearsed lines that have been spoken before. He declines. Making his way upstairs, he looks over his shoulder and tells everyone to take it easy on me, his long lost son from Chicago. When he closes the door at the top of the stairs, I'm told by a young lady that my father is the Hundred Acre School's answer to Jay Gatsby.

"No obscure references tonight," someone says.

I recognize him as Pierre, a friend of Ryan's, my counterpart in the Homer House. Pierre has a diamond stud in each of his lobes, a cleanly shaved head, and a warm, toothy grin. The girl rolls her eyes at him, telling him the reference is from a classic book. Then she introduces herself to me as Amber, who lives in the Missouri House and teaches English. She's a petite, pleasant looking black girl with grayish eyes and a pile of blonde dreads that sits atop her head like bucked barley.

"He likes to play the host, your father," she said. "But he never stays. He just goes upstairs and drinks cognac and smokes cigars with Nuss."

To my left is Sandra, who mentions to no one in particular that Nuss refers to Dr. Nussbaum.

"He knows who Nuss is," Pierre said. "He grew up here. We're in *his* house."

Then, as though my silence has made him doubt his allegiance, he asks me if I do in fact know Dr. Nussbaum.

"Very well," I tell him.

A few of them ask how it was growing up at the Hundred Acre School. I respond with the first thing that comes to mind:

"Like growing up in a moving car. And the scenery, which is the people, I guess, is always changing around you."

They absorb this for a moment. Then Pierre asks about Chicago. What did I do? Where did I live? Why did I leave? Who did I root for: Cubs or White Sox? I answer all but why I left. The jukebox is playing Stevie Wonder's "Boogie On Reggae Woman." Drinks are being drunk. The first hand is dealt.

"My brother went to DePaul," said Tennille. "He loved it."

Tennille is a tall, buxom Midwesterner with a quick wit and natural talent for flirting. I recall seeing her around campus. She seems to mostly keep the company of the male staff.

"It's a good school," I said.

The finished room we're in is bright and attractive. Formerly the basement of my childhood home, it's now a warm and inviting living space. Oak floors. A sheetrock ceiling with recessed lights. Two leather chairs. A flat-screen TV. A minibar in the corner. A small jukebox. And a card table. Looking around the room, I try to picture it when it was filled with dusty boxes and mouse traps. The young man to my right notices my curiosity. I recognize him from the dining hall, where his dorm's table is adjacent to mine. Fair complexioned with reddish hair and freckles, he has an affable manner about him. His name is either Tim or Tom.

"Diego did practically the whole thing," he said. "Talented dude."

Sandra turns to me and mentions that Diego is the head of the maintenance department.

"Let's not forget *my* contributions; I installed the bar and the TV."

This comes from the source of my evening's invitation from earlier in the day. He sits across from me, two beers in front of him on the card table.

"You're a real fucking MVP, Dave," says the slouching, dough-faced joker to his left. "Mr. P.E. We couldn't get along without you, babe. Now don't forget, you're *big blind*, bitch."

This must be Scotty, who feigns impatience over all the small talk. He pretends to admonish Dave as he reminds him of the rules. Then he looks at me and rolls his eyes, telling me it's become a tradition for him to constantly explain the game's rules to Dave.

After a few hands, all of which I lose, the conversation turns in another direction. Sandra, throwing her cards on the table, asks if any of us have heard the latest news about the dead girl. The song on the jukebox suddenly ends. After a moment, a new one plays. "Jesus is Just Alright" by The Doobie Brothers. Down to my last five chips, I play it safe and toss my cards onto the table.

"I heard Rollie talking to Annie about her autopsy results."

Between Rollie and Nussbaum, they have quite a few contacts downtown. They always have, as long as I can remember. This would allow them such privileged information. Sandra turns to me and mentions that Annie is the school nurse.

"And?" Tennille said.

"And, the girl had a ton of amitriptyline in her system," Sandra said. "That's what Rollie said."

The hand is between Scotty and Tim/Tom. Neither of them say a word. They just toss a few more chips on the pile until Scotty lays out his cards. Tim/Tom slaps his cards face down on the table while Scotty collects his winnings.

"Do you guys know how many of our kids take meds with that in it?" said Sandra. "It must be dozens. That's what Rollie said. This thing is *not* going away."

"What did you expect?" said Dave. "The body of a local kid has just been found on our campus. Of course it's not going away."

For the next several hands, I bet conservatively. One chip at a time. The conversation veers all over the place. The dead girl and its effect on the school. Students who are especially disturbed by it. The Molotov cocktail from the other day. Kids who were recently caught smoking, screwing, swapping meds. I listen, but don't engage. Tennille is coaxed by Tim/Tom to tell the story of the late-night threesome she discovered in her dorm just this past spring.

"Ah, girls will be girls," said Scotty. "Do tell."

She has a way with a story, understanding the benefits of pauses and inflections and details. And just as she's getting to the part where she walked in on the young ladies, the door at the top of the stairs bursts open and the Old Man hurries halfway down to the middle step. His face looks long and wired, like he's just been the victim of some dreadful accusation.

"Louise just called me. The police found a car on the highway, along the edge of the campus about a hundred yards before the onramp. And not ten minutes later, she finds *guess who* lurking around the school? Dimitri Ames. Louise and a few others managed to subdue him, but they had a hell of a time. According to her, he was going bullshit. And still is. I could hear him in the background when she called. I'm going to need some help."

Dave stands up and finishes off one of his beers. Rollie begins to head back up the stairs, asking the rest of us to please stay behind. Before I even know what I'm saying, I tell Dave to sit down. I'll go, I tell him, standing up.

The Old Man turns to look at me. I announce to no one in particular that I'm nearly broke - not to mention stone sober. Dave looks at Rollie.

"You two figure it out. But we need to move. And quickly."

Tossing my last few chips onto the table, I make my way towards the staircase. Dr. Nussbaum yells down for us to hurry. My father takes a moment to study me. Then he turns and hustles up the stairs. I follow him, wondering what life is like for other fathers and sons our age. Before I can begin to imagine, and when I'm literally on his heels, I hear Sandra say something - it's something I've also considered when Rollie delivered his news moments earlier:

"A hundred yards before the onramp? That's where they found Dimitri's car? Interesting. Isn't that pretty close - if you cut right through the woods there - to where they found the body?"

Another voice - I believe it's Dave's - says how Dimitri Ames is a predator and he never trusted him from the moment he met him. The Old Man wheels around to look at me.

"I'm right behind you," I tell him.

CHAPTER 8

Ben Reed was my only coworker in whom I ever confided. Mild-mannered and quick-witted, Ben is about ten years older than I am. Over the years, we played squash on the occasional weekend, bitched about the same colleagues, and had lunch together a few days a week at a deli around the corner from our office. He's always been an easy confidant. I told him when I was planning to propose to Laura. I told him about Grove Garden Estates. About Laura's pregnancy. And, during our meal one afternoon, about the fetal ultrasound.

"They go through hell. I admit it. With the tests and checkups, and not to mention the actual pregnancy. It's a nightmare. *We* could never do it. I know all this."

"Of course you do," Ben said, biting into his sandwich. "We *all* know it, Gray."

"So what's one more test? Especially after the news we've gotten. It just seems irresponsible not to go through with it."

"Justine wanted no part of any of those tests," Ben said, smiling at an attractive young woman taking the table adjacent to ours. "She was adamant. You know Justine."

I had met her only a few times, but I nodded anyway.

"Women see it differently than we do, Gray. They don't need to know what we need to know. Because there's only one option for them: have the baby."

I asked if he was ever worried during Justine's pregnancy. He smiled and told me that his wife's composure was infectious.

"You know Justine," he said again, sipping his iced tea.

I sat back in my chair and wiped some mustard from the corner of my mouth.

"Listen," he said, "there's some kind of bond between the mother and what's growing inside of her. We can appreciate it, but let's not bullshit ourselves that we can ever understand it. I once read about a pregnant woman - she was in her third trimester - who defended herself against a Rottweiler. She was pretty beat up, but she survived. She was interviewed, and was asked how she was able to summon the strength to fight. It was her *baby*, she said. She just kept picturing herself holding that baby of hers in a few weeks. I remember she said that there was nothing, let alone a fucking dog, that would ever deprive her of that right."

Finishing off the rest of his sandwich, Ben told me it would all work out. It was simple, he said. If I wanted peace of mind, I was going to have to pay for it.

"They have a lot of cards to play when they want something," he said. "We have *one*. We have to lay out cash, my friend."

He explained. Take Laura on a trip. Book a romantic weekend at a bed and breakfast. Hilton Head or Savannah or the Outer Banks.

"Don't use it as leverage. Book it first. Then, tell her you booked it and that it will be the perfect spot to go after the stress settles from this ultrasound thing. She'll be so taken with the idea of the vacation, plus your initiative, that she'll see her way to appeasing your stubborn ass."

I thought about this for a moment. It seemed logical. And, knowing Laura, it had the potential to work. She always complained that we never traveled as often as she would have liked.

"Not to mention this trip might be your last for a while. Look at it as your last hurrah before the baby comes. Another good selling feature."

Ben leaned back in his chair. He sighed before taking a long sip of his drink. Then he looked at me. Probably he noticed the apprehension in my face.

"It's going to be fine. She'll take the damn test. You'll get the results. They'll be negative. You'll go away for a few days, forget all about it, come back, have a baby, and live happily ever fucking after. Trust me."

My sense of wonder was piqued. Ben's idea, as well as his take on women, was reasonable. But I must've still looked unsure when he said what he said next, which piqued an entirely different sense of wonder:

"Ask your neighbor about these tests. He's a doctor, isn't he? I'll bet you anything he'll relieve some of Laura's stress. That'll help your cause, too. Right? After all, what are neighbors for?"

. . .

One of Laura's cravings during her pregnancy was lasagna. She couldn't get enough of it. What really appealed to her was the cheap, frozen kind. Stouffer's was her favorite brand. And she had to have orange soda with it. Lasagna and orange soda. So this is what I prepared for her the Friday evening I made my proposal. Like the meal, my rhetoric was simple.

"Just so we have all the facts. I think that's important."

Though I couldn't get the word *responsible* from my mind, I was careful not to use it. This was Ben's idea. He surmised that by using it, she could interpret my meaning to suggest that she was behaving *irresponsibly*. She could therefore become defensive. Then, according to Ben, I'd really have my work cut out for me. The plan would be to keep it neutral and light. Which I did, refilling her plate and glass in between humble, soft-spoken pleas.

"And what do we do once we know?" she asked. "What's the purpose of this information?"

Pausing for a moment, I repeated myself:

"Just to know."

Her position, she explained, was as simple as my own. She valued the surprise of the experience. The excitement. The spontaneity. As an adult, she argued, there are so few opportunities for such sensations. She wanted the pregnancy to offer all of this.

"But if something's wrong, sweetheart, I think we should know beforehand."

She looked at me. The faintest trace of orange soda was on her lower lip.

"And what if something *is* wrong?" she asked.

"Then I think we should know."

"And then what? What happens after we know?"

Turning away, I focused on a painting on the kitchen wall. It was of a European bistro where a lone couple sits under the twilight, drinking wine and staring at one another. It was done mostly in yellows and reds. I knew it was a wedding gift, but I couldn't remember who gave it to us.

"We'll deal with it," I said softly, turning back to Laura.

She was about to say something when I cut in:

"You want the element of surprise? You want excitement and spontaneity? Well, I can guarantee all of that and more. I can *guarantee* it."

I went on, telling her that we were in for something unlike anything either of us had ever known. I laughed and told her it was going to be wild. I said that I could hardly stand all the surprises we had waiting for us - the joy and excitement of starting a family. Hesitating for a moment, I reached across the table and ran my finger over her lips.

"All of that's not going away with some stupid test," I said. "Trust me."

I told her I could sweeten the deal for her. Then I reached for my phone and found the confirmation of the two first class tickets to Key West I purchased that morning. Sliding it across the table, I reminded her that she had plenty of vacation time coming up. She picked up the phone and studied it for a moment. Her tongue slid behind her top lip while her eyes became focused and sharp. I knew that expression. It meant she was trying to play it cool, but was actually excited.

"Is this the best bribe you could come up with?"

I said it was. She tapped her fingers on the screen while pretending to think. After a moment, she leaned towards me and said there was a way for me to sweeten the deal even further and ensure that I would get my way. Now *I* pretended to play it cool. Leaning back in my chair, I asked what it was. With deadpan delivery, Laura hesitated for a moment and then asked for me to bring her the last piece of lasagna.

· · ·

Glenn Kilburn had grown a beard. Not a self-pitying or lazy man's beard. And not a bushy or spotty or an up-to-your-cheekbones beard, but a good beard. The kind that the tanned, chiseled TV stars so effortlessly grow. The kind that draws attention to an already attractive face, complementing it, and giving it a shaped masculinity and even an enigmatic quality.

I was able to chart the development of this beard on a daily basis. Glenn, who worked evening shifts at Saint Joseph Hospital in the city, could be found at my house most days upon my return from work. Laura, who always arrived home at least two to three hours before me, would be entertaining Glenn. They'd be drinking - always straight whiskey on ice for Glenn, and orange soda or cranberry juice for Laura - and talking and laughing and getting to know one another. Glenn would leave almost as soon as I walked in the door, but never before downing his whiskey and telling me I was lucky to have such a winner or peach or gem of a wife. He would clap me on the shoulder and thank Laura for her hospitality.

"Should a doctor be drinking so much?" I'd ask once Glenn had left. "Seems a bit reckless."

"He's a grown-up."

"I suppose."

"And he's quite the character."

Laura said this with a modest degree of affection. She was getting to know Glenn Kilburn, and must've liked what she was learning. And because Laura and I weren't the jealous types, she never felt the need to justify his presence in our home or assure me that Glenn, after as many as four or five whiskeys, was behaving himself. What she would share instead were trivial anecdotes about Linda, his soon-to-be ex-wife. They would all end the same way: with her declaring that Glenn likely endured unbearable shallowness, coldness, even cruelty.

"The poor guy," I would say, barely concealing my sarcasm.

One evening, just minutes after Glenn's hurried, half-drunken departure, I asked Laura what she thought of his new beard. And I'll be goddamned if she didn't make a face I knew all too well. A face that tried to play it cool, but was a thin disguise for something else - curiosity maybe, or some kind of keen interest that imposes itself on matters it likes to ponder in private.

"I didn't really notice his beard," she said.

"Really?"

"Yes, really."

"Well, it's there. Trust me. It's all over his face."

"Then I guess he grew it in the right place."

"But you're saying you haven't noticed it, right?"

"Maybe I'm just not as observant as I should be."

I was on the verge of breaking this ruse wide open with some self-righteous gesture or comment that would expose it and in fact embarrass her a little. I didn't, though. I stopped myself. It's just a beard, I thought. Besides, I knew better than to antagonize a pregnant woman.

• • •

Aside from waiting on the results of Laura's amniocentesis, there was a lot of additional drama during that summer. A colleague of mine, Marty Nye, lost his wife in a rock climbing accident. She was forty. That same week, Laura's mother, Abby, was driving home from a luncheon with friends when a motorcycle darted out from a side street and crashed into her. Abby was seriously shaken, and her Volkswagen was totaled. The man on the bike, though okay, was banged up pretty badly. And, finally, Laura and I would learn one morning that Great Caesar's, our favorite restaurant, had burned to the ground, killing one employee and severely burning at least three others.

"It'll be nice to get away," Laura continued to say after each tragedy.

We were both looking forward to Key West. The last trip we took, nearly two years prior, was to Wind Lake, Wisconsin. And though it was pleasant, it was with Laura's siblings, their spouses, and their children.

It was never clear to me whether Laura was anxious about the amnio results. All that was clear was that she was never interested in the test to begin with. The reluctance she felt was something I often thought about. It bothered me. We were usually in agreement. Movies, food, politics: Whatever the matter, we almost always saw it the same. Yet I never got a sense of how she wanted her family life to be. She managed to keep hidden whatever her mind may have conjured on the subject. Of course she wanted what every parent wants - to see their kids play and laugh and grow and fall in love and fall down and get back up and become the type of adult to give thanks for how they turned out - yet there was no denying that I married a woman whose levels of acceptance and even forgiveness transcended my own. And by a lot. In fact, all I can recall ever hearing her say was, simply, *I want to be someone's mother.* Maybe it's just that elementary for women. Maybe men are more ego-driven, and their progeny must be constant and glorious tributes to them.

Women, meanwhile, are swept up in the miracle of their bodies and the godlike sensations they want to feel forever. Maybe everything else, comparatively, becomes unimportant. Maybe, when you've been gifted such abilities, and can perform in some divine-like fashion, nothing else really matters.

We had waited a total of twelve days before we heard from Dr. Rose's office. It was a Thursday when we received the news. It was a brutally hot day. I remember learning that it was the hottest weather on record in the city in ten years. I arrived home from work to find Glenn in my driveway. With a drink in his hand, he was walking back to his house. Guiding me towards him as though he was an air traffic controller, he greeted me with a faint smile. When I stepped out of the car, he took a seat on a large landscaping rock in his front yard and watched me approach him.

"Mr. Grayson, the man of the house," he said, sipping on his ice, "welcome home."

The glass, as usual, was one of ours. I wondered if he was returning them.

"Good day for a drink," he said. "It's brutal out here."

The truth is he didn't look the slightest bit affected by the heat. With a black golf shirt, army-green shorts, and leather flip flops, he appeared cool and comfortable. I, on the other hand, started sweating the moment I stepped from my car. Agreeing with him about the heat, I mentioned that it was the hottest day on record in ten years.

"How's the journalism business? Always a lot to report on, I'm sure."

"Like your business, I imagine, it's unending."

We both agreed that as long as we did our respective jobs well, we'd probably never be out of work. Then Glenn said something that I found interesting, something that suggested to me that he was not only stacking us up side-by-side for the purpose of comparison, but that he had done it before, and possibly several times. I'm not sure if this was revealed to me through the quiet, confident way he said it, or in the way his body seemed to go limp a little, as though he was relieved by this small revelation.

"You see," he said, shaking the ice in the glass, "we *do* have something in common. And I bet you thought we were fire and water."

"I never really thought about it," I said, which was a lie.

Setting his glass down on the rock, Glenn stood up. He was probably three or four inches taller than me. I noticed his beard had become fuller.

"That's the kind of stuff I think about a lot," he said. "What connects people. How we're related. All of that."

I nodded my head, wondering if it was the alcohol that was making him approach the precipice of sentimentality. Glenn and I stood there for a few moments, not saying much of anything. After a while, I told him I should head inside to see Laura.

"She's waiting for you."

I half-expected him to offer me some type of assurance that he had just enjoyed my wife's company, that she was helping him through a difficult time and there was nothing more to it than that. But he said nothing of the sort. We said goodnight and headed our separate ways. But just as I was about to enter the house, Glenn called my name from his front lawn:

"You know what else we have in common?" he asked. "All of us, I mean. We all just want to avoid a major tragedy in life. If we can pull that off, well, that's a hell of a thing, isn't it?"

He never waited for a response. He just turned and went inside his house. The empty glass was left behind on the landscaping rock. Laura was on the phone when I entered the kitchen. Later, I would find out it was with her father. She barely greeted me when I walked towards her and whispered hello. Just a slight nod. She stayed on the phone for a few minutes, mostly listening and confirming what she was being told. When she hung up, she looked at me with an entirely new expression. Her mouth moved into a slightly pursed position, and her eyes appeared dark and defeated. It wasn't an offensive look, yet its foreign quality made me worry that it might be her new face forever.

It was with this face that she told me our news. She had spoken with Dr. Rose, who had called in the afternoon. They had a lovely talk. Dr. Rose was positive and encouraging. She had some literature for us to read. Some on the science of what we were facing, and some on the psychological end.

"She's good at what she does," Laura told me.

She began cleaning the kitchen. First, she wiped the counters and polished the stovetop. Then she began reorganizing the fridge, removing its contents and running a sponge over the glass shelves. Taking a seat at the table, I decided to let her non sequiturs and trivial domestic gestures run their course. This took a few minutes. During that time, I was able to articulate what I wanted to say. But when her pretense of busyness finally halted, I forgot every word.

"What are you thinking about?" she asked.

The truth was that my mind was not at all focused. Probably it was swimming in confusion, but I could articulate nothing. So I lied.

"Glenn's beard."

She asked if I was serious.

"I can't imagine that in all your visits with one another, the topic of his beard was never once brought up. Yet you maintain that you've never even noticed it."

Staring at me with cold eyes from across the kitchen, Laura called me a bastard for coaxing her into taking the amnio test. She glared at me for a few moments and then stormed past me towards the stairs. After some time, the door to our bedroom slammed.

My mind felt like it was now able to unfurl a complete thought. And it became focused on Glenn Kilburn. But not on his fucking beard. Instead, I was focused on what he had said to me earlier from across his front lawn - about how what we all have in common is the hope of avoiding a tragedy in life. He was quite the philosopher, Glenn Kilburn. I thought of how he looked and sounded when he said this, how he must've felt slightly self-conscious to deliver such a heady statement to a neighbor he hardly knew. Suddenly, my mind, as though on a timer, cleared all these thoughts and made room for only one: the notion that it was a very real possibility that Glenn Kilburn had in fact learned the fate of my family hours before I did.

CHAPTER 9

There was never any choice but for Rollie to have a relationship with Old Brookview's police department. It's part of running a therapeutic boarding school in town. His students occasionally run away or shoplift downtown or cause a public disturbance. Or, they find the body of a dead girl in the woods on their school's campus.

Because the Old Man is so protective of his kids, he views everyone in town as an outsider. The local cops are no exception. Rollie knows what the town thinks of his students. They're seen as pariahs - poor, mysterious creatures who are damaged and sometimes dangerous.

Since the murder, though, he's cooperated. He's given the authorities the freedom to scour the premises, ask questions, and collect evidence. The Dimitri Ames situation is different. I think the Old Man is not only fed up with catastrophes at his school by the time this occurs, but he must feel that he has the upper hand in this one. This is a situation where I believe he feels *he's* the victim. He's been duped by this young predator. And then, once Ames was confronted, he had the audacity to be belligerent, going so far as to threaten the Old Man.

To show up at the school late at night, get caught sneaking around, and then get mouthy, and even physical, goes well beyond ballsy. And there *I* was. Not hundreds of miles away, sleeping soundly in my own home. Not living anything resembling the adult life I thought I'd be living as a grown man. But tramping through the familiar grounds of the HAS in the dense summer darkness, supporting my father, helping him subdue a complete stranger.

By the time we reach the scene, which has progressed from the woods behind the girls dormitories to just outside the SOD office, Ames is pretty much wound up. He's throwing his arms in the air, darting from side to side, and cussing at Louise and the other security staff, Jimbo and Paddy, both of whom are paunchy, middle-aged men. Louise shines a flashlight in Ames' face while she rests her other hand on the butt of a thin club holstered at her hip.

Ames is telling the threesome that they have no authority over him and to fuck off, that he's done nothing wrong. The cops are on their way, Louise tells him, and it's they who can decide. When Ames spots Rollie hurrying towards him, with me and Nussbaum in tow, he laughs. It's the kind of laugh filled with fresh terror and an uneasy heart that can't decide between obstinacy and deference.

"Six on one," Ames says. "What the fuck?"

"My thoughts exactly," says the Old Man, spreading his arms and lifting them in the air. "What the fuck?"

"I still have friends on campus."

"I don't give a shit. This is private property. You're not welcome here."

Ames becomes still. For a moment, no one speaks. The fist of light thrown around from Louise's hand finally settles on Ames' face. He's tall, dark-haired, and cleanly shaven.

"Look out now," Ames said, his smile wide and brash, "he's going to start quoting fucking Nietzsche or something."

"Nietzsche?" I said, "you wouldn't understand it if he quoted Scooby Doo."

Jimbo and Paddy laugh. The Old Man turns to me.

"What I mean," I said, capitalizing on the tacit approval I assume I have from everyone, "is that you're obviously not a bright guy. My father has apparently asked you several times to disassociate yourself from this place and everyone here. But you don't seem to grasp that simple concept."

"So," he says, with pitch-perfect smugness, "you're the new me. Well, aren't you just Daddy's little fucking hero?"

He laughs to himself before telling me to go to hell. Louise turns towards the Old Man and quietly mentions that the police are on their way. Ames says to no one in particular that he's done nothing wrong, that he still has friends on campus.

"We know all about your friends on campus," Louise said, turning to my father. "When we found him, he was by himself, near the woods behind the girls dorms."

She continues, telling the Old Man how she sent Jimbo to the Missouri House to check on Lindsay Lowe. Jimbo, Louise's newest security staffer, hoists up his pants and comes to her side.

"She was there, Mr. Loveland," he said. "Reading in the lounge. Fully dressed, I might add. But in her day clothes. I asked if she'd been out of the dorm tonight and she said she hadn't."

Jimbo added that he didn't believe the girl. So, with her dorm staff present, he questioned her two roommates, who were also wide awake, but in their beds. It took them a minute of scared glances at one another to relent and reveal that Lindsay had in fact snuck out before she made them swear not to tell. She was gone for about an hour, the girls had told him.

"The fuck does that prove?" says Ames, more in a naturally inquisitive way than with hostility. "Maybe just that no one in this shitty little psych ward is competent enough to do their job."

Nussbaum, who's standing off to my side, calls Ames an arrogant little shit. Suddenly, as if stung by some mad, invisible archer, Ames lunges towards the doctor with his teeth bared and his breath heavy with hate and humiliation. Before I know what's happening, I extend my arm, which Ames runs directly into. I then find myself curling it around his neck and bringing him crashing to the asphalt. I hold him while he violently kicks up his legs and flails in a futile effort to grab at my face and hair. Louise turns the light on us as we struggle on the cool, dry pavement. The Old Man is suddenly hovering over us, his wide eyes appearing shocked and pleased.

"I guess you shouldn't kill him, Gray," he says dryly. "After all, the cops'll be here soon."

Two officers, Jerome and Bagley, end up arriving within a few minutes. Ames does not go quietly. He writhes under their force and spits out sharp bits of indignation towards those who watch him get cuffed and folded into the backseat of the cruiser. Mostly, he looks between me and my father, who begins naming all of Ames' charges to Officer Jerome: trespassing, assault, resisting arrest. He says these with an annoyed energy as though there should be more to comprise the list.

"Rollie, leave the police work to us, okay?" the officer says.

"I want to press charges," my father tells him.

"We're looking at a class A misdemeanor," says Officer Jerome. "Criminal trespassing."

"What's that?" asks the Old Man, "a slap on the wrist?"

"It's taking him downtown, it's processing him, and it's a fine."

Rollie emits an exasperated sigh. He bites his lower lip and points his chin outward ever so slightly, a habit that flashes in my mind as something he did when I was a kid. It means he's willing himself to have self-control.

"What if I told you he sexually abused one of my students?" my father asks, gritting his teeth and pinching the bridge of his nose.

Officer Jerome is a solemn looking black man with a powerful build. He folds his arms across his sturdy chest and asks if there's proof.

"C'mon," the Old Man pleads.

"Rollie, I know what you're dealing with right now. This is the last thing you need. That's for damn sure. But we're in the business of proof. Until then, he's just some punk you fired, who's not over it yet."

My father shakes his head. Leaning towards the officer, he reveals that there's more to the story.

"There always is," says Officer Jerome.

"He threatened me. The day I fired him, he threatened me. He told me I embarrassed him, and that he would do the same to me. But on a much grander scale. Nuss here was a witness."

Unfolding his massive arms, the officer turns to get a look at Ames, who's sitting motionless in the back of the cruiser, staring ahead. Turning back to Rollie, the officer says they'll do all they can. Bagley, an older man with a graying moustache and neatly slicked hair, calls for Jerome to wrap things up.

"Listen, Rollie," says Jerome, "we know you're trying to buy this place from Roarick, so you probably have a lot at stake. I understand that."

My father suddenly views me out of the corner of his eye.

"But the best we can do is to see that this kid keeps off the property. But to accuse him of what I think you're accusing him of, well, again we come back to the burden of proof."

The Old Man points out where Ames' car was discovered, close to where the body was found. Then he states, almost inquisitively, how perpetrators often revisit the scene of their crime. The officer looks at his watch.

"Proof," Jerome says again.

Grumbling over what he knows is nothing more than lawfulness, Rollie hesitates for a moment before extending his hand to the policeman.

"I'm hoping this is the last I see of that kid," the Old Man says, motioning towards Ames. "But I guess we'll see."

After the officers leave, my father and I walk through the campus. A thin, hammock-like moon rests easy in the sky. An evening breeze gathers.

"This place is a regular slice of heaven, isn't it? Just as I remember it."

No response. I continue:

"Hell, who could blame you for wanting to buy it? Makes sense to me."

My sarcasm is the quiet kind, tempered with an indiscreet hope that my antagonism will eventually escalate to the level of verbal sparring.

"The Joni House," Rollie says, as we pass by the tiny clapboard Cape. "Your mother lived here for an entire summer. In that staff room."

Smiling, he points to the rear of the house. He explains how there was a shortage of female dorm staff that summer, so my mother acted as interim. The story - if it qualifies as one - was told to me before.

"The kids loved her. As you can imagine. She used to read to them like they were a kindergarten class - short stories, poetry. They would sit at her feet, in a circle, and she would read to them. That's precious stuff."

I tell him I can imagine that. He nods his head and walks on, just slightly ahead of me, towards the woods where Ames had just been discovered.

"Was there a plan to tell me about your little takeover?"

"Don't be condescending," he said, turning around to face me.

"Well?"

He bites his lower lip and takes a deep breath. He suddenly looks younger. Like his consternation has rallied his heart into beating a new tune set to vibrant and kinetic melodies. This is strangely inspiring. I almost want to let him have the upper hand in the argument.

"Well," he says, "how about you tell me what the fuck is going on in your life and I'll tell you what's going on in mine?"

Cupping my jaw into his hand, he shakes my face a little, his gaze somewhat endearing.

"Okay," he adds, releasing me, "I'll start. I'm buying the place from Roarick. The deal's not yet sealed, but it's in the works. Now seems like the right time. I've put in a hell of a lot of years, not to mention money, and I want it to finally be mine. He's asking a price I can manage and I can't see walking away from the opportunity. It's always been in the back of my mind, and it's honestly beginning to feel like a now or never situation. So it's gotta be now. And I'm glad you'll be here, hopefully, to see it through with me."

"That's it?"

"You want more? Okay. Out of left field, I'm getting hit by the Fire Marshall, who's breaking my balls over the sprinkler system in the dining hall and the stairway in the Missouri House. Not up to code, I guess. And it's going to cost more than $20,000 to fix. Not to mention we had another withdrawal today. Your turn."

"Are you trying to further prove my argument against buying this place?"

"Your turn."

"What would you like to hear?"

"Gray."

"I'm serious. What would you like to hear?"

"I was thinking maybe something about my former daughter-in-law or the baby who would've been my first grandchild."

"It's late. I'm exhausted. My arm is starting to hurt from ramming it into that moron you hired once upon a time ago."

The wind suddenly starts to gather. The Old Man begins to say something, but stops himself. He puts his hands on my shoulders and looks me in the eye for a moment.

"I guess tonight's not our night. Take care of that arm," he says before mumbling a little and then walking away.

My amazement over my father buying the HAS, I realize, is absurd. Nothing would change. Maybe deed possession and property taxes. But that would be about it. What bothers me is the ruined possibility that he'll ever pack up and walk away from this place. Not that there was ever much of a chance of that to begin with. Still, though, the obligation factor would increase. It would have to. Rollie Loveland: overseer *and* proprietor of Old Brookview's famed Hundred Acre School. Unbelievable. Why now? After all these years.

A morbid and selfish thought crosses my mind: my father's passing. What will *my* obligations be? Would he actually will the place to me? And what would his expectations be for his only child? Pushing it out of mind, I conceive a new thought: Dimitri Ames. Feeling my arm that clotheslined him into submission, I straighten myself up and begin walking back to my dorm. It's late. The praise I award myself for my instincts suddenly gives way. Is it possible that what occurred this evening has nothing to do with instincts? Is it possible that it has more to do with an allegiance to my father? An allegiance that has been dormant for so much of our lives. And one that found us working in concert for the first time in as long as I can remember, and for quite possibly one of the strangest and most indefinable causes.

. . .

The boys in the Homer House are at war. Albert has locked the dorm's gaming system in his footlocker and has hidden the key. He claims Alex and Dustin have been cheating at certain games by receiving online tips. Cliff has pleasured himself on J.J.'s pillow twice this week. Hawaiian Punch - Noah - is being accused of stealing Andrew's watch.

Yet it's Nick Russo who wins the prize. Over the course of a couple of days, he has filled Cal's acoustic guitar to the brim with his own urine. The instrument, which also houses some of the boys' rolled-up dirty magazines, was stored in a closet, so clothing and shoes have also been soiled. Nick's punishment is to replace the guitar and clothing, as well as scrub down the entire dorm. He accepts these consequences - not from me, but from Reese, one of HAS's youngest administrators - with unabashed hostility.

I'm told by Reese that bad behavior is magnified during the summer session. The HAS kids will have to wait until the end of August for their next vacation. Reese has been at the school for a few years now, and he assures me this is the pattern. There's resentment over being in school while other kids - *normal kids* - are traveling, sleeping late, and reveling in forgetting what day of the week it is. Acting out then becomes the norm for the HAS student.

I don't doubt this. But I believe there's more. I'm beginning to become attuned to the boys in the Homer House. What makes them tick. What sets them off. What rules and creeds they devise and respect and live by.

There's been no previous rivalry between Nick and Cal. In fact, their perversity and defiance makes them the closest thing to a male counterpart either can tolerate. They can be seen together tormenting the same student, riffing off of one another, basking in their sick competition. So it's an unprovoked act, this guitar stunt. Completely random in its destructiveness, uniqueness, and foulness. Nick is like that, though. I've watched him turn against his supporters in the blink of an eye. A true loner, Nick will sneer at anything resembling genuine camaraderie, unless it's guaranteed to be fleeting or superficial. If one of the boys sides with him as he argues or bullies, they're sure to be his next target. Cal, who's not too far ahead of Nick on the evolutionary chart, is initially taken aback when he learns he's not an exception to this. Resilience in the shape of preternatural apathy has a way of finding human beings who thrive on selfishness and hollow relationships. So it's no surprise that Cal is more disturbed by the vandalism of his guitar than he is over a betrayal from a fellow HASER.

"I loved that guitar," he announces one afternoon at lunch. "You know how many times that thing got me laid?"

The other boys at the table laugh. Ryan reminds Cal of the new instrument Nick will be purchasing for him.

"But not in time for this weekend," Cal points out. "I had my shit all ready to go. I was gonna do a nice little ditty that I was gonna dedicate to all my boys here."

The upcoming talent show is an annual summer event, something the kids seem to anticipate with unusual pride. Not that there's an abundance of hype - there isn't - but I do find it remarkable that here is at last something, besides their own impediments, that is being considered and taken seriously. I find their interest downright surprising. They talk about the show during class and in the dining hall and in the dorm. Handmade posters have been made and hung in various locations around campus. *Show off your talent!! Impressions, Songs, Monologues, Jokes, Skits, Dances. TALENT SHOW SIGN-UPS AT THE SOD OFFICE.*

"Encourage as many kids as you can to sign up," Rollie urges the staff. "Or to just come and watch. This is probably one of the best distractions we could ask for right now."

The talent show is my father's pet project. He came up with the idea when I was a kid. Always acting as emcee and general overseer, the Old Man would try in vain to enlist my help in the behind-the-scenes. Building a platform stage. Screening the acts with him. Acting as gofer during rehearsals. I refused everything. Then, the evening of the production, he'd try to entice me to attend with him. He'd endorse the talents of his kids, promising me absolute entertainment. Impressions, Songs, Monologues, Jokes, Skits, Dances. He did this year after year. I refused every time.

• • •

The Dimitri Ames invasion seems to have had a genuine effect on the kids.

"I know where he's from," I heard Caitlin, a self-deprecating earth mama, tell another girl in the pavilion. "He told us like fifty times. I say we find his house and burn it to the ground."

"What a motherfucker!" the Homer House boys sang out in unison one morning.

"It's pathetic," said Bridget, a girl in one of my classes. "He probably has a dick the size of a baked bean, which would explain why he can't get a girl his own age."

There's no condoning Ames' behavior. He's violated more than just a professional code of conduct. He's preyed on the very essence of those things they all have in common. Their lack of sound judgment. Their impulsivity. Vulnerability. Neediness. They are protective of their campus, their world, and of their own kind. Ames is now, and forever will be, an outsider.

Lindsay Lowe. Her name is circulating the campus for the second time this summer. Speculation ignites the curiosity of many. She has been impregnated and her intention was to run away and marry Ames that very night. Another one: Ames has been living on and off again in Lindsay's dorm and was caught while sneaking back in. My favorite: She told the Old Man off, pleaded her devotion for Ames, and received parental permission to be picked up by the former teacher in the most furtive of ways.

The truth, which is explained to the faculty by Dr. Reynolds, Lindsay's therapist, is simpler than all of these:

"We confronted Lindsay the very next day," Dr. Reynolds, a fair haired, middle-aged man with permanent dark pools under his eyes, announced at a staff meeting. "Naturally, she was quite inhibited. Her mother thought it best if she came home for a while. A change of scenery, we all agree, will do her good. She'll be back when the time is right."

Two boys in one of my classes, Matt and Adam, have taken a special interest in the situation. They're friends with Lindsay. Adam, who must weigh well over two-hundred pounds, is a bear. His baggy clothing, faded black t-shirts and an assortment of three-quarter length camouflage shorts - everything he wears looks like thrift store treasures - hangs judiciously on his bulky frame, never defining or revealing bulges or rolls. He rarely smiles, but is far from a miserable kid. Witty, cynical, and somewhat worldly - he's lived just outside of London for three years and in the heart of Amsterdam for two - Adam is happiest when he's arguing. And not just with anyone, but with those he considers worthy opponents. Among his favorite topics are religion, occultism, sixties counterculture, and anything having to do with John Lennon. Nothing seems to please him more than inspiring a dialogue with anyone who will partake, and guiding the discourse to a plane where he will barrage his well-respected adversary with arcane facts and references, causing his target to be nearly punchdrunk with defeat.

Adam had seen in Lindsay someone in need of protection, a lost and lonely girl who could probably never articulate such a need, but who would never deny it, either. So he took on the role of big brother. And this worked out quite well since his best friend, Matt, happens to be head over heels in love with the girl. At just about the same height as Adam, Matt is lean, longhaired, and fresh-faced. He has boyish looks and a constant expression that seems just on the verge of bewilderment. These attributes help to offset Adam's seriousness as the boys make appearances together as a duo. By no means branded as a HAS student, Matt could pass for your ordinary American teenager. Aside from a school phobia and some self-esteem issues, which he manages to keep under control, Matt's only real eccentricities are his penchant for hats and harmonicas. His head is always covered in something; he has several caps boasting one of many sports teams from his native state of Ohio, not to mention a Panama hat, a porkpie hat, a fedora, a beret, and others I can't quite categorize. And then there are his harmonicas, which he plays everywhere he goes, but without so much of a trace of formality or affectation. It's as normal and natural to him as taking a breath.

"I've got one in every key," he tells anyone who's interested.

Then he names them all: one in A, B, B flat, C...

His worship for Lindsay Lowe is known among students and faculty. He's fine with this. I witnessed some of his classmates tease him about his obsession. His response, always, is to shrug it off.

"What can I tell you? She's pretty much perfect," I heard him say before carelessly blowing into one of his harmonicas.

The Dimitri Ames situation must have him up at night. As far as I can see, no jocularity abounds about this. No playful teasing. No mention of it, even. He must've been crestfallen after the illicit affair surfaced. Not only was it likely a blow to his ego, but to his relationship with Lindsay. After all, Matt and Lindsay are friends. Good friends. And she hid a profound secret from him. But when the news of her recent late night rendezvous broke, Matt's expression seemed to change a little, occasionally resembling the stoicism of his good friend, Adam.

Each morning, the boys look out my classroom window, sizing up the Old Man's Winnebago, discussing it in technical terms, asking me questions to which I have no answers. Then, when class lets out, they head outside where they circle the vehicle, study it together, and point out God knows what.

"We could get this thing running," they tell me as though I've challenged them on the matter. "Talk to Rollie for us, will you?"

Aside from the boys' tendency towards arguments and harmonicas and hopeless mobile homes, they have another pastime. It's one that I'm told is catching on, especially in certain higher echelon towns. Dumpster diving. My questioning of this during the last few minutes of class one day is met with incredulity.

"It's exactly what it sounds like," said Matt.

I ask them to explain. Put simply, they tell me it's rooting around in dumpsters in search of buried treasure.

"There's a science to it," Matt said. "It's more involved than just picking through garbage."

"He's right," said Adam.

The other HASERS in the class, a morose boy named Will, and Sloane, the first female skinhead I've ever seen up close, eavesdrop on our conversation. The boys tell me about their recent exploits. Adam found a skeleton clock downtown by the professional building. And an old wooden cigar box behind the drugstore. And a stash of Saturday Evening Post magazines. And a footrest he's currently refinishing. As for Matt, well, he's been in a bit of a slump for a few weeks now. His last interesting discovery, though, was right here, on campus. And it's this that has prompted the boys to share their hobby with me in the first place.

"Tell him," Adam said.

Matt looks at the other two students in class. Then he leans in towards me and lowers his head.

"It was in the cans behind the Homer House," he whispers.

"We're not limited to just dumpsters," Adam points out.

"It was just a few days before Rollie fired Dimitri," said Matt.

"Tell him what you found," Adam coaxes.

"Confirmation," said Matt. "Confirmation that he was sketchy from the start."

He found several boxes of blank checks, he explained. They were in different names and addresses, all from Old Brookview.

"I told Rollie," he said, his voice suddenly flatlining, "but he was dealing with the other Dimitri thing."

Adam chimes in:

"That's not all he found. I believe there was some drug paraphernalia to speak of. Let's not forget that."

"Some empty sleeves of rolling papers," Matt said.

As though I've challenged the veracity of these findings, Adam, with a powerful show of persuasion, tells me that the articles no doubt belonged to Dimitri. Other effects, he tells me - crumpled lesson plans and dorm reports with Ames' name on them - were alongside the contraband. Both boys study me for a moment, as though waiting for a counter to their claims. Adam, squinting his eyes a little and cocking his mouth, suddenly becomes pensive:

"I'd bet anything he had something to do with that girl's murder," he said. "No doubt."

Matt nods in agreement. The boys continue to study me, waiting for a reaction. To appease them, I nod. Lowering his voice, Adam leans towards me and says how they've found some interesting items here on the HAS campus, most of which have been from the trash of dorm staff.

"One of those old CB radios. A bunch of Playboys from the 1980s. A couple of Zippo lighters. A fish tank."

All I can think of is the litany of worries a HAS teacher endures in their job: summoning the mental and physical stamina to last a weekend on-duty; not getting woken up at 3:00 a.m. over some trivial squabble; the sodium content in Mickey's chicken marinade. Now these boys have alerted me to one I had never previously considered: being conscious over the contents of my garbage.

• • •

News of outsiders at the Hundred Acre School travels fast. It's often cause for speculation among students as well as staff. The visitors, a man, woman, and young girl, were seen roaming the campus before being escorted into the Old Man's office. They were an attractive threesome. One report stated that the woman, blonde, slim, and in her forties, seemed close to the verge of tears. Another said that the young girl, around seventeen, hung close to the woman's side with her head bowed low. The kids conjectured. Maybe an interview for a new student. Maybe the family of a current student about to withdraw from the HAS. In any event, the trio was holed up in Rollie's office for nearly two hours.

Because of this, for the first time in all the years since its inception, Rollie misses the talent show. He asks that a few of the staff share emceeing duties. So Tim/Tom and Tennille share the mic and usher the acts on stage. Most students are in attendance. Those uninterested must go to the pavilion where a few staff members supervise a showing of *Cool Hand Luke*.

The dining hall is made up to resemble a dinner theatre. Tables and chairs are pulled back from the rear of the room where the stage is set up. A makeshift curtain is suspended over a tautly drawn rope that runs the length of the stage and is tied at both ends on flagpole platforms taken from a couple of classrooms. Lighting and music are done by two students, who crouch in front of the stage with iPhones and multi-colored spotlights. This is my first talent show.

I find a vacant seat next to Amber and Scotty. I have a good view of the stage, as well as the Homer House boys, who sit together in a tight cluster, two tables to my right. The lights dim and the show begins. Tim/Tom and Tennille, standing in front of a drawn curtain, start things off with a series of impromptu impressions of staff members. I only know two of their subjects, and they seem like accurate renderings. From there, they introduce the first act, a girl named Margot, who plays piano and sings an original number. The song, sad and slow, has a catchy chorus: "The light you light is the light in me," which causes the crowd to eventually sing along. The next act is Josh, a brawny kid I teach in one of my American Lit. classes. He does a five minute comedy set. He talks about when he was a baby: He didn't have a first word, but first letters, which were *OCD*. He tells a story about his fear of sitting on Santa Claus's lap when he was a boy, how his parents would drag him, against his wishes, to tell the corpulent, bearded stranger what he wanted for Christmas. The punchline of the joke is that it happened in the middle of May in some back alley near an abandoned apartment complex. For his closing bit, he tells a story about how his mother once found a Penthouse magazine in his room and as a result registered him as a local sex offender. He exits the stage amid much applause. Tim/Tom and Tennille, still laughing, take the mic and comment that Josh's material was all original.

Next up is the girl who serves breakfast on the weekends - I think her name is Courtney - and she sings a mid-tempo ballad she wrote, accompanying herself on a twelve-string acoustic guitar. A boy I recognize from his frequent visits to the Homer House, parodies Cassius' soliloquy from Julius Caesar. He performs it impeccably, and though the original context might be too esoteric for some, the deftness of articulation gets him a nice reception from the crowd.

Scotty turns to me and tells me I must be impressed with the parody - being that I'm an English teacher. It's on the tip of my tongue to tell him I'm really not an English teacher. I opt to smile politely and agree that it's impressive.

More acts follow. Comedy sketches. Songs. Impersonations. Monologues. Dumpster-diving Matt even reads a poem, which he describes as an ode to something indescribable:

I held your breath for you for an entire second.
Upon promising its return, you said I could keep it,
so I did, for the rest of the day.
That night, you ran and sang and built a cathedral of whispers.
We never mentioned much after that,
but I always wanted to know,
what exactly was I holding of yours?

Matt exits the stage. The crowd applauds. Again, Scotty turns to me. This time he says nothing. I nod. During a flawless performance of "Dueling Banjos," which two boys each play on saxophones while seated in a humorous face-off, I'm tapped on the shoulder by Louise, who has just entered the dining hall. Her expression looks sunken and almost bereft of color. Pressing her face to my ear, she whispers that the Old Man is requesting Nick Russo. Nick, in a subtle show of defiance, takes his time rising from his seat. Louise, watching the saxophone piece, waits patiently before escorting the boy from the building.

The talent show ends with what Tim/Tom describes as a last minute addition. The curtain parts and Dan Hart steps on stage with a black acoustic guitar and a stool. The kids yell *Dan Juan!* at him; some shout out requests for Lou Reed and Pink Floyd songs. Unfazed, Dan sets himself up, adjusts the mic and begins his song. After a few strums, he stops to tune the instrument a bit. Then he leans into the mic and says something to the crowd:

"I don't really remember writing this song. But friends of mine tell me that I must've written it. It's called 'Escape Artist.'"

His singing voice is nothing like his speaking voice. It's strong and self-assured. Dan's stage presence is stoic and even calming. He seems at ease up there playing and singing. The tune is memorable and its lyrics belie the kid's age:

Back roads are so beautiful
There's angels in the dust
I swear I've seen 'em all before
They know my wanderlust
Temporary dreamer
And temporary dreaming
Working hard to get somewhere
And tryin' to find some meaning

The show ends and the lights flicker on. Tennille commandeers the mic from a male student who begins singing "We are the Champions." She wishes everyone a pleasant evening and asks all on-duty staff to escort their kids back to their dorms. Following the Homer House boys outside, we find Nick sitting on the front steps. He's hunched forward with his elbows resting on his knees. It takes me until I walk past him, down the steps to the gravel walkway, to see that he's smoking a cigarette. And though I'm focused on Nick alone, I can feel the Homer House boys all awaiting my reaction to this blatant misdemeanor. Before I can say a word, Nick rises, takes a step towards me, and flicks the still lit cigarette over my head.

"Ready?" he says, walking past me to join the rest of the boys.

When I enter my apartment, I find I have a visitor. My father is sitting at my desk, thumbing through some magazines I purchased in town the other day. When I walk into the room, he doesn't get up.

"Comfy?"

"I like what you've done with the place," he says dryly.

We both scan the unadorned, wood-paneled room that probably looks as sparse as it did when Dimitri Ames did God knows what in this very space.

"Let me guess," I said, taking another step inside the room, "you're here to put these little princes to bed - maybe read them a story?"

He rolls up the magazine he's been reading and looks through it towards his shoes. Laughing a little to himself, he says how he's got a bedtime story for *me* instead. The couple he met with in his office, he tells me in that solemn nonchalance he uses when he wants to show off his self-control, were Nicole D'Ambrosio's parents. They called earlier in the day and asked to meet with him this evening.

"Very nice people. We spoke for a while. The way they're handling themselves, well, it's a hell of a thing. I can't imagine what they're going through. It's unthinkable."

It takes a moment for it to register that Rollie must've considered the torture in losing a child.

"They received news from their daughter's friend, news that came as quite a shock to them," he adds.

Nicole D'Ambrosio's friend, a girl named Paige Vickerman, accompanied the couple to meet with Rollie. The news, he tells me, lowering his voice to just above a mumble, is that their daughter knew Nick Russo.

"Knew him quite well," he tells me, pointing the rolled up magazine to the wall behind him, through which is Nick's room. "The little fucker seems to have kept this detail from everybody - including the police."

My mind suddenly flashes back to a crude conversation some of the Homer House boys had one afternoon. It was mostly Noah and Cal doing the talking. Nicole D'Ambrosio was the focus. Yet what I remember more about that day was Nick. He was reticent. And he didn't join the depravity; he just took it in, considered it for a bit, then walked away. A coping strategy, perhaps. Maybe it was a way of creating emotional distance so he wouldn't reveal himself.

Rollie continues. Nicole's friend, who also knows Nick a little, was reluctant to say anything about their relationship. She may have been trying to protect Nicole. It's doubtful, he adds, that she was trying to protect Nick.

"What does Nick have to say about this?" I ask.

"Not a damn thing," he says, dropping the magazine to the floor. "Right now, he's scared. And he should be. And he's covering right now with his typical machismo. But he knows how serious this is. My guess is he knows something about what happened."

The girl's parents wasted no time in contacting the police, the Old Man tells me; and with the help of Paige, they revealed what they know about their daughter's relationship with Nick.

"I spoke with the cops tonight, shortly after they left. It's just a matter of time until they pay Nick a visit."

The Old Man reminds me that the boy is legally an adult and can therefore be questioned by the authorities without a parent present. Then he urges me to keep this matter to myself. Nick, he says, is unstable; for now, the key is to keep him safe and calm.

"Oh, and there's this," he tells me, pulling out a folded sheet of paper from his pocket, which he hands to me.

It's a picture, printed from the internet, of a white-gold Tiffany's ring that has Roman numerals circling the band.

"Nicole's folks told me about a ring she wore. *That* ring. It was a gift from her grandparents. From what I gather, it's worth a few bucks. A prized possession of hers, based on what her folks tell me, and something she never took off. Apparently it was missing from her body. We asked Nick about it. Naturally, he says he knows nothing."

Ryan, the Old Man adds, also has a copy of the picture. Then he says there will be a discreet yet thorough room search the following day when Nick is in class. I tack the picture on the bulletin board above my desk.

"Still, keep an eye out for that ring. If he has it, who knows what he'll do with it? He might show it off or try to sell it. If he's smart, he'll swallow the goddamn thing."

"You're really intent on buying this place? Your life expectancy *has* to be compromised with having to deal with this type of thing."

He opens the door to my apartment and steps outside into the cool night air.

"Why now? After all this time? I could've seen this ten years ago. But why now?"

Twisting his beard a little, my father looks at me with caution. He starts to say something about my mother before stopping himself. After a moment, he reminds me to keep an eye on Nick and a lookout for the ring. Then he wishes me a goodnight and turns to walk away. Stepping outside, I urge him, to his back, to answer my question. He stops in his tracks, but doesn't turn around.

"You want to talk about *life expectancy*?" he asks, his voice filled with a casual sternness. "Yet you've left your own life close to a thousand miles west of here. Are you ready to talk about *that* with *me*?"

I don't respond. He nods his head and continues making his way towards the center of campus.

It's an uneventful evening in the dorm. The boys stay up until close to midnight, watching a movie and harassing one another. Nick, I notice, who is usually at the center of at least some of the action, has skulked quietly away and fallen asleep atop his bed with all of his clothes on. The rest of the boys leave him alone.

I do something tonight I've never done since I've been an employee at the Hundred Acre School. I check on the boys while they're sleeping. Slipping in and out of the four bedrooms, I find them to all be out cold. Deep breathing and snoring and crickets just beyond the thin walls all swell up into a steady rhythm, infusing a strange and even peaceful air about the Homer House.

Then there are the dorm reports. Then a little late night TV and some reading. It's just after 2:00 a.m. when I finally drift off to sleep. That's when the knock comes, fast and forceful. I can tell it's not my front door, but the one that opens into the dorm. It's close to 3:00 a.m., though it seems like my head touched the pillow just moments ago. I stagger to the door, feeling the fickle weight of exhaustion propel me towards what must be another trivial late night drama; I'm even half-planning a mini-lecture about coping skills and conflict resolution. J.J. is standing there, wide-eyed, bare-chested, his wild red hair looking like a paint can explosion on top of his head.

"So I get up to take a piss," he begins, his craggy voice narrating as though we've always been mid-conversation, "and notice the room's quieter than usual. Nick's always making a ton of noise in his sleep. He's got that smoker's cough. Plus, he's always twisting and turning."

He veers off course, digressing on Nick's bad habits and how he's the poster-boy for undesirable roommates: the fingernail clippings; the dried up, days-old food festering on his bureau; the uncompromising allegiance to what J.J. calls the lamest music ever, stuff dads listen to. Moving him towards the point of his story with the ugliness of my yawn, he clears his throat, snarls a little bit, and comes out with it:

"He's gone, plain and simple," he says, looking somewhat pleased over the potential chaos his discovery might instigate.

I don't bother with the inquisition. Or even a search of the dorm. I just thank him and reach for the phone behind me. J.J. leans against the archway and watches me as I fumble through the campus directory. After a minute, I find the number I'm looking for. As I wait for the other line to pick up, J.J. and I make eye contact. He no longer looks pleased; his eyes have softened into a watery pool of white, and he now appears vulnerable and boyish. This makes me feel guilty, and I try not to convey, through my voice or mannerisms, that I'm actually relieved that I will not have to sleep under the same roof as Nick Russo, who, by daylight, will surely emerge as a murder suspect.

CHAPTER 10

Entire days went by where Laura and I didn't speak to one another. During that time, our house was not filled with hardened stares or that type of palpable tension that makes everything smell like a relentless, driving rain. It was simply silent. Yet this silence was a bear that had our whole lives wrapped up in its enormous arms.

Mornings were especially a shame. Some recent traditions - helping Laura stretch for fifteen minutes; making breakfast as she read the paper aloud before I listened while pretending to mock the writing of some of my colleagues - were all but abandoned. They were replaced by segregation. Shower routines and eating and tidying up: These were all done with the detachment of two people who were new to the world and hadn't yet figured out its function.

One evening I fell asleep at my office. By the time I awoke, it was past 2:00 a.m. Forgoing a call to Laura, I crashed on a leather sofa in one of the break-rooms. When I returned home the following night, a silver coupe was parked in my spot on the driveway. Entering the house, I was met with distant chatter that seemed secretive and anxious. There were several voices, all intertwined and bleating hard-nosed theories about this or that. I followed them through the kitchen and towards the deck in the rear of the house. Laura and her parents were sitting around the patio table, drinking, arguing, and picking at what looked like California rolls and Szechuan chicken. Citronella candles were lit and placed at both ends of the deck as well as on the table. It was dusky out, but the August heat smeared the early evening air with its heavy breath.

I slid open the screen door and stepped outside. Luke, Laura's father, was in mid-sentence - a bona fide history buff, he was making some reference to McCarthyism - when he was nudged by his wife, who was the first to see me. They all stared at me for a moment. Laura, whose expression was barely concealed by the mostly sheer citronella smoke, seemed relieved. Looking mostly at her, I asked if I was McCarthy or Murrow in Luke's analogy. She smiled a little and said they were all worried about me. I told them I had fallen asleep while working late and that I was fine. Luke sighed a little and swigged at one of my cheap bottled beers he had been holding. Abby, Laura's mother, stood up and told her husband they needed to be going.

I walked them to the driveway and thanked them for keeping Laura company. Luke said *someone* had to keep her company, that it was a needy time for her right now and she needed to be surrounded by people who were reliable. Abby, her expression drawn and embarrassed, hurried him towards their vehicle. I commented that I liked what must have been a new car. Abby, delighted over the change in subject, pounced on this; she expounded on the various models they were looking at and the shady salesman and the headaches involved in making the purchase. I told them it was nice to see them and to have a pleasant night. Luke began backing out of the driveway when he suddenly stopped the vehicle, which emitted a short, halting screech. Leaning out the window, he called for me to come to him. Then he turned to his wife, who I could hear was telling him to mind his own business, and silenced her.

"That's my grandkid," he said, pointing towards the house. "He's got - or *she's* got - an automatic family here: grandparents, aunts, uncles, cousins. Do you see what I'm saying?"

His voice was even and under control, but it used a tone I had never heard from him before. It sounded like a newsman reporting on a recent tragedy.

I told him I understood. Which I did. There was never a moment when I felt on the verge of asserting myself. I respected Laura's parents too much to subject them to my self-righteous ramblings.

"That's all," he said. "That's all I have to say."

Nodding my head, I thought about extending my hand for him to shake, but he had rolled the window up and was tearing out of the driveway before I had the chance. Laura was still outside, sipping seltzer from a straw and sitting with her legs pulled up onto her chair. I sat across from her and waited for her to say something. As I waited, I realized that the night before was the first time we had slept apart since we were married. I wondered if she knew this, too, and would capitalize on it. Throwing my head back against the chair, I asked how she was feeling.

"Fine. Tired, but okay."

"This is a hell of a thing."

"It is."

"I don't know," I said, "part of me wants to divide myself up, so I can make every possible decision available; this way I could examine the different outcomes. And part of me wants to stay whole and just make the one decision I've been obsessing over."

Laura put her feet to the ground and leaned forward. She reached towards me and took hold of my hands. She started to say something before her voice trailed off like it had forgotten to preserve itself. The smell of citronella was suddenly getting to me.

"Let's not deal with this tonight," she said. "Let's just be ourselves. Remember what that's like? Let's just be ourselves and eat in bed and make fun of bad TV."

Sitting up, I remarked that I was surprised by this. Not talk about it? Especially after all the silence, as well as my disappearing act the previous night. Laura said it was good that I was surprised, that if we still had the power to surprise one another, well, then we were in a good place.

We ate in bed that evening. We made fun of bad TV. And we made love. And I was closer to my unborn child than I had been since that day Dr. Rose called with her news. So close that I swear I felt the warmth of its blood and fluids, and the easy, miraculous throbs of its tiny heartbeat. So close that the shame and disgust I felt were as looming as the black August sky.

I gave Laura that one night - and I'm glad I did; it was for both of us, really, but I recognized that it was just about all I could afford to give to her.

• • •

There was hardly a shortage of books on what we were going through. I went online and found at least a dozen. Maybe this should've given me comfort. How remarkable, I should've thought, that so many others before us have endured similar trials and were able to chronicle them for our benefit. But I wasn't comforted. The truth is that I couldn't have possibly felt more indifferent about anyone else's story. This might be an enormous character flaw on my part. Or it might mean that I was standing at the shore of the rest of my life, gazing out beyond the new ripples and chrome-colored horizon, and I was truly alone in every breath I took over this thing.

Expecting Adam: A True Story of Birth, Rebirth, and Everyday Magic. Count Us In: Growing Up with Down Syndrome. Life As We Know It: A Father, a Family, and an Exceptional Child. Even the titles were off-putting to me. I could imagine the formula for each story: initial shock; aggressive denial; vehement anger; gradual acceptance; unparalleled enlightenment and reward and love. I wasn't in the market for hope over God's grand plan. I was looking for the book about the miserable hardships the child and family would endure; the fractured and forever unrealized expectations for a normal family; the chronic burdens; the constant heartaches; the discrimination; the angelic, selfless wife who was oblivious to it all.

Hope in the face of some imminent spasm of nightmarish turmoil is merely false advertising when you're dealing with intelligent human beings. It's a hand-grenade handled by an idiot. Sooner or later... No, I wanted a book on fear. Unadulterated and unfiltered fear. I wanted exposure and insight into enough fear to fill a fucking stadium. That seemed to be the right amount to alter Laura's DNA. But I knew no such book existed. It was up to me.

Life with Laura had resumed. Yet our time together was still strained. Things were cordial enough, but the tension between us was unbearable; we were as careful with it as though we were handling something that might wither at any moment. I had yet to sit her down and explain myself. I felt sick over the thought of having to do this. I couldn't fathom having to say the things I felt. I wanted her to know them. How could she not know them? How could she force me to articulate what I was ashamed over feeling? Didn't she inherently know her husband? Weren't we the same person with the same pure and true visions of family and future? Yes, she mostly knew where I stood on the matter, but there was an incendiary passion, a wild-eyed certainty that knew no absolution, no relenting, and it was these things - if I were to be completely fair - that she couldn't have possibly known.

"Their side isn't as complex," Ben assured me during one of our luncheons. "Trust me. It's not. In fact, it's very simple: All she'll hear is you asking for her to hand over her most valuable possession. And it's not going to happen that easily."

"That's a ridiculous analogy," I told him. "We're talking about a human being, not a fucking Rolex."

He laughed into his lemonade and told me I had a point. He said he was therefore at a loss and that it looked like I was on my own.

"Okay, so my argument is a selfish one," I said, thinking aloud, "but I'll be careful how I present it. I'm not going to make it all about *me*. Because really, it's not. I'll be sure to focus on the positive, which, of course, is how we can always try again. That's positive, isn't it? We can always try again."

Ben's smile sobered a little. He put his sandwich down and wiped his hands on the napkin draped across his lap. After a moment, he responded:

"Just be careful. This thing is like one of those big hurricane vases. Be careful how you fill it up, and what you fill it up *with* - because if you're careless, if you're not looking closely enough, or if you overfill the thing, it could shatter into a million little pieces."

He looked at me with fey concern. Then he picked up his sandwich again and told me that *that* analogy was in fact a pretty good one.

. . .

While I was in the throes of restraint over this matter, Laura went about quietly pursuing her own fate as though ignorant of how I felt. And she did so with an unabashed fervor that made it all seem just on the threshold of being disingenuous. As she was nearing her fifth month of pregnancy, her belly began to swell; so one day she came home with a few hundred dollars in maternity clothes and asked me to sit at the edge of our bed as she tried on each outfit - some more than once. Not necessarily interested in my feedback - I offered none - she talked about style and comfort. At random times she would tell me the baby was kicking inside of her. Then she'd stop what she was doing and clutch her stomach, always with a sense of privacy like I wasn't in the room, and always with a faraway expression like she was straining to hear some distant, beautiful music.

She even bought a book on quilting. Her intention, she told me one evening, was to make an alphabet tapestry she saw in a baby magazine to which she was now subscribing. Bringing things to a head was her most obtrusive gesture, which involved her parents, who showed up one evening for dinner. Ushering our guests into the house, Laura greeted them, looked at me, and flashed a complicated spiral of a grin before joining them in the living room. Luke, who had recently begun to invest in wine, brought along an expensive looking Bordeaux, which he handed to me, asking that I open it and let it breathe for a while. Then he offered Laura a small wrapped package he had also been carrying. She took it with great delight and opened it carefully.

"Just a little something," Luke said.

Laura removed the last bit of wrapping paper, revealing the gift to be a white 5x7 ceramic picture frame. Resting the frame against her stomach, she stared down at it with silent awe.

"I thought it would be perfect for the baby's room," he said.

After a moment, she looked up at her father and mouthed the words *thank you*. Then she handed the picture to her mother, who admired it for a moment, commenting that Luke had been greatly anticipating giving his daughter the simple token. The photo was set down on the coffee table and the three of them made their way into the kitchen and out onto the deck.

I stood there for a few moments, listening to distant, inaudible chatter, grinning to myself, wondering about the limits of my self-control. I looked down at the photo, which I couldn't make out from the way it was facing. So I picked it up and laid it face down on the table. Then I poured a large glass of the Bordeaux for myself, slugged it back, poured another, and made my way outside to join my family.

The three of them, during dinner, flung a little web of conversation and hung from it for the entire meal, protected by their laughter, their egging on of one another, and the comfort of knowing how to finish each other's stories. They talked about a semester Abby had spent in Angola as an undergrad; Luke's 1968 Camaro that was stolen shortly after they were first married; an old boyfriend of Laura's who had reportedly entered the monastery. These were stories I was vaguely aware of, but there was clearly no place for me in any of them. The stories themselves were not only impervious to outsiders, but so was the way in which they were told. I was the invisible audience, blacked out by the blinding spotlight which shone on Laura and her two closest allies. So I sat there, in my own house, at my own table, the faint trace of an absurd grin on my face, drinking Luke's expensive wine, sneering to myself, looking at my watch, growing braver by the minute as I was now gathering the intensity needed to unleash my argument.

Every so often, in the middle of one of Luke's feigned tirades about his daughter's juvenile flings, or Abby's introspective musings on African culture, Laura would flash me a look. It was a fleeting look, all but a second, but I was able to get a good sense of it. It was proud and patient and I knew its purpose. And it was not to see if I wanted a second helping on my plate. Or if I was paying attention to her parents' cleverness. It was to let me know that she had a camp in her corner.

This reduced our dilemma to the most superficial ground. It trivialized it to an insulting degree. It assumed that I was so easily swayed, so fickle, that she simply needed to remind me about this thing called family in order for me to have a change of heart. It was true that Laura had her family; they were close-knit and available to be a part of our new life. Meanwhile, I had no one. Rollie was neatly tucked away on the east coast, brilliantly playing the surrogate father-figure to other people's children. Nothing would ever bridge our two worlds. I knew this. I was fine with this.

By the time dessert had been served - Abby had made and brought along a vegan cheesecake - the topic of conversation had shifted to the baby.

"Give my grandkid a taste of that cake," said Luke. "He'll never believe his grandma managed to make it taste all right with that hippie recipe of hers."

Abby rolled her eyes and looked at Laura. She told her that her father was convinced she was carrying a boy, so he always used the *he* pronoun when he spoke about the child.

"Well, if they would end the suspense and find out already," Luke said. "The guessing games might cease. But until then, I'm planning on a boy."

He turned towards me when he finished saying this. Reaching for my wine glass, I half closed my eyes and took a hearty swig.

"You've been awfully quiet tonight, Gray?" he said. "What are your thoughts? Boy or girl?"

If the circumstances were normal, I would've said that I didn't think about it one way or another. That I had no preference or premonition. I would've said that we just want a healthy baby. But at this point, this would've been a foolish thing to say.

"My *thoughts*?" I said, looking around the table.

It occurred to me just then, at that very moment, that I was beneath them all. I was. Here we were, a family, a real family, who was doing its best to bond, to break bread together, to warm some corner of the world with outstretched arms to an unborn child - *my* unborn child - who we all knew would be unlike any child we had ever known, and I was the only one who wanted no part of it.

These are educated people, I thought. They know what we're dealing with. They know this is a tornado that will suck away our old life and spit out a new one, and that new one will do its best to bewilder us. They must've known this - and were absolutely okay with it.

"What about names?" Luke said, tiring of me and my long pause. "Any names being thrown around?"

Laura said we had discussed names, but we wanted to keep them a surprise. Then she looked at me and asked if we should share them with her parents. When I didn't respond, she changed her question to *could* we share them with her parents. I still didn't respond. My gaze was fixed right through her, still, steady, full of hot, wiry anger that I thought must've changed my looks and my voice and my molecules forever.

"This isn't right," I finally brought myself to say.

The sound of my words, which were sharp and breathy, spoken as though their destination was some lifelong catharsis, surprised everyone at the table. Abby stopped cutting a second piece of cake for herself and looked up. Luke folded his hands under his chin and drew a perplexed expression. Laura, who I could tell had been massaging her belly, suddenly stopped and waited for me to continue.

"This isn't right," I said again. "This futile attempt at subterfuge. Cheesecake and ex-boyfriends."

"What the hell is he talking about?" Luke asked, looking at his daughter.

Laura exhaled. It seemed like her first full breath of the evening. And at that moment, her body appeared to let up a little, restoring her to her former self, which is to say she abandoned the sanctimony she had so enjoyed throughout the evening.

Excusing myself from the table, I made my way into the living room, where I suddenly felt the effects of the alcohol I'd been drinking. My head felt crowded, filled with taut, warm stars and simple confusion. I could hear the others mumbling as they said their goodbyes. After some time, Luke and Abby strode past me, bidding me a somewhat forced goodnight. I reached for a book on the coffee table and pretended to flip through it. It was a biography of Arthur Miller. Without looking up, I said goodnight. Laura appeared in the doorway from the kitchen and waved to her parents as they left.

"This all feels like someone else's life," I told her.

"You're being dramatic."

"*I'm* being dramatic? What about your little fucking coup d'etat with Mommy and Daddy? That seemed pretty dramatic to me."

"Don't mock my family."

"So now they're *your* family?"

"You know what I mean."

I started to say something, but Laura cut me off. Things change, she told me. So you alter your expectations to accompany that.

"This is too big a change," I said. "I know myself. I know what I can handle."

She told me we could handle it, especially with the help of her family. There would be challenges, yes, but we had support. I pointed out that it was not just what I *could* handle, but what I *wanted* to handle. I reminded her that we did have a choice in the matter.

"Not me," she said.

I told her to spare me the self-righteousness and that we did have a choice.

"*I* don't," she said again.

"But you *do*," I said, raising my voice a little. "You do have a choice. And it's simple: Destroy *us* and all we've become together over the years or we try this again in the future."

As the gravity of that statement took hold, I added that it was low to have involved her parents in the matter. I said I didn't care if she enlisted the entire state of Illinois to her side, that it was still between the two of us.

"Can't you see how this baby is already loved by so many?" she said, her tone foreign and dogmatic. "This will be a great family."

I told her it wouldn't be. That it couldn't be. That it was all fucking wrong. I said I had seen families like the one we would have. Growing up, I had seen them and heard about them from my father. They were beleaguered. Absolutely beleaguered.

She shook her head as if to say I had made a foolish comparison. So I started with the statistics. The average lifespan for a person with Down Syndrome is mid-fifties. Common health risks are thyroid problems, heart disease, hearing and sight problems. Leukemia. Poor immune systems, bone muscles, nerves, joints. You name it, I told her. The list goes on. I could tell she was taken aback by my stats, however vague they might've been. Either she was shaken by a new possible reality or floored that I'd obviously been looking into the matter. She sat down on the other sofa and threw her head back.

"Have you taken the time to do any research? Are you even bothering to educate yourself on what we'd be getting into? Or are you too proud to concern yourself with facts right now?"

She didn't answer. Staring up at the ceiling, she said in a wistful murmur that we would be wonderful parents. I told her I agreed, but only at another time. It had to be at another time.

This is when the conversation became desperate for Laura. A levee burst and she began to sob. Then she started repeating all of her previous arguments in succession. Her litany became a frantic burst of mournful pleas. Imploring me to think about it some more, she asked that I let her have her way, that she would never ask anything of me ever again. I told her she was not seeing my motivation. I loved her, I said. Plain and true. And I loved our life together. And all that love would be compromised if these excruciating burdens were placed upon it. I told her it was inevitable. Then I said something she didn't like:

"Trust me."

With this, she sat upright and looked at me. Then she let me have it. She called me arrogant. I was being selfish and short-sighted, she said. She asked how I would be able to look at myself again. And how would we be able to look at each other? What would we tell our parents and friends and colleagues? Was I that callous, she wanted to know? Could I really ask her so flippantly to do this thing? Through her tears, she said I would regret this decision forever.

"So you'll do it?"

The moment I asked this, I knew I had marked myself as a primordial, conscienceless slob. There was no turning back. She stopped crying at once. It was as though I had snatched away her sadness and swapped it out for shock. Hoarsely mumbling to herself in tired disbelief, Laura stood up and walked towards the staircase. Moving slowly, she held her head in her hands and said something about a prediction her parents had made coming to fruition. Then she turned to me, her eyes puffy and red and full of defeat.

"If you make me do this, I'll never be the same again. *Nothing* will ever be the same again."

With that, she headed upstairs for the night. Left alone, I wandered around the house, cleaning up after our guests, replaying the events of the evening over in my head. Laura's final words resonated. *Nothing will ever be the same again*. I knew her intention behind these words. I sensed what she was envisioning for herself if, in her words, I made her do this thing. And I sensed what she was envisioning for me as well. These thoughts made me shudder.

When I passed through the living room again, I noticed the picture Luke had given to Laura earlier in the evening. It was still face down on the coffee table. I picked it up and turned it over. It was a 5x7 frame with a circular photo on the left and an empty spot on the right for an identically sized picture. The matte in the frame was oatmeal-colored and nicely matched the background of the picture, which showed Laura as a little girl - she was probably two years old - dancing with her father. And though I had never seen the picture before, I knew its significance. She had told me how she and Luke used to dance often to one of his all time favorite songs, the Nitty Gritty Dirt Band's version of "You are My Flower." This was a father/daughter tradition they did for years, and one they even resurrected at our wedding. In the photo, Luke, who wore a moustache and thick sideburns, held Laura securely to his chest and elevated her just a few inches above him. Her eyes were wide with delight; her mouth was agape, showing off two uneven rows of perfectly tiny teeth. It took a few moments of staring at the picture, inspecting not only the people in the foreground, but the dated furniture and wallpaper and stereo in the background, to see what Luke must've had inscribed at the bottom. Centered perfectly in a fancy font were the words *Hold forever tightly to your beautiful flower*. I read the inscription several times as though its meaning might suddenly change. Then, as though the gift was part of a crime scene I had just disturbed, I carefully placed it back in its exact position on the coffee table before I turned in for the night.

. . .

Two days later, on a rainy Sunday morning, Laura delivered a speech that appeared extemporized, but I knew must've been steeped in hours of contemplation. I was reading the paper at the kitchen table when she appeared before me. She wore a look of concern that flashed at me like some wayward warning. When she spoke, her voice had a vacant quality like it had lost whatever parts it needed to sound lifelike.

"I'm strong. I know I am."

Thus began what would be a humbling journey down a path she thought she'd never travel - to a grotesque wilderness, barely trodden, blinding in its overgrowth, and miles away from what she saw as a place of logic and compassion.

"I've never been one of those sad cases who's always needed a man around. I can stand on my own - and have, many times. I know what I think and feel, and I know how to express them both. My sense of purpose and priorities are rock solid. I know where I've been and who I am."

I didn't interrupt as she went on. Setting the newspaper down, I folded my hands across my stomach and listened to my wife's detailed character profile. What she revealed was all true. She spoke of her virtues as though they were up for an award and her own endorsement might sway the judgment. With a voice that seemed like it could at any moment burst into a dirge, Laura moved from her strength as a woman to her rootedness and loyalty to her family.

After a pause, she turned her head from me, took a step back, and leaned against the wall. What she said next must've sounded surreal to her own ears. The words had to have cut into her, dragged around her insides, and left her feeling eviscerated:

"I know my limitations. And I know how it would be raising this baby by myself. It would be very difficult."

She went on, mentioning how it would be hard even with her family's support. She declared how she was profoundly tuned in to the needs of such a child, adding that she had begun her research the day Dr. Rose had called with the news. As she continued her campaign against single-motherhood, I found myself losing focus on her arguments; I was dwelling instead on what they signified: Laura had made up her mind to finally see things my way. Not only this, but she had actually considered leaving me to have and raise the baby herself.

Her face was flushed and taut as she finished with one final point:

"*We* came first, you and I. So I'll honor that. But I do this knowing that you are not honoring me - my principles, my values. So after we do this, all that we will have together is absolute uncertainty."

Neither of us spoke. My heart was skittish inside my chest, and I felt it anchor down under the weight of this silence. Laura was examining me in a thoughtful manner, her eyes wider than usual, her lips parted ever so slightly. A decision had finally been reached. And I believe she was considering whether I understood the gravity of what our fate might be. For a moment, I was overcome with a strange feeling that I needed to somehow talk her out of it. I couldn't believe it: A decision had finally been reached.

CHAPTER 11

My father laughs a short, stuttering kind of laugh when I announce to him that it should be me who calls Eileen Russo.

"I wouldn't put you through that," he tells me, cupping my shoulder. "First off, the woman's not all there. Trust me."

"This happened on *my* watch. Nick was in *my* dorm and I was probably the last to see him."

"I recognize that, but it's times like this where *I'm* the expected messenger. Let's call it the shittiest part of the job."

I understand what he means. I know the circumstances whereby he's had to deliver dreadful news to parents about their troubled child. Over the years, there have been other runaways. Not to mention the occasional overdose. Probably the worst calls were the couple of suicide attempts and pregnancies.

"Let me give you a glimpse of the apple not falling far from the tree," he says.

Ushering me into his office, the Old Man dials the woman's number and puts it on speaker phone. Then he props his phone against a Newton's cradle he's had at the edge of his desk for as long as I can remember. Eileen picks up after only a couple of rings. The Old Man, his arms crossed tightly around his midsection, reveals his purpose in calling with modest, breathy reserve.

"What am I paying you for, Rollie? Isn't it to keep Nicky safe? I thought that was the whole point of your place. Shit, it turns out you can't even keep him, *period*."

"For whatever it's worth, I have faith in Nick's abilities to take care of himself and make sound decisions until he returns. Safely."

"The reason Nicky's at your fucking school is *because* of his poor decision making."

"I understand that. But Nick *has* made some progress. A lot, in fact."

At this, Eileen launches into a tirade about the boy's father. She says Nick is just like his father: selfish, impulsive, hard-headed. She tells Rollie that her ex-husband is now living on a houseboat somewhere off the coast of New Brunswick. Following this is the sound of broken glass. Probably dishes. Through this, she curses her son, her ex-husband, the Old Man, and the Hundred Acre School. The sound of shattering glass distorts her words as she speaks. Rollie, staring blankly at me, lowers the volume on the phone before telling the boy's mother he has additional news.

"Regarding the recent tragedy that happened here on campus, well, it seems that Nick knew the victim. Personally. I'm sure you have questions, Eileen. We all do. But for now we have to put those aside and wait for Nick's return. I'm sorry I don't have better news for you."

"So am I."

"One more thing," the Old Man says, "when he comes back - or *if* he comes back - I think it's safe to say that the police will have a few questions for him. There's no doubt there."

"Well," the woman says, laughing recklessly into the phone, "I think it's only fair to tell you that Nicky, like his father, fucking hates cops."

She hangs up before any response is offered. With a weary grin, the Old Man bellows out a discordant trumpet sound while pretending to pull out his hair.

"I told you I would've made the call," I said.

"You did. But trust me when I tell you we have not heard the last from Eileen Russo. In fact, my bet is that the next time we hear from her it'll be in person. I'll gladly turn the reins over to you at that point."

"That's fine."

Laughing over my nonchalance, Rollie says that Eileen Russo over the phone is one experience, but in person is another altogether.

Staff members begin calling informal meetings out of their dorms to vent their worries. The Old Man finds out and calls a meeting of his own.

"I can't control everything that goes on here," he opens with, "but we sure as hell don't need anymore off-the-grid get-togethers. Dimitri had a few of those for himself, and it stands to reason that Nick Russo did as well."

The staff listens as he speaks. He pauses on occasion to clear his throat. His voice, measured and conciliatory, has a hostage negotiator quality to it. But his appearance tells the real story of how he's holding up. His hair is barely brushed, his clothes are wrinkled, and his beard needs trimming.

"We're all dealing with a lot right now. But we'll deal with it together. No secret alliances or factions. Please."

The meeting is short. No one asks questions or makes suggestions. The Old Man ends on a typical note:

"Aristotle defined tragedy as a representation of an action that is whole and complete and of a certain magnitude. A whole is what has a beginning and middle and end."

This draws perplexed gazes. Pausing for a moment, he rubs at the back of his neck before continuing:

"I think we're now somewhere in the middle. I'd love to be nearing the end, but we're not. We will be, though. In time, we will be."

Nick's peers don't seem broken up over his absence. Concerned maybe. I can see it in their wizened expressions when they talk about him. They congregate and whisper and search for symbolism. What does it mean, this vanishing boy? Are things unsafe? Should I be planning *my* escape as well? Probably they ask themselves these questions. And as soon as they see the cop car appear on school grounds the morning after his disappearance, the big question is asked, and it's one I hear more than a few times: Do you think Nick killed that girl?

Officer Jerome and his partner walk the campus with their slow, heavy strides, accompanied by Rollie and Louise. They jot the occasional note in their pads. Students who pass the foursome regard them with unnerving awe. It's lunchtime when the officers finish with my father; he meets me on my way to the dining hall with both cops in tow. They want to speak with me next, Rollie says. There's hardly cause for a search warrant, he tells me.

But this doesn't mean we can't volunteer some of Nick's possessions if it'll help them find the kid.

"Search through Nick's things," my father advises, "and give them whatever they want."

"Should we be contacting a lawyer?" I ask.

The Old Man shakes his head at this suggestion. Then he turns from me and the cops and makes his way towards the dining hall. After a few seconds, he calls over his shoulder, to no one in particular, that we're all here to cooperate.

I escort the police into Nick's room, which I proceed to search under their supervision. The older officer, Bagley, takes out a plastic bag for evidence. He asks me a series of questions about Nick: his mood the night of his disappearance; anything he might've said or done that could be useful; any altercations between me Nick, or perhaps between Nick and another student; what I might've known or suspected about his relationship with Nicole D'Ambrosio. My answer for each question is concise and probably unhelpful.

I ransack Nick's closet and dresser. I strip his bed and overturn his mattress and rifle through old shoe boxes filled with papers and personal effects. A few letters seem to interest Jerome, so he asks me to put them in the plastic bag. They also collect a hardbound yearbook from a former school, a 5X7 framed photo of Nick sitting at the base of the Samuel Adams monument, and a few odds and ends. No white gold Tiffany's ring is found.

"Is any of this helpful?" I ask.

"We'll know soon enough," says Bagley.

"We connect the pieces," says Jerome, "and see which ones fit, which ones don't, and which ones are missing."

Next up, says Bagley, is to find out the nature of Nick's relationship with Nicole D'Ambrosio.

"That's exactly what's next," says Jerome. "When's lunch over?"

Throughout the early afternoon, a series of informal interviews are conducted with a few of the Homer House boys as well as others who know Nick or have class with him. The officers use the therapy lounge, and together, with Rollie in attendance, interview one after another. By the time they leave - they question close to two dozen students - the school's energy has changed. So many faces no longer appear weathered with anxiety; they now seem fixed with a sullenness ripped from a Depression-era photo.

After dinner, the Old Man takes the podium. He looks hungover. Straightening his glasses, he addresses the room:

"The police are on our side. So please continue to show them your cooperation. We all appreciate it. By now, all of you know about Nick Russo. We're doing what we can to assure his safe return. If you know of anything that could help, please let us know. As far as his relationship with...with the girl...well, not much has been revealed. Again, if anyone has something to say..."

He stops talking. No one else speaks. It seems unclear if he's offering an opportunity for someone to say something right then and there, or if he's finished with his remarks. The silence carries on and he returns to his seat. After a few moments, he stands up again, remembering the evening ritual he temporarily forgot:

"Dining hall is excused."

• • •

Dr. Nussbaum doesn't have to go out of his way to find me on my weekend off. I'm napping during the hot, late afternoon when he knocks on my door. He enters with a blithe expression as though I should've been ready and expecting him rather than groggy and sticky from the summer's heat. He asks for a glass of water and then moves into the TV room.

"Let me guess," I said, filling a clean glass under the tap, "poker championship tonight and I'm invited to keep score."

When I bring him the water, he's sitting comfortably, his hands folded behind his head. He thanks me for the drink, takes a sip, and sets it on the floor by his feet; after a moment, he smiles and tells me he's being nosy by checking on me.

"I'm fine."

"Of course you are. You're here, aren't you? Working, eating, talking, surviving. I know you're *fine*. Shit, most of us are fine."

"Hell, if that's true, you'll be out of a job before you know it."

"Speaking of jobs, how're you feeling about yours?"

Blase, I tell him. Then I add *ephemeral*. Then *confounded*. His eyes glance upwards as though my words have precariously stacked themselves in the atmosphere and might tumble at any moment. Then, when he doesn't respond right away, I add a trite and meaningless coda:

"It is what it is."

"Because your father and I were recently discussing a few things. We're wondering if you might get more involved."

"Involved with what?"

Most of the staff are major contributors, he explains, mentioning Amber's weekly book group and Tennille's almost daily jazzercise classes and Dave's comic book club and Carrie's wind instrument workshops. He goes on and on, touting the eclecticism of the faculty, their commitment, their generosity.

"Rollie and I were thinking about what *you* could offer."

"Maybe I can do something with time travel. Build a time machine with the kids, show them how it's possible to go back in time."

Nussbaum, taking a sip of water, appears accepting of my sarcasm. He wipes his mouth with his hand and allows me to continue.

"After all, *I* did. Sans the time machine, of course. But I *did* seem to go back in time, didn't I? I mean, I move away from this place, get an education, a job, a wife, a home; then one day I wake up to find that I'm living in the fucking Homer House with Cliff and Cal and Albert and the rest of the gang."

Not missing a beat, Nussbaum says he and my father already have something in mind for me. A writers group. It makes sense, he says: I'm a writer. And, a lot of students show promise in this area. The campus is bursting with songwriters and poets; one student, Nussbaum tells me, has even begun a novel about a blind man who plans a bank heist.

"It'll hardly be a stretch, Gray," he adds, handing me his empty glass before we make our way towards the door. "You're already teaching English."

"If you can call it that."

"You might find it one hell of an experience. And I know it'll please Rollie. It'll be one less thing for him to worry about."

"*This* is what he's worried about? Me not having enough extra-curricular activities? He's got a murder victim, a runaway, a police investigation, and throngs of fucked up kids and irate parents, and you're telling me that my sparse schedule is keeping him up at night?"

"That's what I'm telling you, Gray."

"Well, then I can't decide if I'm honored or just fucking mystified."

We step outside into the hot sunshine. The air is still and heavy. A trio of girls walk by the Homer House singing an old Motown song. The campus is otherwise quiet under the stifling summer heat. Nussbaum puts his hand out to me, which I accept. I do this, not knowing if I'm entering into some type of gentleman's agreement for this writers group.

"You should get off campus and enjoy your time," he tells me. "It's important to have an adventure here and there."

Then he takes a step towards me and puts his hand on the back of my head.

"For the record, you didn't just wake up one day and find yourself in the Homer House. There was a series of events that led to that. When you're ready - if you're *ever* ready - let me know, and we can discuss it. I know it's on Rollie's mind a lot lately."

He leaves me with what must be one hell of a dumbfounded expression. I can sense it. My lips are pursed to the side and I'm flaring my nostrils and squinting. It's an SOS to no one. A nonverbal gesture that signifies the very question I posed just moments ago: How is it that the Old Man, who at the moment has more burdens to contend with than ever before in his life, has possibly found the time to think about and worry about and talk about his fully grown son?

· · ·

The absence of mail and phone calls has reinforced my new life at the Hundred Acre School. I've unofficially been given expatriate status. With the exception of my paycheck, there's never a thing in my mailbox, which is located in the school's main office. So when I receive an envelope addressed to Grayson Loveland in plain, somewhat crooked print, and containing no return address, I'm taken aback. No one from my old life, except for Ben, even knows I've relocated.

What makes the most sense, of course, is Laura. There wouldn't be much detective work involved in her tracking me down. It's possible she still has some loose ends to tie up with me - maybe some additional legal documents for me to sign. But the writing on the face of the envelope is clearly not from her hand. With a strange sense of excitement, I rush back to my place and tear it open. Inside are a few photos of a pretty young blonde girl with dark blue eyes. One of the pictures is a school photo, the girl posing against a white backdrop, her smile, though lovely, is a bit forced. Another is of her lounging by a pool in a black bikini, sunglasses atop her head, pulling her hair away from a tanned, unsmiling face. The last one shows the girl sitting on a blanket in the middle of a dense wilderness. Her feet are together and her legs are open; she isn't wearing any clothes. She's looking up at the photographer with a blank expression. It's this last photo that has a short message scribbled on its back in bubbly red ink. *Dear Nick,* it reads, *A little something for those quiet moments. No sharing!*

Without pause, I make my way to my father's house. Handing him the envelope, I inform him of its anonymous sender. With no questions asked, he pulls out the photos and examines them; before even turning the lurid one over to read its subtle come-on, he quietly muses what I of course already know:

"Nicole D'Ambrosio."

. . .

I recall one of the first writing courses I took in college where the professor, Dr. Eloise Buttrick, a solitary woman with a haggard look and a foul disposition, would regularly state her mantra to the class with the subtle and perfectly honed didacticism that suggested she had believed in her maxim and thought it wise and clever: "A fact is an anchor, a truth is a sail," she would say. The context of this statement would be vague, which suggested she felt it would suffice for any occasion as long as it pertained to the act of writing. Buttrick had probably long before surrendered the notion that she be linear or lucid in her teaching. Her erudition and years of experience would have allowed her this latitude, which came at the expense of her students.

The metaphor nevertheless stuck with me through the years. It might be one of the few moments from my studies I ever employed in my life as a journalist. So now I use it again at the Hundred Acre School for my writers workshop. It's what I start with. Standing there in the dining hall, our home-base, looking down at the nine kids who've shown up for our first meeting, I need an opening, a foundation, a solid bit of profundity they might buy into. No one asks me to explain. Yet I add how they should aim for nothing but truth telling in their writing, leaving facts to the historians. Then a boy raises his hand and asks if this still applies if they're interested in writing a memoir.

"I think it does," I tell him. "To a degree, though."

One of the girls raises her hand and suggests everyone state their preferred genre, what they wish to get out of the group, and so forth.

There's Meredith, one of my own students, who's interested in poetry and gothic fiction. There are two students, Kay and Marilyn, who claim they don't really write, but enjoy reading other people's work. There's Dorian, a skeletal, oblong faced boy who describes his writing as S.J. Perelman-ish with a twist of Penthouse Forum. There's a boy the others call Booth - short for Boothroid, his last name - who's written a nearly two-hundred page manifesto that delineates certain intricacies of a particular video game he's fond of. He's interested in having it proofread, he states quite proudly. There's Jess Singer, the boy who's begun a novel about a blind man planning a bank heist. He claims he's four chapters in and now lacking direction. There's Dan Hart, who's elusive in his purpose. He just acts coolly and says he likes to write. And there's Adam and Matt, who claim they're collaborating on a screenplay about the Altamont disaster of 1969. Adam adds that Matt writes poetry and short stories that will "blow your balls off."

Once these informalities are over, the kids, huddling around the perimeter of two tables pushed together, look to me to see what's next. I'm tempted to tell them I'm not sure how to articulate what I know about writing - that I'm not even sure *what* I know. And if I *was* able to discern what I know, how would I teach it? I want to announce that I'm not a teacher, and that these days, I'm not even really much of a writer.

"Maybe someone can share something they've brought with them," said Meredith, probably sensing my unease. "And we can critique it."

Dorian volunteers. Flipping open a beaten green notebook he produces from under his chair, he fingers through the pages until he finds the piece he describes as a "fluffy little bit of filth." He promises it won't offend anyone, adding that what he's about to read are the beginning lyrics to a rap song one of his characters will be singing. He reads from the page, affecting a husky rapper inflection: *I'm standing in the river, I got the piss shivers, and my nutsack is turning to blue. Like a thousand fire-ants, I'm tryin' to get inside your pants, and maybe fuck your sister, too.*

Some of the boys laugh. Most of the girls roll their eyes and tell Dorian he's an idiot. One of the non-writers, a Muppet-ish, pocket-size girl named Kay, asks about the character who will be singing these words. Dorian describes him with some authentic details, using words like misogynistic, hulking, primal. Kay considers this for a moment before she begins her critique.

"I liked it. But I'm just not sure how believable it is. I mean, if they're in a river, chances are, the girl - the object of desire - probably won't have pants on to begin with."

Without missing a beat, Booth, in as sincere a delivery as any sad teenager could muster, says he was thinking the same exact thing. Then he asks a series of unrelated questions - all toxically boring - on mechanics. He asks about semicolons and verb tenses and prepositions. The kids look to me for the answers. As I give them, Booth hurriedly scribbles in the margins of his manuscript. We move on to Meredith, who's just finished a short story about a young woman who develops an obsession with touring the Edgar Allan Poe House and Museum. Her character, a twenty-something named Rory, ends up selling her possessions and forfeiting her life to live vicariously through the icon. Meredith asks about the character's development, the story's plausibility, and whether her ending appears forced. All good questions. And some mostly useful responses from her peers. Except for some encouraging nods, I offer very little. They seem satisfied with this arrangement.

Dan Hart, sitting properly, and minding his own business, suddenly becomes the group's focus. Kay announces that he's written some song lyrics, which must be shared - they're *that* good, she adds. The other kids encourage Dan to open his binder and read aloud his newest tune. With his head cocked back and his hands folded across his stomach, Dan says he's not in the mood; besides, he casually mentions, they're not *that* good. Adam swipes the binder and asks if he can read them. Dan says he doesn't care. With Kay's help, Adam locates the page and reads, affecting a full, formal tone:

> *You look so good when you're down and out*
> *Like a full moon does in May*
> *But tell me what you mean when you look at me and shout*
> *That tomorrow cancels off today*
> *Your queens and jokers are ruling your deck*
> *You've lost each one of your kings*
> *You say they were damaged, weak, and a wreck*
> *And you're looking for a man who sings*

He's asked who the "you" refers to. And what he means in the third and fourth lines. And, most importantly, if he's the "man who sings." His answers are vague. But never self-important.

The conversation soon veers from Dan's song to Nicole D'Ambrosio. Booth asks Dan if he's having nightmares about the evening he found the girl's body. Dan shrugs.

"I heard her parents were on campus meeting with Rollie," said Jess.

"They probably think it's some conspiracy by the student body," said Adam. "Fucking elitists."

"Their daughter was *murdered*," Meredith points out in a steady but vexed tone.

Arguments ensue over the next few moments. Was the girl raped? Were drugs involved? Will the cops contrive evidence to target the Hundred Acre School?

"She probably OD'd or something," said Adam. "And they came up with this whole murder thing."

"She was strangled to death, you asshole," says Meredith.

Adam tells her she's taking it too personally. It's not like she knew the girl, he says. The meeting breaks up within moments of this. I announce that we can reconvene this weekend while I'm on duty, if they're interested, or still speaking to one another. Meredith asks if at some point the group can read something I've written. My files, I tell her, are in disarray, but perhaps when I'm more organized. Following Meredith, Matt and Adam leave together. So do Kay and Marilyn. A few of the remaining boys wander off by themselves and a few remain behind, jotting down odds and ends in their journals or loose scraps of paper. Dan Hart and I exit the dining hall together.

"We got a little off course there," I said.

"Just a little."

"Nice song. Let me know when it's finished."

I start to walk away when Dan says something that gets my attention:

"That night wasn't the first time I saw a dead body."

Turning to face him, I ask him to repeat himself, even though I've heard him clearly.

"I know I'm supposed to be traumatized, but I'm not. Don't get me wrong, it's a shitty thing to see, but I've seen worse."

Nodding my head slowly, I take a few steps in his directions. When we're standing within arm's reach, he continues. It was his sister, he tells me. It'll be two years this fall. She cut her own throat with a survival knife she had taken from Dan's bureau drawer. His parents were in Baltimore visiting relatives. It was Dan who found her.

"I don't know what to say."

"Same here. It's bizarre that all of us in this place are encouraged to talk about what we've been through - to our therapists, to our dorm staff, to Rollie - but most of what we've been through has made speech pretty fucking obsolete."

"Then I guess it's good we've got our little writers group."

Dan nods before he turns and walks away.

Adam and Matt bring coffee and donuts to our next session. It's a chilly and rainy Sunday. We meet in the dining hall a few hours before dinner. The weekend has been a nasty one. Thunderstorms and gray, bleak skies. The same nine from our first session are present. This surprises me. I figure fickleness runs in their bloodstreams. But here they are. And looking for what? Inspiration? Candor? Enlightenment?

Warmed by the steaming coffee, they soon get underway. Jess Singer begins. He opens by sharing the plotline of his book, which intrigues the other members. Then he explains where he wants his story to go and some ideas he has for his main character. But he's overwhelmed, he admits. It's not writer's block, he says, but rather the acute feeling of wanting to further his commitment to his project, yet not knowing how to do so.

"It's like getting out of bed," Dorian says. "You know you have to. You know you'll be in the eye of a shitstorm if you don't, but it's practically impossible sometimes."

"Like today," said Kay. "Today was one of those days for me."

Meredith, sipping her coffee, offers advice to Jess. She urges him to plod through it no matter what.

"You've already begun," she said, "so that's out of the way. And that's the most brutal part."

Marilyn commends Jess for undertaking an endeavor such as a novel. Matt adds that he lacks the discipline for anything of the sort. Adam reminds Matt about their screenplay in progress. Then he urges him to share his newest poem. Matt, adjusting his ball cap, thinks about this for a moment. Then he stands up and produces a thin stack of fresh photocopies from inside his notebook. He hands them out, but doesn't read aloud:

I'm begging you to please be hungry.
And I don't beg easily these days,
but you need your nourishment.
I know this.
You can trust me.
It was me who told you that time
about the heavy makeup that made your
eyes look like wild green toddler toys.
So let's wander down through the mazes of ruinous heartache,
down to where the moonrise trembles in its vibrant melodies.
And there, I will not beg again.
I will ask.

I will ask you to remember that this is not a poem:
It's a brick through your window.
And it's not a love letter:
It's a single crooked footprint
on a lonesome, rain-drenched road.

Dan Hart is the first to comment. He states - more to himself than to Matt - that the piece is vivid and has a certain strength to it. A few of the others agree. Specific lines are mentioned - the ones about the makeup and mazes of ruinous heartache - and guesses are made as to their inspiration. Kay and Marilyn lead this charge, asking sheepishly if the words are for Lindsay Lowe. Adam, wiping his hand clean of donut powder, claps his friend on the back and says of course they are.

Once the girls exhaust every synonym for *romantic* and *thoughtful*, leaving Matt red, embarrassed, and mindlessly pulling at the brim of his hat, talk turns to Lindsay Lowe.

"When's she coming back?" Dorian asks.

Heads turn to Matt. He shrugs. He hasn't spoken to her, he says. Meredith suggests giving the poem to her as a welcome-back gesture when she does return. Matt, seeming to consider this idea for the first time, his eyes suddenly brighter, says maybe. Then, as though cued to damage a hopeful moment with crass insensitivity, Booth ponders aloud whether Lindsay has been seeing Dimitri Ames while she's been home. The others don't pounce on him for this. They quietly groan and roll their eyes. Adam, probably sensing that the silence is allowing his friend to torture himself with wild imaginings, turns to Booth.

"You must get used a lot by the ladies," he says.

"Why?" asks Booth, confusion swatting at him like a featherweight's jab.

"Because you're an enormous douchebag."

As fast as the insult is delivered, all attention swerves away from the boys and towards the main dining hall entrance, which rattles as it's swung open. Austin Roarick, sporting a haughty grin, makes his way over to us. He's wiping small beads of rain off his face. Putting his hand to his ear, he asks if he's correct in thinking he heard something about douche as he entered. Sounds like a real think tank, he says, still smiling with a smugness that seems practiced. Then he offers me his hand and says it's good to see me.

This is delivered with such deliberate authority that it seems to jar even him, thus unraveling his pretentiousness, leaving him with a silly little boy looking smile. Straightening from my slouch, I accept his handshake. The kids are eyeing him acutely.

"I was told you were in here, but no one warned me you'd be discussing feminine hygiene."

It's unclear whether or not he was going for a laugh with this - he made the remark with such a rushed zeal - but he doesn't get one. The kids almost immediately turn back to their discussion on Matt's poem. Austin, with his large, clumsy hands, swipes a cinnamon powdered donut from the table and moves in closer to me.

"I need boxes," he says with exaggerated authority as though the kids might cease their discussion and suddenly scurry to meet this need.

Soon he will be moving to a new place downtown, he tells me. Briarwood Condominiums. I'm aware of them, I tell him. Construction began on the modest, hazelnut-colored complex during my first or second year of college.

"It's just temporary," he says to no one in particular. "But it sure beats the hell out of your arrangement, doesn't it?"

"I guess it does."

"The truth is I'm thrilled as hell about it. It's worth my rent going up just so I won't have to write that check out to J.R. anymore."

The condos, neatly tucked behind the town's Stop & Shop, is one of the few pieces of prime real estate not owned by Austin's father.

"Working on a Sunday," he said, studying the donut in his hand like it's some complicated fossil. "So devoted, Mr. Loveland."

The kids are back to discussing Lindsay Lowe. I hear Matt admit to having written some of his finest poems about her. Lowering my voice a bit, I tell Austin that I'm obligated to work every other weekend. It's part of the role of a HAS employee, I tell him. I have no choice but to work. This last comment halts his first bite of the donut. He now seems inspired.

"That's what we get when we work for daddy, isn't it?" he says, a flash of ignominious defeat suddenly appearing in his face

It's clear he's waiting for me to appreciate this insight of his, this connection we share, which he's already mentioned at our first meeting a week ago.

"I suppose it is."

"Though I'd say our job descriptions are slightly different," he says, bringing the donut to his mouth for the second time.

"Right again."

Once more he seems inspired. Tossing the donut back into the box, Austin takes my arm by its bicep and pulls me towards him, away from the circle of students.

"How do you do it?" he asks, his words spoken through bared teeth. "How do you get into a pool with crazy and expect to come out intact?"

It's a difficult gig, I tell him, but I'm managing.

"Because I'll tell you what I think: I think Rollie is putting you at risk. I do. He's chucked you in the deep end, hasn't he? He's chucked you in the deep end with no real regard for the danger it might bring to you. And there *is* danger. Just look around, for Christ's sake. This shit is dangerous."

I turn back towards the kids. A few of the boys are writing. Kay and Marilyn are flirting with Dan Hart while Meredith offers Matt some critiques on his poem. They pay me and Austin no mind. Studying him, I consider whether it's even possible for him to actually have any prominent points about my life or my relationship with my father.

"Don't get me wrong," he continues, "J.R.'s been putting me in danger's way ever since I can remember. That's how I've always looked at it - as being put in danger. When you don't provide someone with what they need to thrive - with what they *deserve*, really - you're creating a situation where tension and conflict reign. Am I right?"

I know he isn't really interested in my answer. So I don't offer one. I just listen to his continued rant. He goes on about his father.

"The man is an egomaniac," he tells me, clapping his hands together in front of his chest like he's about to karate chop a stack of boards. "Not to mention a workaholic and a bully. My father's business practices are becoming obsolete; he's in over his head and refuses any type of partnership."

Then he starts in on the Old Man, whom he calls naïve.

"Rollie's no businessman," he says, "let's be honest. You know that. Sure, he can spit-shine these kids to make them look presentable to the community for an hour, but it's a thin veneer, isn't it? He's no more a businessman than you are a teacher."

Before I can defend these accusations - the truth is that I would need time to do so - he's pulling me towards him, farther still from the kids, and firing out questions about Rollie's desired acquisition of the Hundred Acre School. Do I know anything about his financial situation? Are there any silent partners? How far into the process is he? Do I personally think he'll pull off owning the school?

"Wouldn't your father be a better source for this information?" I ask. "He must know."

He tells me that on the subject of the Hundred Acre School, his father is standoffish. Austin's voice, low and measured, betrays a hunger for this information. So I throw some empathy his way, revealing that I'm just as ignorant of the affair as he appears to be. Which is the truth.

Probably sensing that in the last several minutes he's just laid one hell of a burden on me, he sucks in his gut and says he'll collect his boxes now and let me get back to the kids. Noticing Adam and Matt, who've moved towards the periphery of our conversation, Austin asks them to give him a hand. After a dubious pause, they follow him into the kitchen. In a few moments, they emerge, each of them piled high with cardboard boxes, which they help load into Austin's car, parked just outside the dining hall. By the time the boys reenter, they're damp and breathless. Austin follows them inside and says how he almost forgot their gratuity. Then he hands them each a one dollar bill.

"I might need help moving a few things, boys," he says, looking more at me than at them. "So, when I'm ready, if you want to make a couple of bucks, and if you can get...permission, or *leave*, or whatever."

Adam says they might be willing to help, but they would have to first negotiate price.

"Businessmen," said Austin, again looking at me.

Losing what appears to be a desire to leave on a courteous note, he leans into me and says one last thing about my father:

"There's a faction in town, and I'm not saying who they are or how many there are, but this faction wants nothing more than to see Rollie fail."

"Then it'll be interesting to see who ends up being disappointed."

Austin heaves a sigh, but he says nothing. We stare at one another for a few seconds.

"I'll be in touch, boys," he calls over to Matt and Adam.

By the time he's out the door, I find myself mumbling with the contempt of a shopkeeper who's just staved off a thief. Yet I'm conflicted. I want to have at least a little compassion for Austin. It's obvious he hates the Hundred Acre School. His reasons, though, are far different from my own. What we share - likely *all* we share - is looking to our fathers as the cause of this hatred. Austin is no doubt a less than wonderful human being, but this might be due to the permanent second-class citizen status his father has inflicted upon him. As for my own relationship with this place, I'm convinced it's simpler: It stole my one surviving parent from me.

Years ago, back when we were kids, Austin could have easily been a student at the HAS. With his poor social interactions and "repeat offender" predilections, he would've fit right alongside these headcases. I'm on the cusp of venting this to the others as a way of explaining his crassness, but I stop myself. I don't want to offend them with the comparison. Besides, I have no doubt that these kids, in every possible way, are several cuts above Austin Roarick.

. . .

At dinner that night, my father pulls me into the kitchen to thank me for not revealing anything to Austin. Mickey, paying us no mind, is sharpening a cleaver on a piece of whetstone while watching a baseball game on a tiny flat-screen mounted on a far wall.

"What could I possibly reveal? I know nothing."

"He's a nasty little prick. Am I right, Mick?" the Old Man hollers over to the chef.

"You're right, boss man," Mickey says, clearly ignorant of what we're discussing.

"Always poking around, always asking questions about this place," says the Old Man.

Austin's relationship with his father, Rollie tells me, has been impaired for a long time. He's resentful that J.R. won't pay his debts as well as make him an equal business partner.

"J.R.'s confided in me a little over the years," he tells me, "which is what leads me to think that we need to beware of this character."

Mickey curses at the TV before dropping the slab of whetstone on the prep table. I glance up at the game. Mickey catches me and says he's made a hefty bet with his brother-in-law.

"Beware of Austin?" I ask, turning back to the Old Man.

"Absolutely. He's dangerous."

I can't help but laugh at this. Abrasive, maybe. Socially inept, perhaps. Even pathetic, in a way. But *dangerous*?

"How so?"

"Grayson, don't you know that anyone who has nothing going for him but desire is dangerous?"

I shrug over his comment. Then, turning away, I comment softly to myself, but loud enough for him to hear:

"Funny you should use that word."

"What word?"

"Dangerous."

He waits for me to continue. I don't. It would be absurd to share with him Austin's inane theories about my relationship with my father. So I turn my attention to Mickey and ask him the score of the game.

CHAPTER 12

It wasn't relief I was feeling. And it wasn't anything resembling a sense of victory. I felt like an obese shadow cast upon some rippling silkscreen; I was awed over my own spectacle and mass, but aware that I had used up all of my actual power. It was spent. Spent on a miserably unpopular decision.

It was a brutal August. Record-breaking heat waves. Relentless and mood altering. The city was especially unpleasant. It felt dirty and overcrowded. But I looked forward to work everyday; it was a refuge from the wreck that was my home life. Laura and I were sleeping in different rooms. We stopped sharing meals together. Conversation was limited to the details of the procedure that was to take place on August 11th.

Dr. Rose, meeting with us in her downtown office, told us time was of the essence. We didn't ask many questions. Laura, her eyes puffy and her mouth tightly drawn, sat with her hands folded in her lap and mostly looked out the window. I half listened to the doctor explain risks and aftereffects while I studied a collage of photos on the wall behind her desk. I counted nine pictures in total. All appeared to be of her kids. As far as I could tell, the pictures were of three different children, two boys and a girl, in various stages of their lives. The range looked to be from around two or three to fifteen or sixteen. Most of the photos showed outdoor activities. Snowboarding and field hockey and playing in big piles of sunburned leaves.

All three children were blonde and attractive. They had white teeth and easy, endless smiles.

I found myself focusing more and more on the photos as the meeting progressed. I was hoping Laura would notice them as well. A few times I even came close to commenting on them. My mouth opened and I jerked forward a bit, but no words would come. "What lovely children," I would've said. Or "Beautiful family - so healthy looking."

I began staring long and hard on purpose. My hope was that Laura would notice my staring and begin staring herself. Then she would understand. But I knew that wouldn't happen. I felt like I wanted to pull those photos off the wall and force them upon Laura. I wanted to leave her alone in that office, just her and those goddamn beautiful photos. I'd come back in an hour and ask if she understood. But I knew she never would.

When our meeting ended, Dr. Rose told us she was required to ask us something. She waited a moment. Looking more in Laura's direction than in mine, she asked if we wanted to know the sex of the baby. I turned to my wife, who said nothing, but began nodding. The question was asked again, this time directed only at Laura, who continued moving her head up and down.

"A girl," the doctor said.

Laura stopped nodding. She began clawing at her purse with her fingernails. Studying her profile for a bit, I found that she had instantly morphed into a complete stranger. I imagine I appeared the same to her. Dr. Rose opened a drawer and produced a couple of business cards. She handed one to each of us, advising us to call the number and make an appointment. This was a delicate matter, she said, and the woman whose name was on the card would prove useful.

The next afternoon, which marked three days before our visit to the hospital, Luke showed up unannounced at my office. He asked if we could talk. We found a quiet stairwell. He paced the small landing for a few moments. Aside from his breathing, which was fast and steady, he seemed to make no sound at all. Then he looked up from his pacing and smiled a generic and forlorn smile. He explained that no one in the family knew where he was. He had taken it upon himself, he said, and no one was responsible for the visit but him. He added that we would be keeping the visit between the two of us.

"We've always gotten on well, haven't we?" Luke said. "From the start, I mean. I'd say as far as son-in-laws go, you're a fine one. And you lucked out with the likes of me, if I do say so myself. Are we in agreement?"

I told him I agreed. Then I started to embellish upon what he had said, but he was quick to cut me off. He was focused and serious like I had never seen him before.

"I don't appreciate smoke being blown up my ass," he said, "and I imagine you feel the same way. So I'm going to get down to it. You're too smart for me to condescend to you, and that's not my style anyway. But there's one thing I know a hell of a lot about, and that's being a parent. I've been doing it for decades - for four different kids I might add - and doing a goddamn good job of it."

Luke paused long enough for me to agree that he was a good father. Even though his present intentions were mostly clear to me, I still felt the need to encourage him by being agreeable. He went on, telling me that he and Abby felt privileged to be parents. He said they knew people who took parenting for granted. This, he said, was a shame. He added that men far more articulate than him have put down in words the beauty and immensity of being a parent.

"Hell, I'm talking to a writer. And a good man. You are, Gray. You're a good man. You've been good for Laura and I know you've made her happy."

He paused and took a deep breath. Then he poked at his temple with his index finger before continuing. He brought up religion, saying how his family was not a religious one. He talked about faith and virtue and how these things, as far as he was concerned, were only useful when they applied to people, not deities.

"Faith in people and faith in self," he said.

Then he told me a story about Rick, Laura's oldest brother, who had a serious heart murmur when he was a baby. He was operated on when he was just seven months old. Luke explained that after the natural reaction to this - fear, dread, anger - he changed. And the change, he said, came about like it was meant just for him at just that moment in his life. And it was profound and everlasting. Raising his voice a bit, Luke asked if I could guess what he changed into. I shook my head.

"A superhero," he said. "Don't laugh, because it's true. A superhero. Because that's what kids do: They turn us into superheroes. We'll do anything for them - and we do. So I found that I had this power. And the more I thought about it, the more intense this power became."

That power, Luke admitted, was simply hope. But it was as potent as anything a superhero can wield. And it encompassed his sick child, who eventually recovered.

"Forgive me. I'm rambling. Parenthood, religion, my children. And I probably broke my promise that I wouldn't condescend and that I'd get right down to what I had to say. We both know why I'm here. Because I'm a parent and I want you to feel what I feel. And because I'm a parent and I don't want to see my daughter devastated. I want to help you from making what will lead to the biggest regret of your life."

My heart began beating quicker. My mouth, suddenly parched, seemed heavy and dumb and without the coordination to speak. I grunted a little before he went on.

"That's what it is. I want to help you. And Abby and I are prepared to do *anything* to help you. We love you, Gray, and we love our grandchild. This is our family."

He said that a few times: *This is our family*. Then he reached into his pocket and took out a folded white envelope, telling me again that this visit was between the two of us. And as he handed me the envelope, he told me that its contents were also between the two of us. I took it from him.

"Please don't misunderstand me. I'm a parent, and because I'm a parent I happen to know the difficulties of such a responsibility. This is to help you and Laura with those difficulties. It's just for starters."

I tried to see through the white paper, but it was one of those security envelopes. Luke told me to open it. I tore off one side and pulled out its contents. It was a personal check for $20,000.

When I looked up at him, he turned away and faced the cold, gray wall. My mouth still couldn't formulate a response. We stood in that stairwell for a few moments, neither of us speaking. The only sound was our breathing, which I couldn't tell apart. Finally, Luke broke the silence:

"This is all very complicated. I realize that. Abby and I *both* realize that. I don't know if my being here today makes it more so, but it's only my intention to make things easier. This should be an easier time, don't you think?"

He wasn't looking in my direction when he spoke. His gaze was settled on the wall behind me. My voice suddenly worked. I told Luke I had many thoughts about the situation between me and Laura, and that most of them had already been voiced to Laura. I told him I wasn't a religious man, either - something he certainly knew about me - and how my instincts were informed by trust. And this trust was something I felt very deeply. Like my love for his daughter, I said, which came above everything. If he could ramble, so could I.

"Laura and I need to focus on each other right now. And nothing else. And that's why I cannot accept this."

Luke stared at the check I handed back to him. Then he looked up at me. It was with hard and penetrating clarity. He knew. Certainly he knew. He knew my bit about Laura was bullshit. She wanted nothing to do with me. Nothing. And he knew this. When he wouldn't reclaim the check, I laid it at his feet. He continued to burden me with his lucid, all-knowing gaze. It was making my skin itch to be there with him in such close quarters. Promising that I would keep our visit between the two of us, I turned from him and descended the stairs. I had no destination. When I reached the next landing, I could hear Luke above me, shredding the check and mumbling to himself. By the time I was three floors beneath him, he shouted down to me a question I *had* considered on occasion, but was too exhausted to begin answering:

"What does your father think about what you're doing? Does he realize what a selfish prick he has for a son?"

• • •

Throughout Laura's pregnancy, the Old Man received minimal updates. He understood that I would never share anything beyond the superficial. Never before had I offered him any true depth in the way of personal anecdotes, so why would this stage of my life be any different? He likely expected me to be terse on the topic. When we spoke, which was infrequent, I would hardly address the baby. And my responses to his questions would be little more than matter-of-fact. Laura told me I was punishing him for not living close by. We both knew it went beyond that.

She encouraged me to send him sonograms and to call more frequently. Of course I never did either. So Laura took it upon herself to text him the occasional photo, always accompanied by a quick message that she was feeling well and his grandchild looked forward to soon meeting their grandpa. None of that mattered. I planned to sever whatever enthusiasm he might've felt over our unborn child with a simple two word phrase. It was a phrase I had worked out shortly after learning what Dr. Rose had told Laura on that brutally hot Thursday. The phrase would be used a lot over the course of a few weeks. Anyone who knew we were having a child would hear this phrase with genuine solemnity. *Unexpected complications*. This was true on so many levels. But I would never be called on to explain it. No one would ask for specifics. *Unexpected complications* had the perfect mix of ambiguity and pathos to it. After the condolences, the matter, god willing, would be dropped.

I understood that my father wouldn't be satisfied with this. It's not that he would badger me for the story, or demand that I get into the minutiae. That wasn't his style. He was conditioned to provide the necessary space and distance. Allowing me to feel whatever I would feel: This would be his focus. He would let me have my time. But that time would be limited. His job, after all, has always been to get to the bottom of pain.

The truth is that besides Ben there was really no one to talk to. I believe I was feeling the appropriate emotion over this. It wasn't shame. And it wasn't regret. It was tricky - sort of in between relief and malaise. I was thankful for Ben, though. Writers listen like no one else. They understand what expression or gesture or response of theirs might coax more of those private ruminations to the surface. And their truest and harshest judgments, which one should understand are as acute as any, are often set aside for their work. So I accepted that I could someday become manifest in a story Ben would write. His anti-hero might be confused, lonely, misunderstood, reviled. And Ben, perhaps struggling to capture this man's true plight, would recall his good friend, Grayson Loveland.

Our lunches together, ostensibly for unwinding - they were actually full-fledged bitch sessions about my marriage - suddenly changed. Ben, being the professional he was, took on an MFA intern from Columbia College. No longer could I discuss with my friend and colleague my family's woes. Or seek his counsel on how I handled a delicate situation.

The intern's name was Andrea and she joined us for lunch each day. She had a quick wit and was a natural conversationalist. What had been a male dominated jaunt, full of frightful honesty and shots at wisdom, had turned into a mélange of coyness and innuendo. It was harmless flirting, but evident to any onlooker. We were mentors, me and Ben, and this girl, who couldn't have been a day older than twenty-four, was in awe of us. We were, after all, doing what she wanted to be doing. From her flattery to her looks - she had long, straight black hair, a killer smile, and skin as fair and perfect as white honeysuckle - Andrea proved a timely distraction for me. It helped, too, that Ben told her nothing of my situation. As far as she knew, I was unburdened and not at all the son-of-a-bitch my family took me for. I was grateful for the levity - especially since things were only worsening at home.

. . .

A few days before the procedure, Laura found me in the bathroom and said she had been thinking long and hard on something she wanted to share with me. I was about to shave and had just lathered my face. Studying my razor for a moment, I noticed it had begun to rust a little. With my fingernail, I tried to scrape the rust out, but it wasn't the flaky kind. It was permanent. Laura watched me do this for a few seconds before she spoke:

"I want to go to the hospital alone."

She conveyed this in a quiet, casual tone, like she had just discovered her independence and it was a triumph she hadn't fully grasped.

"What are you talking about?"

"I'm not interested in having a conversation about this, or certainly an argument."

As I studied her, I could see she was concentrating on her breathing. Like a singer ready to release a wordy or difficult verse. She appeared to have nothing left to say. I wanted to comfort her. I wanted to hold her head in my hands, put my face to hers, and remind her that we were in love. I wondered if I had any strength left to offer her, or perhaps words about fate or family. Something prevented me from doing any of this. There was a palpable force driving us from one another. I felt it every time we were near. It was cold and relentless and I knew she felt it, too; it was probably all we had in common at that point.

I didn't press the matter. I only asked who would be going in my place. She didn't respond. Then I added a pathetic attempt at sensitivity when I said I didn't want her to be alone. Again, no response. She wheeled around and left me there alone, the shaving cream now thinly transparent and dripping from my chin. Rinsing the blade in the sink bowl, I brought the razor to my face. On my first downstroke, I cut my right cheek. The blood ran through the white foam on my face, crisscrossing slowly, carving out some obscure symbol on my cheek before finally clotting into a thick puff of red-stained cream.

· · ·

Ben's mother was having hip replacement surgery and he wanted to be there. *There* happened to be Salt Lake City, so he flew out with Justine and their two girls. Before he left, he wished me the best with everything, demanding I call him if I needed to talk.

"Give Laura our best," he said.

He added that he knew I'd be a comfort to her during the procedure, that I would hold her hand and ease her mind and say all the wonderful things she needed to hear. Nodding my head, I forced myself to keep silent, my shame stabbing at me with steel prongs.

"Just take care of your mother. We'll be fine."

"At least I know you'll be in good hands during lunch," he said, his smile glib and slight.

"Why's that?"

"Oh, come on," he said, moving in closer to me and lowering his voice. "If hormones were people, that girl would be China."

"What does that even mean?"

"Don't tell me you don't see how she looks at you."

I rolled my eyes at this and told Ben he was delusional. Sure, I said, Andrea might've been a little flirty, but it was only because we were newspapermen, something she envied.

"Besides, you're the one she's in awe of," I said, not entirely sure whether that was true.

"To her, I'm an old man, like a hip uncle. But you, you're like the cousin."

I pointed out that it wasn't possible to be hip if one used the *word* hip, and that if I was the cousin, well, wouldn't that be incestuous?

"Just behave yourself. The last thing you need right now is just about everything that girl has to offer."

Any other time, Ben's remarks would've been taken lightly. Innocuous banter. Guy talk. But I found myself considering the possible truth of what he was saying. Part of me wanted it to be true. I needed to feel worthy of someone's affection, even if that someone was a stranger.

That stranger sidled up to my desk the first day Ben was gone and asked me out for lunch. The next afternoon would mark Laura's visit to the hospital. Focus was difficult to achieve that day. My mind felt like it had come unhinged and was affixed only by some sinuous fiber. So when Andrea invited me to accompany her, I didn't answer; I just stood from my desk and said "after you."

On our way out of the building, she said she had a new place in mind. She said I must've been sick of the deli Ben and I frequented. Her presumptuousness was remarkable to me. Here was this young, attractive grad student, still paying her dues, and she was eager to test my malleability. It appeared to be deliberate. She might've been asking herself how willful I was. Or maybe she was a young woman who easily grew tired of certain foods. Part of me was hoping it was more complex than that. She took me to Heaven on Seven, the city's famed Cajun cuisine joint. Though I had never been before, I lied when she asked if I had.

"Ever drink during your lunches with Ben?"

"Occasionally," I lied again.

The first thing she told our waitress to bring us was a carafe of white wine. I noticed she was looking at me as she placed the order. Probably to see if I balked. I didn't. She told me she loved Cajun cooking, that her family was from Louisiana and she had a taste for hot spice in her blood.

"Can I order for us?"

I told her that would be fine. She ordered the Cajun fried oyster salad, which she said we would split, as well as two Louisiana Catfish Po' Boy Sandwiches. When the waitress took our menus, Andrea added that she would like to keep the wine coming, that we were celebrating.

"What exactly are we celebrating?" I asked.

"There's always something to celebrate," she said, raising her glass.

"You're not one of those hedonists, are you?"

"Hey, everyone needs something to believe in."

The wine was sweet and cool. After two full glasses, I realized I was getting drunk. Drinking in the afternoon was something I wasn't used to.

We discussed books and movies. She told me some of her favorite authors were Raymond Carver and T.C. Boyle. I told her I approved of her choices. Film was a different story, though. I could identify only one of them that she mentioned.

"Well, you're an old man. What are you, like thirty?"

I hesitated for a moment before telling her I was thirty-three.

"So old," she said, finishing off her wine.

When she put her empty glass on the table, she began studying my face. Then she reached out her hand and touched my right cheek with the tips of her fingers. She smelled of sweet vanilla.

"What happened?" she asked.

For a moment, I didn't understand. Then I remembered my shaving mishap.

"Poor baby," she said when I told her. "You need to be more careful."

After a few moments, she told me I looked wonderful for an old man. That I would no doubt age into one of those attractive, silver-haired men young women threw themselves at.

"And you'll love every minute of it," she added.

"Why do you say that?"

"You're loving *this*, aren't you?"

"And what *is* this?"

"*This* is our celebration."

The waitress brought our salad and an extra plate. As Andrea divided it up, I told her it was important that she understand something.

"What? T*hat*?" she asked, pointing to my wedding band.

She looked unfazed by it. In fact, her smile suddenly became wicked. I was about to say something when she broke in, her voice low and breathy:

"The old man has some experience under him. That's all. Nothing wrong with that. Besides, find me one who doesn't."

• • •

The next morning, Laura snuck out while I was asleep. I knew it would be at least a couple of days before I'd see her again. I could feel a transformation underway. We were in store for a different life together. Laura would have to spend some time living inside her new body. She would be asking herself if she could still love me after the procedure. The emptiness of the house revealed these things to me. There was something about the quiet that struck me. As I walked around and slept and ate and tried to read, I could only focus on the miserable quiet. It carved out a place in my mind and resuscitated realities I had tried to destroy. Picking up my phone, I almost called Luke and Abby; I knew they were with her. It would've been an impossible call to make. The day wore on. As evening approached, I figured the procedure was over with. Relief and dread were staging a vicious duel in my heart.

Laura was probably resting now. Or sedated. If she could dream, God only knows what her mind would produce. Freud contends that dreams are gifts we give to ourselves. Their purpose, he claims, is to allow the psyche to act upon dormant impulses we attempt to stray from in our daily lives. If this is the case, then Laura must've dreamt about doing away with her husband, the selfish prick, the man she thought she knew and loved, the cause of her life's most violent heartbreak.

Two or three times I grabbed the keys to the car and made my way towards the front door. One time I even stepped outside. Dusk was approaching. The heavy August air, full of a sticky kind of silence, made me sleepy. When I thought I heard my phone ring, I ran back inside. No one was calling. And I knew they wouldn't. I was of no concern anymore. I didn't deserve an update. I wasn't allowed to support my wife through the ordeal, or say my goodbyes to my child. Yet I had support to give and goodbyes to offer.

Anger began to take hold. It lasted long enough for me to smash a bowl and two glasses in the sink. The feeling then turned to regret. Suddenly, as though the broken glass radiated some type of conscious-altering spell, I began to wonder if I had made a terrible mistake. I picked up my phone and called Stevie. She and Laura were as close as sisters could be, and I knew they were together. The line rang once and went to voicemail. When I called back, same thing. I slammed the phone down so hard that I cracked the screen.

I found a liter of rum in the cupboard, which I began drinking straight from the bottle. It tasted terrible. Hard liquor on its own never appealed to me, but there I was, storming around my empty house, cursing, slamming into walls and furniture, slugging mouthfuls of fiery piss in a bottle. The effects of the alcohol seemed to take hold instantly. The inside of my head felt like a hot jacuzzi jet had been turned on. By the time I was drunk, I found myself lurking outside the baby's room, walking back and forth past the doorway, which was ajar by a few inches.

When I entered, it dawned on me that I hadn't been in the room in quite some time. Probably weeks. It was a small room. But pleasant to look at and stand in. As I ran my hand across Laura's stenciled clouds and stars and Man in the Moon, I recalled the single afternoon she produced this effect, turning common walls into something beautiful, and doing so with such ease. That's how Laura did everything related to being pregnant and preparing for the baby. Like she was born to do it, or had done it before. And that's the kind of mother I knew she would be. A natural. Like it was a simple and logical extension of who she was.

As though I was seeing it for the first time, I examined the furniture in the room. The crib the Old Man paid for was sturdy and attractive. The other pieces, a small nightstand, a bureau and changing table, the antique rocking chair Luke refinished, were all well crafted and equally impressive, their dark honey-colored wood flawless and clean. I flipped through the closet full of clothes. Each season was covered. There were white and yellow pajamas with hedgehogs and bears on them; tiny t-shirts embossed with the words *Cutie* or *Babyface*; overalls and sweaters and even a rain parka. The clothes smelled freshly laundered and were organized according to season and size.

As I drank the last bit of rum from the bottle, I noticed the picture frame Luke had given Laura. It was placed on the windowsill across the room, its sides fitting perfectly within the perimeter of one of the window's rectangular panes. Dusk had set in and the inside of the house was darkening. But I could still make out the picture of father and daughter; I could still see the empty space slotted for our own photo; and I could see the words Luke had had inscribed at the bottom of the frame.

I did all I could to convince myself into believing that I belonged in that space, among all that newness and potential, but I felt like nothing more than an intruder. I suddenly found myself wondering what would happen to the room. Would it change? Would it remain untouched? Would a child ever occupy it? Would Laura ever live out her motherly ambitions in all its perfect warmth and whimsy?

Without another thought, I wound up and threw the empty rum bottle towards the picture of Luke and Laura. My aim was off. The bottle missed the picture and hit directly above, smashing the window, which exploded all over the room. The picture, unscathed, rocked a little, but remained in its exact position on the windowsill. The gesture, which was pathetic to begin with, was made even more so when, without missing a beat, I began cleaning, picking up handfuls of glass and dropping them into the tiny wooden trash can that had blue and silver stars hand-painted by one of Laura's coworkers.

The doorbell suddenly rang, startling me, causing me to gash my left hand on a piece of glass. The blood spilled out onto the hardwood floor, making an ominous Rorschach pattern. Covering the wound with my mouth, I ran downstairs, taking three steps at a time, ricocheting off the walls, bleeding all over myself. Luke or Abby, I thought. It had to be. They were here to tell me that Laura was okay and that she loved me and needed to see me. Everything was going to be fine; they would assure me of this on the way to the hospital. We were a family. And families run into these types of situations from time to time.

When I opened the door, I was face to face with Glenn, who wore an expression that had little more to it than the pretense of concern. Pulling at his beard a little, he began sniffing the air in front of him. The alcohol on my breath must've been strong.

"Hey, neighbor," he said, a trace of mockery in his voice, "everything okay?"

"Fine," I said, trying not to pant.

"I was in my garage when I heard glass shatter."

"A little mishap. That's all."

Motioning to my hand, which by now had bled all over my clothes and bare arms, Glenn said I had a pretty deep cut. Then he stepped inside the house, pushing past me, and asked where the first aid supplies were. I let him help me. After he bandaged my hand, I washed up and put on clean clothes.

"I'm obliged to offer you a drink," I said.

"*Obliged*? What is this, the wild west? Just being neighborly, that's all."

I told him I insisted.

"Well, you're out of whiskey, unless Laura recently picked up some more."

Annoyed that he knew the contents of my liquor cabinet, and anxious to continue drinking, I filled two glasses with gin, passed one to Glenn, clinked my glass against his, and collapsed on the couch. As he drank, Glenn moved around the room, examining a painting or a lamp or piece of furniture, and making idle conversation about the weather and the booze. After a few moments, he refilled his glass and raised it in the air before downing the entire thing. Then he looked at me and remarked that he preferred whiskey, but gin would suffice.

"How is it being in that house all by yourself?" I asked.

A wild smile lit up across his face. He sniffed at his empty glass before refilling it.

"Were you embarrassed to tell people what happened with your marriage?"

Glenn said he made well into the six figures so he wouldn't have to feel embarrassment. As arrogant of a statement as this was, it somehow sounded almost charming coming from this man.

"Do you enjoy being a doctor?"

"Get a few drinks in this guy and his inhibitions go AWOL."

I apologized if I was making him uncomfortable. Glenn said it was no problem, that he thought it was about time we got to know one another.

"Let's put it this way," he said, "I'm pretty eager to see all the ways I can disprove Fitzgerald's claim that there are no second acts in American lives. And I plan on having a whole lot of fucking fun doing just that."

Then he laughed and said how I must appreciate the reference since I'm a writer. He added, somewhat soberly, that he did some writing in college. Short stories, he told me. He even had one published in his school's literary magazine. Setting his glass down on the roll top desk, he ran both hands through his hair, trying to recall its plotline.

"It was called 'Daybreak Diner.' It was very noir-ish. Had a lot of dark humor and clever dialogue and everyone carried a gun and smoked cigarettes."

I recalled Ben's philosophy on writers. It was simple. He explained it to me one afternoon after a colleague, according to Ben, unjustly received the Studs Terkel award. He said there were three kinds of writers: creators, critics, and klutzes. The creators, Ben contended, had an original voice and could *always* make something out of nothing. The critics, though, excelled only at academic writing and nothing else; they could write, but never anything with blood and bone and soul to it. As for the klutzes - according to Ben, these pervade the journalism profession - they couldn't translate a coherent or original thought to paper if their lives were at stake.

Glenn, with his perfect beard and his brashness, struck me as a klutz. The idea of him writing was absurd. His inspiration, after all, seemed to be his sports car and his salary and his name tag that said *Doctor* on it. I couldn't imagine there being a time in his life when truer muses existed for the man.

He filled his glass again. Then he turned to me with a solemn expression and said his divorce would be final within the month. With his eyes averted towards his liquor, Glenn told me he was glad for one thing:

"No kids. That makes it all pretty bearable, even entertaining at times."

He smiled at this last part, but his smile faded as though whiplashed by the seriousness of the mood he just created. Eyeing me with thoughtful intent, he asked what I was doing home. If I had considered his question for even a moment - as well as the brightness in his eyes when he said it - then I would've realized he knew what today meant for my family. But I didn't consider it, so I lied.

"Laura's staying with her parents. They just bought a new dog - a boxer - and she's helping them train it."

The spontaneity of the lie was not enough to rescue uneasiness from setting in. I began to think about what he might've known, what Laura had told him, what pep talks he might've given her in my absence. Glenn was our only neighbor, so he would naturally find out. In his own way, he played along with my story.

"I'm not sure how manly of a drink this is," he said, holding up his glass. "Gin. It's not bad, don't get me wrong. And I sure as hell appreciate anyone who opens their liquor cabinet and rings the come-and-get-it bell. But it just doesn't have that same effect as, say, whiskey. Whiskey turns you into either a poet or a brawler. It makes everything throb - your hands and head and heart. You want to break another man's neck, paint your own Sistine Chapel, and bed every broad who enters your path. I've been drinking it for years and I swear the size of my balls have grown because of it. And we're not talking dead weight, either. We're talking muscle mass. Gravitas. I think about this type of stuff. I think it's important. It's a conversation that should be had more often. Who's a man and who's not, you know? And what *makes* him a man. It's not just about who drinks whiskey and who doesn't; I know that much. It's a hell of a lot more than that. I think all the real men are the ones holding their breath as all the others walk by - that's why a real man's chest is always puffed out. And he's mocked for it. Which he accepts. You know why they're holding their breath? Because their bodies have imbibed all the burdens that no one else will take on, and they're holding onto them. With pride. They'll never let them go. The burdens have become part of them. They take on the burdens for all men. They have to."

For the briefest moment, I considered laughing. It would've been forced since I found nothing he said the least bit amusing. I found it sententious. Not to mention strangely out of character. Was this man really a doctor? Talking about bedding broads and the size of his balls. He sounded like a suburban Neanderthal. I was glad I stifled the laugh when I saw his expression after delivering his dissertation. He was working his lips into a tight circle and bobbing his head ever so slightly while he stared through the glass of gin. Either he was waiting for me to respond, or he had to allow his words to safely launch into the atmosphere before he resumed common activity. Either way, he seemed inspired, moved by his own philosophies, inebriated by the high-flown sound of their cadences.

"So who are the real men, Glenn?" I asked, feeding into his bold gray rhetoric like a damn fool. "How do I spot them? Will their faces be turning red from holding their breath for so long?"

This brought him back down. He laughed. Then he finished off the liquor in his glass and set it on the desk.

"Change that dressing before you turn in for the night," he said, pointing to my bandaged hand. "Keep it clean."

Walking him to the door, I decided to press a little further. So I asked him again how the real men could be spotted. I don't know if I was taunting him or seeking some subterranean insight he might've possessed. Clearing his throat, he looked me in the eyes. Then he inhaled deeply and seemed to hold it for a long time.

"It's not easy," he said, turning his back on me and walking outside. "But know that they're everywhere. And they're not just your cops and your firemen. The problem becomes spotting one if you're not one; you don't always know what to look for."

He thanked me for the gin, putting emphasis on the word *gin*, and walked across my lawn, back towards his house, which may have been larger than mine, and certainly was as empty, yet hardly seemed so. My stomach began to churn and I felt like I could've been sick just then.

"Oh Laura," I said aloud. "Laura, Laura, Laura, Laura, Laura, Laura, Laura, Laura."

I took a breath and then said her name some more, rolling over its first syllable towards the second one with a kind of caution in my voice that bespoke the detachment I truly felt from my wife. She had grown more fond of Glenn after talking to him and spending time with him. This gave me such a crushing sense of loneliness that I thought for a moment I might actually throw up.

My hand then began to ache, which reminded me of the broken glass in the nursery. I was startled when I entered the room again. There was my blood, dark and glossy, spilled out onto the floor in an ugly coagulated mess. There was a lot of it, too - a hell of a lot more than I remember there being.

CHAPTER 13

My father assists me and Ryan in giving the Homer House boys a pep talk. I'm glad he does. It can't be denied that I've made progress communicating with them. I've finally won the right to urge them out of bed or to unclog the toilet or to cease with the pig-pile before someone gets hurt. But I have to imagine that any serious talk will feel too forced. Ryan, who comes off like the mellow uncle no one ever thinks to disobey, has accomplished this feat now by rote. I've been at the school for a little over a month, and I believe the Homer House boys and I have struck a tacit agreement: They show civility towards me, heeding what's reasonable, and I don't dare put on the pretense that I've somehow earned the right to be there with them, living under the same roof, deflecting conflicts, observing the coursing tumult of their own personal hells. Never do I fool myself into thinking I've made any headway with them, but the arrangement we have, however tenuous in anyone's mind, has become functional.

The pep talk is my idea. And Ryan, as well as the Old Man, thinks it's a good one. We're all wondering if they have information about Nick, but might be unwilling to share it. The boys listen to Rollie, who sits on the hearth in the Homer House common room; he finesses them with tactful rhetoric, using humor, which never appears labored. It's an impressive display. There are a few matters to bring up - where Nick went the night he slipped out into the dark; his relationship with Nicole D'Ambrosio; maybe even something about that Tiffany's ring that's gone missing.

With drawn expressions, the boys listen. This isn't a lecture about divvying up dorm snacks or using discretion when self-satisfying urges strike. One of their own is missing, and they know the gravity of the matter. Aside from the occasional head nod and glance at one another, they're tuned in to what Rollie has to say. He talks about the progress Nick has made. He praises the boy's strong personality, describing him as *willful* and *his own man*. He mentions his sick-with-worry mother back in Vermont, awaiting a phone call to tell her that her son is safe.

Ryan, cued by the Old Man with a fleeting look, adds that our doors are open, so please be forthcoming with any information. Then, more in the spirit of inclusion than competition, Ryan asks if I have anything to add.

"Nick's much better off *here*," I announce, "than he is wandering the streets of God knows where. This is a good place, and it's where he needs to be right now."

My statements are met with silence. Not that I was expecting some tearful admission of Nick's whereabouts, or an impassioned plea to escape consequences for withholding information. After a moment, Ryan asks if anyone has any questions. Cal's hand shoots in the air. He asks if it's normal to be able to pinch your testicles particularly hard without even a hint of pain.

"Because I swear, just last night, I applied vice-grip pressure, and nothing," he shares with deadpan delivery.

With that, the mood buoys back to its juvenile frat house state, replete with laughter and obliterated attention-spans. Using a fraction of the austerity of his dining hall voice, Rollie dismisses the boys. A few stay behind and turn on the TV while others retreat to their rooms. Ryan, who's on duty, produces a hacky sack and leads two boys outside to the front porch. My father follows me back to my room.

"If they want to tell us something, they will," he says.

"Do you think they know anything?"

"Hard to say. Nick is a fiercely private kid when it comes to just about everything. But if he *was* getting laid - and those pictures suggest he was - then chances are good that he wanted others to know."

"Turning those over to the cops must've been brutal. The girl's family has to be devastated."

Rollie doesn't respond to this. Stuffing his hands into his pockets, he makes a smacking sound with his tongue and leans against the fridge in my kitchen. I recognize this coyness. It rears its head when he's either backed into a corner or considering whether he wishes to compromise his principles. It doesn't take him long to come out with it:

"I'm going to handle this a little differently. A little tact and ploy."

"What's tactful about not involving the cops?"

"They're already involved. I just don't want them to get any wrong ideas."

"Like what? That Nick dabbled in photography?"

"A little update for you, my son: In addition to the cops and the fucking fire marshall being up my ass, I now have the local health inspector threatening to shut down my kitchen. Forget bad things happening in threes - we'll be approaching double-digits before dinner."

He explains how he received some phone calls over the past couple of weeks. And then surprise inspections. And then bad news. And then costly ultimatums.

"I just need as little aggravation right now as possible. The photos are between you and me."

"And whoever sent them."

"And whoever sent them," he repeats.

"Nick?"

"I don't know. Maybe. But it's a damn rare thing for a high school kid to part with a nude photo, let alone one of the girl he lost his cherry to."

"I feel like it's a damn rare thing for a high school kid to even *own* a nude photo. A physical one, I mean. What is this, the nineties?"

"Good point."

"By the way," I add, "no way Nicole was his first."

Rollie assures me that this is the case, adding that Nick is all talk.

"*You* know this kid. Do you think he did it?"

"That's a thought in progress. I haven't yet made up my mind."

Turning around, he opens the fridge and takes out my last bottle of beer; he twists off the cap and takes a long swig before handing it to me. It's been a long time since we've shared a beer.

"You took a chance that I wasn't going to say anything to the cops about those pictures. That's quite the display of confidence. How'd you know?"

Grabbing for the beer, the Old Man laughs a little in spite of himself. After a long drink, he hands the bottle back to me and tells me I'm giving him far too much credit, that he's improvising as he goes, like one of those stoned-out beat poets I used to make him read years ago. I nod over the memory.

"The truth is, my boy, I'm about as uncertain over all of this as anyone is. Pretty fucking scared, too."

He's quick to change the topic before I have a chance to respond.

"By the way," he says, "Are you aware of what you said to those kids a little while ago about this place? I'm not sure if you were caught up in the moment, being polite because I was right there, or listening to your subconscious. Either way, I was floored."

I tell him I have no idea what he's talking about, that I have no recollection over anything I've said about the HAS. Cocking his head a little, he stares at me as though I'm guarding easily gotten-to treasure. I'm sure he's looking for me to press him further. I don't. I just stare back, waiting for him to tell me. Neither of us get our way.

• • •

Four days later, on a bright and breezy Monday morning, Rollie calls an emergency staff meeting before breakfast. A few therapists have already arrived on campus - at the Old Man's request - and they, along with Louise and her security team, man the dorms while we meet in the dining hall.

"Just last night," he says, wasting no time, "Lindsay Lowe tried to take her own life. We received word from her mother early this morning. She found Lindsay, at a little after midnight, passed out in her father's car, which was running in a closed garage. There was a note and an empty bottle of sleeping pills in the passenger seat."

Some of the faculty break down a little.

"She's alive. But she's in bad shape. She hasn't regained consciousness. I'll make the announcement after lunch. Maybe by then we'll have some new information."

No one asks questions or makes comments. Even Rollie seems at a loss for words. After a moment, he articulates what many are probably feeling:

"There's a goddamn wildfire burning around here. It's contained for a day or so and then it's raging the next. Useless analogies aside, I don't know what else to say. We had another student withdraw yesterday."

Many of the kids, he warns - not all of them, but some of them - will be hit particularly hard by the news of Lindsay. Some will have real sadness, while others, referred to by the Old Man as emotional opportunists, will do their best to assimilate to the grief. Either way, he warns, some reactions will be explosive, so be prepared. Therapists will be around, he says, and the name of the game, for the next few days, will be damage control.

Some of the staff file out of the dining hall. Tennille and Amber walk past me, wiping away their tears. Tim/Tom puts his arm around Sandra and offers comfort as they approach the Old Man, who sits slumped forward on a tabletop, exhausted, sunken into himself, his weary face the perpetual rest stop for countless worries. I suddenly feel very aware of my own expression, which must appear stolid. And all I can think of is Matt. Hat and harmonica collector. Precocious poet. Best friend to Adam. And, of course, Lindsay Lowe devotee.

The writers group, which initially decided to meet two times a week, begins meeting nearly everyday. Mostly it's to discuss Nick Russo, Nicole D'Ambrosio - and now Lindsay Lowe - and any other melodrama, however minute, they collectively feel warrants some commiserating.

"There's your fucking study in irony," said Adam, a few days after the news of Lindsay has been revealed. "The staff are put in place to do everything in their power to keep us from *wanting* to swallow a goddamn bullet, and yet it's none other than a staff member who's responsible for nearly destroying this girl."

The group has been speculating for days as to what drove Lindsay to such desperation. Some say humiliation. Some say rejection. Some say a need for attention. These are all guesses that take into account the one common denominator that is Dimitri Ames. No new information has been revealed to Rollie, and thus to the students. Lindsay's family is no longer in contact. The last Rollie heard - two or three days ago - is that Lindsay is still unconscious.

Adam's comment draws lean, focused glances my way for the briefest of moments. I'm staff, and therefore on the opposing side. Yet what I have going for me, and what has thankfully become well known, is the story of my altercation with Ames. And so when his name is brought up during the writers group one afternoon, I don't mind Dan Hart turning to me with that mordantly sober look of his and saying how he wished I had broken Ames' neck that night. Secretly pleased over the acknowledgment, I choose to ignore it and focus instead on Matt, who has not attended the group since word first broke of his muse's suicide attempt.

"He's refusing to come," Adam announces. "Tortured artist shit aside, he's pretty fucked up over it. *I'm* fucked up over it, but he's *really* fucked up over it."

The timing couldn't be worse, Adam explains - the boys are just beginning to wear down the Old Man into letting them take a crack at fixing the Winnebago. Not to mention, he adds, their recent dumpster diving has been fruitful, some of their best ventures yet. One in particular stands out, he says, reaping them something spectacular from behind Sali's Pizza just the day before Rollie made his Lindsay Lowe announcement.

"It's got to be one of our best finds ever," he says, beaming.

The boys are beside themselves with excitement, Adam says. And once Matt is himself again, they'll show off their find to the group.

No new writing is critiqued. No comments or questions about syntax or sentence structure, either. Meredith, who's badgered me nearly every meeting to bring in my own writing, has relented for now. The focus, for the time being, seems to be inhaling and exhaling. The kids are busy keeping themselves alive, their heartbeats strong and quick and heard, just by talking to one another. The climate of the school feels the same. Everyone waits for good news, or any news, about Lindsay.

It's business as usual - classes and activities and therapy - but the typically charged pace seems reset to selfless introspection. Even those who don't know Lindsay very well take an interest. The Homer House boys, for instance, who are so often consumed with their pubescent antics and snarky belittling of everyone and everything, ask me for updates on her condition. Meanwhile, Matt has become a campus pariah. He attends classes infrequently, spending the better part of his days tramping around the school in laps, blowing lonesome notes on one of his mouth harps, listening to music, peering into classrooms with a sullen, faraway look in his eyes, and getting a special pass to shoot pool by himself in the pavilion. His dorm staff, teachers, friends, therapist, and the Old Man, have all spoken to him. They don't believe he's a threat to himself.

"He's literally placing himself at the center of the campus," Matt's therapist, Dr. Reynolds, observes in an email he sends to the faculty, "which, I believe, is not only deliberate - Matt, after all, is a young man who has a strong need for people - but also quite helpful when it comes to the task of us watching him. This is what he wants: to be watched. His sadness, in a sense, is on display, which I do not for one moment believe is an affectation. It is real and deep and he wants us to know it. So please know it. That's all I ask at this point."

• • •

A much needed distraction occurs a few days later when a young woman drives a chargold, dust covered Jaguar onto campus, parking it not in the guest lot, but rather in front of the SOD office, where many suspicious eyes regard it as though at any moment it might turn into a racehorse and bolt into the wilderness beyond the campus. The owner of the car is a short, thin, fit woman, probably around my age, with big, deep eyes, a tanned face and body, and short, black hair that sweeps over her forehead in breezy wisps. On the back of her neck, curling out from under her left ear, is a small tattoo of a thin, yellowish vine with a fully blossomed flower in its center.

Lunch has just ended and the campus is strewn with busybodies, now anxiously regarding this stranger. Seemingly at ease on the HAS campus, the woman takes delight as she looks around, greeting students and therapists and administrators and anyone who passes her. She introduces herself as Vee Scarret-Rosewell, former student at the Hundred Acre School, which, she adds with less levity than one might think, makes her a HAS-BEEN. The Old Man, emerging from the dining hall in mid-argument with a female student about her downtown privileges, throws his arms around Vee and tells her she looks wonderful. She kisses his cheek and blushes a little. Then, informally, the Old Man makes an announcement - to anyone within earshot - that Vee is a distinguished HAS graduate. He turns to her so she can confirm when exactly this was. Fifteen years ago, she says proudly.

Returning students. My father lives for this. He'll drop whatever's at hand and talk with them, searching for his school's imprint on their new lives. He won't hesitate to fire off question after question about how they've been getting along since they were a HAS student. He wants to know. Hell, he *needs* to know.

With his arm draped over Vee's shoulder, Rollie asks if he can escort her on one of his favorite pastimes: the campus tour. She obliges, and the two of them, in all of their energized nostalgia, part through the cast of onlookers to go view all that has changed in the past decade and a half.

Vee's story, which she willingly shares that night in Rollie's basement over poker and beer, may as well have been the story of every HASER, past, present, and future. It features addiction, depression, suicidal tendencies, periods of clarity and inspiration, relapses, various therapists, various meds, more clarity and inspiration, and then, for Vee, a feverish existentialist bout of approaching adulthood and its many real and frightening responsibilities.

"I had a baby," she says, fingering through some poker chips. "That sobered me up pretty quickly. It scared the shit out of me is what it really did. Which I guess is what I needed."

Amber asks Vee about her experience at the HAS. Her response is that she put everyone, herself included, through absolute hell. The Old Man, surprising everyone this evening by playing host in the flesh rather than from afar, denies this, describing Vee as willful and tenacious. She turns to him and reminds him how she changed her name for a while, demanding everyone at the school call her by her new Celtic name, Agrona, goddess of war and strife. Laughing, the Old Man admits he forgot about this.

Tennille asks Vee about her baby, who we learn is a little girl named Chloe who's just turned seven this summer and is now staying with her father for the week. She scrolls on her phone to find a photo before passing it around the table. When it gets to me, I regard the picture politely - the little girl has dark green eyes, a sinewy, devilish smile, and wears a blue dress with white butterflies on it - before passing it to Scotty.

"I remember you," Vee says, claiming her third jackpot in a row.

It takes me a moment to realize she's talking to me.

"Really?"

I wait for her to say something else. Anything. Like maybe how I always had my nose in a book when she saw me. Or how it was nice to see me again after all these years. But she just sizes me up from across the table, smiles a little, then takes her phone back before putting it in her purse. Maybe there's nothing for her to say. Maybe fifteen years is too long to remember details about someone who never made much of an impression. Or maybe she *did* have something to say, but was being courteous. Embarrassed a little, I sip my beer and fold my hand without looking at my cards.

The silence is broken almost immediately when Vee announces that Rollie has told her about all the recent turmoil on campus. She says that in all her time as a student, the most drastic thing that happened was when the school lost power for a few days after a bad storm. Then she thinks on that for a moment, adding a disclaimer:

"I mean, aside from the sex, drugs, and drama that happened on a daily basis."

The Old Man pretends to block his ears over Vee's remark. The night goes on like this. Small talk. Drinking. Texas Hold'em. I barely speak, except to make a bet or thank anyone who occasionally passes me a beer. Something about this Vee woman - or, really, what she said to me - puts me in a pensive-like state. I could've packed it in and gone back to my place to finish grading papers or read Vonnegut's *Jailbird*, which I'm halfway through. Yet something's compelled me to stay. Vee's piqued my imagination with her remark. It's made me wonder what she might've recalled about me, but refuses to share. It's hard not to sit there wondering what kind of a prick I might've been fifteen years ago and how that left an impression on a then depressed adolescent. I could've thought about this back at the Homer House, but it seems more proper for some reason to do it here, in my father's basement, with Vee Scarret-Rosewell sitting across from me, downing the fancy beer Tennille brought, hustling her way through another hand while claiming it's all beginner's luck.

The evening dies down at around midnight. The staff, most of them a little drunk, thank Rollie, shake hands with Vee, and stumble out into the darkness and back to their dorms. The Old Man offers Vee - for what seems like a second or third time - the small apartment above the gym. She reminds him of the B&B in the center of town where she'll be staying for a few days.

"Is this what the staff did when I was a student? Got drunk and played poker?"

"Probably."

It's just the three of us. Rollie takes a break from straightening up before sitting down with me and Vee. In his hands is a bound manuscript, about an inch thick, with a clear plastic cover framing a baby blue title page. Drumming his fingers on the book, he turns to me and says that Vee has a favor to ask of me. He's clearly pleased, smiling a great big helium-filled smile that looks so full and airy, like it might fly off his face at any moment. It was difficult, he admits, to control his excitement while the others were around.

"Vee's written a book," he says. "It's a memoir about her three years here."

When I turn to her, there isn't a trace of boastful pride on her face. Rather, she seems to be beaming over her mentor's enthusiasm. She lets him do the talking. He finished it this afternoon, he tells me.

"It's a hell of a read," he declares. "Beautifully done."

Leaning back in his chair, the Old Man confides that he's always secretly hoped a former student would chronicle their experiences at the HAS. This way, he says, the place would survive long after he's gone.

"Forever," he adds, looking at me. "It would survive forever."

The memoir's been accepted for publication, which is set for late fall. Vee's in the process of cleaning up the manuscript, tying up a few loose ends. And what better way to tie up loose ends than by having some fresh perspective? And what better perspective than HAS students? She wants a handpicked group of them to read the manuscript - she has a stack of bound copies in the Old Man's office - and provide candid feedback. Not on spelling and semicolons. But on her ability to capture the spirit of the school, the intensity of the therapy, the immeasurableness of the shame and guilt that are so deeply embedded in being a student at the Hundred Acre School. Vee turns to me and says it was Rollie's idea to approach me.

"You've got your writers group," the Old Man points out, "there must be some good candidates there to read Vee's book. I figure between that and your classes—"

Absently nodding my head, I think about Meredith's honesty, and Adam's straight-faced intensity, and Dan Hart's cool instincts. The Old Man slides the book across the table to me. It's titled *Miserable Bitch: A True Has-Been Story*. I have a group of students in mind, I tell her. They're bright and artistic and brutally candid. Vee says this probably describes the majority of the HAS population. It did when she was there, she adds.

Three days, she tells me as we all walk up the basement stairs and outside into the pleasant night air. That's how long the kids have. And then she's heading back to Poughkeepsie.

"No problem," I tell her.

"No problem," Rollie repeats, adding that Vee will probably want some face time with the kids once they're done reading.

She agrees. The Old Man bids us goodnight, adding that he'll see us tomorrow. Then he covers a yawn with his forearm and disappears back into the house. It's on the tip of my tongue to now ask Vee what she might remember about me, but I don't. Instead, something compels me to reach for the manuscript clutched against her breast and ask to see it.

"Of course."

Staring at its glossy cover under the moonlight, I offer to read it.

"You're more than welcome to. I'd love feedback from another writer. Your dad was bragging about you earlier, Gray."

The way she says my name sounds melancholic. Taking a deep breath, she looks around with her eyes half shut. The night is still and cool. Summer constellations dot the sky in sharp, bright points.

"Rollie wants you to take this place over someday, huh?"

"Why would you think that?"

"It's all in there," she says, pointing to her book. "See if you can find it."

Then she turns away from me and walks on ground that is probably as familiar to her as it is to me. It takes me all night, and well into early morning, to finish reading the manuscript. The book is well-written. It's clean and sharp. Vee's style is understated. She recalls her time at the HAS with unerring clarity, musing on her medication and therapy and living away from home among "one hundred fellow fuck-ups" as she frequently dubs her peers. She explores her anger and humiliation and depression. And, practically functioning as a character unto itself throughout the memoir, there's the school. She describes it vividly. Praises it at times. Curses it at others. Her relationship with the place, she states in the book, is like any other complicated relationship. Which is to say it's burrowed a deep and permanent space within her, releasing itself in spurts of memory at the best and worst of times throughout the years, either inspiring or devastating, but always finding a way to break the heart.

To my astonishment, I'm in the book. Towards the middle, a few pages into a chapter mostly devoted to the dread Vee and other students felt over being profiled by uneasy townspeople, enters Rollie's son, Gray, described initially by the author as appearing just as tortured and troubled as many of the students I refuse to acknowledge. I'm described as handsome, brooding, too self-aware. It's noted that I hardly interact with the students when I visit the campus, that I barely look up from my reading to regard these troubled lepers.

The author states that it was rumored that I composed the school's mission statement, which she prints in its entirety; she states that my authoring of this mission statement proved, undeniably, that I was conflicted. On the one hand, I had obvious contempt for the school, quietly sneering at its conventions, passively ignoring its members, but on the other, I must've possessed, on some level, a profound appreciation for not only the emotional strife the students endured, but of the monumental undertaking of the school's overseer, my father, Mr. Rollie Loveland. She ends up coming to the conclusion that I'm simply resentful and probably petrified. Resultantly, her hostility towards me is tempered; by the end of the chapter, it changes into what she calls "a bizarre brew of envy and pity."

After lunch, I run into Vee as she's crossing the street. Her hair is wet and slicked back and she's wearing a yellow cotton dress. She appears somehow younger than she did the evening before. I tell her I've already given out the copies of her book to a group of handpicked students. Thanking me, her attention is focused on my messenger bag, out of which protrudes the corner of her manuscript. As I produce it and turn it over to her, I briefly consider saying how I didn't get around to reading it, that I probably wouldn't, and good luck with its publication. But I suddenly find myself praising her efforts and even referencing specific parts. Vee says she appreciates the feedback. Writing the book, she says, consumed the better part of three years - and however taxing it was, she adds, it was worth it. She changes the topic to the Old Man, telling me she just learned he's trying to purchase the school from J.R. III. She says it's about time. All I can do is nod.

"Speechless over the matter?" she asks.

"I have more to say on it than you can possibly imagine."

"I have to tell you that I'm surprised to find you working here."

"And where would you expect to see me working? Keeping in mind that I'm a complete stranger to you."

"I'm sorry if that came across as rude."

A car whisks by. The driver, a middle-aged man, stares at us as we stand on the side of the road.

"It wasn't rude. I apologize."

Holding her book to her chest, Vee looks up at the sun for a moment. Then she tells me she's spoken to some students today.

"What a trip," she says, "it's like coming home again."

"I know all about that."

She smiles and thanks me again for helping her with the book; she'll be in touch to follow up with her anonymous readers. Before she walks past me, she apologizes again if she was presumptuous. When she's still within earshot, I call after her:

"It must've been difficult to capture all that truth. For your book, I mean."

She thinks on this for a moment. Then she says it *was* difficult, that it was like capturing a wild animal with hopes to tame it and learn from it and even live with it for a while.

"Sounds intense."

"It was, I suppose."

"And what's the payoff?"

"The *payoff*?"

"What's the end game? The point? The payoff?"

"It's just a map," she says. "Nothing more. Just my own personal map. And it shows this odyssey that I trekked, this unfuckingbelievable odyssey with heroes and villains and darkness and light."

"And let me guess," I said, careful to eschew any mockery from my tone, "it reminds you that you're here, still breathing, still alive."

A somewhat guarded smile finds its way on her lips, which I notice are glistening a little. After a moment, she moves towards me with a couple of steps before responding:

"Of course. Can you think of anything in this world that's more important?"

During Vee's three day stay in Old Brookview, she breezes in and out of the HAS, leaving in her wake a stoic kind of hopefulness the kids are all too glad to observe. I see her walking the campus with the Old Man or Dr. Nussbaum, or talking to a group of students on the front steps of the pavilion, or listening to someone play guitar by the benches in front of the SOD office. She always looks up and offers me a warm smile. Brief, sincere, and full of self-assurance. I find myself wanting to ask her about including me in her book. And what else she remembers - fodder she may have left on the cutting room floor - or any exchanges we might've had back then. I clearly left some kind of impression, and I want to better understand why. We're all fascinated by the perceptions strangers have of us. Our shrewdest mysteries are still firmly intact at such a faraway vantage point. It's only later, upon knowing us, that myth becomes dispelled, uncertainty dissolved, and our image becomes as common as daylight.

Vee meets with her readers for an hour during her final afternoon in town. Thanking them for their feedback, she says the book is as much for them as it is for her. With a firm promise to Rollie that she'll send him an on-the-house published copy, she drives back to Poughkeepsie to collect her child and resume her life. I never ask about her decision to include me in the book. Her true motivation. Her actual memories. I suppose I'm content to think that her inspiration must've sprung from a source that holds firm to those elusive moments, the ones that try their damndest to trick us into believing that they're nothing more than trivial; thankfully, there are those among us who know better.

. . .

The night after Vee leaves, at around 2:00 a.m., Rollie gets a visitor he tells the staff about the next day. Dimitri Ames. Drunk, disheveled, and reeking of alcohol, Ames showed up at his house, demanding to discuss Lindsay, claiming they're in love, something he's certain the Old Man is trying to stymie. He's sick with worry, he says, since her attempt on her life. Desperate for news on her condition - the girl's family is refusing his calls - he's at his lowest. Belligerent one minute and weepy the next, Ames' fickleness, according to the Old Man, was both maddening and amusing.

Standing on the front porch of Rollie's house, the two went at it. Ames would make a pathetic threat, retract it, bawl into his hands, curse my father, then beg for information. Rollie steered the conversation from Lindsay Lowe to another topic altogether. Nicole D'Ambrosio. Ames' reaction to this, as the Old Man put it, was interesting: His face turned the most unnatural shade of red before he bowed over the side of the porch and threw up all over the Old Man's bed of tiger lilies.

"Let's talk," Rollie said, ignoring Ames' vomiting. "I'm up for it. Let's get it all out in the open. Let's talk about all these young girls you seem to be so fond of."

He was bluffing, of course. But Ames didn't know this. Wiping his mouth, he cooled off at that moment and asked for a glass of water. My father, sensing a possible breakthrough, told him to stay put. Then he went into the house for a drink; when he came back, Ames was gone, the only sign of him choking the flowerbed below.

• • •

More mail for Grayson Loveland. Another single white envelope with the same handwriting as the last. Again addressed to me with no return info. Inside is a handwritten letter on lined paper, composed in blue ink. It reads as follows:

Dear HAS,

I know what you're all thinking. You're thinking I'm a guilty piece of shit who killed that girl. Why else would I run away, right? Well, "that girl" wasn't just "that girl" to me. She was Nikki. Yes, I knew her, which by now is probably common knowledge. Can you fucking believe it, a lowlife shitstain like me with a gorgeous girl like that? I'm not going to say we were in love. Because I don't really know what we had together. What I do know is that it was better than anything else I've ever had in my life. Not that it was perfect. It wasn't. It didn't need to be perfect. It was just this thing that we discovered together. And this thing considered each of us a human being. Human beings who needed something we seemed to get from each other. Sound lame? Maybe. But that's how it was. I've never been the kind of guy who gives a fuck what others think. And I'm still that guy. So think whatever you want. I don't care. My purpose in writing this is to say simply that I'm still out here. And that's enough for now. What else is there to say? Except maybe a shout out to the Homer House boys! What up, fellas!

Nick R.

"Does it sound like him?" I ask the Old Man when I show him the letter.

"It's a little angry," he said, "so in that sense, yes."

"Can we be positive Nick sent this? How about a handwriting sample? Ask one of his teachers."

The Old Man likes this idea. We agree that confirming that the letter was written by Nick will at least tell us he's safe. A few interviews reveal that Roger, Nick's math teacher, oddly enough, is the only one to have a useful sample. It's obvious from the way the ms are all pointy and lopsided, the way the capital Bs are bulbous and top heavy, the way each word is spaced out a good centimeter from the next, that it's a perfect match.

Laughing in spite of ourselves, Rollie and I agree that though successful, we are nevertheless pathetic in our attempt at amateur sleuthing.

"Why the hell is he singling me out? I barely know the kid. Why wouldn't he send it to you?"

My father has an immediate answer to this. Loyalty. Nick, despite what others might think of him, is truly loyal. And he recognizes his home on campus as being the Homer House. So it's to the Homer House he'll send anything he wants us to have.

"But why to me? Why not to one of the boys, or to Ryan?"

"Again, loyalty. It may sound strange. But I think he feels like he owes you."

"Owes me what?"

"The closest thing to an explanation."

"Why?"

"Because he disappeared on *your* watch."

"Seems like an odd thing for him to be considering."

"This kid is one for considering odd things. Anyway, there's another matter - a more important matter."

Trepidation has suddenly snuck itself into his tone. He thinks for a bit. I prod a little.

"It's just that I can't help but wonder why he takes the time to write and send a letter like he does - when clearly he has better things to do like staying under the radar - yet he makes no effort, none really at all, to deny the murder."

. . .

Three days later, during breakfast, the Old Man takes the podium and announces he has something for everyone that's been in short supply for far too long: good news. Lindsay Lowe has regained consciousness and is expected to make a full recovery. Applause is at first moderate, yet steady sounding and real. It then gathers momentum and soon becomes rousing. Scanning the sea of faces, I spot Matt. Seated, and still holding a fork full of food, he's massaging his temple with his thumb, a quietly satisfied look on his meditative face.

The writers group welcomes him back the following afternoon. Not that there's much fanfare. There isn't. Just Adam announcing his friend's return with a slap on the shoulder and a brief chastisement for holding up their great dumpster diving show-off. Adam points to the table where the Old Man sits everyday among the therapists and administrators. Mounted on the wall just beneath the window is a tabletop jukebox the boys installed earlier in the day. Its chrome is as faded as the pink and white song tags behind the abraded glass. It's scuffed and worn, but the machine appears intact and the installation looks clean. Sali's, the downtown pizza joint, is doing some renovations, the boys tell us, and they swiped this after spotting it wedged between rusted out bathroom fixtures at the bottom of a dumpster.

Walking over to it, some of the kids comment that they can't believe the boys knew how to install the machine. Others can't believe Rollie let them install it by his table - or install it *at all*.

"We're wearing him down for the Winnebago," Adam says. "I think the jukebox was his way of giving us an inch, testing our abilities."

Meredith flips through the sleeves of song selections. They've rigged the machine so it doesn't require money, Matt tells her. Then he asks someone to pick a tune, something that will be the group's unofficial anthem. Meredith sees something she likes. B9, she says. She presses the buttons. After a moment, "Shake Your Groove Thing," plays from the scratchy speakers. Dorian asks if Meredith can play Black Sabbath instead. Then others begin making requests. Before long, though, they accept the tune she's chosen. There's even some foot-tapping and head-bobbing. This soon turns into full-on dancing. Ridiculous dancing. Uninhibited dancing.

"What do you think?" Adam asks me in the midst of some absurd shimmy.

"I think we here at the Hundred Acre School like to offer and encourage a wide diversity of experiences, from writing screenplays and poetry to dancing to the song stylings of Peaches and Herb."

"That's hardcore," he says.

"That's what we're all about here."

Matt ends his odd leg kicks and display of zero rhythm to tell me how he recalls the song from a movie. Meredith, who sidles up to me and ceases with her own bizarre jig, also has something to say:

"Interesting," she says, "that you're using the *we* pronoun when discussing this place. Before, I believe, it was *them*, wasn't it? Now it's *we*. Don't you think that's interesting?"

"Incredibly," is all I can think to say.

• • • •

That evening, J.R. III's silver Lexus, one of his many cars, pulls onto campus moments before the cop car with its flashing lights and wailing siren. This is in the middle of dinner. The kids and the staff must be used to these sightings by now - strange vehicles and persons on their school grounds - that they react accordingly. A few quizzical stares. Some obstinate mutterings. Even a little apathy. But as far as shock or incredulity, no way.

Rollie, his phone pressed into his ear, is halfway out the door when he suddenly halts. All eyes are upon him when he looks in the direction of the Homer House table and yells at me to follow him. I'm swallowing my last bite of one of Mickey's better meals - a perfectly cooked fillet of cod in some kind of lime salsa - when I find myself hurtling towards the door and out into the warm night, side by side with my father.

The commotion is near the Homer House. The cop car, its siren off, but lights still flashing, is angled in front of my private entrance. J.R. III's Lexus is angled the other way, so both vehicles form a V against the building. The cop, a thickly built woman, probably in her early forties, with a braid of black hair swinging from her duty cap, is speaking with J.R. III. The security team of Louise and Jimbo are sandwiching who is clearly the reason for the chaos: Austin. He's puffing his chest out and jabbing his hands into the folds of his love handles. It's still light out - light enough to see his expression, which is both subdued and worried. When he sees me and Rollie, he shifts his weight and nods in my direction.

"Jimbo caught him walking out of the Homer House," Louise tells us.

"Just as plain as day," adds Jimbo.

Louise mentions they discovered a rear window with a torn screen. Austin snorts an ugly laugh at this. His father, now at his side, silences him with a piercing glance. Jimbo turns to me and says that Austin told him I'd given permission for him to enter the dorm. After learning this, Jimbo contacted Louise, who didn't believe Austin's story. She immediately phoned the police, and eventually the Old Man, who I sense is looking at me.

Before I can respond to the absurdity of Austin's lie, he announces that his father is still the owner of the school. This is *fact*, he says. Then he adds that he works for his father and it's his father alone to whom he'll answer. J.R. III turns to his son, pauses for a bit, then thrashes him upside his face with an open hand. Austin barely flinches while his father strikes him several more times. In between each blow is a quick, hostile rant. The featured words are *useless* and *pathetic*. The abuse is rough, but not enough to gain Austin any defenders. And it's over in a moment. A quick, angry burst of violence. No police interference. No outsiders expressing judgment. J.R. III apologizes to everyone and tells his son to get in the car. Austin begins to explain that his own vehicle is nearby, but soon stifles himself. He climbs into the Lexus, avoiding eye contact with the crowd. Sunken into himself, all his bravado and hopes for nepotism vanished. Before father and son embark on the winding road that cuts through the campus, the campus they *do* rightfully own, the silver Lexus pulls alongside me and rolls down its driver-side window. J.R. III leans his head out just slightly and looks up at me.

"I'll assume you're foreign to the feeling of being an absolute embarrassment to your own father. You seem like you've got your shit pretty well together. That's good, you know. Rollie appreciates it, you not being a goddamn embarrassment. Fathers everywhere appreciate it. Hell, *I* appreciate it."

Looking past him for a moment, I fix my eyes on Austin, who's staring stonily ahead, his face contorted into a miserable shadow against the oncoming twilight. There's no doubt he's heard every word of this. The window suddenly shoots up and the Lexus drives off.

. . .

That night, I'm on duty. Minutes before the boys settle down, hysteria erupts. Yelling and cursing and confident accusations. Several of the boys, J.J., Cal, Noah, and Cliff, are involved. Their things, they say, have been moved or misplaced.

"Blow me!" Noah shouts at the boys, "I didn't fuck with your stuff!"

"Punch, you do have a habit of *borrowing* our shit," says Cal.

"Fuck off!" says Noah, his eyes beginning to water.

He swears up and down that he's touched nothing, and, in fact, *his* things - cologne, watch, ukulele - have also been tampered with. More boys begin coming forward - Alex, Albert, Dustin - claiming similar charges. It's then brought up that Nick's things especially have been disturbed. It's not clear if anything's missing, but definitely moved.

"It's like Punch ransacked our shit looking for his missing balls," says Cal.

With clenched fists, Noah, gritting his teeth, encroaches upon Cal. I extend my hand out to his chest and tell him I believe him. His eyes continue to water. Then I turn to the rest of the Homer House boys who've gathered in the name of what they naively regard as some great mystery, and I tell them it's a lousy time to begin turning on one another. No one asks me to explain myself, so I mention again that Noah, their roommate, their sometimes friend, and most likely their only Hawaiian connection, is innocent. Then I give a brief dissertation on short-term memory loss and explain to them that they're too young to give in to such an inconvenience. They agree in an endearingly dumbfounded way. Lots of tired, sideways glances and slow head nods. So I remind them of Austin and his father and the police and all that occurred just hours earlier.

"Oh yeah," Cal says, "that fat fuck. I forgot all about him. I guess we all did."

"Not Gray," says Noah. "Gray didn't forget about him."

All eyes are suddenly fixed upon me. So I agree with Noah, that I have in fact remembered Austin.

"More importantly, though," I added, "I'm positive the police will also remember him."

The boys nod. They seem satisfied. In their own way. Satisfied enough, I suppose, to drop the misunderstanding and head off to their rooms in peace to settle down for the evening.

CHAPTER 14

There was that one dream, stark and brutal as anything I could imagine. It was the kind that ties itself so tightly around reality that it takes a bout of sweat soaked breathless panting and feverish blinking to break from it long enough to calm down and see my wife lying there beside me in the late night darkness. I began to lose track of how many times I'd been woken by this dream. It seemed like every time I shut my eyes. And it became impossible to go back to sleep. So I'd sit up in bed, breathing deep, loud breaths, hoping to wake Laura. I secretly wished she would hear my distress and pull me down towards her and console me with whatever she had left to offer. I couldn't help but wonder what exactly that might be. But she never did this. She continued to sleep the impossibly heavy sleep of one who's fought in a war and has lost everything and foolishly thinks they can regain it in the morning with a fresh, blinding sunrise. Ben told me I was being too hard on myself when I suggested the dreams were some kind of divine punishment.

"Maybe I deserve it," I told him one morning, cornering him before he could even get a cup of coffee in him. "Maybe I'll be plagued for the rest of my goddamn life."

I didn't tell him I was beginning to question the decision I had forced upon my wife. Ben knew me. So I was fine with him knowing my entitlements and arrogance. We were, after all, kindred spirits in these ways. But I could never have him thinking I was full of such serious regret, something I wasn't even certain of myself. Such regrets signify defeat. And men seldom admit to other men they've been defeated, especially at their own hands. Perhaps on the tennis court or golf course where there's a finite score, a winner and loser. But not in ways where it truly counts.

"It's natural for your mind to be fucking with you right now," he said. "Your world has just been given intense shock therapy, for Christ's sake."

Part of me was hoping he'd be harder on me, that he'd agree that these dreams were a type of cosmic intervention, a harbinger to dark times. Instead, he put his hand on my shoulder and told me I knew better than to buy into the notion of interpreting my dreams.

"Maybe," I said.

"*Maybe*?"

"It's just so goddamn heavy. The dream."

"Of course it is," he said. "What's *occurred* is pretty goddamn heavy. That doesn't mean you need to break out the tarot cards and start looking for signs."

Ben was right in everything he was saying. But being right wasn't enough to deter me from obsessing. I thought about the dream like it was some looming prison sentence I'd be forced to serve once I got my affairs in order. From night to night, it was more or less the same. Laura never returns from the hospital. No phone call. No word from her family. Days go by and nothing. All my attempts to reach out are futile. Then, one day I receive a letter. Laura has fled to some remote part of the country where she's given birth to our baby. It's her intention to raise the child by herself, which she does. And proudly. And she meets a man, a man more accepting and generous than her husband. A man who gives her the life she and our child feel destined to live. She resigns to never tell our child about her real father, the coward, the quitter, the selfish, hurtful prick who threw it all away so he could free himself of explanations and excuses as to why his family wasn't like he had hoped it would be.

But Laura *had* returned to me. And her return, I soon discovered, was as terrifying as the dream. The haunting possibility of her absence, and the bloated sadness of her presence: Each loomed in dark hanging gray things that I couldn't push away or tear down or remove long enough to examine and understand them. She was different, too. And not just in her belly, which flattened after a few weeks. Her voice had changed. Its vibrancy had been dialed to zero and replaced mostly by sheepish, inaudible mutterings. Her movements had also changed. What was once a breezy and self-assured stride gave way to an awkward delicateness, as though she feared her most important organs might disconnect inside of her body at any moment. And her eyes – they now seemed colorless and opaque, the kind of eyes torn from the pages of a children's grim fairy-tale where good encounters evil for the first time and is struck so hard that it has no choice but to change forever.

We ate most of our meals together. We spoke about baseball and the weather and the lousy economy. She thanked me for replacing the broken window in the baby's room. We slept in the same bed. We dressed and undressed in front of one another. And time went on.

We eventually had a small memorial service for the baby. For family only. It was me and Laura and her parents and siblings and their spouses and children. It was through a local parish. The headstone was blue pearl granite with flowers etched around its perimeter and an epitaph that read *Emma Elizabeth Loveland, Beloved Daughter, Granddaughter, Niece, Cousin*. The dates were at the bottom. I wasn't consulted on any of the details for the service or the stone.

Through all of this, I never contacted my father. I'd end up waiting several more weeks before sending him my *unexpected complications* text. In my message, I said I'd call him, and I asked for him to please not be in touch. We were fine, I said. Laura was fine. It was all fine. We were doing better than we had anticipated.

One evening, Laura and I, lying in bed, began to embrace. We fell asleep in one another's arms. When I woke at a little after midnight, her arms were wrapped around my neck and we were nose to nose. Her breath was warm and her breathing steady. Inching back a bit, I studied her face. It was flawless in the dark, neutral and unburdened, all traces of its sorrow gone. I wondered about the dreams *she* might be having. Maybe I could slip back into them, I thought. There must be some smooth crawlspace in there that I could wedge myself into, some smoky recess where I could hole up for a bit, count to a million, then rise and wade my way through the density and be seen and heard and loved and understood once again. I promised myself that if I made it I would do everything I could to remain there, boldly and proudly intact, forever claiming it my true and righteous place in this life. By the next morning she had woken before me and was out of the house without a sound. She came home at close to 9:00 that night, missing dinner and eventually falling asleep on the sofa in the living room. This pattern continued over the next few days. I never spoke a word about it.

I made the mistake of researching the procedure Laura went through in the hospital. Countless websites came up when I entered my search. Many of them, I would learn, based on their abrasive and even hostile wordings, were Christian anti-abortion sites. They were unforgiving in their brutal depiction of the process. Forgoing all professional nomenclature, they relied instead on hard-nosed, tactless language that, once I cross referenced with less fanatical sites, proved nevertheless accurate. Words I had never considered - *dismember* was among them - were used often, and in the most casual of contexts. The procedure seemed as invasive and horrifying as anything I could imagine. This cemented my guilt over not having been there. Absorbed with the sting of self-loathing, I considered sending bitter tidings to some of these sanctimonious Puritan fuckers, but the effort hardly seemed worth it.

My instincts were failing me. There was a desire to tell Laura I knew what she'd been through. That it must've been unthinkable. Or surreal. Or both. Or maybe she was numbed to the entire experience, having shut herself off from it so as to not break down. But I was wary of offering sympathy. Sympathy would only support the animosity I knew was there.

We began seeing less and less of each other. Her family whisked her away whenever they could, and she'd often spend entire evenings and weekends with them. She returned to work around this time, and began volunteering at the Pleasant Pantry, a local soup kitchen. When I saw her, it was brief and hurried. The way she regarded me reminded me of that noncommittal way an exhausted tour guide regards their party. There's a little boredom, a little distance, a little waning perfunctory courtesy.

The way I viewed her had changed. Laura, to me, was someone who had actually suffered. And I began to hate her for this. The suffering validated her sorrow, making me feel more unworthy than ever. As I thought of what it was to suffer, to truly suffer, I found myself thinking about Rollie's school, a place where suffering was imbued into the atmosphere. And though I grew up with this all around me, I always managed to avoid it at any cost. Certainly I could brush up against it and look it in the eye over a quick meal or a walk through campus, but I would never learn its source or feel the dire weight of its tendrils. It wasn't my place to. Or interest. And I knew early on that it would never be my vocation. If it was at all possible to exist on the opposite side of such suffering, for as much of my life as possible, then that's what I would strive for.

Laura and I had become a different entity from what we'd once been. What this meant was obvious to us both. Yet it wouldn't be anything we'd discuss. She was too busy erasing me from her life and I was too immersed in self-pity and my unreasonable contempt towards her. This isn't to say we were apathetic over the idea of reconciliation. Laura, I found out through an appointment card she left on the kitchen counter, began seeing a therapist. She didn't tell me about it, opting to go alone, showing her notion of reconciliation to perhaps be a bit self-centered.

Dr. Eugene Gaskell, Family Therapist, had his work cut out for him. Meanwhile, I'd prepared a speech about focusing on the two of us, getting back to our roots, taking up new hobbies together like meditation and kayaking, and, eventually, trying to once again start a family. I went so far as to write the thing out, wordsmithing it to death, softening parts, infusing it with levity here and there. Then, as though I'd be auditioning any day, I set to memorizing the thing, practicing it in the car on my way to work, or as I tramped up and down the grocery store aisles, or while I drifted off to sleep every night, somehow hopeful that my words, in all their spanking glory and precision, could restore the ruins that only seemed to be piling up.

Bringing up the topic of trying again seemed perverse to me. For a lot of reasons. It meant that Laura and I would have to talk about being intimate with one another. Aside from that one evening in bed, as well as seeing each other in the nude on occasion, we hadn't so much as shared a meaningful kiss for the months since she had returned from the hospital. We had reached an impasse that seemed so firm, so unrelenting, that I told myself, despite how foreign and grotesque it appeared, it truly must've been our destiny.

There was also the issue of whether I still wanted a family. Searching for those elusive moments of sudden introspection, I waited to be told this by some higher power. I waited. And like a goddamn fool, I listened. All in vain. If it was this simple - and it might've been - I was not to be the heir of such conveniences.

So I revised my speech again - I kept the part about children - and psyched myself up to deliver it. I chose Halloween for some absurd reason. But the holiday came and went without so much as a word on the subjects of family and future. So I tweaked the speech once more and picked Thanksgiving. That too passed. First snowfall. When the Bears win three in a row. There was no opportune time. My words, muted by their own inertia, were destined to die a slow, silent death until someday they flaked off the page entirely and were swept away to that long lost place of all that is unspoken and unanswered.

I was grateful for the few certainties that did grace my thoughts. They might've been sparse in number, but they were rock solid, and as devoted to me as my confusion. One was that I still loved Laura. This was true. I knew it. I felt it. But I suspected restlessness in that love, some remote hint of wanderlust and anxiety. Like it had gotten a glimpse of an approaching conspirator ready to change its form and function forever. The other was that I knew I couldn't live the rest of my life playing the role of a villain. Some men are better equipped for that than others. Martyrdom only goes so far. It begins to lose whatever flair it has around the time the leaves change. I'm not an animal; like the song goes: a time to dance, a time to mourn. I suppose I was just aching for some guarantee that the mourning would not blight all that could be beautiful between the two of us.

Since I could only prevaricate on the matter, I thought some research might counter the inactivity. So I investigated the chances of me and Laura having another child with the same condition. Everything I came up with told me it would be next to impossible. The most current study indicated that the issue is due to a random event. That's how it put it: a *random event*. It said that it occurs during the formation of the sex cells, something I already came across in my initial research months earlier, and that there's no evidence to suggest parental behaviors or environmental factors play into it. All evidence showed we'd be safe. It said that it having happened even *once* was a fluke.

Someone especially as young as Laura was in the lower risk category. At only twenty-nine, she was years away from the at-risk age of thirty-five. This was all good news. I should've been relieved. I should've been sharing my findings with my wife and dusting off my speech. Whatever energy I had, though, was directed at trying to dismember a thought that suddenly entered my mind: What Laura and I had made with our love for one another was something that horrified me.

I tried to repress this. But it kept at me. Was it some kind of sign? Or was it, like my research told me, a *fluke*? All I knew was that I'd begun to think of all Laura and I had together, all we were capable of, in very different terms.

I threw myself headfirst into work. Work meant routine. It meant stability. And it meant Andrea. As the year was ending, so was her internship. With a few weeks to go before the end of her college semester, and all of her requirements fulfilled, she spent most of her time loitering at my desk, or texting me short, clever quips about topics as diverse as the Johnstown Flood to the chief differences between certain Cajun and Creole dishes. I always contemplated whether I wished to play along. And I always ended up doing so.

Then there were our lunches at the deli. These were always threesomes, with me and Ben holding court, each of us trying to be droll and self-deprecating, all the while vying for the girl's attention. It gave me little pleasure that I was winning. It was clear that she respected Ben - she bought nearly every book on journalism he recommended - but it was impossible to miss the way she gazed at me from across the table, or how she smoothed her hair in slow motion whenever I said something even halfway witty. Ben was fine with this. He must've thought it all harmless and even restorative to my brutalized ego. Or maybe I was hoping for as much.

There was one day, a couple of weeks before Christmas, when I didn't see Andrea all morning. I found myself thinking about her - the clever comments she'd fire off, and even her scent, which seemed as much a part of her identity as her intellect. Half tempted to ask Ben her whereabouts, I resisted, refocused myself, and got back to work. Then, at about 11:00 a.m., I received a text from her that read, "I know something's wrong." Maybe I was over-analyzing those four words too closely, but I found them fascinating. With the "I" in her message, she'd entered herself into an equation that had *me* as its center. Her message could've said, "Are *you* all right?" or "How're *you* doing?" Her way seemed intent on getting me to think about the "I," which was *her*. It appeared to me to be as brilliant as it was egocentric.

Not to mention she proved adept at reading my moods. The signs had to have been discreet. Never one for public moping, I knew I'd been successful in maintaining my professionalism. Only Ben was subject to the spectacle of watching me ramble through my sorrow, and that was during stolen moments throughout the day. Yet Andrea was somehow on to me and my troubles. I liked guessing how this came about. Maybe she had studied me from afar and discerned that something didn't seem quite right, something so subtle and apparent only to the most skilled watcher. Or maybe she had been observing my lunchtime banter and mannerisms and was told by some womanly instinct that I seemed to be going through the motions, and probably had been for a while.

For too long, I sat there, deciding how to respond, or if I even should. I typed and deleted a series of replies; some were elusive, some sarcastic, some serious. None of them made it past my own eyes. I did, though, eventually settle on "I'm fine," before getting back to work. Which meant pretending to look busy as I awaited her response to my laconic text. Nothing was sent.

Then, thirty minutes after her initial text, she made an appearance at my desk.

"It's freezing out," she said, "so grab your coat and meet me by the elevators."

All I could do was stare at her with a puzzled half-smile. When I started to say something, she leaned into me, her hair brushing against the side of my face.

"You're not *fine*," she said, hitting that last word with enough forcefulness to suggest maternal concern.

Then she reminded me of the temperature outside and walked away. Before allowing that dangerous lull to settle - the kind that brings with it the inconvenience of contemplation - I sprang into action, dug up my jacket, and met her by the elevators. Aside from a black felted wool peacoat, she was bundled in maroon gloves and a scarf that draped her breast in a purely decorative sense. She looked five years younger than her actual age.

"What's the plan?" I asked.

The elevator doors opened and we got in. We were alone. I recall wondering at that moment whether anyone in the office was watching us. Yet I never took the time to look. Even now I wonder whether it was fear or apathy that stopped me from doing so.

"The plan," Andrea said, as the doors slid shut, "is to stage my one woman intervention and see if it's a success. God knows you need it."

When we stepped outside, I felt like my lungs were going to collapse. The air felt colder than it had just a few hours earlier. The sun was out, but hung uselessly in the sky, like a mirage, warming nothing, signifying some blurry, burnt-out distant planet. Andrea hailed a cab and we climbed into the backseat. She told the driver to head towards East Grand Avenue. Staring out the window, I played it as cool as I could by refusing to ask where we were headed. This is what she would be expecting. Or maybe she knew I'd be thinking this way and had anticipated my taciturn cooperation. Either way, I said nothing until after the driver, a lean, bearded man probably in his sixties, looked in the rearview and asked Andrea to specify her destination.

"Good question," I said.

"Take us to where the vast slate of possibility looms like the fine arc of the bluebird's flight," she said, looking at me with a recklessness I hadn't yet seen in her.

I couldn't help but laugh aloud over her abstruseness.

"Who talks like that?"

She laughed, too, asking what I thought of the line. The driver cussed under his breath at a fellow motorist, who darted out too quickly from a side street.

"Very nice," I said.

"*Very nice*? That's all?"

"Is it yours?"

She was saved for a moment by the driver, who asked again for a destination. Still looking at me, she told him the Four Seasons Hotel on East Delaware. I knew she was waiting for me to say something. So I didn't. I'm not sure I could've if I had even wanted to. My throat felt swollen and my voice suffocated. All of my insides felt like they'd been scalded with hot water. After a few moments, Andrea told me that the line about the bluebird's flight *was* hers; she said it was from a poem that had recently been accepted by some underground publication.

"Very nice," I managed to mutter again, not thinking at the time that it was either cocky or romantic that she was quoting herself.

Though it felt much longer, the drive lasted only a few minutes. My thoughts were pure one moment and then impure the next. Andrea sat beside me, looking out her window, quietly humming along with whatever melody was playing inside her head. When we pulled up to the hotel, I paid the cabbie with a twenty dollar bill and didn't ask for change.

Andrea was already at the front desk when I entered the lobby. Even though it was nothing more than a reprieve, a slight stay of execution, I fell into a sofa and sank into it as much as my body would allow me to. After a few moments, Andrea called for me. She didn't use my name, which I thought might've been deliberate. We took the elevator to the thirty-seventh floor, neither of us speaking the entire time. A new melody must've replaced the previous one in her head, the new one more mischievous, filling the elevator with a manic energy.

As I followed her down the hall, I suddenly remembered Ben. I'd forgotten about our lunch. He'd be looking for me - and probably Andrea - come noon. This seemed like a possible out. It might not have been the strongest excuse - and I don't imagine that even at the time I thought it would work - but I tried it anyway. Andrea, unlocking the door with the keycard she was given, took hold of my chin in her gloved hand and told me Ben was taken care of. He was meeting with her professor, she told me, to discuss her internship and submit his evaluations.

The room was a suite overlooking the lake. It had a large sitting area and a separate bedroom, all tastefully decked out in a modern French style.

"What do you think?" she asked, closing the door after she ushered me past her.

"Very nice."

She rolled her eyes and told me I was being trite. Then she removed her scarf and gloves and threw them in my direction. Picking them up from the floor, I asked her if this hotel was where she hosted all of her one woman interventions. Tossing her coat on a garish purple sofa, she smirked a little before walking around and inspecting the room. She said it was perfect. I asked my question again, not sure what I expected or even wanted her to say. Walking over to me, she asked why I thought she'd brought me to this hotel, to this room. My hesitancy made her sit down and get comfortable.

"What do you think my intentions are? I'm curious."

Whatever she was willing me to say sounded good in my head, but was nothing I could bring myself to voice. I settled on quoting her - something she was apparently fond of - when I mentioned her intervention.

"And is it working? Do you feel better just by being in this wonderful suite? I think it's perfect, the perfect place to celebrate the new year."

Andrea explained how she and some of her friends had rented out a room for a New Year's party they'd be hosting. And this was why she'd brought me this morning: to inspect the room. I sat down next to her.

"Right now, yes, it's just a room," she said. "A beautiful, empty space. But come New Year's, it will be awash in toasts and kissing and resolutions. I've always loved New Year's. It's a rejuvenation, isn't it? A starting over. It can be thrilling. What do you think?"

The humiliation I was feeling was tempered with relief. A New Year's party. She was planning a fucking New Year's party. There was no doubt she must've known the assumptions I had. And it must've empowered her. After all, I blindly followed her to a luxury hotel, asking too few questions.

New Year's, I told her, was absurd. I was smiling when I said this. Being a smartass was my way of celebrating a little; I was off the hook, so I figured I could have some fun with her. Not to mention, I did feel the need to retaliate and reclaim some of my dignity.

"In that case," she said, "I hope your invitation goes straight to spam."

"That'd be a real shame," I said, probably more sharply than I had intended, "missing out on all the keg stands and college pranks."

Her mouth went agape in a playful manner as she re-crossed her legs. Her tone, while she assured me how the party would not be a sorority bash, was coy and sophisticated. She added that many attendees would actually be friends she'd recently met at the paper during her internship. Her expression sobered a little when she told me that my wife was also invited.

After a moment of half-hearted sniggers, I rose from my seat and said I had to be going. Handing her the scarf and gloves I'd been holding, I told her the room was lovely and that it would be a fine party. As I made my way to the door, Andrea called out to me that we hadn't yet inspected the bedroom. The concierge, she mentioned, told her she could take her time. She asked if I was interested. The momentum I had achieved in rediscovering my pride couldn't be compromised. I knew this. So I paused a moment before saying what I said next:

"I know you've learned a lot during your time at the paper. Ben, no doubt, has taught you well these past several months. He's a wonderful mentor. And even though the internship is essentially over, here's one more lesson, from me to you, writer to aspiring writer: Avoid, at any and all costs, no matter how tempting it may be, quoting yourself. It's in bad taste."

This was said with some temperance so as to buffer the blow I was hoping it would cause. This girl, I thought, needed to be put in her place. But rather than being defensive, she responded with a confident answer:

"I don't agree, Mr. Loveland," she said, her tone playfully mocking her role as the dutiful pupil. "In fact, in many cases, in *most* cases, quoting yourself, though certainly brash, might be the only time you'll ever hear the sound of your own words in a conversation. It can be thrilling, especially when you sneak them in there just so and watch the reaction of the person you're talking to. Try it sometime."

With the ringing condescension of these last few remarks tolling in my mind, I turned and walked out of the room, and the hotel. Two days later, Andrea finished her internship. I saw very little of her during her last day. She sent me a text that read, simply, "Take care and good luck." There was also a BTW that had her address, which I stared at for a long time before taking a screenshot and then deleting the original message.

• • •

Christmas came and went without even a trace of joie de vivre between me and Laura. We went to her parents' and opened presents and ate and drank and went through the motions of being a family who had something worth celebrating together. I was on the periphery of every tender moment that occurred, which seemed fair penance, and one I could endure with at least some stoicism. My presence was enough of an affront for Laura to tell me, the day after the holiday, that I would not be accompanying her to her family's on New Year's Eve.

"I'd like to be with my parents," she said, "and I'd like to avoid putting them through what we just put them through on Christmas."

"I understand."

"Thank you. I appreciate that."

The effortlessness of the exchange tricked me, for just a moment, into believing that things were peaceful between us. And perhaps they were. But it was peace without honor. It was the kind with long, uneasy silences that might at any moment produce a sudden declaration of war. I knew for certain that if my wife could've caused her own disappearance, a bold and permanent one, that she would've in the blink of an eye.

New Year's Eve found me pulling a disappearing act of my own. I went into the city late in the afternoon and ate at a dirty Thai joint with peeling wallpaper and books of matches used to steady the tables. Then I went to a forgettable movie, through which I fell asleep, and finally some shopping where I picked up some overpriced shirts I didn't need. When I arrived back home, it was close to 9:00 p.m. Laura was gone, but had left a foyer light on for me. As for Glenn's house, it was an imposing black mass of darkness.

My plan was to lie in bed and watch TV before drifting off to sleep. Clad in my pajamas and ready to turn in for the night, I noticed a liter of liquor on the bureau by the window. It was a sight so out of place in my bedroom that I had to walk over to it and hold it just to convince myself that it wasn't an oversized bottle of perfume. It was whiskey. The bottle was a little more than halfway full. And two empty glasses were pushed to the rear of the bureau. They were adjacent to Laura's journal I hadn't seen in months. I sat at the foot of the bed and flipped through its pages. Laura's letters to our unborn daughter. Poetic and personal, the letters were so uplifted with that rare, singular quality of late-night earthy candor, that you're not even sure you recognize it at first. One entry was a whimsical rhyming couplet poem about the kicking sensation she had felt in her belly. One was about deciding on a name. One was a list of twelve reasons why Laura had already fallen in love with the baby. They each started with "because." The first and last one read the same: *Because you're doing a remarkable thing: You're making us a family.*

Pictures Laura had taken of herself when she was pregnant were tucked into a pocket in the rear of the journal. With her eyes averted just slightly from the camera, and her expression demure in all of them, the photos seemed to capture a spirit that was now entirely alien to our lives. Putting the book back on the bureau, I inspected the two empty glasses. They each had smudges around the rim, as well as a few droplets of whiskey that were so slight they were almost clear. I suddenly found myself wondering how and when my bedroom had been turned into a den of alcoholic sentimentality. The thought hadn't yet achieved the gravity it needed to be truly brutal. It was simply bewildering. Like seeing the creases of unanticipated anguish transform the once pleasant face of a loved one. It's an eventual race towards personal dread.

Then I began studying our king-size bed in the middle of the room. It didn't look the same to me. After a moment, I realized what was different. It was the pale blue comforter, which was usually so taut that it resembled a flawless patch of sky. It now lay across the bed in a loose and somewhat wavy fashion. It had to have been disturbed sometime during the day, I thought. Or maybe I sat on the bed at some point. I couldn't remember. I tried, but for the life of me I couldn't remember.

CHAPTER 15

I wasn't there, but I heard it got nasty between the Old Man and Eileen Russo. She made the four hour drive alone from Montpelier to find that her son *was* in fact missing, the local police not terribly sympathetic - they did initiate an "attempt to locate" - and a HAS campus not necessarily in mourning. Words were exchanged outside Rollie's office as students were passing to their next class. Sandra was nearby. She reported that Mrs. Russo was nose-to-nose with my father, shouting that he was a "second-rate overseer" as well as an "asshole." Rollie, according to Sandra, didn't budge, but told her to "please lower her voice." The confrontation ended when the Old Man turned his back on the woman and walked away.

I believed my father when he told me he was apologetic to Eileen. He said it didn't take long for her to find an opening in his vulnerability, wedge her way inside, and trounce on him with the weight of all her grief. He said he thought her grief wasn't even about Nick's disappearance. He seemed to think it was just about Nick, period.

Some think Eileen should've shown up at the HAS earlier. Rollie is among them. He might've told her as much. He's apt to look for signs of neglectfulness in the parents of his students. I think it's his way of cutting his kids some slack - a plea with himself to gather and store the sympathy he seems to think they're entitled to. It's discreet. A sleight of hand, really. Rarely does he offend. Eileen Russo might've been an exception to this.

She chastised the Old Man. Then she went downtown to fill out the proper paperwork at the police station. Next on her agenda was to see Nick's room. The Old Man escorted her himself, watching in silence in the doorway as she perused her son's belongings. According to my father, Eileen, as she fingered through clothing and magazines and basketball cards, vacillated between concern and contempt. She prayed aloud that Nick was all right; then she cursed him up and down for running away. She was optimistic one moment, stating how he'd soon return, unharmed and contrite that he'd caused so much worry; then, in a flash, her mood darkened and she swore the boy was a constant burden, and that he may very well have murdered that poor girl, so it'd be best if he never showed his face again. Almost the moment she uttered this, she was close to tears as she retracted it with sobered authority.

I seemed to have been next on Eileen Russo's itinerary. She finds me at my place just after dinner. I have the night off, which I spend folding laundry and watching *Papillon*. It's raining outside, so I invite her into my kitchen. I can smell liquor and cigarettes on her breath. She tells me I must be Dimitri Ames' replacement and that she's heard about what's happened with him. The pause she takes after saying this suggests she thinks I might gossip and reveal additional details. Instead, I apologize for her son's disappearance.

"It was on *my* watch."

"I know it was," she says, wiping some rain from her forehead.

Eileen Russo is a slender woman with deep blue eyes. She has nice teeth and an even, full-faced tan, and yet she still wears too much makeup. Probably she was attractive ten years ago. Now, though, she looks like a woman who's earned her lines worrying about life's injustices while she babbles herself blind at some dive bar as the local hustlers and whores shoot pool and chase shots and one-up each other's hard luck stories.

"What do you *do* around here in your free time?" she asks, poking her head around the corner to glimpse into the other room.

I tell her she's looking at it. Her top, a thin, low-cut summery thing, is wet with rain. It's sticking to her, and she begins pulling at it. Modesty doesn't seem to be a priority. After she's satisfied with her shirt, she asks if I want to have a drink with her at a tavern she's discovered near her motel. Lying, I tell her I don't drink. She makes a few sarcastic remarks before poking around my place some more. We end up in the TV room together. Before I can offer her a place to sit, she makes herself comfortable.

"I appreciate Rollie not turning Nicky's letter over to the police," she says. "As well as those pictures. What I *don't* appreciate is his implication that my son is a fucking murderer."

Eileen explains how she's reconfirmed for the Old Man that the handwriting on the letter is Nick's. Then she disparages him, threatening to sue the school for defamation of Nick's character and for negligence in losing him. When her tirade runs its course, she settles back into her seat and watches the movie.

"My son is very private," she says, breaking the silence. "So he doesn't tell me everything; and God knows I don't *want* to know everything. But a parent knows how their child feels about things. All sorts of things. It's a special power we have. Sometimes it's the *only* power we have when all our other powers have been stripped from us - when they grow up or shut you out of their lives."

She asks if I have any children of my own.

"No."

"You're still young," she says, smiling.

"It doesn't feel that way lately."

"If you ever do have children, you'll understand what I mean. Your father knows. He knows for sure."

Smiling some more and pulling again at her shirt, Eileen tells me that her son was in love with Nicole D'Ambrosio and that there was no way he would've hurt her.

"I just can't help but feel like someone owes me," she says, sighing. "I know how that sounds, but it's how I feel."

There isn't much for me to say. Probably I'm not taking the time to consider her plight and what she's entitled to. She makes it a point to ask me. She asks if I think she's entitled to *something*. I tell her she is. Pulling at her shirt some more, Eileen asks where my bathroom is before excusing herself.

I finish folding my laundry. Then I sit back and watch *Papillion*. The famous scene is approaching where Steve McQueen jumps off the cliff. This feat, I remember reading, was performed by the actor without a stunt double. Such balls. Balls of galvanized steel. Balls I wonder if I'll ever possess.

Just as I'm considering my balls, Eileen Russo walks into the room without a stitch of clothing on her body. The first thing she does is draw the blinds, which are opened slightly. The expression on her face seems inquisitive. It's as though she isn't entirely sure she's nude and needs me to confirm it for her. I take a quick glance at the TV - McQueen has just thrown his makeshift raft from the cliff - and then back to Eileen. She has a good body. It's toned and tanned and completely hairless. Her breasts are larger than I imagined. She walks over and straddles me. Neither of us say a word. Her expression turns meditative. Before I know what I'm doing, I have my arms around her and am pulling her into me. And though I can't see the TV, I can tell by the film score that McQueen has made the jump.

• • •

The phone wakes me up at around 10:00 p.m. Stumbling in the dark, I answer by the fourth ring. It's Austin Roarick.

"We probably need to talk," he says. "Not now. But at some point. Don't you think?"

I'm still processing who it is, so I don't answer him.

"Maybe you think I owe you an apology," he says, "and maybe I do. Maybe I was being presumptuous in involving you in that matter the other day."

"Okay."

"So for that, I apologize."

"Fine."

"But I know you'd understand if you knew the...the full scope of this thing. *You* more than anyone. I know how that sounds. We don't know each other well, but there's common ground with us."

He pauses.

"You saw how J.R. talked to me."

"What were you doing in my dorm?"

"Not now. We'll talk. But not now."

"What do you want to talk about?"

He pauses again.

"Lot of things. Business opportunities. The common ground we share. And you, Gray. I want to talk about *you*, and the look you have when you're at that place. I know that look. I bet you even have it right now at this exact moment. But you may not even know it. It could be creeping in and taking over. And I might be able to help you stop it."

"What the hell are you talking about, Austin? Listen—"

"Not now. We'll talk."

Within a few moments of hanging up, there comes a knocking at my door. So there's barely time to process the odd nature of the phone call. It takes a moment for me to realize where the knocking is coming from. It's at my door leading into the dormitory. Quickly, I check on Eileen. She's still asleep, splayed out on the futon, wearing only her black bra and underwear. After I put on my clothes, I open the door to Ryan, who wastes no time in telling me that my father has just been taken to Yale-New Haven Hospital. He holds up a scrap of paper for me to take. It has the necessary information on it. Barely awake and still adjusting to the light, I yawn and accept the paper. My reaction to what he's told me probably seems too tame. So I begin to explain how I'm having a lazy night, watching TV and napping. But Ryan, in a brusque tone I've never heard from him - even when he speaks to the kids - tells me to get myself together, get rid of my *guest*, and to make the drive into the city.

• • •

The following day brings with it pleasant weather. The sky is clear and the sun is already hot by 8:00 a.m. A thin wafer of moon hangs in the morning sky. Beads of rain from the previous night hover on blades of grass, making them into armless stick figures. The Homer House boys are in typical form during breakfast. Noah and J.J. flick bits of cereal at Albert's head. Cal announces to everyone that he's convinced Cliff never washes his hair, and that his bottle of shampoo is probably semen collected from his many notorious bouts with himself. Andrew, cursing daylight and breakfast and the HAS, sits miserably in his chair, his arms folded across his chest in defiance. Ryan ignores all of this. He's been trying to initiate a conversation with me and get news on the Old Man's condition. When he finally manages his question, he asks it with the sincerity of a Boy Scout. Christ, he even looks like a Boy Scout. Maybe it's the bright lights on his still boyish face, or maybe it's how his eyes widen a little and his forehead rolls back, revealing a concern that's been toiled over and now at last needs satisfying. I can see a subtle gloom hiding behind his eyes, a gloom that's real and brought about by devotion to my father. It makes my stomach drop.

"He's okay."

"What happened?"

"They're not sure."

"What'd the doctors say?"

I can tell by his tone, soft and appeasing, that if I'm firm enough with him, the matter will be dropped.

"That he needs to rest."

Excusing myself, I leave my breakfast mostly untouched and head over to my classroom where I make a CLASSES CANCELLED sign that I tape to the door. Whatever the consequences might be for this seems unimportant to me. The students will find something to do. Some, after rejoicing, might break back into their dorms and go to sleep. Others will fish out their cigarettes and retreat to the woods for some morning respite.

Without a plan or destination, I get in my car and drive. I pass through the center of town and out into some remote neighborhoods I tramped through while growing up. The houses I once knew from parties and old friends bear an unwelcoming look. The maintenance and restoration they've endured through the years - the freshly sealed driveways, the bountiful new gardens, the modest additions - show off just enough proud change to make me feel like I've missed something by not witnessing their progress.

It's hard to know how to feel about Old Brookview. And now, with this summer, it's even harder. I tell myself I should resent it. Dismiss it. Neglect it. This is too easy. So I challenge myself for brief moments to feel the weight of nostalgia and joy and regret. I feel like I need to finally have a conversation with someone about the responsibility one has for his hometown - and the responsibility it has for him. This is a conversation I've never had before, and one I've rarely considered through the years. Until now - now, when it suddenly seems like an important conversation to have.

I find myself pulling into the winding dirt driveway of Saint Stephen's Cemetery on Horsepond Road, a rural little snippet of road that bends around one of Old Brookview's newer and more posh developments. It's been years since I've been here. Probably the last time was before I left the

Northeast for good. The cemetery lawn is green and trim; beds of sunflowers and stained wooden benches line the narrow drive.

My mother's site is easy to find. It lies in the middle of the first row of graves on the northernmost tip of the graveyard. I recall the Old Man, on more than one occasion, bragging about this location. It was perfect, he'd tell me. Her summer view, he would say, was of those big-faced sunflowers. As I walk towards her gravesite, I can see a bouquet resting against the black speckled stone. They're white lilies. Only somewhat wilted and worn, they look a mere two or three days old. The site is kept clean. Its grass looks healthy and fed. The stone itself is attractive. With its pristine gloss and rounded corners, it stands out among the dull, faded, and forgotten ones.

It's easy to imagine my father making regular visits here. He probably gets dressed up in one of his clean collared shirts and fancy ties. He wouldn't mind getting on his knees to pull up any crabgrass or wipe away leaves and moss that might've gathered at the base of the headstone. Then he probably rests the bouquet in an upright position. There might be a list he's brought with topics to discuss and news to tell. There would be no maudlin pleas or fits of wild temperament. Sure, he may smile over some memory of shared youth and rebellion he'd muse on with restrained fervor, but he'd keep it together. These visits, he'd tell himself, must always be pleasant. They're all he has left of my mother. So there'd be no room for bouts of mercurial behavior.

As for me, where my mother is concerned, I don't ever feel on the verge of some breakdown, or that I'm readying myself for a headfirst dive into a pool of self-pity. I handle it. Which is not to say that I don't have thoughts about what could've been or should've been. Here's one: What kind of son would I have turned out to be if my mother had lived? There's always a bit of guilt that accompanies this thought. It seems selfish. Like I should be contemplating her memory, or legacy, or the void she left in the world, or in our family, or if there's an afterlife and whether she's now a baby or a butterfly, or if there's a heaven, and if she's in it, and what her celestial charge might be. Thinking about what type of son I might've been always ends up being a fleeting thought. Probably since it's too painful to think about the son I actually *am*.

An elderly man kneels in front of a modest headstone a hundred or so feet away from me. I can hear him speaking to his loved one as he wipes his brow with a handkerchief. The sun is hot and the air is still with barely a morning breeze. I find myself trying to listen to what the man is saying as though I'm in need of my own inspiration. The truth is that I'm not sure what to say - or if I'm supposed to say anything. Perhaps being here is enough. It might be self-consciousness or a lack of imagination. It might be that I'm terrified of what might come out. Or that I'm terrified that *nothing* will come out.

Despite the anarchy in my mind, I begin speaking. I start with an acknowledgment that I don't know what to say. That takes only a moment. Then I pause a bit before commenting on the weather. Then, as though the sunlight takes aim at my uncertainty, barriers begin to be burned away. I begin talking to my mother. I talk about the HAS and Old Brookview; I tell her I'm working for the Old Man, which seems as miraculous as anything. I talk about memories I've been told we have from those first three years of my life - our heady conversations on *The Wizard of Oz*; her homemade cornbread I apparently helped make; our equaled enthusiasm for Halloween. Illinois comes up. So does Laura. And my job at the paper and my move back east. Then I pause for a moment and look around. The elderly man has gone.

"Laura got pregnant," I say aloud. "It took us a while, but she got pregnant. She loved the way it made her feel. She wasn't one of those complaining pregnant women; she was grateful and overjoyed, which, to me, seems the right way to feel."

A troupe of black-bellied birds fly overhead. Splayed out against the sky, they look like a spray of aimless buckshot. There's more to tell my mother. So I get as comfortable as I can and continue. The foreignness of the moment is overwhelming. But I continue. My voice has a strange atonal quality to it.

I know for certain that I won't be telling my father I was here, that I saw this place and the blackbirds and his white lilies and had a heart-to-heart with my mother, who's been gone for thirty years of my life. He would dwell on it for sure. And have countless questions over what led me to this place on this day. Besides, there would be another matter to discuss with him, a matter I was not at all looking forward to.

• • •

The next couple of days drift by in a sort of languid haze. Rollie returns to the HAS, is greeted with modest fanfare for his good health, and resumes his role as patriarch. I hear him tell his story over and over again, unassumingly, and to anyone who asks. But to me it's old news. I learned it before anyone else did a few evenings back when I called the hospital during my drive into New Haven. He was treated for exhaustion. It was hardly life-threatening. The staff and students, when they hear this, express their relief. When I first heard it, from a nurse named Diana, as I was pulled off the interstate, I barely contemplated a moment before I drove to a shitty black brick tavern called Bebe's where I nursed beer after beer while observing the regulars play bar trivia.

Upon his return to the school, my father doesn't bother tracking me down. Not to mention Ryan never says a word to me about Eileen Russo, who eats lunch one afternoon at the Old Man's table before her departure back to Montpelier. She leaves without so much as a word to me. Even by Hundred Acre School standards, this lack of accountability seems odd. No admonishments for canceling my classes the day following the Old Man's hospitalization. No preachy lectures imbued with dense philosophical rhetoric from my father. And no word from Eileen Russo about whether or not she now feels compensated for her many troubles. I'm not certain whether I should be grateful or wary. All of this indifference feels like a conspiracy. Like everyone's gathered and put to vote whether or not Gray is worthy of their time. The consensus might be that he's not, that he's just a mirage projected from the past of this place, cast out into a temporary space and time; and one that might dissolve if ignored long enough.

• • •

Matt and Adam call out to me the weekend following Rollie's return to the HAS. Covered in smears of black grease, they are hauling engine parts back to their dorm when they spot me on my way to the dining hall to grab some breakfast.

"Did you hear about our good friend?" Adam asks.

"Our good friend?"

"The one who likes young girls a little too much," Adam says, looking gingerly at Matt.

"What happened?"

Matt takes over the story. Dimitri Ames has been arrested, he beams. He was picked up in the northwest part of the state. The Litchfield County

Sheriff's Department apprehended Ames in a sporting goods store after he tried to purchase a paddle board with a stolen check. Since the check was from a resident of Old Brookview, its authorities were notified. Word of the arrest got back to the HAS through Officer Bagley, who knew Rollie's prior dealings and suspicions where Ames was concerned.

Relief suddenly washes over me since I know the Old Man will now be preoccupied with this new Ames situation rather than the disappointment he feels over the fuck-up he has for a son. The temptation to say the wrong thing, to gloat even, is too great. So I pause myself, step back from the boys a little, and ask what they're doing with the engine parts.

"Take a guess," Adam says, motioning to the Winnebago, which rests in its usual spot alongside the Virginia II schoolhouse.

Its hood is open and spark plugs and connecting rods and pistons are neatly laid out on a blue tarp in front of it.

"My father gave you lunatics the green light?"

"Not only that," Matt tells me, "but a decent budget for repairs."

"You guys are just swimming in good news today."

Adam sums up the matter nicely:

"It's about fucking time."

• • •

Nussbaum finds me that evening during an outdoor basketball game between the Missouri House girls and the Homer House boys, who've accepted a challenge and are now losing by close to twenty points. He's anxious to talk about the Ames saga. Speaking briskly as we pace up and down the sidelines of the court, he times the volume of his voice with the cheers of the game's onlookers. Pulling me away from the crowd, he tells me that the authorities, since the arrest, are leaning on Ames over the Nicole D'Ambrosio case. They know the girl's approximate time of death and are thus looking into Ames' whereabouts during this window. Working against him is his joblessness. Ames, having recently been fired from the Hundred Acre School, now has to come up with an alibi.

"This is the break we've been waiting for," he says.

A girl from the Missouri House makes a shot she claims is a three-pointer. This is immediately debated by the boys. An argument erupts.

Nussbaum, ignoring the melee, says how much the Old Man is looking forward to owning the school. It's in the works, he tells me, and will soon be finalized.

"Who knows where your father would be if it weren't for this place?"

He surveys the grounds with a prideful gleam in his eyes. The argument escalates between the boys and girls. Supporters for both are on the court, raising their voices, swearing, drawing imaginary lines on the asphalt with their feet.

"Honestly," he added before heading towards the dispute, "I think sometimes it's all he's got."

• • •

Two more days pass and my father and I still haven't spoken. We see plenty of one another from a distance - at the dining hall, at staff meetings, around campus – but we maintain our own space. I've staged a few brief conversations in my head, yet they just swoosh around like puddles trapped in a shallow divot. There's no doubt I owe him an explanation for the night he was rushed to the hospital. But, like Eileen Russo, I feel entitled to something as well. I'm just not sure what.

I have visions of packing up, sneaking out in the middle of the night, and forever leaving the Old Man to his chaos. At least then there won't have to be any talking. We'd each settle into our own lives, and whatever debts we felt towards one another would be forgiven with enough time and indifference.

Then something happens. Something that brings him to my door one evening just as I'm finishing off a bottle of wine.

"Are you drunk?"

Relieved that it's him who speaks first, I offer him a brief smile before inviting him inside. He looks well. His hair, which is combed back and styled, looks like it might've been cut earlier in the day. He carries himself with the strength and purpose of a general.

"Well?"

"No, I'm not drunk. Just relaxing on my night off."

"Good. Because it's important you're sober for this. We had a visitor earlier today. A girl named Paige Vickerman - a close friend to Nicole D'Ambrosio."

The girl, he tells me, had accompanied Nicole's parents when they paid a visit to the Old Man the evening of the school's talent show.

"The night Nick disappeared," he adds.

Paige had come alone this time. And she brought some tragic news with her. A friend of hers and Nicole's, a boy named Quinton Sandrey, overdosed the previous night and died in his sleep. His parents found him in his bed this morning. According to Paige, Quinton was popular. It's true that he was a regular in the principal's office, as well as being no stranger to Old Brookview's law enforcement, but he was still regarded as a kid with a future. He played lacrosse and was supposedly being looked at by Rutgers. He dated pretty girls and had friends and a stable family life and even the nagging distinction of being the only boy in his class to have appeared regularly on the cover of various clothing catalogs. He modeled professionally during his middle school years, giving it up when he was old enough to consider it too emasculative. Nevertheless, it affectionately earned him the nickname "GQ" among his peers.

A brief pause allows me to absorb the surprise I feel over the Old Man's talk not being a father/son one. It's equally surprising that the news isn't related to the school.

"This town must be cursed," I said.

"Well, it's rallying right now from what Paige told me. Quinton's friends are coming together to show their support. From what the girl told me, they're working around the clock to keep the family in meals for as long as they can."

"What the hell kind of consolation is that for losing a child? I've never understood that."

"There's more."

Paige told Rollie about the drug problem in her school, *my* old high school. There are the potheads, the most timeless faction. Content to come to class high on occasion, they space out, sneak food, and scribble images of retro bands on the legs of their faded jeans.

There are the elitists, a group who not only have the funds to buy the more expensive drugs, but the connections to do as well. They dabble in ecstasy, cocaine, even heroin. These kids are often honor roll students who call their parents by their first names, drive pristine hand-me-down Mercedes, and have tanning beds in their houses.

And there are the more experimental kids. They trade pills and take obscene amounts of acid and create their own hybrids out of whatever they can find in their parents' medicine cabinet. Usually athletes or adrenaline junkies of some sort, this group cares about appearances. Which speaks to their preferred method of ingesting mostly legal drugs. It's this last group of which Quinton was a part.

"A drug of choice for a lot of these kids is Amitriptyline," says the Old Man, "which is found in antidepressants. You see where I'm going with this?"

"I think so."

"Paige told me that she and some of her friends, on several occasions, would go downtown to buy pills from none other than Mr. Nick Russo. That's how he met Nicole."

Nick, my father reminds me, had his downtown privileges. So it was hardly a feat for him to set up a modest enterprise and make a few bucks off these local kids who probably regarded him as some sort of adolescent outlaw.

"Where do you think he's getting his supply from?" I said.

"Good question."

"And I wonder how modest of an enterprise it was - or still *is*."

"I asked Paige the same question."

In Rollie's mind, Nick's disappearance is related strictly to Nicole's murder. He considered that the boy was too devastated to cope with the loss, or else he was guilty of the crime. But now, it's just as plausible that Nick wants to be unfettered so he can continue with his business venture.

"Paige had something to say about this right away," says the Old Man. "She told me that when Nick and Nicole began seeing one another, which started about six months ago, he stopped selling almost immediately."

"Do you believe that?"

He shrugs his shoulders.

"She also assured me that she hasn't seen him in weeks."

We stand there in my kitchen for a few moments, neither of us saying a word.

"That's it. Just thought you should know. You're his dorm staff, after all."

Just as he turns to go, I ask how he's feeling. Without missing a beat, he says he's feeling like for the first time in nearly a decade that he needs a vacation.

"You should take one. God knows you should take one. Go lie on a beach somewhere and have a couple of cocktails. This place—"

I suddenly interrupt myself, clearing my throat a few times before starting and stopping meaningless sentences. After a bit of this, I come out with it, revealing to my father that I was banging Eileen Russo as he was being rushed to the hospital, that I don't know for sure how it could've happened, or why I did it, but it happened nonetheless.

"I'm not proud of it. And I'm not even sure why I'm telling you."

There's no doubt, I admit, that he has more important things on his mind. His mouth, as I speak, forms into a little "o," and he absently nods his head every so often. He appears neither stunned nor disgusted over my admission. There's more, though. There's the part that concerns the two of us, the part where I didn't show up at the hospital, and instead found a bar where I got drunk enough to forgive my selfishness. That's the part he must be waiting for me to get to.

"As far as why I never came: I don't exactly know."

Folding his arms against his chest, the Old Man clears his throat a few times. Then he fills his cheeks with air for a few seconds before exhaling.

"Well, when you do know, maybe we can talk. Really talk. Not just about that, but about everything. Because I think we're past due, don't you?"

"I suppose so."

"You suppose so?"

"I think we could stand to talk, yes."

"Good," he says, walking past me and out onto the porch. "And as far as banging Eileen Russo, at least you're surrounded by licensed therapists who can help you deal with the post traumatic stress of *that* ordeal."

Then he snickers a little before walking away. Later that evening, as I settle down to sleep, I begin to think about the Sandrey family and whether they're eating the food that's being brought to them. Then my mind drifts to how and when the bereaved get hungry. And the practice of offering them food. It isn't a matter of understanding the practice; I understand it perfectly well. The assumption is that the grief-stricken cannot be bothered with trivial domestic chores such as cooking. They're expected to dedicate themselves fully to their sorrow. What intrigues me about this is that it seems like, in times of great loss, it's become the most offered and accepted form of solace. No one wants speeches or psalms or empathy when their world's brains have been bludgeoned. With all the ways humans pride themselves on how sophisticated they are, really, when it comes down to it, words and gestures can't compare with a noodle casserole or eggplant parmesan. We may walk upright and speak with fire and eloquence; hell, we may play golf and chess and eat other species, but we're as primitive as jackasses when it comes to coping with loss and offering condolences. Take your poets and priests, your philosophers and therapists, and put them side-by-side with food for the bereaved - maybe a fancy dish; maybe a simple one; maybe one with carefully chosen and expensive ingredients; maybe one made with what's left in the cupboards. Either way, the food will win out. Always. It has a certain logic to it. A comfort. A simplicity. And it'll always win out.

I wonder about Quinton Sandrey's neighbors and family friends, and if any of them are good cooks. That raises an important issue as to whether or not the offerings can be procured from a business. Is the gesture rendered futile if they are? Does the giver need to toil in the kitchen for endless hours to truly show their support? It seems absurd, but all I can hope for is that the family will score some halfway decent meals. Ones that will keep for a while. Maybe chili and chicken curry and stir-fry and pasta. And I hope that they won't have to worry about returning kitchenware. Then I think of Nicole D'Ambrosio's family, and I hope the same for them during the fresh horror of their own tragedy.

Exhausted, but unable to fall asleep, my thoughts turn to Laura's and my loss. The vividness of the ordeal is decked out in such bright remembrances that it seems like it's compacted into a handful of hours that happened earlier in the day. I recall Laura being well taken care of. For months, it seems, she had the compassion of an ever bustling society of siblings and coworkers, and, mostly, her parents. When she wasn't being whisked away to a spa or salon or shopping spree, her phone rang incessantly. As did our doorbell. Strange cars were often parked in the driveway. And, of course, there was the food. Sweet potato casserole. Chicken piccata. Mushroom stroganoff. Lovingly sealed in blue and pink and clear plastic Tupperware, it was all for her. I never actually watched her eat any of it, but I saw the before, which was the fresh, hearty, untouched food, covered securely and stored neatly in the fridge, and then the after, which was an empty container, soaking in a bath of cool, soapy water and its own crumbs. I don't know what you have to do or who you have to be to get offered food in a situation like that. It's true that I made some selfish decisions, and that I concealed what happened from my own father, and that I became closed off and embarrassed, and at times cruel, but hell, I was hungry, too.

CHAPTER 16

I must've lost count or lost interest, but either way, I stopped keeping track of how long it had been since Laura and I had sex with one another. Eventually, for some reason, the matter stopped being depressing. Time fell through the air in dangerous acrobatic twists, and its crash landing made it and everything around it unrecognizable. So the lack of intimacy became the norm.

"Seduce her, for Christ's sake," Ben said over the phone one evening. "Do I really have to go through this with you?"

There was no levity in his voice when he said this. It was evident that he was becoming worried over my situation.

"Candles, music, whatever. Or a getaway. What about a getaway?"

I reminded Ben about my last attempt at this; the tickets I bought to Key West went unused, costing me over $1,000. He paused. I could hear Justine in the background.

"Listen, I'm not saying the sex is everything," he finally said, "but its absence is pretty serious."

Laura's birthday was at the end of the month, I told him. Maybe I could plan a party. I could rent out a space and get her family and coworkers and friends in on it. Then at the evening's end I could capitalize on her joy, and, possibly, with some luck, break our slump. Ben, I could tell, had muted his phone and was likely talking with Justine. Probably he was running my idea by her. When he returned to our conversation, he sighed and told me that my idea was a decent one. With his terseness and tired tone, I barely believed him.

• • •

Of course I thought of my father when I made an appointment with a therapist. His name was Dr. Jerome Forrest and I learned about him from Ben's sister-in-law, who described him to me in a text as her "pocket sized savior." In parenthesis, she revealed that the doctor barely scraped by at being five feet tall. My appointment was for a Wednesday afternoon. I called his office three times in two days to verify the details - the day, the time, the building. Dr. Forrest's secretary identified herself to me as his wife, Shannon. She was tolerant and even good-natured over my obsessiveness. During the third call, I told Shannon I grew up with therapists all around my neighborhood. She joked that as a result I must be exceedingly well-adjusted. Initially missing the joke, I told her I was. Then, forgetting I was speaking to his wife, I began asking questions about the doctor. Was he any good? Where did he attend school? Was he as short as the rumor said he was? Shannon advised me to visit his website and said they looked forward to meeting me in person.

The notion of therapy was surreal to me. These men and women were not mystics or magicians. They were fellow human beings who had enough ego to consider themselves capable of helping someone too fucked up to help himself. They had read some books and taken some classes. That's all.

I started to think about the therapists I knew while I was growing up. There had been a lot of them. The gregarious Dr. Homer Wald's legacy lives on in the dorm whose name he inspired. Dr. Whitaker was a pale yet pretty woman who always wore her reddish hair in a tight bun that made me think of a ripening tomato; I secretly wished she and Rollie would marry. Dr. Lawrynowicz was a deep-voiced, heavyset man who was always looking for his glasses, clipboard, or keys. Dr. Nussbaum was and still is my father's commandant. Dr. Hines, who used to call me Graymalkin, won a few bucks on Jeopardy in his mid-twenties and liked to mock this long-faded triumph.

I thought about the human suffering they all must've been privy to, the abuse and neglect and despair and hopelessness. I wondered how that might've affected their state of mind and how they elicited such weighty matters from teenagers; they needed a special power to establish that type of trust. There's no doubt that I regarded the therapists differently than I did the rest of the Old Man's staff. To me, this elite group of bookish men and women with glasses and dated wardrobes and sincere, understanding smiles, were pathetically brave. They were stuntmen and stuntwomen, hurling themselves into wreck after wreck with full creative force, stepping brilliantly to the dysfunction, not sideswiping it, but taming it and naming it and learning how to master it somehow.

The same could be said for my father, who I began to think a lot about during this time. Not only him, but his school and his kids. I found myself tramping through the HAS campus in my mind, remembering the scent of cigarette smoke when the wind gusted in a certain direction, recalling the stares of suspicious students as I talked to my father outside of his office. It was remarkable for me to consider that I shared meals with kids my own age who had done heroin, attempted suicide, pierced their nipples, bartered with sex, told their parents and teachers to die.

"How does it work?" I asked Ben. "Do I just start talking? Or is it Q and A? Will he ask about my fucking childhood?"

"How am I supposed to know? I've never been fucked up enough to need therapy. But in the movies there are always head games between patient and doctor. So *there's* something to look forward to."

His joking was just what I needed. I was becoming anxious about the appointment. But Dr. Forrest's stats all looked good. He was well-educated and qualified and was a handsome man to look at. He took nearly every type of insurance and his website was accessible. Still, I didn't know what to expect. What would I say during our first session together? Where would I begin? How much would I reveal? Would the onus be more on the doctor or patient? Something else I thought about was whether or not I would lie. I truly thought about this. And it made me more anxious. It made me feel like whatever truths I had to offer might not be enough - that they might vilify me in the doctor's eyes. They might cause Dr. Forrest to judge me and side with Laura and her parents and friends and coworkers and even the fucking strangers Laura had probably won over as allies. Then I began to get angry. Calculating the money this guy would make off of me when he couldn't even see my position infuriated me all the more. I told Ben over the phone one evening that I thought therapy was a bunch of shit.

"Well," he said, "come Wednesday, you'll find out for sure."

His memory of my appointment was both impressive and suspicious to me. Clearly, he was a good listener, remembering small details - two things I'd always known about Ben - but something told me he was keeping track of this thing. There was no doubt that he was relieved I'd made the appointment. He joked that it would free up a lot of his own time. On a serious note, he said it would do me a world of good. But I began to think those were euphemisms for his real sentiments, which might've been that I had fucked up my life and my marriage and another human being. Fucked them up beyond repair, so why not get a jump start on the therapy. I imagined him talking to Justine about it, saying things like, *"Poor Laura,"* and, *"Well, you know Gray. You know how he is and how he likes everything in his life - flawless and up to his unbelievably impossible standards."* I called Dr. Forrest's office two hours before the appointment and cancelled.

. . .

Wildfire was the only restaurant I considered for Laura's party. I'd never been and it was out of my price range. The menu was high-end and the place looked nice enough online. The thought of being cheap and shopping around for the venue that would host my attempt at reconciliation was depressing. So I gave the man my credit card number over the phone and booked it.

"Sounds too fancy," Luke said when I told him my idea. "Too much pomp and circumstance. Laura's not going to want all that."

"Want all what?"

"Laura doesn't like surprises."

I recognized right away what he was doing. He was trying to make me question how well I knew my wife. This business of not liking surprises wasn't at all true. I didn't argue. We hung up the phone and I called back a few hours later and spoke with Abby.

"What can we do?"

I asked her for a list of friends and coworkers and their contact info. The guest list, along with everything else, would be my responsibility, I told her.

"Just tell the rest of the family," I said. "That's it."

And pray that my efforts aren't in vain, I wanted to add. Before we got off the phone, I thought about telling Abby that I loved her. I had never done so before. My affection wouldn't have been misplaced, but I thought it might come off as pandering. So I just thanked her before hanging up. Then I felt a pang of regret that I wasn't more demonstrative. So I wrote out a brief text that read, "Thanks for everything. Looking forward to seeing you both. We love you very much." Staring at my words for a few moments, I ended up deleting the last sentence before sending the message.

. . .

"Have you thought about moving?" Ben asked during lunch one afternoon.

This was like a boulder flung from space, landing at my feet. He said it was something to consider, that it would foster the new beginning I was looking to establish between me and Laura. I liked the idea so much, without needing even a moment to contemplate its magnitude, that I managed to convince myself I had been the one to come up with it.

"Stands to reason," he said. "You're working on getting your head on straight, right? Might as well deck this thing out with other changes, too. Besides, how attached to that house are you?"

Ben didn't know I cancelled my appointment with Dr. Forrest. I wanted him to believe I was the kind of man who could buy into something like therapy, especially for the purpose of saving my marriage. He called me that Wednesday evening, hours after he figured my first session had ended, and asked if I was okay. Nothing more. Just if I was okay. I said I was fine and that I appreciated the call. For a moment, I thought about lying and saying generic things like how cathartic it was; or detailed things like Dr. Forrest twirled his pen while I talked; or hopeful things like Dr. Forrest was able to perfectly articulate the type of relationship he feels Laura and I have.

"I suppose we're not *that* attached. It is just a house. I mean, if things had gone according to plan, who knows?"

"If things had gone according to plan, we wouldn't be having this conversation."

Lately, Ben had grown a bit harsh with me. Even his sarcasm had an edge to it. It was often delivered in quick, solemn bursts of words that always seemed chewed up and spit out with ragged intent. Even the polite grins that used to accompany his remarks soon gave way to no eye contact or affect - or worse, a sort of stoic indifference I had no problem detecting in him. I told myself it was because he was in a rush for me and my wife to fix what had become broken. That he was worried and wanting only the best for me, which he decided must've been Laura. I told myself it was *not* because he was harboring some very real contempt towards me that he would show through such meager gestures.

There was the Cadman Brothers disaster. There was the shortage of neighbors. There was the 3200-square-foot home with only two people occupying it, absently floating from room to room, hoping the largeness of the place would be enough to contain their burdens, wondering if the other was at home, praying at times that they wouldn't be, but terminally aching when they weren't. I imagined us once again living in the city. This appealed to me. People. Culture. Distractions. A return to our roots. When things were simpler. When they were free from the signposts of heavy responsibility.

I found a townhouse on Milwaukee Avenue. The online photos were impressive. With its freshly painted rooms and refinished oak floors, it was described as move-in condition. There was another one, on N. Lakeview, with generous walk-in closets, a newly remodeled kitchen, and high ceilings. Then there was the one on E. 13th Street. With its views of the lake and harbor and Museum Campus, the doorman building unit had granite countertops and cherry maple hardwood. It had Laura's taste all over it. I arranged for a private showing with my checkbook in my back pocket. After the tour, the realtor, Janet, an attractive fifty-ish woman with blonde highlighted hair and a pretty smile, told me the place would be sold by the end of the week. Looking out of the living room terrace at the cold, dark water of Lake Michigan, I suddenly felt a calm wash over me that I hadn't felt in a long time. It was a complete feeling. Like my nerves had been rewired by the high altitude of the apartment. I suddenly didn't give a shit about the past or the future or whether fate had driven me here to this spot on this day, or if Janet herself was some sort of alchemist who had altered my consciousness by advertising such a nice place and luring me to it.

I asked for her pen and wrote a check for the $5,000 deposit. She told me I was a smart man. Letting the flattery settle for a moment, I cleared my throat and stumbled for a bit, trying to get some words out. Janet, probably in an act of deference, avoided eye contact as she looked at her leather folio and slid my check inside. Then she flashed a warm, inviting look, which told me I was cleared to speak. So I asked her, with as much savvy as I could muster, if, assuming special circumstances, the money was refundable.

• • •

"This is wonderful," Laura kept saying throughout the evening.

As her guests approached her, she would embrace them and say how she was glad to see them. Then she would add, to no one in particular, how nice it all was, the restaurant, the company, the food. Yet she never once turned to me as I followed her around like some idiot schoolboy, overseeing her affection towards others. I kept at it, though, staying close to her side, shaking hands with the husbands of her coworkers and friends, men I'd met on occasion at previous gatherings, asking banal questions about what they did for a living and if they thought we'd really be getting that big snowstorm predicted for the upcoming week.

As the evening wore on, Laura and I eventually separated. I gravitated towards the bar, and she continued to work the room, soaking up as much good cheer as she could. I found myself watching her interactions, hoping she would turn suddenly away from her conversation and call for me to come to her side once again. Or that she would at least take pause for a moment, search the room, point me out to her friends, and raise her glass to me with a thankful smile.

Ben and Justine couldn't make it - both of their girls had food poisoning - so I was on my own. There would be no one to clap me on the back in front of Laura and tell me I was one hell of a guy for putting this thing together for my wife. It was pathetic that I needed this. But its simplicity would've been a starting point for me and Laura. Instead, I had to endure the imagined scrutiny I figured I was under from everyone in the room. They all knew about me. They knew I was the one responsible for the hard to define thing that had happened to my wife. They knew. *A party*, they must've thought. *A party as consolation. What a guy.*

Abby found me by the bar at around the time I began to feel a buzz from the four beers I had. She ordered a couple of glasses of white wine. I told her she looked lovely, which was the truth. Her hair was shorter than it was the last time I saw her, and it was pulled away from her face in a tortoise shell hair clip. She wore a little makeup, which I decided was uncommon for her. It was all very becoming.

Considering whether Laura would look like Abby in twenty or thirty years was always something I liked to do. It pleased me to think that she would. And for some reason it made me feel closer to Abby. But looking at my mother-in-law now made me wonder if I'd ever be able to find out this potential likeness for myself.

She greeted me with a light rub to my shoulder. I wanted to tell her how I was happy to have her in my life and how I enjoyed not subscribing to all those stale, unfunny jokes that were supposed to define our relationship. Instead, I complimented her appearance and thanked her for coming to the party.

"You did a terrific job, Gray. She's having a wonderful time."

There was a trace of melancholy in her voice when she said this.

"Good. I'm glad."

The bartender presented two glasses and handed them to Abby. There was no one else in line at the bar, so we stood there for a few moments, neither of us speaking. Finally, after some time, Abby took the wine and turned to me with an earnest look. She pursed her lips and then took a deep breath.

"We miss you, Gray," she said before kissing my cheek and walking away.

This arrested my beer buzz almost immediately. I wondered if Laura was among the "we" who had missed me. And if conversations had taken place where I was mentioned in a nostalgic light. Perhaps she was planning a seduction of her own. Any thoughts that Abby's comment was obligatory were disregarded with a shudder as I asked the bartender for my fifth beer. My mother-in-law's sentiment, I reasoned, was a portentous gesture, a carefully thought-out offering. I told myself it must've been not only Laura's humble message being delivered by her magnanimous mother, but a quiet plea for me to once and for all embrace and live by the rectitude of this thing called family.

Just as I was sorting this all out, I heard a man's voice, a familiar one, cut above the rest of the voices in the room. The voice was proud and commanding. Like it was pleased over how it sounded, and wanted others to be pleased as well. As I scanned the room, I had the feeling that my head had just been emptied of the thoughts it had contained only seconds earlier. And then when I spotted Glenn Kilburn by the L-shaped buffet table, I was certain that what Abby had said to me was as meaningless as my efforts would prove to be for the evening.

He was talking to two of Luke's friends, men I had briefly met a few times through the years. They were all laughing and getting the attention of those around them. Glenn was wearing a dark navy suit with a royal blue dress shirt and no tie. He was now clean shaven, and I could see, even from faraway, that his hair, which never warranted much notice, was neatly combed and parted meticulously to the side.

The bartender, I realized from his tone, had been trying to hand me my beer. I took it and drank. And I watched Glenn. The men he talked with seemed rapt by whatever he was saying. There was no doubt that Glenn was a talker. A real connoisseur of conversation. He was a doctor. And probably a well-traveled doctor. He would have stories of Morocco and miracles and medicine. Taking another good long sip, I made my way towards my neighbor and his entourage.

"*Here's* the party planner," Glenn said when he saw me approach.

We shook hands, all the while his remark searing itself into my brain. I *am* the goddamn party planner, I thought to myself. He told me I looked well before stating that I must know Ron and Ethan, the two men he was entertaining. I shook their hands and told them it was nice to see them again. Glenn, it seemed, was not about to explain his presence to me.

"Having a nice time?" I asked.

He looked around and commented on the aesthetics of the place. Then he told me that my family and friends seemed to be enjoying themselves.

"Seems that way," I said, probably a little drunkenly.

Ron and Ethan excused themselves to the bar.

"No drink?" I said, swigging at my beer.

"Not tonight. I'm on call."

"Me too. I'm on call, too. It's nice to be on call, isn't it? Keeps you on your toes."

There was no doubt I was drunk. Yet Glenn seemed amused at my absurdity.

"You sure I can't get you a drink?" I asked, finishing off my beer.

"No thanks, neighbor," he said, looking around the room.

"I'm sorry to say, Mr. Doctor-man," I said, trying to pull back on the sarcasm, "that we won't be neighbors for much longer."

He seemed to refocus in my direction before asking what I meant. Pulling my phone from my back pocket, I began scanning through it, looking for the pictures of the E. 13th Street place. Luke suddenly appeared, carrying two drinks in his hand. He gave one to Glenn, who took it and thanked him. Glenn called him *Luke* when he did this.

"Gray was just telling me about some big future plans he's got," Glenn said.

My mind went blank for a moment. The noise in the room seemed to suddenly stop. It felt like all eyes were on me, waiting for me to prove I was in control of something. When I looked down at the photos on my phone, I remembered my intentions. Both men waited for me to say something. But my confidence was shaken.

"Aren't you on call?" I finally said, motioning to the drink Luke had given to Glenn.

"It's ginger ale," Luke answered for him. "Now what about these big future plans?"

Glenn reached out towards me and took my phone from my hand. Then he rested his drink on the buffet table behind him and swiped his finger over the screen.

"Nice place," he said.

Luke looked on as well. Then they shared a glance that had a perfect synergy to it, a steady, artful focus, like they were rehearsing for a spy film and the cameras might be rolling. Luke started to say something, but stopped himself. It was nice to see us, he said, but he needed to find Abby. As he walked away, he touched Glenn's shoulder.

"Nice place," Glenn said again, handing me my phone.

I took it from him in haste and told him he wasn't family, that the party was mostly for family and that he was not family. A few of the guests nearby stopped talking and looked over at us. Calmly, Glenn told me Luke and Abby had invited him. Perspiration was beading up on my face, and I could feel my shirt sticking to my chest and underarms.

"You're not family," I said again.

"Take it easy, Gray," he said, his voice softer than I'd ever heard it.

"We're moving," I blurted out, waving the phone wildly in front of me. "Laura and I are moving. To a new home. Where only *family* are invited."

By this time, most of the guests had quieted. I spotted Laura from across the room. She had been talking to her sister. But now she was focused on me and Glenn, a hard, uncompromising expression turning her face into a maelstrom of discontent.

"Happy birthday, babe!" I yelled across the room. "We're moving on up! To a deeee-luxe apartment in the sky-aye!"

Then I turned and hurled my phone against the wall behind me. It ricocheted back to me, landing at my feet. When I turned to face Glenn, he looked as sincere as I'd ever seen him. This made it all the more difficult to stare him down for a moment before spitting in his face at point blank range.

• • •

"You know what mob men do after a hit, don't you?" Ben asked when I told him what had happened. "They lay low for a few days. They find a quiet spot and they lay low."

"Where the hell am I gonna go?"

"Somewhere warm. Jesus Christ, get out of this city and find a beach somewhere. Have a few drinks. Clear your head."

Ben's advice was becoming redundant. I understood that he must've found it more and more difficult to respond to what was happening to me. Still, I was fed up with his vacation ideas. He needed to shadow me for a few days so he could see Laura's eyes when she looked at me. He needed to come to my house and smell its new smell of whiskey and wood cleaner. He needed to hear the sounds of my life, which were silence and memory and regret all bleating out a weary cacophony every time I had a thought.

"Do you want to stay at my place for a while? If things are unbearable for you, you're welcome to stay at my place. We've got the room above the garage."

"You're a peach, my friend."

"Actually, what am I saying? You've already got a place, don't you? A whole apartment. A beautiful, brand new apartment. Your very own bachelor pad."

The realtor was understanding over the matter. She even laughed over the lie I told about Laura wanting to look at other places and how her indecision was the story of my life.

"You know what they say about a happy wife," she said, her feminine politeness a refreshing sound to me.

"I certainly do."

But really I had only a slight idea at best. My check, she told me, would be shredded the moment we hung up.

Three days after Laura's party, I texted Andrea, asking about her job search and her writing and if she'd eaten any good Cajun food lately. She responded a few hours later, saying she'd recently returned from a weeklong jaunt to Panama with some friends. We went back and forth for a day or so, sticking mostly to simple pleasantries. It was a Monday evening when she called. I answered on the first ring. It took me declaring my boredom for her to invite me to a hotel.

"Why the fuck not?" I said, barely hesitating.

"Are you sure?"

"What was it you said about the vast slate of possibility?"

"About that: I decided you were right."

"Right about what?"

"About quoting oneself. It's in poor taste."

"What made you come around?"

"I think you just got inside my head."

During my drive over, I decided to sleep with her. Not because I had to have her. And not for revenge, despite how easy it had become to imagine what Laura had been doing for the last couple of months. So I'd sleep with Andrea. And nothing would be solved. And life would only grow more complicated. Of this I was sure. Yet I'd sleep with her.

The thought of touching and smelling a woman up close thrilled me. I needed to feel the soft fuzz of miniscule white hairs against my body. I needed to feel like a human being again - like I wasn't a pariah, a burden, a fucking saboteur.

Andrea had changed her hair and put on a little weight since the last time I'd seen her. Her hair was darker and shorter. It was bold and flattering. But it was the additional few pounds that really caught my attention. It was also flattering. Her breasts were larger and her curves more pronounced.

There was a light in her eyes when she greeted me at the door of the room she'd rented. Her scent was all around, filling the space with a dense, lusty air.

"When was the last time you did this?" she asked.

The question caught me off guard. It wasn't clear whether she meant sleep with a woman or go behind my wife's back. The former excited me because it insinuated *sex*, which pleased me to think was on her mind. The latter implied I was a two-timing prick. As I made my way into the room, Andrea slowly backed up, all the while looking intently into my eyes. She was wearing a short, strapless black dress with a sort of built-in belt that was wrapped just a few inches below her breasts.

"When was the last time you did *this*?" she said, pulling a joint from her cleavage.

My expression lit up. I went from feeling seduced to feeling an almost starstruck awe. Sex *and* drugs, I thought to myself. She threw the joint at me, which I caught in a cup I made with both hands. Her brother and his girlfriend, she told me, had driven out from Penn State to visit her, bringing along a healthy quantity of the stuff. They had all smoked some together before going to a concert in the city, so she could vouch for its efficacy. Sex *and* drugs, I thought again.

"It's been a while," I said, unable to recall the last time I'd gotten high.

We set ourselves up in the room's small sitting area and went to work on that joint. It was well rolled and it burned slowly. Andrea looked sexy as she got stoned. She held the joint like a cigarette and took long, even drags. Her eyes shut as she inhaled. And she never had difficulty holding the smoke in her lungs. When she exhaled, she did so with her mouth, and in graceful streams that made me think a genie might appear at any moment. After a few hits apiece, I asked about the room's smoke detectors. Andrea laughed, choking a little and prematurely blowing the smoke out at me in a cloudy burst.

It didn't take long before I was feeling it. We let the joint burn out before setting it on one of the end tables. Andrea curled herself up on the couch and told me she was high. We began to talk. First about nonsense. Our conversations veered all over the place, from her brother's girlfriend, who Andrea said was beautiful in a 1950's movie star kind of way, to the description of a candy bar she wanted but couldn't remember the name of.

Declarations were random. Transitions were nonexistent. Non sequiturs were abundant. I talked about Norman Mailer and a new deodorant I was using and an idea I once had for a sitcom about an ex-con bail bondsman who was raising his teenage daughter on his own. We both agreed that the bail bondsman facet of the show allowed for a lot of humorous conflicts.

Conversation flowed. We laughed in all the right places at one another's contributions. And we'd congratulate the other if they made it back to a topic we abandoned without resolve. At one point, Andrea shot up and said she almost forgot about something special. She had planned ahead, she boasted. Then she walked past me, towards the closet, where she rummaged around for a few moments. When she returned, she was cradling two large bottles of pink lemonade, a big bag of pretzels, and a box with a pound cake in it.

"A great combo," she said. "Definitely my favorite in times like these."

I sat up almost immediately from the slumped mess I'd become on the overstuffed sofa. We went to work on the food and then smoked the rest of the joint. That's when the conversation took a turn into new territory.

"How do you feel?" she asked.

"Like I'm in high school," I said, cutting a second piece of cake.

"Not what I meant," she said, her voice singing the words at me.

"Oh. I get it. You wanna play therapist with me."

She smiled. The bottle of pink lemonade was in her lap, both her hands wrapped around it, mindlessly massaging its neck and label.

"No, I wanna play *doctor* with you."

When my eyes widened at this, our expressions locked and we both burst out laughing. Pound cake debris flew from my mouth and onto the floor.

"But we can start by playing *therapist*. If you want, that is. It'll be foreplay."

I'd always managed to be elusive with Andrea where my marriage was concerned. But she clearly knew there was a story there. Why else, she probably figured, would I be at a hotel with her on a Monday, smoking pot and eating pound cake? So I talked. And I told her everything that had happened to me and Laura in the last year. Without interruption, she listened, shifting her body a few times on the couch, but always maintaining focus on my story. She barely blinked. It was more than the pot, too; I could tell she was genuinely fascinated with what I had to say. Aside from the story, which seemed compelling on its own, there was confirmation given that I was not some cardboard cutout: I had a past, a wife, domestic troubles, a grown-up's life. My story ended with me being at the hotel with Andrea.

"I'm not saying I'm justified in being here. I'm not saying I'm a victim in any of this."

"Then how *do* you see yourself?"

Alone is what I wanted to say.

"I don't know."

For a while, we didn't say anything. The room suddenly seemed darker than it had before. I picked up a few crumbs of cake from the floor and put them on the table in front of the sofa. Andrea started to say something, but soon stopped herself.

Finally, after a few moments, she said, "I would've done the *exact* same thing you did. Truthfully."

Now it was me who couldn't speak. She continued. My decision, she said, was courageous and difficult and right. She quoted Gertrude Stein - something having to do with instinct. I couldn't listen to her. I couldn't stand to hear her take my side over Laura's. I needed her to side with Laura. Maybe then I would've slept with her. But she was singing my praises and telling me I was brave. Then, in nearly the same breath, she asked if I wanted to stay the night. This seemed to sober me immediately. I stood up and brushed myself off. I felt as though I could've cried at that moment. Really balled like a baby. I knew it was in me somewhere, a dam of tears ready to burst, shuddering my body and swelling my eyes. But I didn't cry. It wasn't the time or the place. And Andrea wasn't the person to coax something like from me. I couldn't stay, I told her, heading for the door. I wished her luck, which we both knew meant that we'd never see one another again. There was no necessity in explaining myself. That would've implied I owed her something. But because I didn't want to make her feel foolish, and because I was still a little high, I thanked her for the pink lemonade and delicious pound cake.

The drive home was a treacherous one. My adrenaline kept me on the right side of the road. I felt somehow empowered. Yet I had no definitive speech or course of action where Laura and I were concerned. All I knew was that I felt the unrelenting strength to demolish the brutalized parts of our past, to overcome them and spite them and do away with them forever and make peace with my wife and have a baby with her and for the rest of my life feel the soft fuzz of *her* miniscule white hairs against my body.

It was close to 11:00 p.m. when I pulled into my driveway where I parked next to Laura's car. Both garage doors were open. The house was cold and dark. I'd wake her up, I thought. It didn't matter if she'd been sleeping for hours. I'd wake her up and tell her what I was feeling. We'd sit in the dark of our room together, and with my words and her faith in them, we'd reinvent the true grace of the love we once shared. The house, I soon discovered, was empty. A sinking feeling found its way into my stomach.

As I walked next door, I discovered I was following footprints in the inch or so of snow that covered the ground. They led to Glenn's front walkway, which was neatly shoveled. His front light was on, as were a few on the second floor. I knocked on his door as though it were mid-afternoon. I began to sweat a little. My mouth was dry and I could still taste the pot from earlier. But I was sober. The foyer light suddenly came on. I heard voices. There'd be no confrontation, I told myself. That was all over with. We're adults, not jealous teenagers.

Someone began descending the stairs. I forced a calmness over myself. Glenn opened the door. He was dressed in a black Princeton sweatshirt and blue jeans. The way he smiled, slight and modest, suggested he was expecting me. I took a deep breath and told him I was there for Laura. It had been an extraordinary evening, I told him, one of a kind, really, and I needed to collect my wife and go back to our home and talk with her. There were no hard feelings between me and him, I said, and it would remain this way. I understood everything, I said. Understood completely. My voice was steady while I looked him in the eye as I spoke.

Pausing a moment, Glenn turned around and looked up the stairs, which were behind him. Then he faced me again and stepped outside into the cold February air. He closed the door behind him.

"Gray," he said after a few false starts, "This is a hell of a thing we've got here. It's the stuff of a Hollywood movie, I guess you could say. And maybe someday it'll actually make one hell of a story. But I don't think it's the ending you're looking for."

Grumbling over his analogy, I told him I wanted to speak with Laura. He sighed. I started to move past him and he stopped me with his hand on my chest.

"For now, I'm the best you're going to get. Not what you expected, I realize, but that's how it is. What can I say?"

Then he moved his hand from my chest to my shoulder, which he gave a slight embrace.

"That being said," he added, "I think *we* should talk."

CHAPTER 17

Adam and Matt select a song from the jukebox - the Faces' "Ooh La La" - and explain to the rest of the writing group why they have dumpster diving on their minds. After Dimitri Ames' arrest, the boys came forward to the authorities with information about the blank checks they'd found in his garbage. They even kept a few, which they turned over during their interview with the cop who visited them a day earlier. They admitted how it had been tempting to test their own luck by going downtown to pass a few of them.

"Make out a few for cash," said Adam, "and keep your fingers crossed. Problem is it's too damn easy to get away with. Which is what leads to doing it again and again. Which is what leads to getting caught. Which is how dumbfuck got caught."

"Fucking conman," said Meredith, "and thief."

"Let's not forget *rapist*," said Kay.

"He's not really a rapist," said Dorian.

An argument ensues over whether it's fair to call Ames a rapist, given that what happened between him and Lindsay was consensual. Matt interrupts by saying it hardly matters. Meredith's initial point, he emphasizes, is that Ames is a petty criminal, not a murderer. And this, Matt says with reserve, is unsettling. The group agrees how they were convinced of Ames' guilt over the crime. According to Rollie, Ames, who was formally interrogated about Nicole D'Ambrosio's murder once taken into custody, had a successful alibi. During the window of time in which the murder could've occurred, Ames was at the Red Roof Inn in Milford with Lindsay; the girl snuck out of her dorm and met him on the interstate behind the campus. And though he checked in under an alias, the security cameras confirmed that it was in fact Ames. With obvious disappointment in his voice, the Old Man tells the staff that Ames is no longer a suspect. Word of this spreads quickly.

Matt announces to the group how he's okay. Lindsay, he adds, wrecked him, it's true, but he's grateful for it. Without her, he says, he'd have no muse for heartache.

"At least this way," he tells the group, "I've got some credibility."

"You've got credibility crawling out of your ass," says Adam.

The boys are excited about an upcoming gig to help Austin Roarick move into his new condo. Roarick, who might as well be banned from the school after the Homer House incident, has hired them for a few hours. Yet the boys have no intention of telling him the real reason for their service. It has nothing to do with the meager fifty dollars he's offered for them to split. Nor does it have to do with boredom or campus politics or any of that. It's the dumpster diving. The boys, whose didacticism on this topic is oddly charming, even poetic, are looking forward to getting a little dirty. Someone has recently moved out, they explain, and Roarick will be moving in.

"We're bound to get our hands on *something*," says Adam. "And if there's no treasure to be found, we'll just steal some of his shit; he's only the son of a powerhouse."

"Speaking of sons of powerhouses," said Meredith, looking at me with faux sternness, "when will you let us read some of your stuff? This *is* a writers group, isn't it? And you *are* a writer, aren't you?"

Both questions have easy answers, but I don't respond. I find that I'm focused on the school's mission statement hanging at the far end of the dining hall; I'm tempted to point out that this, in a way, is in fact a writing sample of mine.

• • •

Dan Hart has again become the talk of the campus. And it's not his beguiling charm or sexual exploits that are being discussed. It's his unwillingness to get out of bed. For two days, Dan is holed up in his room, quietly refusing to leave his top bunk. His dorm staff can only do so much, so the boy's therapist, as well as the Old Man, are brought in on the matter. Nothing works. He can't be roused with humor or bribery or threats. He's apparently showing no signs of aggression. He's simply depressed. His first few meals are withheld as a means of leverage. At the twelve hour mark, though, his dinner is brought to him by one of his dorm mates. Most of the meal - fettuccine alfredo, green beans, and a brownie - is left untouched. I overhear a few of his peers mention how it must be serious since Dan isn't even playing his guitar. And if he's truly abandoned the instrument, then this standoff might very well be for real.

It's impossible to fault the kid. His malaise appears well-timed. And though no one's certain whether this bed-in is some sort of statement - he's barely speaking, other than to say how tired he is - it's nevertheless regarded as sensible recourse to the constant oil spill of bad news. Stay in bed. Smooth the pillow. Find solace and warmth under soft cotton covers. Others eventually follow suit. It starts with two girls in the Minnie House, then one more in the Helen House, then a group of boys in the Miles House. And thus a movement is spawned. Students from nearly every dorm stage a revolt, refusing to rise from their bunks and attend meals, classes, therapy, activities. Most are too fickle and relent after as little as an hour. Some hold out longer, lasting until lunch or until classes have ended for the day. Others manage to chalk up a full day, lying there in their pacific glory, sleeping, starving themselves, taking one for the team, somehow communing with Dan Hart, Hundred Acre School's de facto insurgent.

The Homer House is no exception. A few of the boys instigate their own movement. Andrew, Cliff, and Dustin take hold of their new cause with fiery grit. Ryan offers to deal with it, so I'm free from having to extemporize some plagiaristic pep talk on why greeting the new day in the face of all this summer's strife is oh so important. As this is happening, J.J. finds me on my front porch and asks if we can talk. He has news about the ring.

"What ring?"

"The one you and Ryan have pinned up on your bulletin boards," he says coarsely. "The picture."

It comes back to me. Nicole D'Ambrosio's Tiffany's ring. The one with the Roman numerals circling the band. J.J. says he and the others know it must have something to do with Nick; this became evident, he tells me, the day the Old Man rounded them up one by one and asked if they knew of the ring's whereabouts.

"You found it?"

"Noah and Cliff did. But a bunch of us were there."

It was discovered in Nick's mattress, he explains, hidden inside a thin slit made towards the bottom of the bed. Recalling my search of the kid's things, I'm positive I looked there, recognizing it as one of the more obvious hiding spots for contraband.

"Where is it?"

"That's the thing," he said, infusing his tone with a sort of languid importance, "Noah took it; he claimed to be the one to really find it, so he gave it to Alexis Peterson. I guess they're a thing."

I know Alexis Peterson. She's a short haired, serious looking girl with olive skin and a large diamond stud in her nose. She's a frequent visitor at the Homer House.

"She has the ring?" I said, taking out my phone and calling the Old Man.

"She did the last time I saw her," he said.

"When was that?"

"Tonight. At dinner."

The Old Man picks up on the second ring. He's on campus, walking with Nussbaum. Incredulous over my news, he reminds me of the search I did in Nick's room.

"I know."

"Then how do you explain this?"

"I *looked* in his bed. I know I did."

He says I must've done a half-assed job. Assuring him I did not, and reminding him that the police carefully surveyed my search, I encourage him to track down this Alexis girl. He pauses for a moment; I can hear him give the girl's name and dorm info to Nussbaum. I can't tell if what he says next is to me or Nussbaum, but it happens to be the same question I'm also considering:

"Is it possible someone planted that goddamn ring there?"

. . .

On a humid Friday evening, at about 7:30, Nick Russo walks through campus, a plastic grocery bag stuffed full of clothing and personal effects slung over his shoulder, and a cold, defeated gaze torturing his face. Attention has now shifted away from bed-ins and found jewelry. Nick's reappearance happens upon the HAS campus like some cool, spindly efflorescence. No one is looking for something to occur. No one is waiting for this kind of change. But they accept it. They accept it with what must now be automatic anxiety. It resembles something out of a student film where the actor, a novice whose self-consciousness might be his best asset, is given limited direction, so he accepts carte blanche to play it any way he sees fit.

Nick moves slowly through the campus. He passes fellow students who are clustered in small groups, gossiping, hacky sacking, skateboarding. They stop and watch him; his forward motion is awkward and stunted. No one approaches or calls out to him. No girls become weepy or euphoric or relieved. He's viewed from afar, regarded as though he's some beautiful stranger who might at any moment empty a pocketful of dangerous secrets. The front steps of the pavilion become home to Nick's burden. When he sits down, it's with the modesty of an understudy making their debut. He crosses his legs and leaves his bag by his feet. The campus buzzes.

Nick's been gone for six days. And now he refuses to speak. Not to Dr. Reynolds, his therapist. Not to Roger, his math teacher, who makes a big showing of welcoming him back. Not to me or Ryan, who conspire over a lie, telling him the Homer House boys have missed him. Not to Rollie, who escorts him into his office, which becomes Nick's temporary quarters. The Old Man wants him eating and sleeping in there at first, away from the others. Jimbo is assigned to watch him.

After calling the police and Eileen Russo, the Old Man leaves Nick to himself for the rest of that first night. By the following morning, the kid will be plied with questions. Nick, who seems to shut out the energy around him, no matter how tense or claustrophobic, is unrelenting in his vow of silence. It seems authentic, which raises some eyebrows. He tells no one to fuck off or to leave him alone. He doesn't reveal that he's sorry. Or innocent. Or hungry. He merely slouches a little into himself, tilting his head as though his thoughts, whatever they might be, are an abacus, content to add up nothing of consequence. Questions about his absence and sudden return are greeted with blank indifference. Rollie asks Nick about his downtown enterprise. And the ring, which has been confiscated from Alexis. No response to either.

In all likelihood, Nick's days at the Hundred Acre School are numbered. My father must be tortured by this. He'll see it as a personal failing. Expulsions at the HAS are rare. The cops have been investigating Nick's drug dealing as well as involvement with Nicole D'Ambrosio. At this point, there's no proof of either, yet they'll have their turn with the kid. For now, though, they're allowing Rollie to keep the boy on the school's premises where he'll be made to feel safe long enough to drop his guard and explain himself.

His return rouses kids from their bunks. They want to see for themselves. To them, the name *Nick Russo* must carry with it some sort of spectral connotation. There's been so much talk in the time he's been gone. Imaginative stories and theories. There's one that had him fleeing to New York City to oversee his drug business. Another had him hitchhiking to Maine to meet up with his deadbeat father, who would try sneaking him over the Canadian border. And there was one that named him Nicole D'Ambrosio's murderer and had him evade the police long enough to destroy incriminating evidence. It's this last one, and this last one only, about the D'Ambrosio girl, that everyone seems to entertain with earnestness.

. . .

The writers group has morphed into a social club. The kids still show up with their work, but it's hardly anyone's focus. A poem or story excerpt might be read aloud, but before any real commentary is offered, talk turns to whatever shining catastrophe burned brightest that day. Dan Hart, still confined to his bed, might've held his position as the foremost subject on everyone's mind - the fourth day of his reclusion is upon us - but his story has been superseded by Nick's return. The unanswered questions are on everyone's mind. Where did the kid run off to for six days? What exactly is his involvement with Nicole D'Ambrosio? Is he really a drug dealer? Why did he come back? Why is he refusing to speak? What does he have to hide?

Today the group is sparse. There's Dan's absence along with Matt's and Adam's, who are helping Austin move into his condo. Those present are on the topic of Nick's relationship with Nicole D'Ambrosio.

"It's crazy," says Dorian. "I can't picture it, the two of them together."

"You didn't even know the girl," says Meredith. "How can you possibly judge?"

"I don't know Nick, either, but I still can't picture it. He seems like the exact opposite of who girls like that usually go for."

"He's a thug," says Booth.

Kay dares him to say this to Nick's face.

"I'll say it to his face," says Dorian, "what's the worst he'll do? He's a fucking zombie now anyway. It's been, what, two or three days? And he hasn't said a word."

"It's a cool little contest, isn't it?" says Kay. "Between Dan and Nick, to see who can hold out the longest."

"Poor Rollie," says Marilyn. "He must be ready to lose his mind."

My thoughts exactly. The estimates for the building repairs came back at double what he anticipated. And because he has a triple net lease, he's responsible for the full cost. Not to mention he's lost five students. His nerves must be frayed, and he's certainly spread thin, yet he's holding it all together. Minutes after being grilled by a parent over the phone, the Old Man will sit down in the dining hall with the girls from the Joni House and flatter them with funny stories about their own progress. After meeting with Old Brookview's unrelenting law enforcement for the third time in a week, he'll spontaneously announce a pool tournament in the pavilion, offering prizes of gift cards and breakfast in bed. He continues to thank his staff for the job they're doing. And he puts his hands on their arms when he speaks with them. If the context is right, he'll quote Carlyle or Camus about strength or will. The love he has for his school has never been in question. But seeing it this way, as a grown man, who now understands at least something about achievement and loss and the grim nature of time, is not easy.

My father has watched me closely this summer. I've felt him searching for signs of recognition. He wants to see how much of me he can put to a song he understands and can later sing to Nussbaum or to himself, and how much of me will remain those stubborn notes caught in a mysterious transition between two dueling harmonies. But I wonder if he knows I've been watching him as well. That I've looked at him from across the dining hall, from across campus, and pretended we're absolute strangers one moment and then as close as a father and son can be the next. That I've pictured my mother at his side, happy and youthful looking, flirting with him in front of the students, her long, silken fingers playfully grazing his shoulders, her smile wide and real and harvesting all the Old Man's moments of gladness and grace.

Sometimes I imagine the Hundred Acre School as the Wild West. I imagine it's outlaw country, parched, desolate, and with its good guys and bad guys. There are things buried in the earth here, I imagine, some sacred and others evil and profane. And as the students roam the grounds, their hard, rebellious heels digging into land my father wants to call his own, they feel the spirit of these things. And though they choose to not talk about them most of the time, they know and understand them. They understand the sacredness and they understand the evil and profane. It's Rollie who sometimes guides these steps of theirs. But sometimes he does not. Sometimes he'll let them walk where they wish to walk. This is not easy for him to do, but he does it. He does it because he knows he must. And they, the students, might even, depending on their mood, the moon, their meds, be grateful.

The group calls it quits for the day. It's dull, they decide, without Adam and Matt and Dan.

"Unless Gray wants to share something he's written," said Meredith, feigning a schoolteacher's demeanor.

"I thought we were trying to *avoid* dull," I tell her.

Meredith rolls her eyes before leading the group out into the late afternoon sunshine. I'm not far behind. A few Homer House boys greet me as I head back to my place. Two girls are sitting on the Old Man's front porch as I pass his house. One is braiding the other's hair. They smile at me. As I move past them, I can see Matt and Adam pacing near the entrance to my apartment. When they see me approach, they stop moving and watch me walk towards them. Adam says something to Matt, but I can't hear what it is.

"You boys are apparently the glue," I tell them from a distance. "We decided it's too dull without you, so we cashed it in. How flattering is that?"

Matt's hair looks like someone tried to blow his head off with an industrial fan, and the sweat on Adam's shirt has soaked it to a new, darker shade of black. They're both out of breath.

"Can we talk to you?" asks Matt.

I invite them into my place and give them each a towel and a glass of ice water. As I look at them now out of the glare of sunlight, it's plain to see their expressions. They each have the look of a man who's come back from a long vacation to find his estate in disarray. There's a lean, hard focus in their eyes, and a worry on their lips I haven't seen on either of them. They remind me that they were working for Austin, helping him move into his condo.

"So we're unloading stuff off the truck he's rented," Adam explains. "A shitload of boxes, and *some* furniture - a little sofa, a desk, and a small kitchen table with a couple of chairs. We're not talking about big pieces here."

The boys tell me how Austin was obnoxious. He teased Adam about his weight and Matt about his harmonica breaks. Plus, he frequently changed his mind as to where he wanted this or that.

"We must've moved certain boxes three or four times to different rooms," says Matt. "And we're not talking about lightweight boxes, either."

He really put them to work. They're earning every cent of that miserable fifty dollars he's promised. As soon as the boys take a moment to rest or drink or blow a melody, Austin is in their faces, calling them pussies, saying how he should've hired some of the public school kids.

"His dickishness is baffling," says Adam.

"He acts like he knows us," adds Matt. "Like he's some beloved uncle or something."

So there's little time for the boys' true purpose in being there. Besides, the dumpster is locked, a minor problem with which the boys have contended before.

"But it's not like we even had time to put much of a plan together," says Adam, "let alone execute one."

By the time the truck is cleared out, Austin announces that he wants to go back to his father's house and load up an armoire. The boys, who have pretty much cut their losses, agree to go. At least they'll get to check out J.R. III's waterfront palace.

"Who says size doesn't count?" says Matt, shaking his head. "The guy lives like a rock star."

The real attraction, though, wasn't the house; it was the twenty yard dumpster out in front of the house. Austin told the boys he'd been using it for days prior to moving out. An act of subterfuge was needed.

"Some people are cool with you going through their shit," says Matt, "and others, not so much. He seemed like the kind of dude who definitely wouldn't be having it."

After moving the armoire into the truck, Matt asked for a drink. When Austin escorted him into the house, Adam would go to work.

"He's smaller than me," says Adam, pointing at Matt, "but I'm faster."

"True," adds Matt.

The boys decided Matt could blow into his harp to warn of Austin's return. The plan works. Matt even coaxes a house tour out of Austin. Adam has plenty of time. But nothing strikes him.

"It's a lot of old clothes and books," says Adam. "Some furniture, too - a beat up leather recliner, a foot stool, stuff I could never take with me without him seeing."

Knowing he's on borrowed time, Adam starts his ascent up and out of the dumpster. It's when he's balanced on the ledge of the thing that he sees, half buried in a mass of garbage, a thin spiral notebook with its creased red cover flipped open, revealing a six word sentence written on its first page, over and over, from top to bottom, in neat, careful rows. Easing himself back inside the dumpster, Adam fishes the notebook out; he turns the page only to see the sentence written on the next one, and the next, and the next. He screws up his eyes while standing up to his waist in junk, double and triple checking whether he's actually face-to-face with what resembles a sort of demented grade school exercise.

Adam stashes the notebook down his pants and waits for Matt's harp to blow. Austin then drives them all back to the condo, where the boys help with the armoire before heading back to the school on foot to see me.

"You've got the thing?" I ask.

Matt lifts up his shirt and produces the notebook. As he hands it to me, he wears a stoic expression that betrays an almost relieved gaiety that he for once is exempt from any trouble or scrutiny. Both boys look on as I open it to its first page.

"Lovely," I muse to myself.

"There's more," said Adam. "Thumb through it."

There must be close to twenty pages, front and back, with the same blunt six word sentence written over and over and over. My mind suddenly flashes back to Austin's odd predilection back in high school. The epithet "Repeat Offender" proved more fitting than anyone could've known back then.

I'm on the verge of asking the boys why they chose to confide in me. Instead, I tell them I'd like to hold onto the notebook.

"Keep it," Adam says. "Publish it. Put it online. Do whatever you want with it as long as it fucks this guy over."

"Do you remember what condo unit he moved into?" I ask.

"Of course," says Adam. "Why? What are you going to do?"

"I'm not sure."

"Do you want us to go with you?" Matt asks.

The heartfeltness of this gesture makes me blush a little. I immediately consider whether I'd be friends with these boys if I was their age. They are smart and interesting and likeable. Yet I know that I probably would've misjudged them before shunning them completely. The shame I feel over this causes me to put my hand on Matt's shoulder and politely decline his noble offer. He doesn't wince. Or show the slightest sign of discomfort. He simply stands there, looking up at me, his posture impeccable, his eyes bright and unblinking, and without knowing it, and certainly without any fault of his own, lays the biggest guilt trip at my feet.

• • •

It never seemed as humid as when I arrive at Austin's place. The sun has sworn off the cool frost of the moon and is battling to blaze the sky into a great lake of ash. I'm already sweating by the time I reach his front door. His unit, like the rest of them, is plain to look at. Its weathered clapboard needs a fresh coat of stain, and the grounds can use a feminine touch. It's quiet. Besides some distant chatter from a young couple walking their black dachshund a few units away, the only sound I hear is that of my own breathing. It's fast, motorized breathing, running only on adrenaline.

The notebook is in an old orange backpack I found left behind in a closet in my apartment. I knock loudly on the door. No approaching footsteps. No signs of life. But I can sense a certain kind of energy from within. The kind that's poised and may be released at just the right moment with just the right momentum. Maybe it's the heat that makes me feel this way, or maybe it's the quiet.

Austin opens the door and greets me with what seems like terminal suspicion. His face is drawn and the whites of his eyes are bloodshot. This all takes a moment to wear off, and before I can say a word, he's turned himself into a convivial host with his hand outstretched towards me and a glint in his expression.

"Are *you* looking for some work now? Because your boys took my last dollar."

Feeling the absence of a smile on my face, I shake his hand. He studies me for a moment before looking over my head towards the parking spaces in front of his unit. I'm struck by the urge to say something non-confrontational, so I ask about Matt and Adam. He invites me inside his place. I accept the offer and find myself standing in his tiny foyer, which is really no more than a dozen cream-colored ceramic tiles. A few short feet away is a maroon carpeted staircase. On the landing are enough boxes to make it nearly impossible to turn and negotiate the rest of the stairs. The former resident must've been a smoker because the place has a stale, rotten stink to it, like all the air within it has been wrung out by large, filthy hands.

"They're a couple of pissers, those kids. Not great workers - especially the fat one - but they're amusing as hell to listen to. I swear they have their own language."

"They're good with their hands. Putting things together. Taking them apart. Figuring them out."

"What kinds of things?"

"All kinds."

"Example?"

"They installed an old jukebox in the dining hall. And they've been working on Rollie's Winnebago."

"Pretty good."

"It's an important set of skills. Don't you think?"

"What?"

"Putting things together. Taking them apart. Figuring them out."

"I think it probably is."

"It was never my strength. I think at one point I thought it was. But it's not."

Austin leans into the wall and crosses his feet and hands. I notice there are no lights on. The place is dusky. Yet I can see him clearly. There's now something rigid in his face. A tautness. Like his muscles are working hard to hold back a slideshow of expressions that'll give away every emotion he's ever felt.

"But I think I'm getting better at it. Actually, I think I've gotten better at it since I've been working for my father. What are you good at, Austin? Any special skills?"

"This is the most I've ever heard you talk."

"I guess I have a few things to say."

"You didn't come over here to talk about your father. Or about those two pissants. Did you?"

"I think it was you who said we'd talk in the future. Well, here we are."

"What do you want?"

He takes the time to force a nasty grin after he says this.

"I want to know what *you* want. We can start there and see where it takes us."

It's out now - the closest I can come to any type of accusation, ambiguously disguised as meaningless repartee. I can tell he's intrigued. He has the look of a man on the verge of exploring a foxhole. We stare at one another. There's a brightness in him that I believe I've missed in our previous encounters. It seems to live in his skull and get parceled out through his eyes and mouth, just a bit here and there, enough to satisfy social situations, but not enough to dispel whatever darkness he could claim.

"What makes you think I want anything?"

"Everybody wants something," I said.

"That's true."

"What were you doing in my dorm that day?"

"In *your* dorm?"

"Do you want to argue over semantics?"

He smiles a broad, arrogant smile.

"I don't want to argue over *anything*."

"Then why don't you tell me?"

He straightens himself out and leans in to take a good long look at me.

"Well, I'll be goddamned. It's happened, hasn't it? As much as I thought it wouldn't happen, it's happened. You've been indoctrinated. You're one of them."

"We're not talking about a cult, Austin. There're no factions here. And if there ever were, you and I were never on the same side. Do you understand that?"

My stomach suddenly bottoms out. I have mixed feelings about having insulted him. Who knows this man? He's certainly not the simpleton I'd once pegged him as. But pulling back now will be devastating. We're already in his pathetic kingdom; I sure as hell don't need to give him the power by putting my mettle on the guillotine.

"What if I told you I know what you were doing in my dorm that day? That I know you left a little something behind. A little something my boys found. Would you still want to focus on semantics and factions and all of that?"

Sighing, he turns his back on me and begins to walk around, sidestepping boxes and pictures and rolled up rugs on the floor.

"You asked me earlier if I had any special skills," he says, examining a painting of an old woman playing the violin with her eyes closed. "Well, I do. It's the ability to recognize who in the room has power and who doesn't - a pretty simple skill, actually."

After he brushes some dust from the top of the picture's frame, he leans it against the wall. Then he takes a few steps back and examines it.

"But it doesn't stop there," he continues, his back to me. "It's also recognizing how much power the other person has and what they can do with it. And how comfortable they are with it - how it suits them. Not to mention whether they're an asset or a threat."

Turning towards me, Austin laughs a little and says that he considers himself an expert on the matter. He could write a book, he tells me. Give lectures. All of that.

"Working for a man with, let's face it, more power than you could ever imagine, will imbue this trait," he says.

"And is this skill of yours being put to use right now?"

"Of course it is."

"And?"

"And what? Do I have my answers?"

"Well, do you?"

"Of course I do."

"I'm curious."

He turns back to the painting of the violinist. A dog barks in the distance. After a few moments, Austin wheels back to face me. He's not smiling.

"It's getting dark in here. The summer is winding down. And it's getting dark earlier. And I don't have electricity yet. But even in the oncoming dark, I can see your face perfectly well. You've got a new look now when you talk about the HAS. It's not the one I remember from years ago, or even a few weeks ago. It's different now. It used to have a certain blankness to it, a kind of robust blankness, as if the hate you felt was too big to fit your face. So you had to ration it or conceal it or something, I don't know. But now, I don't know exactly who I'm talking to, so I have to be careful. But I'm asking you to leave here and discontinue whatever path you think you're on. Go back to babysitting. It's less interesting, true, but it's much safer."

I don't know what to address first: the notion of this hatred I supposedly once wore in my face, or the rambling threat just laid at my feet. My brain, in a daring show of virtuosity, tricks me, and goes for neither. It conspires with my mouth and asks him about Nicole D'Ambrosio. Upon mention of her name, he regards me in a new way. There's a stern thoughtfulness to his expression, like the look a father might have before he reproves his child for behavior that may blight the family name. The composure in his mannerisms - a slight licking of the lips, an occasional knuckle crack, barely audible inhaling - nearly forces an apology out of me. Then I remember what I'm carrying in the orange backpack strapped to my shoulders.

"Did you know her?" I ask a second time.

"What're you doing here?"

"Did you?"

"Tell me."

"You first."

"Gray, when you're powerless, you can't just make some up on the spot. The stuff's not forged in a lab. It's given to you - or you take it."

"Is that what *you* do?" I said, cinching the straps on the backpack. "Do you take it?"

"It's not made in a lab," he said again. "Either you have it or you don't."

"I'll tell you what," I said, swinging the backpack into my hands, "I do have something. And it's enough for now, enough to put you in touch with some situations *no one* wants to be a part of."

I throw the bag at his feet. He takes a quick, wayward glance down at the thing. Then he laughs a little to himself. After some time, he says he's a businessman. His eye, he admits, is on the Hundred Acre School. Close to three years ago, a young developer named William Medhurst made J.R. III a reasonable offer on the HAS property, which he thought ideal for what would be Old Brookview's first gated community. High-end homes with several fireplaces and tray ceilings and bonus rooms the size of fast food restaurants. J.R. III turned down the offer. Medhurst came back with another. J.R. III turned that one down as well. Medhurst's calls eventually went unanswered. Yet his perseverance did not waver. He got in touch with Austin, who assured the entrepreneur that if he was made a partner in the endeavor he could make things happen. The two then began collaborating on how to buy the property.

"There's a whole Shakespearean thing going on with my father and me," he said. "You've been teaching that shit, haven't you? So you should understand. *He's* the one with all the best lines. These wonderful monologues - all this perfect poetry. And it's all on ambition and reputation and accomplishment. And then there's me. And I'm fighting for a fucking part. And I've *been* fighting - been fighting for a long time. So when no one was looking, I made up a part for myself. Made up my own lines and stage direction and everything. And I discovered it's a part I play pretty goddamn well."

"And what does this *part* of yours entail exactly? Does it stop at the Fire Marshall and the Health Inspector? Or does it go beyond that into something desperate and depraved? Something that'll forever affect this town and its people? And my students? And you and your family? And me and Rollie?"

The words come straight from my gut; they're processed there by some new will I feel enter my blood through the oncoming twilight, and they're forced out in the same cool, natural way a trumpeter might blow a run of notes.

Austin begins talking excitedly, explaining his new drive to prove himself. He stutters a bit when he speaks. And he veers towards tangents about business ethics as well as my relationship with my father. Through his ramblings, he manages to explain how he initially saw me as a potential ally, someone who disdains the Hundred Acre School as much as he does. He had therefore planned on asking me to make things difficult for Rollie to purchase the school. To perhaps talk him out of it. Or at the very least supply any pertinent financial information on Rollie's acquisition of the property.

By the time he stops talking, I can barely see his expression. The dusk has turned him into some three-dimensional charcoal drawing. But I can see the top of his figure leaning towards the backpack on the floor. I break the silence with the evening's simplest question:

"What did you do?"

"I made up my own part, like I already told you."

"That's a meaningless response."

"You're not at all qualified to say that. You're not. You're not the son of James Roarick III. You're a fucking nobody, in *my* house, talking to me about *my* life, trying to get inside *my* fucking head. You're not some moral voice here. You're a fucking nobody."

He isn't yelling, but his tone has risen. And his breathing, which earlier had been his best kept secret, is now gruff and labored. What suddenly runs through my head is that Matt and Adam are the only ones who know where I am.

There's nothing left for us to say to one another. All that remains is written over and over again on page after page in a red spiral notebook. As I walk outside, he kicks the backpack at me, demanding I take it with me. I don't respond.

The evening is still and awful. Nothing moves. I'm both relieved and surprised when my Jeep starts and takes me down the road, back towards the Hundred Acre School. When the place is within eyesight, I see a crowd of people clustered around the dining hall. As I approach, driving at half speed, I see that they're mostly students. Dozens of them. Many of whom are simply standing still, gazing up towards the sky. The moon is in the east, on the other side of the dining hall. And the stars are cosmic smears, hidden behind dense layers of humidity. When I roll my window down, I can hear voices. It isn't until I pass the building that I see, in my rearview mirror, the sudden movement of some figure on the roof.

Parking the Jeep, I make my way over to the spectacle, only to hear the clean, bright sound of guitar chords coming into focus. Mixed throughout the crowd of mostly students are my colleagues. Sandra is there along with Tennille and Amber. Administrators like Reese and Victor are also there. And the Old Man, who is tapping his chin with his phone, is there. And they're all focused on that guitar sound; it plays quick, inspired bursts of melody before it quits. It's lovely music, even amid the heat and confusion. As I join the crowd, planting myself next to a girl I recognize from a speech she'd given on recycling a few days earlier, I can now see the source of everyone's attention.

Dan Hart is on the roof of the dining hall. Sitting just atop the peak, his legs are splayed out in a crooked diamond shape. He holds firmly to his guitar, pressing it into his midsection, strumming minor sounding chords that sound like nervous bird calls. Through the dusk, I can see him clearly. He looks leaner and lonelier than the last time I saw him. That was days ago. Now he's close to thirty feet from the ground. A small group of girls, who stand directly below him on the concrete, ask him to come down. They're not bawling or begging; they tell him he needs something to eat and someone to talk to. The Old Man lets them do this. Aside from a few hollers to come down or to play "Free Bird," most of the crowd just looks on.

Dan's not interacting. The songs he plays are truncated bits of ragged poetry. They last no more than a few seconds before he stops and then gazes down at his instrument. This goes on for some time. Then, clearing his throat, he speaks, to no one in particular:

"I feel like a melody is sometimes an excuse for a lyric, and that a lyric is sometimes an excuse for a melody. I don't think either is the case with this song. It's called 'Ten Minute Song.'"

At that moment, the Old Man dials 911. Dan, as if sensing his time is limited, begins the song. It has a pleasant mid-tempo melody to it, some major and minor chords played up and down the neck of the guitar. As he sings, he projects his voice well. For someone who's lazed around for days, and has had little nourishment in that time, he sounds strong. We all watch and listen. Though the verses are tuneful, the lyrics are nearly indecipherable. But not the chorus. For some reason, it rings with such clarity, such pleasing contrast to the rest of the song, that by the time it comes around for the second and final time, I find myself singing along in my head:

There's barely time
To speak my mind
And let you know where I'm at
So here, my love, is a ten minute song
Sung in three minutes flat

He takes a brief solo and then ends the song. Then applause and cheers. Then the girls telling him to come down from the roof. And more requests for Lynyrd Skynyrd and David Bowie songs. Dan's impervious to it all. He just sits, the darkening shadows of his posture resembling some gothic artifice. There's no movement or music coming from the roof. The crowd quiets. The sky darkens. Our wait for something to happen ends abruptly when Dan flings his arms out in front of him, as though offering his guitar in sacrifice. The instrument tumbles away from him, bounces awkwardly on the roof, invoking an awful sounding incantation of sour, tuneless notes, and falls through the air in a dangerous spiral before crashing to pieces on the concrete.

There's little time to react to this. In the next moment, Dan catapults himself from the peak of the roof with every bit of strength he has. For a moment, he's airborne just a few steps from where he was sitting. When his body finds the surface again, he's already out of control, skidding on his rear and his back and his head, turning over as though on fire. The girls below him scream. This helps me find them among the newly minted chaos. They must think gravity is some violent backstabber since I give no warning as I trample them, my arms cradled in front of me like some mad hulk, waiting to accept the crushing weight of sorrow and song and burdens I feel strangely qualified to carry.

CHAPTER 18

We let our cities beguile us. We want them to. We build them that way, alluring and sexual, stacked with hard metal and glass, heartache and promise, perfect views to the stars and all the neatly scrubbed fantasies that drift through the atmosphere on clouds of ether. I fell for Chicago the moment I arrived twelve years ago. Its architecture is breathtaking. Its winters are unforgettable. Its blues are for real. It took me in, gave me shelter, let me wave its flags and sing its songs.

Though we no longer lived in the city at the time of our separation, Laura and I always saw ourselves as Chicagoans. For better or for worse. And when she left me, the city appeared changed. All its subterranean poetry and wild-eyed nostalgia was gone. A riot had occurred and swept Chicago's best parts into the gutters.

After the split, I binged on the city I'd once so loved. It was easy to do. Taking some time off of work, I got a room at the Blackstone Renaissance Hotel where I spoiled myself. No one there knew me. So I indulged on room service and shoeshines, on massages and manicures. No one knew what I'd done to my life and my marriage and why I walked around feeling like my guts were on fire. This decadence was in no way celebratory. Little pleasure was involved. I was going through the motions, reconciling with the city I somehow figured I had let down, working my way towards a sort of farewell. I think I knew I was done with the Midwest. But I would first give myself over to some hedonism. It was all I could do to keep away from the kind of melancholy that holds your head under water until you do the kind of begging that's nearly biblical.

Winter was working up a rather bland farewell during the four days I spent at the Blackstone. And most of what I did there in that time was unhealthy. I ate ribs and cheesecake and pounds of sushi. My room had a mini-bar, which I restocked twice. I drank cold bottled beer and shots of bourbon and tequila and pint glasses of rum and coke. Smoking cigarettes was something I hadn't done since college, but I found myself buying a pack of Marlboro Lights from the store in the lobby. They were repulsive, yet went wonderfully with the booze. My behavior was depressingly banal. But in the aftermath of adversity, there are only so many ways a man can occupy himself. I found most of them. The other obvious one, sex, certainly occurred to me. I even researched a few escort services in the area. This was hardly a feat. I asked the concierge, a beatific Asian man who responded to my inquiry with undaunted professionalism, and even printed out three separate sheets for me from his computer. I gave him twenty dollars and thanked him.

On my last night at the hotel, I considered calling one of the services. Yet I resisted. Not out of pride or discipline, but rather out of self-serving vanity. I denied myself the pleasure of sex with a beautiful stranger, then made a solemn declaration that I must've been saintly to have done so. I even told myself, aloud, that I was not that kind of man. Almost immediately I had to take a drink and turn on the TV in an effort to drown out such sorry behavior.

The four day jaunt at the Blackstone wasn't deliberate. It was in no way some type of planned program of iniquity. Things merely ran their course. By the end, I was exhausted. My plan, which materialized on a subconscious level, was something of a success: I no longer felt like myself. Bleary-eyed and miserable, I avoided mirrors as well as eye contact even with strangers.

Going home didn't seem an option at this point. The thought of setting foot in my own home was terrifying. I couldn't bear to smell the blackberry candles Laura had been burning all winter, or hear the creak of that one floorboard at the top of the staircase, or admit that I was face-to-face with a $500,000 failure. Home was done for. It was an old, obsolete luxury.

Visiting the concierge for the last time, I asked him to find one more number for me. It was for an ashram just outside of Aurora, about an hour from the city. I'd heard about it from Ben. His wife, Justine, had spent some time there with a girlfriend a year or so ago. It was the girlfriend's idea, Ben told me, but Justine came back a new woman, renewed and refocused. When I called, I spoke with a man who identified himself as the presiding Swami. He told me there was available space in their facility for overnight guests. Having no idea what to expect, I thanked him and said I'd see him by early evening. Much of that day was spent walking around the city, ducking in and out of stores and restaurants to warm up for a few moments before once again braving the cold. I had some soup in a Jewish deli and I bought a black wool scarf from a street vendor.

By 5:00 p.m., I got in my car and headed towards Aurora. For most of the drive, I imagined what I was getting myself into. Yoga and lectures and gurus. Maybe some exotic Indian instruments. My ignorance didn't prevent me from fleeting delusions of grandeur. There were moments when I told myself I must've been heading for some kind of change. Real change. The kind that brings with it stories you break out to remember the smell of the dirt that helped grow your new roots and the feel of the vitality that brought you to your knees in gratitude.

I arrived at a little past 6:00 p.m. and was greeted by a kind faced Indian man wearing an overflowing orange robe. He told me I must be Grayson and that we spoke on the phone earlier. He showed me to my room, which had a wooden table and two slat-back chairs, a small cot with a sunburst-colored blanket, and two single shelves hanging beside the room's only window. I washed up in the shared bathroom before being escorted to dinner, which was buffet style, consisting of white rice and yellow peppers, sambar, which looked and tasted like some type of stew, and roti, which is a flatbread.

Besides myself and the Swami, there were four others. Three of them were women, all of whom knew one another. They lived in the city and were married and had young children and jobs at the same hospital. Laughing, they told me they did everything together. This visit to the ashram was their second. The man, who looked to be in his mid-twenties, had driven out from his hometown of La Grange. He was well built and had a doughy baby face that somehow managed to be serious looking. His Texas accent was as sharp and comical a contrast to the Swami's as I could imagine. When they spoke with one another, I half expected them to break into a skit of some sort. His name was Steve Sweeney and it was his first time at an ashram. He worked on motorcycles, he said, and sometimes raced them.

When the meal ended, Swami offered us a cold drink called Thandai. We were told it was a festive drink, but was appropriate anytime. The only ingredients I recognized were almonds, sugar, and milk. Drinking it like some desperate cultist, I waited for it to have a profound effect. It did little more than help ease the spicy taste of sambar. Swami moved us into a common room off of the dining area. It was a large space with a cathedral wood beam ceiling and two enormous octagonal windows that each took up an entire wall. The room was empty of furniture, so we sat on the floor in front of a mural painting depicting many of the Hindu Gods. For the next hour or so, we drank and listened to stories about the Hindu Gods and Goddesses. Then we listened to one another's stories. The women, whose names I found out were Claire, Doreen, and Nina, talked about their kids and jobs and bosses and lives back in the city. Steve talked about traveling cross-country by himself. He said it was scarier than he thought it would be. As I listened to these strangers' stories, I waited to be moved. I searched for a trace of wisdom I could use, something relatable and devastating in its generosity. The truth is, by the time it came for me to talk - all I revealed was my job and my address - I was bored.

Before turning in for the evening, I thought about calling Laura. Part of me wanted her to know where I was, and that I was in search of self-improvement. Knowing she was too smart to be taken in by this, I settled on reading a book I found in my room entitled *Lighting the Lamp of Wisdom*. It proved to be exactly what I needed; I fell asleep within minutes of opening it.

The following morning saw nearly a dozen new arrivals. Most were there for the day, but a few would be staying overnight. We all ate breakfast together before attending the morning's first session, teachings from a middle-aged white woman named Olivia. It was about recreating yourself. She talked about freeing yourself from the bondage of everyday life. The attendees nodded along or looked knowingly at one another as she spoke. I tried to embrace her words and let them rouse me, but I couldn't get past the notion of her being a white woman named Olivia. From there, I tried yoga, taught by a man named Burt who liked to call everyone his "favorite."

He referred to me as his "favorite man with the black sweatshirt." This was when he announced aloud that my half moon pose was approaching eclipse.

For the next two days, I took Sanskrit courses and meditation workshops; I listened to a man play spirituals on a sitar and I ate a lot of yellow-colored foods. The people I met were kind. They asked a lot of questions and told a lot of stories about themselves. They all seemed to want to be nowhere but at an ashram in Aurora, Illinois. All I did, all I said, all I tried to think, was positive. But it wasn't enough. Nothing worked. This must've been apparent during my last day when it seemed that all I could do was roll my eyes every few minutes before looking at my watch.

It was during my last evening that I considered calling Glenn. I found his number and even prepared a brief script on the back of a split pea soup recipe a woman had given me when I feigned enthusiasm for the dish. The script was a bulleted list. It had three points to it. One was how I didn't blame him for what had happened. Another was how I felt everything in our strange threesome had developed far too quickly. The last was that I was hopeful it could all be sorted out with as little strife as possible. Even as I made my list, I knew I had no real intention of making the call. We would speak, sure, but it would be face-to-face, him playing the calm, confident doctor with wisdom and charm to spare, and me pretending I had to strain to see what Laura saw in him, yet all the while knowing for sure.

To my own surprise, I ended up calling the Old Man. He answered on the first ring. It took a few moments of convincing to assure him that I was actually calling from an ashram.

"C'mon," he continued to say.

"I'm serious."

My father and I hardly have the prank pulling kind of relationship. We can be sarcastic and arrogant with one another, but never whimsical.

"Is Laura with you?"

"I'm alone."

He paused for a bit before telling me all he knew about ashrams. Which was not much. A professor he had at Cornell would spend much of his summers at ashrams in New York and throughout New England.

"How long have you been there?"

In his voice was still a trace of the initial disbelief. It had fused with what I recognized as concern. Together, they made a sound that brought me a strange sense of comfort. We talked infrequently, and had little if anything in common, but he knew me.

I told him about Swami and Olivia and Burt. The food, I mentioned, was decent. Yoga, however, was definitely not for me. He listened. And he asked questions that allowed me to talk some more. Then he talked about his school. Things were running smoothly, he said.

"I'm glad winter is over. You remember what winters are like here, don't you?"

Of course I did. They were torturous. Drab and colorless landscapes. Sore throats and snotty noses. Countless days of inertia and coffee breath. Not exactly what the therapist ordered. The kids would no doubt capitalize on this, morphing further into their grizzled moodiness. The holidays were past and their vacation time was over.

"So are you going to tell me what's going on?" he asked.

"With what?"

"C'mon, you're calling me from an *ashram*."

"What do you want me to say?"

"Well, for starters, where's Laura?"

"Not sure."

"What do you mean *you're not sure*? What's going on with you two? I know you've hit a rough patch, but who the hell hasn't? Do you think your mother and I never hit a rough patch?"

I didn't want to hear a story about him and my mother. I didn't want advice or encouragement. So I blurted out a thought that had taken shape in my subconscious. When I said it, I found that I liked how it sounded:

"I'm thinking about quitting the paper."

"What'll you do?"

Another subconscious thought:

"I thought I'd come home for a while."

"*Home* home?" he asked, his voice maneuvering around the shock and joy and sorrow he must've felt over the idea.

"To Connecticut. Yes."

"Alone?"

"Yes."

"Are you going to tell me what's going on?"

"I don't know," I said, surprised by my honesty.

He let the matter go. Then he began telling me how he could put me up and even give me a job on campus. It wouldn't be with the kids, he laughed, but something behind the scenes.

"I'll come up with something," he promised.

I didn't respond.

"Until you get your footing."

We talked for a while longer. In that time he didn't mention Laura again. When we hung up, I expected to feel the dissolution of the optimism we had just fused. The tacit understanding. The solace. The idea of me moving back to Connecticut. I sat in that little square-shaped room on one of those slat-back chairs, waiting for all of it to abate. It didn't. I was stunned. I fell asleep that night to the distant sounds of Indian instruments, a tabla and a sarod and a shehnai, and for the first time since I could recall, I had dreams about the east coast.

• • •

When I was less than ten minutes from my house, I pulled the car to the side of the road and called Ben. I told him I didn't think I could face things. He sighed a little into the phone.

"Let me call you right back," he said.

Since I broke the news about Laura, Ben's sentimentality towards me seemed to waver. He now dealt with me with such brevity, such remove, that I became self-conscious whenever I delivered my bad news to him. Ben lived in Harwood Heights, a suburb just outside the city, in a beautiful brick Colonial with a three car garage, a spacious first floor den, and his wife and daughters. To him, my reality must've now seemed like some grotesque fantasy once it was stacked up against his own. We were no longer working towards the same conclusions in life. My dilemma must've reminded him of what he never wanted to lose. In that way, I was the worst kind of threat.

As the engine ran, I waited. After nearly fifteen minutes, he called back and told me to come over.

"I don't want to be a bother."

"Justine's parents are here, so you're on your own for tonight."

"That's fine."

I told him about the ashram, hoping he'd see it as a sign of humility and self-help. It was important to me that Ben understood that I wasn't cavalier about my situation. Whenever we spoke, I found myself saying things that tried to underscore this point. My worn away spirit had to show, I told myself. But in case it didn't - or in case it wasn't enough, or in case he doubted whether I was still a good man - I put on a bit of a performance, pausing and mumbling and heaving deep, pensive breaths I hoped would clear up any confusion over the matter.

Justine asked me to join their family for dinner that evening. It would be a nice home-cooked meal, she said, looking at me with more tenderness than I deserved. She was a short, attractive woman with the build of a fitness trainer and bright green eyes that looked like they were made from newly erupted lava. I understood what she meant by the home cooking comment. Politely, I declined. She persisted, so I relented.

The evening was pleasant. The meal was outstanding and my wine glass was never far from reach. Justine's parents, Bob and Susan, were spry, affectionate people. In between romps with their granddaughters, they talked about their recent trip to Belize. Justine, in an effort to include me in the conversation, told them I had just returned from an ashram. She mentioned it was the same one she had once visited. I talked about it, exaggerating its effect on me, claiming it was an unforgettable experience. Ben's twin girls asked no one in particular what an ashram was. Without flinching, Ben told them it was where you went to find balance. Justine perked up.

"Nice to meet you, Meher Baba," she said, raising her glass. "Here's to your expertise."

"Excuse *me*," said Ben, feigning defensiveness, "I forgot whose presence we're in. Darling, would *you* like to respond to your daughters' inquisitiveness?"

Smiling, Justine looked around the table, paused a moment, and told Rachel and Robyn the exact thing their father had. We all laughed. Ben and Justine clinked their glasses together and drank. Once the attention diverted to another matter, I witnessed them making playful faces at each other; it was subtle, but it was there - coy, loving, secretive.

"Did you find that for yourself, Gray?" Bob asked me.

"Find what, sir?"

I knew what he meant. I just needed the extra seconds to work out a response in my mind, something witty or profound or maybe endearingly honest.

"Balance," he said.

Attention was now on me. Even Rachel and Robyn, who must've had more than a few moments that evening of wondering who the hell I was, looked my way and awaited an answer to an absurd question. I was a bastard if I said no. I was somehow damaged in the first place if I said yes. Turning to Ben, I let out a little gasp. Ignoring the plea, he took a sip of wine and looked down at his empty plate.

"I don't know," I finally said.

There was a brief pause, followed by the sound of Susan filling her wine glass.

"Speaking of balance," Justine broke in, "what did you think of the food there?"

Not bad, I told her, but nothing I'll miss. I told the story about the recipe of split pea soup I had somewhere in my suitcase. And so the conversation shifted. And at least for a moment it was put aside that I was the dinner guest, the outsider, the interloper with stories to tell, stories to which I couldn't find a proper beginning or ending or even a point.

Ben helped me settle into my room for the evening. It was an enormous space above the garage that was used as the girls' rec room. Boasting a ping pong table and wall-to-wall shelves filled with books and toys, it was carpeted, well lit, and smelled of cookie dough. We moved a few things to make the space around the pullout sofa more accessible.

"This is great," I told him as we shimmied a portable piano out of the way. "If I can't sleep, I can always play 'Chopsticks.'"

Ben didn't respond to this. We moved a dollhouse and a kitchenette together in silence.

"I appreciate everything."

"Of course."

He told me about the bathroom and the towels and the leftover food in the fridge.

"I'm just gonna crash and then I'll be out of your hair in the morning."

"Fine."

We exchanged looks for a moment. It might've been brief, but I understood that something was happening between the two of us. Ben had me in his house. I was eating his wife's cooking. I was sleeping in the room in which his daughters played and pretended. He was unsure how to handle me now. I'd become as elusive and controversial as some midnight drifter. He turned to walk out of the room when I blurted out that he'd barely known Laura.

"I know that," he said, turning to face me.

"We were never a foursome," I went on, "two married couples breaking bread and hitting the town together - that was never us. Shit, I think Justine met Laura two or three times."

"No one's saying otherwise, Gray."

"Then stop acting like I broke up the old gang, for fuck's sake. Because frankly this is all starting to resemble a Woody Allen film."

"I'm not acting like anything. And keep your voice down."

"I'm not gonna corrupt your family. My misery will not harm any of you. You're safe from my bullshit. You're all safe. It's not contagious."

"Stop feeling sorry for yourself."

"That's not what I need to hear from you right now."

"And what do you need to hear?"

"I need to hear you say I'm not a bad man. That you understand me and nothing's changed where we're concerned. I need to hear you say that you'll help me organize a hit on this motherfucker who's banging my wife."

"Lower your voice. And would any of that solve your problem?"

"I don't *have* a problem."

The blood in my head suddenly felt like it was undulating against my temples. I made my way to the sofa and sat down. With the heels of my hands, I began massaging my eye sockets. After a few moments, Ben came closer to me.

"I don't have a problem," I said again, my voice soft and raspy. "I'm carrying something weightier than a problem. I don't know what the fuck it is, but it scares the hell out of me. I think...I think it's something I've never seen before in anyone else. I'm not saying I'm special, but I'm starting to think I have a stranglehold on this thing, like I've cornered the market on it."

"You're fucked up right now. You didn't corner the market on being fucked up. Besides, didn't you grow up in a place where being fucked up was the status quo?"

He was smiling when he said this. After a minute, he sat down beside me. We didn't speak for a while. Then he let out a long exhale and told me I could stay at his place as long as I needed to. All the ping pong and piano I wanted, he told me. He'd already talked it over with Justine, he said, and she was okay with it. I tried to speak, but I couldn't. This was an unexpected act of kindness, a bounty I would willingly accept, but scarcely contemplate. I'd had, after all, far too many thoughts of worthiness and gratitude for the time being.

. . .

Living like some nomadic fugitive, I stayed at Ben's for ten more days. In that time, I kept mostly to myself. I ate next to nothing, grew a little beard, and watched season after season of a show called *Red House* that Justine had recommended to me. I made the drive back to my place on a cold and overcast Tuesday morning. The second I walked in the door I knew I was alone. I checked the garage for Laura's car and found it was gone. The house felt heavy under its burden of silence. A few windows were ajar and a crisp breeze crept through the rooms. The pillows on the sofas were fluffed and angled. The kitchen sink was gleaming. The wood floors looked like they were installed and polished that day. The only sign of life was a crystal bud vase on the island, holding two of the most perfect red roses I'd ever seen.

I snooped for a while, checking my bedroom, the bathrooms, the contents of the hamper, the fridge, even the garbage. Nothing appeared out of place. Pouring myself a dry bowl of cereal, I sat down and called my father. He picked up on the third ring. Little time was wasted before he asked how I was doing.

"I'm all right."

"Is Laura there with you?"

"No."

"Where is she?"

"Good question."

"What exactly is going on out there?"

"Hard to say."

"Try."

"It's sort of shapeless right now."

"Why's that?"

"Because it's still taking shape."

"I can't get a straight answer from you."

"I'm sorry about that."

"Are you still thinking about coming home?"

It was on the verge of my tongue to tell him no, that I'd changed my mind, that I was an adult, and a successful one at that, and I could certainly navigate my way through turmoil and come out ahead and be fine and whole and happy. But the thought of hearing such lies was enough to stifle me.

"I'll let you know."

That evening I took a bath, something I hadn't done in years. For over an hour, I sat in a tub of hot, soapy water and scrubbed my skin until it felt as red and raw as it looked. Then I shaved my face clean and trimmed all my nails. For a while after this, I watched TV in bed and drifted in and out of sleep. On occasion, I would look out the window at Glenn's house to check for any activity. His lights were off and no vehicles came or went.

At around 1:00 a.m., Laura came home. I awoke from my half-sleep the moment she began ascending the stairs. The TV was still on; it was playing *Straw Dogs*, a movie I'd never seen from beginning to end. The volume was a little loud, so I turned it down to just above a whisper. I still wanted it playing when Laura entered the room; the thought of there being no distractions upon seeing one another was unbearable. The moment she approached the doorway, the scene transitioned and the TV went nearly black for a second. In that flash, as I saw her figure standing no more than twenty feet away, I had the distinct feeling that despite all the recent changes in our lives, the most radical one would be happening at any moment.

"Are you up?"

She said this with a voice sweet enough to caress the soft pattern off of china.

"I was just drifting in and out."

My own voice was hoarse and uncertain. When she entered the room, I got a good look at her as she moved toward me on the bed. She was wearing jeans and a black sweater with a pink scarf around her neck that draped neatly across her breast - all very plain, but she looked classy and pretty.

"Are you okay?"

"I'm fine. I mean I'm not *fine*, but I'm okay."

"I understand."

She sat beside me on the bed.

"How are *you* doing?" I asked.

"I'm good. Yeah, I'm actually pretty good."

"Where's Glenn?"

She looked at the TV. It was the scene where Dustin Hoffman's character finds the dead cat hanging in the closet.

"He's next door."

"And how's *he* doing?"

"Stop."

"Well, we can't leave him out. I'm *fine to okay*. You're *good to pretty good*. How's Glenn doing?"

"I'll tell you," she said, all the tenderness in her tone gone, "he was worried about you, too. He must've called every hospital in the city."

"*Glenn* was worried about me? I can't believe you're telling me this. How do you expect me to react to that? Should I give him a fucking humanitarian award? *Glenn* was worried about me. What was he worried about, that I might shoot myself in the basement and lower his property value?"

"He's not who you think he is."

"Who is he then?"

"He's different."

"Different from what?"

She stared at me. Then she took a deep breath before turning her head towards the TV. I studied her face in the glow from the screen. I decided she looked better than I'd seen her look in a long time. There was a new vitality in her skin and eyes and mouth. She knew it, too, because as well as she wore it, there was a trace of self-awareness that only a husband of some years can detect. I couldn't help but wonder if Glenn knew it.

"I don't want to discuss Glenn," she said, looking back towards me.

"What's left then? What's left to discuss?"

"I don't know."

"There must be something we can discuss."

Laura said that whatever we had left to discuss was no longer emotional, but instead practical. I told her this was an ugly thing to say. She said it was true. Then she stood up and went to her bureau, where she opened the top drawer and removed a large manila envelope. Dropping it on the edge of the bed, she told me it was all very straightforward and easy to understand. I could look it over in the morning, she said, and eventually sit down with my attorney and ask any question that might arise. There was nothing to say, nothing to do. Laura looked beautiful standing there, but it was no longer the kind of beauty that would make me breathe easier; if I let it, it might sicken me to no end and drive me to real despair. So I didn't say anything; I just nodded my head and watched the TV, which was showing the last seconds of the movie's most controversial scene between the woman playing Dustin Hoffman's wife and the film's ghastly villain.

• • •

So much of spring went by in a wash of broken moments. I moved in with Ben after he had Justine send me a pleading text to do so. And I hired an attorney I found online. His name was Ed Rawlings, and he told me an uncontested divorce was the way to go. He said it would be the quickest and least expensive means to an end. Laura agreed this was the best option. She said we owed it to ourselves to be civil. I came close to asking what she meant by this, but I never did. With a maddening sense of grace, grace born out of wisdom and temperance, Laura initiated conversations - all on the phone or in text - on how to best settle our affairs. She was staying with Glenn during this time and it was easy for me to imagine the two of them collaborating in their decorum so that Gray, poor pitiful Gray, might learn that winners and losers alike could maintain such dignity.

With three days notice, I quit my job at the paper. There were no parties or pep talks from any of my colleagues. Just a few handshakes and formalities and I was out the door. The loss felt good in an odd way. Even freeing. Maybe since I was the one in control of it.

My phone rang one night when I was playing chess with one of Ben's girls. It was Glenn. He asked if I had a minute.

"I feel like we never really got a chance to talk," he said. "And part of me thinks that's probably for the best, but the other part knows that's not really my style."

"And what exactly is your style, Glenn?" I said, excusing myself from the game.

"To confront things. Always. Like a man. Head on."

"Would that make you feel better? Is that what this is about? I have to be interrupted on a - whatever night this is - so you can feel better about yourself? Well, in that case, let's confront things. Go ahead, Glenn. Confront away."

"It's not all about me. I do know that much."

"Mighty humble of you. Who's it about then? Laura?"

"Absolutely. It's absolutely about Laura."

I didn't care for the way he said this. It sounded to me like it had come from a man who was so sure he knew more than I ever would about those erratic, precious places in the human heart. I fired back.

"Let me guess," I said, locking myself in the bathroom, "you're going to take wonderful care of her. And you're sorry for how it all turned out, but you want me to know how you feel about Laura: You love her and respect her and you just want me to know that she's in good hands and will be given all that she deserves. It's her happiness, after all, that's the most important thing here. And if she's happy now, well then, it hasn't all been for naught."

He barely hesitated before responding. It came out of him so naturally, so automatically, that for a moment I imagined him reading it from a giant cue card held by some fawning, moronic understudy:

"I can't say what'll happen. I really have no idea. No one does. It's impossible to know. Just like you didn't know any of this would happen, did you?"

It took a moment for what he said to register. When it finally did, I found myself speechless. So I hung up on him and turned off my phone. His words buzzed at me, leaving me with a strange sense of comfort and then anarchy. He was either a genius or an asshole; it was difficult to tell. There I was, sitting on the bathroom floor in a friend's house - my only friend in the world - on whatever night of the week it happened to be, the cold clean tile chilling my bones, making me wish for a warm bed, contemplating the possible wisdom of Glenn Kilburn. Thoughts of his former speeches came rushing back at me; there had been one about what it meant to be a man; and there was one on getting through life and averting disaster at all costs. It felt like every exchange I ever had with Glenn left me in a state of exhaustion as I secretly considered the validity of what this stranger had to tell me.

Sitting there on the floor in Ben's bathroom, the bright lights beating down on me, the crisp, sugary scent of unlit candles in the air, I got the idea to call my father. He'd no doubt be there. Possibly even awaiting my call. But I wasn't in the mood. I'd call the following day. Or perhaps the day after that. It hardly mattered. I knew we'd be seeing one another soon enough.

CHAPTER 19

I found out that my onlookers were more concerned with the strange, alliterative phrase I had been mumbling than they were with my three broken ribs, my broken collarbone, and my concussion. I was in and out of consciousness for several hours and spoke these vile, startling words when I finally came back to life. Rollie told me that the words started out as a labored whisper, then evolved more clearly into something worthy of shocking the hospital staff. Everyone waited for me to elaborate, but I simply continued to repeat the phrase. So in between dry gasps and weak coughs, all they heard from me were Austin's six words that Adam had dug out of the trash. Six words that *belonged* in the trash. Six words that would arrest anyone's attention.

The doctors recommended that I stay the night for some tests and general observation. The Old Man signed the papers and then hovered over me for most of the day, joined occasionally by a few of my colleagues who were able to steal away from the school for an hour or two.

"You're scaring the hell out of everyone here," my father said when I began to come around.

"What happened?" I asked.

"You made one hell of a running catch."

A moment passes before I get his meaning. Dan Hart. It all comes back to me.

"How is he?"

"He's a little banged up - mostly his feet and hands - but he's doing okay."

"And how am I?"

"You? Well, you're a scary bastard, but other than that, you're fine."

I ask to see a mirror. A sling is pulled securely around my collarbone and there's a bandage around the top of my head. The Old Man laughs a little, explaining how my scaring people has nothing to do with appearance.

"It's what you kept repeating."

Leaning towards me so that the nurse, a young, pretty thing named Cecilia, wouldn't hear, he tells me that I had said, repeatedly, *Kill a cunt, frame a freak.* It takes a moment for me to register the source of these words before telling my father everything I know. Which is not much. The dumpster diving and the red notebook and my meeting with Austin and how I raced back to campus the previous evening only to find Dan Hart causing one hell of a scene from the roof of the dining hall. My shortness of breath as I speak makes me whisper the words.

He already knows all of this, he tells me. The boys, Matt and Adam, just hours before, had begged Nussbaum to bring them to the hospital with him. There, outside my room, they told Rollie what they knew. He's asked them to keep this confidential for the time being.

"What now?"

"Just rest. That's all you need to worry about."

"What about Austin?"

"We'll look into it. But I wouldn't expect a confession, for Christ's sake. The proof we're talking about is not exactly of the ironclad variety."

Cecilia leaves the room. A heart monitor makes a sudden beeping sound. I ask the Old Man for a drink and he reaches for the styrofoam cup of ice water on the tray in front of me.

"I've got some good news amid all this goddamn grief," he tells me, planting the straw between my lips.

After taking a long and almost delirious sip of the water, I straighten myself up as best I can.

"It's something I've been waiting on for a while," he says.

"I'm all ears."

The deal between him and J.R. III will be finalized this afternoon, he tells me. The necessary papers are being signed and delivered as we speak. He's certainly tired and unshaven, but he looks more pleased than I can recall ever seeing him.

"Congratulations."

My tone must sound sincere because he thanks me. We sit in silence for some time, absorbed in all the hospital smells and sounds that suddenly seem to be closing in on me. Then, as if being a prick will open up the walls, give me back the breath I feel I've been robbed of, I quash the good cheer:

"At least one of us is getting what he wants out of this life."

My father leaves my side at around dinnertime. Doctors and nurses come and go from my room. They speak to me about my condition, which they call stable and improving. Cecilia has become my favorite among them. She does her job well, yet still finds the time to flirt and make me feel like a man. She doesn't call me Gray when she speaks to me; she calls me Hero. It's Hero this and Hero that.

"What's this *Hero* business?" I finally ask while she readies some morphine.

"Isn't that like a true hero?" she says, "as modest as can be."

The idea of how she found out what brought me here excites me. A conversation clearly occurred. Either with Rollie or with one of my visitors. So I leave the moment alone. But as the drug takes effect, I find myself slipping into a dreamy place where I begin wondering about what I've done for Dan Hart. After reliving the details in my head, I think about why I did it. All I can come up with is because he's just a kid. There's nothing more to it. He's a kid. And because of that, he's deserving of something I'm not certain he's aware even exists.

I find myself wishing for Laura. I even say her name aloud a few times. It could be the morphine, or it could be that I long for her to know what I've done. When I close my eyes, I picture myself in a well-lit room with her at my side. She's close to me and I'm telling her about what happened with Dan Hart. After I tell her about his rooftop concert, his sacrificial guitar bomb, his attempt on his own life, she looks at me and says I'm a good man. She continues telling me this - that I'm a good man. I like hearing it, so I sit and listen to her tell me over and over again. When I open my eyes, though, no one's there to tell me anything about myself - nothing about what I've done or who I am or how things might be from here on out. Cecilia has dimmed the lights and left the room. The overhanging TV is on low, turned to a game show, which I mindlessly watch as I think about the following day and what might become of me.

• • •

Rollie urges me to take off as much time as I need. After my convalescence, he tells me, I can come back to work. I suspect he feels that once I recover I'll be turning in my Homer House keys and packing up my Jeep.

"I want you to recuperate at my place," he tells me. "It's not the Four Seasons, but at least you can get away from the kids for a while."

"I'll be fine where I am. The kids won't bother me."

But we both agree that some time off is vital. Breaking up petty squabbles and confiscating cigarettes will not be part of my rehabilitation. Aside from looking ridiculous in my sling and bandages, my movements are slow and labored; I can hardly be effective anywhere. So Ryan pulls double duty in the dorm and the Old Man finds coverage for my classes. My plan is to read and think and maybe even write a little.

Within a full day of my return to the HAS, it becomes clear that this plan will not come to pass. My place has become a social haven. Visitors come and go, checking on me at all hours. Colleagues and students and therapists. Sandra brings me scallion pancakes she's made. We eat together while she tells me about her family who live in Hainan and own a fishery. Amber brings me some of her favorite short story collections by John Cheever and Willa Cather. She stays for a while and we discuss literature. Some girls I don't teach or even know particularly well come by with peanut butter cookies. Nussbaum checks in on me, bringing me a bougainvillea bonsai plant he says will spruce up my place. He tells me the plant's origins and care instructions, tells me to call if I need anything, and leaves. Others come by as well. Tennille and Scotty visit and we play cards. Matt and Adam stop by and tell me they're putting the finishing touches on the Winnebago and how they're certain it'll soon be drivable. Then we talk about The Beatles. Then about whether Austin Roarick is a murderer. Everyone must have Dan Hart on their minds, but no one mentions him to me. They just keep me company for a while before wishing me their best.

The Old Man also drops by. Mostly to see if I need anything and if the kids in the dorm are giving me my space. On my third day back from the hospital, he comes by after dinner. He has a single sheet of white paper in his hand, which he hands to me when I greet him at the door. It's the Hundred Acre School letterhead. It's new. It now has the Old Man's name, Rollie Loveland, as proprietor and CEO of the place.

"What do you think?"

"Your name is spelled right. What else do you want?"

"I promise I won't go overboard, but I want you to know that your mother would be thrilled with this - absolutely thrilled. Beyond belief. I guess that gives *me* a thrill. But it also makes me pretty goddamn sad at the same time."

"Aren't those manic traits?"

"I think they are," he says, laughing a little.

"Well, I guess you're in the right place then."

He follows me into the TV room where I take a seat on the couch.

"Are you comfortable?"

"I'm all right."

"Good. You're looking better."

"I'm feeling okay."

He looks out the window before pacing the room and sitting down beside me.

"Nick's back in the dorm," he tells me, "on borrowed time, of course, but he's back. He's actually talking a little, which is a good sign. He's not telling us shit, but at least he's verbal. We've asked him point blank everything you can imagine - about Nicole and the ring and the drugs. He's a stubborn little fucker. The police are being patient. They're on our side. I just wanted you to know."

"How're the other boys dealing with him?"

"They're okay. They seem to be leaving him alone."

"Probably for the best."

"There's something else. I spoke with Roarick about Austin. I told him what you and I talked about - about what Matt and Adam found at his place. I felt obligated to approach him before anyone else. Call me sentimental, but I've known the man for a hell of a long time, and it *is* his son we're talking about."

"How'd he take it?"

"He didn't defend him. He said he'd look into it."

"So I guess we'll see."

"I guess we will."

Dan Hart, the Old Man tells me, is doing well. He's still in the hospital, where he'll stay for another few days. And his parents have flown in from North Carolina to be at their son's side.

"They'll be bringing him back with them. With the summer vacation coming up, it seems to make the most sense. No immediate plans as to when, or if, he'll return."

"What'll his entourage do without him?"

"He needs to be somewhere else right now."

The Old Man tells me about a program in a hospital not far from Stokes County, which is where Dan is from.

"This upcoming break couldn't be coming at a better time," I point out.

"Am I a thoughtless prick to wanna know what your plans are when it's over? God knows you've got enough to contend with right now without being forced to make that decision."

"Agreed."

"Still, it's been on my mind."

"I'm sure it has."

"And—"

"And it's been on my mind, too."

The Homer House boys can be heard through my walls. One of them - it sounds like Cliff - is singing a tune so out of key that it has to be intentional. Rollie and I sit for a while without speaking to one another. After some time, when the singing stops, he stands up and tells me he'll check in on me tomorrow. What he really means is that he hopes I'll arrive at a decision by then.

That night I grow restless. Too restless to read or watch TV or certainly sleep. So I pop a few painkillers before cleaning my bathroom and fridge and making up my futon with fresh sheets. All the while I can hear the Homer House boys through the walls. They're laughing every few seconds. When I open the door and peer my head into the hallway, I can hear the TV playing. I listen for a moment, trying to identify what they're watching. Then I close my door and reorganize some of my kitchen cabinets. After a while, I venture out of the apartment and make my way down the hall. All the boys, including Ryan, are gathered together in the common room. The lights are off and they're watching *Friday* with Ice Cube. When I enter, a few of them turn and notice me. Cliff, offering me his seat, moves to the floor next to Albert. My injuries are still sore enough for me to accept.

It's only a few idiotic scenes into the film until I notice Nick, sitting quietly by himself on the hearth. He has an awkward view of the TV, which is almost parallel to him. He seems unbothered by this since he appears to be in his own world. When the light of the TV illuminates his face, I can see his expression, which is one I don't recall seeing on him before. He seems content. Like finding his way back to the HAS was a wise move. Yet it was one over which he'd never express his relief; he'd rather sit at the periphery of his friends and find strange solace in their boorish laughter.

When I turn to Ryan, it's obvious he's observed me eyeing Nick. He nods, which tells me I've been away for a few days and things are different: Nick is back in the dorm, among his Homer House boys, who are no doubt regarding him with trepidation. They're at a loss as to how to process his disappearing act, his return, the fate of his former girlfriend.

When the movie ends, the evening begins to wind down. Teeth are brushed, acne cream is applied, shirts are stripped. Ryan and I sit in the near dark of the common room and talk while the boys check off their nighttime rituals. Ryan asks how I'm spending my free time and how I'm feeling and what my plans are during the upcoming summer break. In between answering him, I study Nick, who moves through the dorm like the air around him is piled high with a tower of champagne glasses.

"Do you have my pictures?" he asks when he finally approaches me.

He makes eye contact when he says this, but his voice is muted and little boyish. It sounds like nothing I remember. It takes a moment for me to realize what he's talking about.

"Sure. I've got them."

This isn't true. Rollie has them. He's had them since the day they were mailed to me. And besides Eileen Russo, he's never shown them to a soul. Not to the cops, not to Mr. and Mrs. D'Ambrosio, not even to Nussbaum. Nick follows me into my place and watches me rummage through my desk drawers as I pretend to look for them. I tell him they're sealed in an envelope for safe keeping.

"How are you?" I ask as I begin emptying the contents of the drawers.

"I'm fine."

"You look well."

I mean this. His hair has been cut, which I can now see since he's stepped into the light of my room, and his eyes appear as though they've softened since his ordeal. It's the closest to handsome I've seen him. Suddenly, as I'm looking at him, I can detect Eileen. They share the same low cheekbones and narrow forehead. Not to mention their noses, which are sharp and slightly longer than usual. As though reading my thoughts, Nick tells me he heard I met his mother. I stop looking for the pictures almost immediately.

"That's true. I met her briefly."

He makes a sarcastic comment on how lucky I am.

"She was worried about you."

Rolling his eyes, Nick says how Rollie gets paid absurd amounts of money so his mother no longer has to worry over him. I tell him I don't think parenting works that way.

"How do you know? You're not a parent."

"I'm not a politician, either, but I can still vouch for their sleaziness."

He drops the matter. I can't help but wonder what Eileen told her son about our encounter. It's tempting to ask, but I don't dare. I decide to bring up something else, something I frame casually enough so he might think nothing of it and let down his guard.

"Where did you disappear to?"

"How can you stand living here?" he asks, stepping further into the room and ignoring my question.

"How do *you* stand it?"

"I don't have a choice," he says.

"I'm not sure I do, either."

"What does that mean?"

"It means we've all got a story. All of us."

"No shit."

Feigning an epiphany, I tell him I just remembered that my father has his photos locked away in a safe place. We didn't want them left in the dorm, I tell him.

"I'm not embarrassed by those pictures."

"Okay."

"You guys probably think I'm some fucking pervert, but I'm not."

"Okay."

Before I can ask anything about the photos, he changes the topic to my injuries, then to Dan Hart. We end up talking for close to half an hour. I never would've guessed that Nick Russo and I would have much to say to one another. I listen to him complain about his roommates in the Homer House and how the Mets aren't realizing their potential this season. He listens to me talk about my collarbone and my classes, which I tell him I think I miss teaching. I manage to sneak in a question - Why did you run away? - but it goes unanswered like the last one. He changes the topic back to his mother, who he mentions will be picking him up a few days before the upcoming vacation. Before I can fully envision once again being face-to-face with Eileen Russo, Ryan leans in the doorway for a moment and says it's time for lights out. Nick starts to leave when I decide to try my luck one final time:

"Why *me*? Why send *me* that letter? And those pictures? To be honest, I was surprised."

He starts to say something. His lips move in several directions before he purses them. Then they open wide and turn inside his mouth and into a nervous smile. I find myself feeling sorry for him. To get him off the hook, I wish him goodnight. And even though he returned a few days ago, straggling onto campus like some burnt-out tramp, I welcome him back to the Hundred Acre School. It immediately strikes me as a cruel gesture of irony since I know he won't be back in the fall. The look he gives me, one of almost philosophical grandeur, belies his youth. Like his face is an ancient burial ground and behind it is the spirit of true revelation. He's speechless once again. But just for a moment.

"Welcome back to you, too," he says.

Then we both laugh quietly at what we've discovered is common ground.

. . .

The following day, I return to teaching. It's better than staring at the walls or reorganizing my silverware drawer again. Besides, there are only a few days left before vacation. The Old Man tells me it was getting difficult to find coverage for my classes, and that he actually taught a few himself, which the kids got a kick out of. I also rejoin the writers group, which has been meeting in my absence. They have a gift to welcome me back - it's a collection of short stories by Richard Russo. One story in particular, "The Whore's Child," might be of interest, they tell me, since it's about a writers group.

The kids are anxious to share their new ideas. Jess has been working steadily on his bank robber novel and reads us a recent chapter excerpt where his blind protagonist ingratiates himself to the unsuspecting bank manager at a cancer survivor support group. Meredith has just completed a poem entitled "A New Font in Which to Write." My favorite line is "The knots in her worry once anchored a cruise ship in St. Croix." Dorian announces he's purchased a book on TV writing and is outlining a script idea for a show I've never heard of. Kay and Marilyn tell me that Matt and Adam, who are not in attendance, have not been writing lately. Thanks to Rollie, the Winnebago has been their top priority. He's even allowing them a ridiculous ribbon cutting ceremony after dinner. There they will unveil the vehicle in its new splendor.

There's of course talk of my injuries and Dan Hart and Nick Russo. The kids admit they don't know how to feel about Nick's return. He may be finally talking, they acknowledge, but he's revealing nothing.

"I don't think he killed that girl," says Booth. "There's no way he'd return if he did it. He'd be in Canada or California by now."

"Ever hear of returning to the scene of the crime?" says Jess.

"I don't think he did it, either," says Meredith.

"I heard he's getting expelled," says Jess.

Kay and Marilyn announce that they are undecided over Nick's innocence. Dorian asks me if it's unsettling to share a roof with Nick.

"Because there *is* a possibility that he's a murderer," the boy adds.

I'm tempted to share with them my talk with Nick the previous night. And about the photos he sent me. And about Austin Roarick and what Matt and Adam found in that notebook. But even I don't know what it all adds up to. So I just tell them that Nick, like the rest of us, has some things to sort out. Meredith focuses on my use of the pronoun *us*.

"What do *you* have to sort out, Grayson Loveland?" she asks.

Before I can answer, she fires out another question, one she's been asking since I met her at the beginning of the summer:

"And for God's sake, when can we read some of your stuff?"

"Maybe after vacation," I said, wondering if this is a lie on a few different levels.

There's a ribbon cutting ceremony that night. Under a cloudless summer sky, dozens of attendees – staff and students – gather to watch Matt and Adam start the Winnebago and rev its newly rebuilt engine. Then Rollie climbs behind the wheel and drives it around campus, chauffeuring anyone who wants a ride. From my front porch, I see the boys' work has been successful, as my father circles the school countless times over the next hour. He sounds the horn whenever he passes the Homer House. Finally, when dusk begins to break and there's no sign of the motorhome, I head back inside and shower and shave and settle down with the Richard Russo story collection.

The evening is quiet. I barely hear the Homer House boys through my walls. Every so often Ryan's voice comes across, or Cliff's guitar, or the barely audible sounds of the TV. I reach the fourth page break in the story I'm reading when I hear a vehicle approach the dorm. Its engine sounds steady and strong. Before looking out my window, I can tell it's the Old Man. He beeps the horn a couple of times and I assume it's me he's summoning. Heading outside, I take a guess as to the purpose of his visit. With his refurbished house on wheels, he's no doubt nostalgic and wanting to relive those nascent years with my mother. Or maybe ask me my plans after the upcoming August break. Yet when I see his face through the windshield, I know it's more than this. He has a stern look about him, like he's some military messenger sent to deliver brutally bad news.

He barely waits for me to sit in the passenger seat before putting the vehicle in gear and pulling away from the dorm. Some of the boys are looking out at us from their window; a few others have stepped outside to watch. The Old Man wastes no time before explaining himself. He's just been downtown at the police station to deposit Nicole's cherished Tiffany's ring. Having already been apprised of some recent developments - Matt and Adam's dumpster discovery, my visit with Austin - the police and Rollie have been in regular contact.

"They had some interesting news for me," he says.

Steering the vehicle off campus and onto Wildwood Road, Rollie reminds me of Quinton Sandrey, the Old Brookview teenager who recently overdosed and died in his sleep. Then he tells me that Quinton's younger brother just came forward to the police, revealing how Quinton and his friends bought prescription drugs from Austin Roarick.

"Sounds like Austin and Nick had themselves a little enterprise downtown," he says. "I don't know how the hell they hooked up - or where exactly their paths crossed - but what a partnership. Jesus Christ."

"Did this kid mention Nick?"

"No, he didn't."

The Old Man emits mock laughter. We've been driving on Route 1, which is the main drag that runs through the shoreline. He's been handling the vehicle well. Pulling into a ramshackle package store called Teddy's Liquors, which has been there since I can remember, he parks as far away from the building as he can.

"I feel like a kid again, driving this thing after all these years. Those boys did one hell of a job. You should hear them explain exactly what they did; it'll hurt your goddamn head."

"What are we doing?"

"Trust me, this is the perfect place to be. I've been saving the best part of what I have to tell you for last, and God knows you're going to need a drink before hearing this. I'm buying."

Leaving me in the vehicle for a few moments, he returns with a twelve-pack of fancy imported bottled beer with a rustic brown label that shows a bear playing a banjo. He mentions it's what a lot of his staff drink and he's come to enjoy it. Opening two of the bottles, he hands me one and tells me he feels like getting drunk this evening.

"I haven't been drunk in an awfully long time," he says, clinking our beers together, "so what the hell?"

He takes a long swig from the bottle and sets it down between his legs. I look around outside before taking a sip. Two overweight younger women exit Teddy's, each carrying a box of booze. They load them into their pickup truck, which is parked in the only handicap spot, and drive away.

"What do you think?" he asks, pointing to the beer.

"I think this is the goddamn strangest father/son bonding we've ever done."

Half grinning, he grumbles to himself and finishes off the bottle. Then he wipes his mouth and tells me that according to the police, Austin Roarick has vanished. The expression on his face when he tells me this comes off as prideful, as though he's just announced his firm decision to run for public office. He opens another beer and starts to drink.

"We're going to need something to eat to go with the beer," he says. "Any requests?"

There appears to be nothing more to say about Austin. When I ask for details, the Old Man merely repeats himself:

"The police paid him a visit this evening and his place was wiped out. No sign of him anywhere. Neighbors know nothing. Hell, even J.R. III, according to the cops, knows nothing. Or so he says."

Images flash in my mind of Austin's father relocating his son. Perhaps he made arrangements for Austin to be privately flown down to Mexico or to Nassau to live with his mother. I picture J.R. III dictating the terms. He'd tell his son to keep his mouth shut and do what he's told, which would be to pack his bags, get his passport, and meet him in an hour. He'd lecture his son in their final moments together. He might even strike him some. Then maybe he'd make an awkward showing of affection, wanting to ask his son what the hell he did and why and how it came to that. He'd want to know what he did wrong as a parent, and did he, his son, know how goddamn difficult it was to *be* a parent. Austin wouldn't respond; his stunned brain would be deluged on private thoughts on how it's just as difficult being a son.

Rollie goes back into Teddy's and comes out with two bags of potato chips. We stay in the parking lot and drink beer and eat chips. The package store closes and a paunchy man in a tank top and jeans turns off the lights and locks the front door. Rolling down the window, the Old Man calls out to him that we'll be leaving shortly. The man waves before giving us the thumbs-up sign. We stay there for over two hours, talking about music and literature and my recent injuries. There are no mentions of Chicago or my mother or the Hundred Acre School or any of its students or recent scandals or whether I'll be staying on after the August break.

My father is drunk during much of our talk. He seems at ease, and quite taken with the effects of the alcohol. The bathroom in the Winnebago is functional, so we each use it a couple of times. At a little past midnight, he suggests we head back to campus. All the beer is gone. He's had a few more than me and needs me to drive. After a slurred tutorial on how to handle the vehicle, he switches seats with me and tells me to stick to the speed limit.

Getting stopped by the cops, he says, would be a disaster for obvious reasons.

The dark roads are deserted. And even though I'm buzzed, driving the thing proves easier than I imagined. When I look towards my father, I can see that he's asleep, or passed out. His head is slumped forward into his chest and his breathing is loud enough to be heard above the din of the engine. He doesn't stir when I shake his shoulder or raise my voice for him to wake up. So I continue driving, keeping the Winnebago straight and slow.

It's either the alcohol in my blood or being behind the wheel of what feels like a tank that gives me the idea to take a detour. Either way, before I know it, I'm parked directly in front of Austin Roarick's condo unit. With the engine running, and Rollie snoring beside me, I sit for a few moments and watch the newly abandoned place. There's a sense of relief now that Austin is gone. Yet as I think about our recent visit, and of our conversation as I stood in his home, I can't help but feel a little spooked.

By the time I pull the motorhome in front of my father's house, it's closing in on 1:00 a.m. He's still asleep, his head now leaning against the passenger window. I go into his house where I find a white cotton blanket in the linen closet. After I cover him with it, I decline his seat and remove his sneakers. For a moment, I consider heading back to the Homer House to sleep in my own bed. But leaving him alone seems irresponsible. Besides, the blanket seems big enough for the two of us. So I stretch it across the driver's seat and close my eyes. It's the first time my father and I have slept under the same roof in years.

• • •

I'm still hungover after teaching my classes the next day when Dan Hart finds me in the center of campus. He's wearing aviator glasses and a black Carolina Hurricanes hat; there's a limp in his step and his right hand is bandaged. Walking with him are his parents. His father has a thick head of light hair with grayish streaks running throughout, an athletic build, and the quiet confidence of an F.B.I. agent. His mother, the obvious source of her son's looks, wears her blonde hair pulled back tightly, has golden skin, and the delicate, feminine body of a dance instructor. They're both smiling those faint smiles that have an almost airbrushed quality to them, as though they're last minute additions to their faces. Despite their reticence, no one would ever be able to tell that these are people whose daughter killed herself, and whose son has one failed attempt on record.

Dan introduces me as his teacher as well as the overseer of the writers group. I shake hands with his parents, who ask me to call them T.J. and Lily. They wanted to meet me, Lily says, before heading back to North Carolina.

"Danny tells us you're from Chicago," says Mr. Hart.

"I moved back east at the beginning of the summer."

"Lucky for us you did," says Mrs. Hart.

Dan's father, advancing on his wife's sentimentality, tells me that his college roommate was from Chicago and he would visit him every so often in his younger years. He mentions streets and restaurants he recalls and asks whether I'm familiar with them. We discuss the city a little, its sports teams and blues clubs. Mrs. Hart asks about my injuries.

"Nothing a few good prescriptions can't fix."

"It was important for us to meet you, Gray," she says. "We'll be leaving tomorrow morning with Danny, and we wanted to put a face to your name."

Dan has been standing between his parents and shifting his weight back and forth while lifting his sunglasses up and down on his face.

"So it looks like you'll be missing my last two classes," I point out.

"I guess so."

"We heard about your writers group," says Mrs. Hart. "It sounds wonderful. Danny's always loved to write."

It's unclear whether I'm now obligated to sing her son's praises. I have no experience doing this. Yet it doesn't appear that this is what she's after. But the truth is that I feel strongly that Dan is a fine songwriter. So I mention it, telling his parents that we at the Hundred Acre School enjoy hearing his tunes.

"I hope he'll continue to write," I tell her while looking at Dan.

This is not a reference to his destroyed guitar, yet the smashed instrument comes to mind almost immediately. I now can't help but wonder if he has a second one somewhere, or if he has plans to buy a new one, or if he even wants a new one. Part of me wants to ask these questions. Part of me wants to even encourage him to continue writing and playing. But I know I haven't earned the right to do this, even after what happened that night he was on the roof of the dining hall. He must regard what I did as some type of visceral gesture that carries with it no meaning whatsoever. If ever accused of this, despite wanting to, I wouldn't know how to defend against it.

Dan's parents ask him to say his goodbyes to me before meeting them in the main office where they'll be signing some papers. We shake hands one last time. Mr. Hart tells me I'm welcome in their home if I ever find myself in North Carolina.

"I remember one of our first conversations together," I say to Dan once we're left alone. "You tried to coax me into letting you come late to class everyday."

"I remember."

There's no levity in his tone; he's serious and appears almost embarrassed in my presence. Despite this, I don't alter what I had planned to say:

"I thought you were full of shit if you want to know the truth," I tell him.

"I don't care."

"Sure you do."

"I don't, actually."

"C'mon, *Danny*," I said, curious to see where the conversation might go.

"You don't even know me. Do you think that being my teacher for a few months and forming some fucking writers group makes you my friend?"

"Just confirm it for me. Confirm it for me that you're full of shit. First this *Dan Juan* bit, and now the brooding, suicidal poet. Just confirm it for me."

Peeling the sunglasses from his face, he's wide-eyed and at first speechless. He heaves a few deep breaths and then tells me to go fuck myself.

"Not exactly the farewell I was looking for, Danny boy."

"Are you expecting gratitude? Do you somehow think I should be grateful to you? Because I'll tell you how I feel: I feel like now I have to spend the rest of my life finding a way to look my parents in the eyes again."

My mind goes to the kid's dead sister. It was Dan who found her. She had used *his* knife. It suddenly seemed like a miracle that he could ever walk upright after this.

"Why don't you start by putting these away?" I said, taking the sunglasses out of his hand and putting them in his shirt pocket. "Start there. Your parents will appreciate it. As far as you and I are concerned, I don't expect gratitude. All I expect is that you stand here before me like a young man about to say goodbye to his teacher of a few months. Nothing more and nothing less. No entourage cheering you on. No guitar in hand. No pretense. I understand this relationship. And I understand *you* better than you think I do. So just say goodbye and that you'll keep in touch, even though we both know you won't. But please put the bullshit aside - for now anyway - and shake my goddamn hand."

Thinking on this for a moment, he shifts his weight a little and pushes his hair out of his face.

"Fine," he says, offering me his unbandaged left hand.

"Have you considered all of your admirers?" I said, walking with him towards the office. "They'll probably light candles in your memory."

He smiles for the first time since we've been talking. Then, true to his quick nature, his response is lucid and well timed:

"Would you blame them?"

"Absolutely not."

"I'm glad. Because no man should begrudge another over a well-deserved vigil."

This stops me in my tracks. Dan walks farther ahead before turning to look back at me. He throws his arms in the air and fights off another smile. Then he tells me that he's sure he'll write about the HAS someday and all the madness that's occurred since he's been a student here.

"Do you really think so?" I ask once I catch up with him again.

"Someone should," he says. "Someone definitely should. So yeah, why the hell not?"

. . .

Eileen Russo and Rollie have it out again. Having arrived on campus early that day, she's been consistent with her threats; most of them involve the team of attorneys she claims she's going to hire. To this, my father can say only one thing:

"I think given the circumstances, that's exactly what you *should* do."

This enrages her further. She calls him a bastard and gets in his face and threatens to sue him and his staff.

"I can't protect him anymore, Eileen," he tells her, both of them standing outside the therapy lounge. "He's been unwilling to talk to us since he came back. We've tried to prolong it for some time, but it's a police matter now."

She says it's the job of the Hundred Acre School to get her son to talk. With a little forced dignity, Rollie says manipulation is never part of the therapeutic process.

"Don't give me that *therapeutic process* shit! You wanna know about Nicky and that girl. You have questions about those pictures he sent. And about his relationship with this Austin Roarick character. And there's the issue of the drugs and the ring and the running away. *You* want to know, so you need to do what's necessary to find out!"

"Don't *you* want to know, too, Eileen?"

He's not using guilt; he appears genuinely taken aback by the woman's flippancy. Pointing out the obvious - that these are serious matters, legal matters, and ones that play a vital role in Nick's future - the Old Man takes a gentle approach and softens his speaking voice. Almost immediately, Eileen bursts into tears. Rollie watches her sob for a moment before gently taking her by the arm and ushering her into the therapy lounge.

Nick is on the verge of being taken into police custody. His day began by being put in the back of a cruiser and questioned by two officers all through breakfast and first period. Rollie, now deferring to the cops, made no objections to this. Nick is eighteen, and the police are within their rights to question him without a guardian present. The Old Man still calls Eileen, who was in transit during the interrogation.

"She should be ashamed of herself for waiting this long to see her kid," he told me.

Yet he understands her reasoning. She's stalling. Nick will not be returning to the Hundred Acre School in September, so Eileen, who must be imagining her imminent struggles with her son, realizes that life as she knows it is about to change for the worse.

Nick isn't being fractious with the cops; he's simply vacillating between spells of silence and modestly asked questions of his own - random questions posed with passive curiosity. What type of firearms do the officers carry? Have they ever fired them? How long have they been partners? Do they have to clean their own cruiser? The officers, Stansky and Gladstone, are reasonable in their reactions. They're both mild-mannered men in their forties. They explain to Nick how they each have kids around his age. The boy is unmoved by this. So they explain the seriousness of the matter to him and tell him his cooperation will serve him well. Then they try again, plying him with questions about running away and Nicole D'Ambrosio and Austin Roarick.

"He's not cooperating," Officer Stansky tells the Old Man. "The only time he flinched was when we talked about Roarick, about his disappearance, as well as this so-called confession your boys apparently dug up. He was interested in that."

There's no actual evidence to make an arrest. Eileen continues to remind everyone of this. But Nick is taken downtown, his mother in tow, probably swearing and crying during her drive to the station.

"I want these people gone," said Rollie, referring to Nick and Eileen. "Let the cops have them now. We've done our part."

We gather Nick's things from his room. The Homer House boys watch as we hastily cram boxes and suitcases with everything the kid owns. Once it's all packed, we make two trips to the SOD office, where we store it until his eventual return. The campus settles down for the evening. By 9:00 p.m., it feels like any ordinary Wednesday. A modest card game has begun in my father's basement. By the fifth hand, he gets a call from Louise; Eileen and Nick have returned to campus. The Old Man and I meet them walking across the road towards his house. Eileen is practically pulling Nick by the collar. The awkwardness over her and I seeing each other is belied by the circumstances.

"Tell them what you told me on the way over here," she demands of her son.

The four of us are standing on the side of the road. Nick is weaving himself out of his mother's grasp.

"Tell them!"

Nick laughs scornfully. Rollie asks Eileen to pick up her son's things in the SOD office; they should get a motel room and return in the morning for the necessary paperwork. For now, though, he says, he's had enough.

"The topic of those pictures came up," she says, trying to control her temperament. "I told Nick that he needed to get them back. He started talking about Nicole. And then about those pictures. She was even more beautiful in person is what he said. Those pictures didn't do her justice. Isn't that what you told me, Nicky?"

The kid is smiling with obstinate pleasure. He tells his mother she's wasting her time.

"Tell them!"

Nick says again that she's wasting her time. Rollie agrees and asks her to come back in the morning to settle her son's affairs once and for all.

"He told me why he sent you the pictures," Eileen said, looking at me.

A modest breeze suddenly gathers. A truck drives by with its high beams on. My father tells Eileen he's going to call Louise and Jimbo to escort her and her son from the property. She ignores the threat. Her focus is on me. Maybe she senses my curiosity.

"He trusts you," she says. "He said it was one outcast to another."

The police, she tells us, remained unsuccessful in their interview. But the fact remains that there's no evidence to make a formal arrest. Any narcotics Nick may have sold downtown cannot be linked with anything serious like the Sandrey overdose or the traces of the drug found in Nicole D'Ambrosio's autopsy results.

I start to wonder if Nick would still trust me if he knew I slept with his mother.

"Will you talk with him?" Eileen asks. "Just the two of you. Please."

Rollie points out that Nick has had many chances to speak up. Now, he adds definitively, it's a police matter. She asks me again if I'll speak with her son.

"He's got nothing to do with this," my father says, pointing at me.

There's something compelling me to want to help them. It's true that Eileen is pushy and by all accounts a bad parent. And Nick is by far not my favorite Homer House resident; I didn't care for him from the beginning. He's a bully and a punk. Yet I find myself interested in their plight, Eileen's as a parent and Nick's as a misfit. Maybe it's because she's the first woman I've slept with since Laura. Maybe it's because I can somehow relate to Nick in not being ready to talk about the trauma that's become your life.

My father relents and gives me the keys to the Winnebago; Nick and I take a drive. Almost immediately, I acknowledge the strangeness of our togetherness. Nick, sitting at my side, asks if we might forget about all the bullshit and drive out to Chicago. He says he's always been interested in that part of the country. Then he asks why I left.

"I thought we were going to discuss *you*," I said, taking a turn down a dark beach road.

"It's a simple question."

An animal darts across the street, missing the vehicle's tires by a narrow margin.

"I don't know. It became too big, I think. And too small. It was just the wrong size, I guess. For me, it was just the wrong size."

"And what about *this* place? You grew up here, didn't you? How does *this* fit? After all these years, I mean. How does it fit now?"

It was a good question. I told him it was, too. Then I said I didn't have an answer.

"Weren't you married or something?"

We drive past a stretch of impressive waterfront homes. Nantucket style colonials with red gardens illuminated with floodlights. Restored Victorians with sweeping wrap-around porches. An old high school acquaintance of mine, Jack McShane, lived in one of them.

"Listen to me," I said, "I know you've become known for this sort of macho indifference thing, but I think the reality is that my father is serious about expelling you. So we can either drive around and talk about my charmed life, or we can work on getting some people off your back."

He's been thrown out of plenty of schools, he tells me. This, he points out, is how he ended up at the HAS. Then he asks again about my wife, wanting to know what she was like. I tell him. We drive the Winnebago on side streets and main roads and through the downtown, and I talk freely about my past with Laura. I find it's easy to do so. To the point where I don't seem to come up for air. He learns about the pregnancy and Glenn Kilburn and even my job at the paper. He listens well. When I'm through, he has only one question:

"Can we stop for cigarettes?"

We pull into a convenience store where Nick buys a pack of Camel Lights and an energy drink. For the next hour, he chain smokes as we drive some more around Old Brookview and I listen to him finally tell his own story. He starts with Austin. The two met downtown one afternoon when the older man introduced himself. Weeks earlier, he'd hired a few of Nick's peers for some odd jobs, which is how he recognized Nick as a student at the Hundred Acre School. Not long after their introduction came Austin's offer to sell the boy some pot. Nick accepted. The two went for a ride in Austin's car and got high. Then another offer was made: Austin needed help selling his products downtown. His business was modest, but with the help of someone younger, he figured he'd be able to change that. Nick accepted and soon began selling mostly prescription pills to local kids. This is how he met Nicole. The two hit it off and began seeing one another. Nick became inspired. She was fun and beautiful and interested in him. And though the girl found convenience in her new boyfriend's trade, he gave up dealing almost immediately upon meeting her. His downtown privileges were now sacred, and they needed to be used for spending time with Nicole, not slinging pills to line Austin's pocket.

Nick's ties with Austin were thus broken. There seemed to be no ill will over the split. Meanwhile, there was still Nicole's habit to consider. She was at first content to take the pills Nick would save her from his own meds. This soon proved to be not enough. So Austin became her dealer. And the three of them began meeting whenever and wherever it was convenient - mostly downtown, sometimes on a remote part of the Hundred Acre School that's adjacent to the interstate. As time went on, Nicole's habit increased. She began meeting Austin alone. Soon enough he began making passes at her and telling her she was pretty, far too pretty for Nick. Often, he suggested the two of them get high together, which they did on occasion. Then he'd talk about someday owning the Hundred Acre School property; he told her he was working on a big deal and that it was just a matter of time. Nicole, torn between being disgusted and amused by Austin, told Nick everything of their visits. Nick asked her to only meet Austin when he could go with her. She agreed.

"But she continued to meet him," he said, lighting a fresh cigarette. "Alone. No one knew about their meetings. No one knew about Austin. Not her friends. Not anyone. Just me."

Nicole's substance dependency was increasing, as were the frequency of her meetings with Austin. It wasn't always possible for Nick, whose freedom was limited, to accompany her.

"But she told me about all of them," he said.

"Why?"

"Because he really started to freak her out," he said. "She thought he was a fucking lowlife."

Nick explained to me how Austin would brag about his future business ventures, telling the girl he was on the verge of rivaling his own father. He made absurd claims that he was on his way to becoming a multimillionaire as well as a pillar of the town; then he'd pocket the modest amount of cash from their recent transaction. More disconcerting to Nicole were the advances Austin would make on her. They began as furtive attempts to steal a kiss here and there, but soon escalated to full-on propositions. Nicole, who was anything but demure, nevertheless found it awkward to reject the much older man. She held her ground, though, telling Austin she was in love with Nick. To this, he would sneer and laugh, calling Nick a freak, a loser, and insist that she could find a worthier boyfriend if she picked a name out of a hat.

"She told him off one time," Nick said. "He said some shit about me, so she called him a pathetic fat fuck or something like that. And..."

Nick takes a long drag on his cigarette before finishing what he was saying:

"And he hit her."

That, ostensibly, was the last time she met with Austin. Nick saw Nicole downtown the following afternoon. She was affectionate and in good spirits; she even had some pictures for him, one of which was racy. They made plans to see each other Sunday morning. That would never come to be. He'd never hear from her again. Her strangled body was discovered three days later by two of Nick's own classmates. The corpse was found in the same proximity where Nick, Nicole, and Austin met just weeks earlier.

As we approach the campus, there are questions I want to ask him. Like why he never went to the police in the first place. Or why he considers me a fellow outcast he can trust. Or why he never took the time to proclaim his innocence in the letter he sent. I want to ask why he didn't defend Nicole's memory in the dorm that day, and where he ran off to for nearly a week. Aside from the questions, I want to tell him I believe him. And let him know I'm sorry for his loss. It's obvious that he and Nicole were in love. Maybe they knew each other for a short time, and maybe the relationship was anything but a typical teenage romance, but it's clear that what they had was something he not only believed in, but something that changed him.

By the time I park the Winnebago beside Rollie's house, I know our conversation is over. It has a sense of finality to it and I have no intention of pushing him any further. Maybe there are reasonable explanations for the missing pieces. It hardly matters. Nothing will change. Nick will still be expelled in the morning. His story, he must feel, will be a waste to tell anyone not outcast enough. And his girlfriend will still be dead. I turn off the ignition. Nick is working on what must be his tenth cigarette. He seems calm to the point of sedate. Turning to him, I start to say something. When no words come out, I improvise:

"Those things are killers, you know."

After forming a perfect smoke ring, he exhales through his nose. Then he turns to me with the pack and offers me one, which I accept. The campus is quiet. No lights are on in my father's house. I know it's unlikely that he's sleeping inside. He's probably in his office or the therapy lounge with Eileen, awaiting our return. Nick lights my cigarette and we sit in silence for a while and smoke. I'm surprised to discover that I don't cough. After a minute, Nick turns to get a look at me. Then, leaning his head back on the seat, he sighs a little and mentions how a couple of beers would go nicely with the cigarettes.

. . .

Travel days are hectic. I recall them from when I was a kid. The buzz on Wildwood Road begins a little after breakfast. It's an assembly line - parents and taxis and airport shuttle services drive onto the campus, circle for a while to find a parking space, load luggage and passengers, and head off towards the interstate. Activity in the dorms is no different. The kids are frantic. For many of them, home is where their troubles began. Yet despite such trepidation, Rollie has always encouraged these two-week reunions. "You're not a stowaway," he'll tell the overanxious student, "the Hundred Acre School does not harbor stowaways. Go be with your family and see what happens." As insurance, the kids always have access to their therapist's as well as the Old Man's number.

Usually by early afternoon, all the students are gone and the school settles into a lull of stillness and late summer sunshine. The staff are next to leave. They're often on the road before dusk. Sometimes a few of them remain, reveling in the new calm of the campus. But they mostly all use the time to vacation or to visit their families.

My father stays behind. He always has. Once the school is deserted, he might unwind by jogging or gardening or playing pool in the pavilion. I know how he regards the school: In his mind, it's embodied as the closest thing he has to some sort of detached alter ego. When the students are present, it's next to impossible for him to reconcile with the notion that so much of his own spirit is imbued in the place. When he has it all to himself, though, that changes. He walks around the campus with a soaring sense of quiet pride, no doubt wondering where all the years went, while at the same time considering how many might be left.

So it's surprising - shocking even - when he corners me in the dining hall just minutes into breakfast to announce his plans to take a trip.

"Where to?"

"I thought I'd start with New Hampshire. Pay a visit to Jeanne and Walter."

It takes a moment for it to register that he's talking about my aunt and uncle on my mother's side.

"For how long?"

"Two or three days. Then it's off to Cornell for a day or two. And from there, I'm heading west. I'll stop when and where I feel the urge. I have two weeks, so we'll see what happens."

"You're driving?"

"Of course. In style, I might add."

"The Winnebago?"

"Absolutely."

"If you were any more sentimental, you'd be unbearable."

"If you were just a *little bit* more, you'd be tolerable."

"Fair enough."

As the day's rituals take hold - cleaning and packing and student pick-ups - I find myself considering over and over the Old Man's trip. There was a gleam in his eyes when he told me his plans. This makes sense. The poor guy hasn't had an adventure in years. It's in me somewhere to be happy for him. There's no doubt the trip will turn into some sort of tribute for his youth. It's easy to envision him blasting Cat Stevens, revisiting his old haunts, and talking aloud to my mother's ghost, insisting that she's there with him, guiding his memory into savagely blissful terrain. Picturing all of this does me good. Yet one competing thought that I can't seem to shake is whether I'll be invited on the road with him.

Through the chaos of cleaning the dorm, helping the kids pack, and meeting some of their families, I find myself looking over my shoulder for my father, waiting for him to sneak up on me with the suggestion that I go with him, apologizing that it's so last-minute. This never happens.

I'm instead approached by a number of parents. Meredith's, a tall, intimidating couple with Ivy League swagger, shake my hand and tell me that their daughter has enjoyed her time in my writers group. J.J.'s mother also introduces herself to me. A pleasant woman, she's as redheaded as her son, yet she looks young enough to be an older sister. I meet Adam's father, a heavyset man with a ponytail and a limp in his left leg; he slaps me on the shoulder and says he's heard a lot about me. There's Cliff's parents, who made the drive all the way from Akron; there's Cal's mother, who thanks me for looking after her son. I meet the parents of kids I have in the classroom and in the dorm and in the writers group. Some of them seem as troubled and odd as their children. Some are obviously educated, decent people.

"Meredith tells us you might not be returning after the break," says her father. "We're sorry to hear that. Just a summer fling, huh?"

It never occurred to me that the uncertainty of my return might've become rumor. What's more, it's never occurred to me to say goodbye to anyone in the event that I don't return.

"I'm not sure. Just weighing my options."

"He's gonna quit just so we can't read any of his writing," says Meredith.

"Pretty good detective work," I tell her.

"I know it. But even *I'm* not good enough to figure what those options of yours might be."

"To be honest, I haven't thought them through yet. That's the truth. We'll see."

The girl smiles. After wishing me luck on whatever I decide, she leans in close so only I can hear her:

"Interesting use of the pronoun *we*. Don't you think?"

By the time the students are gone, and the campus is left only with an exhausted staff, Rollie calls a brief meeting in front of the SOD office.

"This sound," he says, pausing, allowing the new silence to resonate for a moment, "has been hard-earned. There's no doubt. We've had one hell of a summer. And I've asked a hell of a lot from each of you. But today, before you leave for your travels and your adventures and your families, I need to ask something more. I need to ask that you leave your burdens here. I'll accept them, all of them. And I'll take them with me on my own trip. There might even be room enough in that beast I'll be driving. Don't get me wrong: I'm no martyr. I just need you all to go away from this place and forget about it so you can come back with openness and enthusiasm."

He ends with a little philosophy. He mentions John Stuart Mill and the principle of utility. It isn't hedonism the Old Man is promoting, but instead simple happiness and pleasure.

Some of my colleagues find me and wish me a restful break. Ryan tells me he'll be spending a few days in New York City with his girlfriend. Tennille, Sandra, and Amber will be biking in Cape Cod. Dave is going back home to Peabody, which he tells me is just outside of Boston. Nussbaum will be visiting his son and daughter-in-law in Atlanta.

"What about you?" he asks. "Will you be holding down the fort here with Louise?"

"Maybe."

"Somebody has to do it."

"What do you know about this trip my father is taking?"

"I know he's looking forward to it, and that it's well-deserved."

"Has he been planning it?"

"You know Rollie's never been much of a planner. Especially for something like this. No, I think it was born out of necessity."

We shake hands and he tells me to take it easy and rest my injuries. He starts to walk away before he suddenly stops and leans in towards me.

"Maybe when he gets back you two can have that talk that's so long overdue."

By dinner time, everyone is gone. The campus is officially on hiatus. Rollie calls to tell me he'll be leaving shortly. He asks that I meet him in the dining hall, where he's looting Mickey's kitchen for provisions to bring on his trip. By the time I arrive a few minutes later, the vehicle is loaded and parked adjacent to the building. He's taken bottled water, dorm snacks, dried fruit, and cereal. He jokes with me that he'll make it look like a robbery to keep Mickey off his back. Handing me the keys to the school, he points out the ones that might be of use while he's away. He reminds me that Louise and her staff will still be on the clock, patrolling the grounds and maintaining security. We end up sitting at his table, looking out the window to a garden of white and purple impatiens, waiting for the other to say something.

"I thought by the end of summer it would be you to get in the car and drive away."

"So did I," I admit.

"No one's stopping you, you know."

"I know."

I start mindlessly flipping through the song selection on Matt's and Adam's jukebox. My father's attention is on the tapestry with the school's mission statement embossed on it. From his seat, he has a perfect view of it on the far wall. He sighs after a while and asks about my ribs and collarbone. I tell him I'm okay.

"I had to dig up some old photos of your Aunt Jeanne last night, you know. It's been a long time. I goddamn near forgot what she looks like. Turns out she looks just like your mother. She used to anyway. I'm trying to convince myself that a large part of my visit is not just to see what your mother might've looked like if she were alive today. I'm having a tough time, though."

"You don't need to rationalize your trip to me. Go. Enjoy."

"Is this place really that bad for you?"

"It's not bad. It's just—"

He cuts in, admitting that he shouldn't have asked that question.

"Now's not the time for that talk," he says, suggesting we wait until he returns.

He adds that he knows this is dependent upon whether or not I'm still here.

"If you do decide to leave," he says, standing up from his chair, "Louise will take those keys off your hands."

He pulls me up from my chair and throws his arms around me, telling me he'll give my regards to Aunt Jeanne and Uncle Walter. I wish him a safe trip. When he makes his way to the door of the dining hall, he turns to tell me that if I'm hungry there's some of Mickey's homemade chicken salad and

Swedish meatballs in the fridge; they were made fresh this morning at his request, he says, especially for me.

Sitting back down, this time in my father's chair, I wait for the Winnebago's engine to start. It fires up after a moment, idles briefly, and recedes into the distance. Turning back to the jukebox, I continue searching through the song selections. There's music by T-Rex and Willie Nelson and Steely Dan and Cheap Trick. On the very last sleeve of songs is one I haven't heard in probably fifteen years. I press K8, and after a moment it begins to play. My mind suddenly wanders to my writers group and our meetings in this very room; I can't help but smile over images conjured by Dorian's crude comedic sketches, or the precocious beauty of Dan's song lyrics, or the romantic grandeur of Matt's poems. And there's Adam's intensity and Meredith's candor and clever ambiguity. They're all out there now, all of them. They're out there with Nick and Eileen Russo. And Austin Roarick. They're out there with Laura and Glenn Kilburn. And with poor Mr. and Mrs. D'Ambrosio. And now with my father. Everybody's out there.

The small jukebox speakers can't repress the gorgeous harmony I'm hearing. It sounds like one voice with multiple lives lived within it. And the harmony rises above the music - the acoustic guitars and the pedal steel and the bass and percussion - with a courage that isn't showy and in fact still has much to prove. I'm grateful for the song, grateful that I'm able to listen to it because of the devotion and toil of two industrious young men who figured that an old wall unit jukebox would go nicely at Rollie's table.

My ribs begin to ache a little and I suddenly feel hungry. I'm grateful for the food the Old Man asked Mickey to make for me. As soon as the song ends, I'm going to get up and fix myself a hearty plate. For now, though, I'll rest my body in the Old Man's chair, reveling in the sweetness of a melody that brings with it both the clumsy mirages of the past, and the strange miracles of my recent summer at the HAS. This is idle time, which suits me well. As does the solitude. My mind needs not a single challenge or shot of wisdom. Yet as much as I long for this respite, and no matter how hard I will myself to bask in it, it's impossible to ignore the weightiness of sitting in my father's seat as I nurse my injuries and behold the school's mission statement I've either been reading or thinking about for the better part of my life.

ABOUT THE AUTHOR

Everybody's Out There is Robert M. Marchese's third book. He has published one other novel, *Nine Lies*, as well as a memoir, *Land of July*. Additionally, Robert has published both short fiction and nonfiction in a variety of publications and literary journals. He lives on the Connecticut shoreline with his family.

NOTE FROM THE AUTHOR

Word-of-mouth is crucial for any author to succeed. If you enjoyed *Everybody's Out There*, please leave a review online—anywhere you are able. Even if it's just a sentence or two. It would make all the difference and would be very much appreciated.

Thanks!
Robert M. Marchese

Thank you so much for reading one of **Robert M. Marchese's** novels. If you enjoyed the experience, please check out our recommended title for your next great read!

Nine Lies

"This important, nail-biting crime thriller about MS-13 sets the bar very high. One of the year's best thrillers."
–BEST THRILLERS